Advance Pr[aise for]
The Pages of Her Life

"The *Pages of Her Life* is quintessential James Rubart and showcases why his novels are automatic must-reads. Rubart's new novel explores courage and self-discovery. The right decisions are almost always hard, and Rubart's deft hand with character and theme shine in his new novel. Highly recommended!"

—COLLEEN COBLE, *USA TODAY* BESTSELLING
AUTHOR OF THE LAVENDER TIDES SERIES

"I'm a slow reader, but I couldn't put down *The Pages of Her Life*. This intriguing story is brimming with wonderful characters and more than a few surprises, including marvelous cameos by characters from another favorite Rubart novel. Immensely thought-provoking, this novel would make a fabulous book club read. I can't recommend it highly enough!"

—DEBORAH RANEY, AUTHOR OF *A VOW TO CHERISH*
AND THE CHANDLER SISTERS NOVELS

"James L. Rubart's writing always delivers characters that echo our own lives, living in a world not too removed from our own. *The Pages of Her Life* is another captivating taste of who we really can be."

—DAVID RAWLINGS, AUTHOR OF *THE BAGGAGE HANDLER*

Praise for James L. Rubart

"In the same thought-provoking style that propels his previous novels, James L. Rubart takes readers on a journey of discovery and self-renewal."

—*BOOKPAGE* ON *THE MAN HE NEVER WAS*

"For fans of classical retellings and dark, spiritual thrillers."

—*LIBRARY JOURNAL* ON *THE MAN HE NEVER WAS*

"Rubart's latest is a complex, contemplative look at the two sides of everyone—the light and the dark—and their war with each other. The unique perspectives and fantasy situations give stunning realizations about life and spiritual truth. This is a novel that begs to be read more than once and discussed with others to get the full impact of its meaning."

—*RT BOOK REVIEWS*, 4 STARS, ON *THE MAN HE NEVER WAS*

"This is no mere novel, but a journey to the soul. Sage, deep, filled with a truth of terrible beauty and the real nature of love."

—TOSCA LEE, *NEW YORK TIMES* BESTSELLING AUTHOR, ON *THE MAN HE NEVER WAS*

"Thought-provoking. Fascinating. Full of spiritual insight. These are just a few ways I'd describe Rubart's latest gem. With plenty of twists and turns to keep the pages turning, *The Man He Never Was* expertly explores the difference between *knowing* and *experiencing*, and asks the important question: What might happen if we could see the person in the mirror as God does?"

—KATIE GANSHERT, AWARD-WINNING AUTHOR OF *LIFE AFTER*

"Richly imaginative and deeply moving, James L. Rubart's story of forgiveness and freedom reaches past the page and into the soul."

—JAMES SCOTT BELL, CHRISTY AWARD–WINNING AUTHOR OF *FINAL WITNESS*, ON *THE LONG JOURNEY TO JAKE PALMER*

"James Rubart has been one of my favorite authors for some time now. I love the way he writes. Imagine Nicholas Sparks, C. S. Lewis, and Mitch Albom collaborating on a novel. *The Long Journey of Jake Palmer* is something very close to that. Highly recommended."

—DAN WALSH, BESTSELLING AUTHOR OF *THE UNFINISHED GIFT*, *THE DANCE*, AND *THE REUNION*

"Rubart delivers a creative, ingenious novel about love and discovery. *The Long Journey to Jake Palmer* will have you thinking, *How do we really see ourselves?* long after the end."

—RACHEL HAUCK, *NEW YORK TIMES* BESTSELLING AUTHOR OF *THE WEDDING DRESS* AND *THE WEDDING CHAPEL*

"If you think fiction can't change your life and challenge you to be a better person, you need to read *The Five Times I Met Myself.*"

—ANDY ANDREWS, *NEW YORK TIMES* BESTSELLING AUTHOR OF *HOW DO YOU KILL 11 MILLION PEOPLE*, *THE NOTICER*, AND *THE TRAVELER'S GIFT*

"The clear message about loving others, relying on God, and focusing on your family leads up to an emotional conclusion. A spiritual and family-centered book that will appeal to readers of inspirational fiction."

—*KIRKUS REVIEWS* ON *THE FIVE TIMES I MET MYSELF*

"*The Five Times I Met Myself* is another James L. Rubart masterpiece."

—SUSAN MAY WARREN, BESTSELLING AUTHOR OF THE CHRISTIANSEN FAMILY SERIES

"Powerful storytelling. Rubart writes with a depth of understanding about a realm most of us never investigate, let alone delve into. A deep and mystical journey that will leave you thinking long after you finish the book."

—TED DEKKER, *NEW YORK TIMES* BESTSELLING AUTHOR, ON *SOUL'S GATE*

"Tight, boiled-down writing and an intriguing premise that will make you reconsider what you think you know about the spiritual realm."

—STEVEN JAMES, NATIONAL BESTSELLING AUTHOR OF *PLACEBO* AND *OPENING MOVES*, ON *SOUL'S GATE*

The Pages of
Her Life

Other Books by James L. Rubart

The Man He Never Was
The Long Journey to Jake Palmer
The Five Times I Met Myself
Book of Days
The Chair
Rooms

THE WELL SPRING NOVELS

Soul's Gate
Memory's Door
Spirit Bridge

the

PAGES

of HER

LIFE

James L. Rubart

THOMAS NELSON
Since 1798

The Pages of Her Life

Published in Nashville, Tennessee, by Thomas Nelson. Thomas Nelson is a registered trademark of HarperCollins Christian Publishing, Inc.

Thomas Nelson titles may be purchased in bulk for educational, business, fund-raising, or sales promotional use. For information, please email SpecialMarkets@ThomasNelson.com.

Scripture quotations in chapter 13 are taken from the Holman Christian Standard Bible®. Copyright © 1999, 2000, 2002, 2003, 2009 by Holman Bible Publishers. Used by permission. HCSB® is a federally registered trademark of Holman Bible Publishers.

Scripture quotations in chapters 35 and 43 are taken from the Holy Bible, New International Version®, NIV®. Copyright © 1973, 1978, 1984, 2011 by Biblica, Inc.™ Used by permission of Zondervan. All rights reserved worldwide. www.zondervan.com. The "NIV" and "New International Version" are trademarks registered in the United States Patent and Trademark Office by Biblica, Inc.®

Scripture quotations in chapter 44 are taken from the New American Standard Bible®. Copyright © 1960, 1962, 1963, 1968, 1971, 1972, 1973, 1975, 1977, 1995 by The Lockman Foundation. Used by permission. (www.Lockman.org)

Publisher's Note: This novel is a work of fiction. Names, characters, places, and incidents are either products of the author's imagination or used fictitiously. All characters are fictional, and any similarity to people living or dead is purely coincidental.

Library of Congress Cataloging-in-Publication Data

Names: Rubart, James L. author.
Title: The pages of her life / James L. Rubart.
Description: Nashville, Tennessee : Thomas Nelson, [2019]
Identifiers: LCCN 2018054927| ISBN 9780718099428 (softcover) | ISBN 9780718099435 (epub)
Subjects: | GSAFD: Christian fiction.
Classification: LCC PS3618.U2326 P34 2019 | DDC 813/.6--dc23 LC record available at https://lccn.loc.gov/2018054927

Printed in the United States of America

19 20 21 22 23 LSC 5 4 3 2 1

For Natasha

"Hateful to me as the gates of Hades is that man who hides one thing in his heart and speaks another."

—HOMER

"Stay strong. Stand up. Have a voice."

—SHAWN JOHNSON

one

Are you still glad we did it?"

Allison Moore looked up from her laptop Monday morning and studied her business partner and onetime best friend, Kayla Brown. Not at one time. Still best friends. At least that's what Allison told herself. It's what Kayla probably said inside her head too. And Allison wished it were true. But she'd discovered that people who say, "Don't go into business with friends or family," have a large slice of wisdom on their side.

Allison didn't have to ask what "it" was. Going out the door. Leaving their old architecture firm, where they'd made gobs of money for the owners and not much for themselves. Now here they were, two and a half years later, working harder than they ever had and still not making much money for themselves. But it would come, wouldn't it? It had to. Their heads weren't completely under the financial waters, but she and Kayla did have to hold their breath far more frequently than they liked.

"Glad?" Allison leaned back in her chair and picked up her heavily caramel-flavored coffee, the only breakfast she'd had that morning. "Yes, I am. Most days at least."

Kayla stepped inside Allison's tiny office and sat in the chair on

James L. Rubart

the other side of Allison's oak desk, the twin to Kayla's. Oak. Not Allison's style. Nor Kayla's. But the furniture had been affordable.

"Me too." Kayla sighed. "I'd rather be poor and free than rich and in the shackles we used to wear."

"I agree." Allison took a sip of her almost-warm-enough drink. "Except when Seattle rain turns into snow up at Steven's Pass and I don't have the money for a lift ticket."

"Our time is coming. With four new major accounts within reach, you have to be feeling good."

"I do."

The air felt stale—the same conversation they'd had too often over the past six months was undoubtedly the reason—and they slipped into silence. Another sip of coffee.

"Am I still your best friend, Al?"

Allison stared at her. The truth? More often than not it was an extreme challenge to be around Kayla. But Allison was committed to the business. And committed to the friendship.

"It's been hard. But yes, you are." Allison took another sip. "Am I yours?"

"I want you to be."

Allison nodded and pushed back from her desk.

"Like you said, Kayla, I'd rather be here running my own business than working for someone else. Not sure I could ever do that again. And you and me? We'll get back to the way we were once we get a little bit of cash flow going. It's just the stress, you know?" She set down her cup and straightened up. "I should get going on these drawings. Promised Kim Kelly they'd be finished this afternoon."

"Girl?"

"Yes?"

"I'm sorry, Al, for what I did on Friday." She placed her hands

2

on Allison's desk. "When I'm wrong I say I'm wrong, and that wasn't in any way called for, making you look foolish because I blew off the appointment, and I'm really, really sorry because I said I would come and then I didn't, because I thought it was too small of an account for us to pitch, and I did tell you that, but I still should have . . . and it was late on Friday afternoon and I wanted to get home to my kids, and to hubs, and since you don't have kids, you don't know what it's like, but it tugs at me, but still, I . . . I was so completely wrong."

Kayla scrunched up her face and peered at Allison, then tilted her head, waiting for an answer.

"Not completely wrong. You were right. They're small. But I got 'em." Allison pointed to her cup and grinned. "So they'll at least pay for our coffee."

"Really? You signed them?" Kayla stood and clapped twice.

"I did."

"Sweet!" Kayla reached back and pulled a slip of paper out of her jeans. "Then there's even more reason to give you this."

She unfolded the flyer and slid it across Allison's desk.

"I signed us up for a Sip and Paint class this Thursday night. My treat."

Allison smiled. "I've always wanted to try that."

"Me too. It'll be a celebration of picking up our latest massive client."

Allison laughed and said, "Can't wait."

Kayla flashed the love sign and Allison returned it. As Kayla spun to go, Allison's cell phone rang. Caller ID said it was her mom. But Allison had no time to talk and at times her mom could be a world champion monologuer. Not a problem when Allison had time to listen. Which wasn't now. She would return the call on her way home. The ringing stopped. Allison's focus returned to her drawing desk, but before her brain could engage, her cell rang again. Her mom. Again. Allison sighed, sat back, and picked up her phone. Deep breath. Explain she couldn't chat and hold her mom to under five minutes. Then finish the drawings.

"Hi, Mom. Listen, I'd love to—"

"No, this isn't your mom, Allison. It's her neighbor, Tara Elsner. We've met a few times. You might remember me."

"Yes, Tara, of course I do." Heat flashed through Allison. "Why are you calling on my mom's cell? Is she okay?"

"Yes, Corrine is . . . Your mom . . . is fine." Tara paused. "Well, not so fine. She was up on a ladder working on the gutters and slipped and fell, and landed on her ankle and broke it pretty badly. Bruised up a little on her right side."

"What?"

"Yes, she's banged up but okay. It could have been far worse."

"What was she doing up on . . . No, no, no, forget that. Where are you now?" Allison stood and grabbed her purse and car keys.

"She didn't want to bother you, but I said you needed to know . . . She was, and still is, I suppose, in a lot of pain, so I borrowed her cell phone because in all the commotion after she called me and I raced across the cul-de-sac to help her, I forgot to grab my cell phone before we—"

"I'm sorry to interrupt, Tara, but where are you?"

"Right now we're in a room waiting for—"

"Are you at the hospital?"

"Yes."

"Which one?"

"Overlake."

"Thanks, Tara, I'm on my way."

Allison hung up without waiting for a goodbye, snatched her

coat, and sprinted out her door and into the doorframe of Kayla's office.

"That was my mom's neighbor. My mom broke her ankle. She's at Overlake. I gotta go."

Allison turned and raced to the front door of their office, yanked it open, and pushed into the hallway.

"Is she—" Kayla's voice was clipped off as the door slammed shut.

Allison growled at the Bellevue traffic crawling up 405 and glanced at her watch. Ten forty-five. Ten years ago you could hit the speed limit this time of day for at least a few seconds at a time. Even five years ago. Now? Lucky to reach half that speed. She tried to calm down. It wasn't a heart attack. She didn't need to race to get there. Allison called Tara back and was told her mom's ankle had been set and she was sleeping. But still. She wanted to get there. Be there when her mom woke up. Tell her things would be okay. Because her dad wouldn't ever be there for her mom again.

Why did he have to go and die? Yes, he was with Joel now, father and firstborn son reunited. But now it was just Allison and her mom. Parker? Sure, he was alive—at least he was three and a half months ago before he'd vanished again—but being alive and being part of their shrinking family were two different things.

Finally she reached her exit and accelerated down the off-ramp as if she could make up the time she'd lost in the river of stop-and-go cars. A light mist from the sky began and she turned on her wipers.

Broken ankle? Falling from a ladder? Allison shook her head. What was her mom doing up on a ladder working on the gutters? Sixty-two-year-old women did not get up on fifteen-foot ladders. At least they shouldn't. Especially not women with frequent vertigo.

Allison pulled into Overlake Hospital's parking garage twenty minutes later. Ten minutes after that, a nurse in the ER gave a quick rundown of her mom's condition, then pointed to a hallway to Allison's left. "Your mom's at the end of the hall, probably still sleeping. She was when I checked five minutes ago."

"Thank you."

Allison clipped down the hall and breathed in that antiseptic hospital smell that always seemed to be covering up a deeper, less pleasant odor hiding in the walls. She slowed as she approached the ER bay, stopped just outside the door, took a deep breath, then stepped inside. Her mom lay propped up in a bed covered by an off-white blanket. "Mom?"

"Hi, sweetie." Her mom gave a smile, her eyes at quarter mast. "I guess I lost my balance."

"They told me you were trying out for the circus."

Her mom laughed. The morphine they'd given her was obviously taking care of the pain, at least for now. "You should have seen the flip. I just couldn't stick the landing."

"I see."

Allison sat and took her mom's hand. Warm and soft. Gentle. The way it had been forever.

"Thanks for coming, Al. You didn't have to."

"Mom? What were you doing up on a ladder?"

"Working on the gutters."

"Why? What would possess you to climb up there?"

"They need fixing. And Parker's not around. And who knows if he'll ever be around again."

"So if Parker's not around, you hire someone to do it."

Her mom turned her head and stared at the rail of her bed.

"Mom?"

"No."

"No?"

"No." Her mom pulled her hand away. "I can do it myself."

"Obviously that's not the case."

"I won't slip next time."

"They told me you won't be ready to do anything for at least a month and a half."

Her mom yanked her arms across her chest. "Then I'll fix them in six weeks."

"Please, Mom. Explain this to me. Why didn't you hire someone to take care of your gutters?"

Her mom turned back and opened her eyes fully for the first time since Allison had stepped into the room. "No, I won't."

"Why not?"

"It's nothing you need to know about."

"Why are you—"

"It's strictly off-limits."

The look in her mom's eyes was full of fear. More than Allison had seen in her mom for a long time. Maybe ever. Whatever it was, Allison had the feeling it was about to change her life.

two

THREE HOURS LATER, AS ALLISON drove her mom home from the hospital, she tried once more to draw out her mom. No luck.

After she asked twice, her mom muttered, "You'll find out soon enough, so let it rest, okay?"

"Find out what?"

Her mom slipped back into silence and Allison tried to shift gears. "How are you doing with missing Dad?"

"I don't."

"Don't?

"Don't miss him."

The same answer she'd given a few days ago. Strange. Only four months since the funeral, and her mom had gone from talking constantly about his passing to not at all. It didn't make sense. They'd been happily married since the day they wed, and now it was as if he'd never existed. The last time Allison had stopped by, all but one picture of her dad had vanished from the walls.

They rounded the corner of the street her mom lived on, the sun now streaming directly through the windshield into Allison's eyes. She pulled down the visor, shielded her eyes, and slipped on her sunglasses.

The maple trees were just starting to bud, but the reminders of a wet, gray Seattle winter hung in the air.

The house would always be home for Allison. For her mom as well. Mom would live the rest of her days here. So many memories. For all of them. The good, the bad, the horrific, but those walls held her history. Parker's. And most of all, her mom's. How many couples could say they'd lived their entire married life in one house?

Allison did a double-take as the one-story home came into view fifty yards away. Was that a For Sale sign in her mom's yard? No, couldn't be. Had to be in one of the neighbor's. But as she got closer she saw that wasn't so. She pulled up to the curb and blinked as if that would make the sign vanish, or move to the next-door neighbor's yard.

"Mom, what is going on?"

"I told you you'd find out soon enough. Now you have."

Allison sat stunned, grasping for reasons her mom would be selling her home. She closed her eyes, gave a tiny shake of her head, and opened them, half expecting the sign to be gone. It didn't happen. She stared at the sign for a few more seconds, then turned off her car, got out, and shuffled over to it.

A bad photo of a middle-aged, plump, smiling Realtor glared out at her. Allison touched the letters on the sign that spelled out For Sale. The sign curled slightly at its edges, which meant it had sat there for a few days at the least. She swallowed and took a slow look at the yard, the house, the roof, the stamped concrete paths leading to the backyard where so many barbecues and games of bocce ball had happened over the years.

She walked back to the car, pulled her mom's crutches out of the trunk, then went to the passenger-side door. Allison opened it and said, "What's going on, Mom?"

"I'll tell you when we get inside."

She lifted her mom up and out of the car, then handed her the crutches.

"Can you do this?"

"Yes," came her mom's sullen response.

It took three minutes for them to navigate the seven steps to her mom's front porch. Three minutes of silence during which Allison's mind tried to come up with answers. Finally they stepped inside, and Allison helped her mom to the couch in the living room. Then she sat across from her mom in the rocking chair her dad had loved. Allison leaned forward, elbows on knees.

"Are you going to tell me now?"

"Would you like some coffee? Some tea maybe? That's your favorite, and that always seems to go better when it's later in the day. Or I could whip up some—"

"No, Mom. You're going to rest that ankle."

"I'm going to need to learn how to use these crutches, so why don't—"

"Stop, Mom. Please."

Allison took a slow breath. Maybe tea was a good idea. Give her mom a moment to settle in and figure out how she would tell Allison whatever the horrendous secret was.

"Why don't I go make us some tea?"

Her mom nodded. "I'd like that, thanks."

Allison went to the oh-so-familiar kitchen, put a kettle on the stove, and waited for the water to heat. She wandered over to the refrigerator and spotted a photo of a midthirties man and a little girl, both dressed to the nines. Over their head was a sign that said, "First Annual Daddy-Daughter Dance!" Probably the son and granddaughter of a friend of her mom's.

A memory rushed into Allison's mind before she could stop it.

She'd been in second grade, more dressed up than she'd ever been to that point in her young life. She was about to go to her first dance. A few minutes before it was time to leave, Allison's mom stepped into her bedroom room and gave a little laugh.

"What's funny, Mommy?"

"Nothing." Her mom's eyes went from Allison's dress to the bow in her hand and then to the quiver of arrows slung around her neck.

"It's just—"

"Do you like my bow, Mommy?" Allison grinned. "I'm a princess, but I'm also a war-ee-or."

"You mean a warrior?"

Allison nodded.

"I didn't know princesses carried bows and arrows."

She grabbed her bow tighter. "If they're a war-ee-or they do."

"I see." Her mom knelt beside her. "But I think you're far more of a princess than a warrior, so maybe we should leave the bow and arrows at home."

"Nope." Allison closed her eyes and wagged her head back and forth. "I'm half and half."

"Okay." Her mom squeezed her hand gently and said, "But I still think you should leave your bow at home. You don't want to scare the other princesses at the dance who don't understand you can be half and half. What do you think?"

"I guess."

Her mom stood and ushered Allison to the door. "We should go downstairs. We don't want to keep Daddy waiting, do we?"

"No!"

As they reached midpoint on the stairs, her dad slid into view and came to a stop in front of the front door. The suit he'd been wearing *earlier had been replaced with jeans, a Huskies sweatshirt, and a baseball hat. Allison stopped and pulled her hand from her mom's grip.*

"What are you doing, Daddy? Aren't you going to wear your suit to the dance?"

Her dad glanced at her, then fixed his gaze on her mom.

"Corrine, can I talk to you for a second?"

Allison's mom didn't answer. She turned to Allison and said, "Hang on for a minute. I'm going to talk to your dad. Go up to your room and I'll be right there, okay?"

Her mom clomped down the stairs, and she and Dad shuffled into the living room and talked in whispers. But Allison didn't go to her room. She padded down the rest of the stairs and sat on the bottom step.

"Did you hear me?" Her dad's voice wasn't a whisper anymore.

"Yes. I heard you. You're going to break a little girl's heart so you can go watch Joel play baseball."

"So you didn't hear me. He's not just playing. He's pitching. In the final game of the season. They win this, they get into the playoffs. If he's the winning pitcher, it sets him up for—"

"He's ten! This isn't—"

"He'll remember this the rest of his life. It's a defining moment."

Now her mom's voice grew beyond a whisper. "And you don't think your daughter will remember what you're about to do to her the rest of her life?"

"She's six, Corrine, so no, I don't think she'll remember it. And it's not like this is going to be the only father-daughter dance they ever put on. Come on."

"Don't do this, Jerry. It's not a good plan."

"I didn't plan this. I just found out ten minutes ago!" The thud of her dad's shoes pacing back and forth on the hardwood floors echoed. "I'll make it up to her. I promise."

Her mom stayed silent.

"Did you hear me? I said I'll make it up to her."

Again her mom didn't respond, and Allison knew the conversation was seconds from being over. She spun and scampered back up the stairs and into her room, closed her door to a crack, sat on the edge of her bed, and waited for her dad to come upstairs. He pushed through her door a few minutes later, a worried smile on his face.

"Hey, princess."

She stared at him for a few seconds before turning away.

"I have some bad news, sugar." He went to one knee. "I am so, so sorry, but I have to change our plans for tonight. I'm not going to be able to take you to the dance even though I really want to."

She glanced at him and then stared at her bow propped up in the corner.

"I promise I'll make it up to you, okay?"

She picked at a loose thread on her dress.

"Okay?"

She nodded. Her dad stood, kissed her on the top of her head, and left her room.

Allison sniffed out a sad laugh as she recalled the number of father-daughter dances they'd gone to after that night. It didn't take long to add them up. Zero is a quick calculation.

She shoved the memory away and poured the tea. After they sat in silence for a few minutes sipping their drinks, Allison set down her cup and said, "Why are you selling the house?"

Her mom rubbed her hips with her palms and glanced at everything in the room except Allison.

"Please, Mom."

"Yes, right." She sighed and pushed the crutches off to the side of the couch. "Now, what would you like to know, dear?"

Allison wanted to blurt out, *Are you even my mom?* The tightness in her stomach grew. Something was seriously wrong.

"What's going on?"

"It wasn't an easy decision, but it's the right one. I talked to my friend Kathy about it at length. She agrees with me. I'm getting older. Who likes to admit that? But it's true. And I have to think ahead. Make plans."

Her mom stopped as if that was all the explanation Allison needed.

"What plans?"

"I suppose I simply realized this is a big house. A lot to take care of. You and Parker don't drop by that much, and even if it's all three of us, it's still a lot of house. I thought it was time to downsize, get something a little smaller, something where I don't have to worry about the yard . . ."

Allison stared at her mom, trying to organize the two million thoughts racing through her mind. Getting older? Her mom was only sixty-two. Yes, sometimes, well, more than sometimes, she acted like she was eighty-eight, but still, sell the house? She was still teaching elementary school, had no plans to retire, and had never even hinted about selling the house someday.

Right after Dad died, someone had asked her, and she'd sworn they'd have to drag her out of the house when it came time. Worry about the yard? Her mom loved the yard. Without her flowers and garden and the hummingbirds she invited into her domain as if they were royalty, she'd be lost. This was insane.

"Do I need to ask why you're lying to me? You've never been good at it."

A sad little laugh sputtered out of her mom's mouth. "Do you remember the first time you caught me in a lie?"

"We were out on the back porch and I asked you if Santa Claus was real."

"You were only four."

"You and Dad stood there with silly looks on your faces. You glanced at each other and you said, 'Yes, of course Santa Claus is real.'"

"And you said, 'I think you're lying, Mommy.'"

Allison lowered her voice. Softened it. "I think you're lying to me now."

Her mom took a long time pulling air into her lungs and even longer releasing it. She looked around the room again, slower this time, as if she was reliving every memory created there.

"Have you ever woken up from a dream and not known for a few seconds whether the dream is reality or your waking life is the reality?"

Allison nodded.

"And when you realize your waking life is the true world, you feel incredible relief, because the dream was your life but upside down? You shake the dream from your mind and the world is the way it should be, right-side up, and the smell of coffee freshly brewed floats down the hall and a new day, a good day, has begun?"

Again, Allison nodded.

"I'm not in the dream anymore, Ally." Her mom's gaze shifted from Allison to the window looking out on the weeping willow in the front yard. "No, the dream is over, I'm awake, but my life is still upside down, and all is not right with the world."

"What happened, Mom? Whatever it is, we can work through it. Tell me, please."

"I wish that were true." She gave Allison a sad smile. "This time I don't think we can work through it."

"What is it?"

Her mom's gaze stayed fixed on the willow tree as tears formed in her eyes. "It's your dad, Ally."

The grip around Allison's stomach made it a challenge to breathe. "What about Dad?"

Her mom folded her hands across her lap and looked at Allison, but her focus cut right through her daughter, not seeing anything at all.

"I'm $550,000 in debt. And they want their money. On a regularly scheduled basis. Money that I don't have."

three

WHAT ARE YOU TALKING ABOUT?" Allison lurched forward in the rocking chair, her hands gripping the arms.

Her mom waved her hands in the air. "Where do I start? Where would you like me to start, honey? From the beginning? That's always a good place to start in situations like this, don't you think?"

Allison forced herself to be patient. To not blurt out a thousand questions at once. "Yes. Sure. Wherever you want to."

Her mom picked at the armrest of the couch and spoke in a sing-song voice. "That's why I have to sell the house. The Realtor says I'll get $150,000 once commissions and paperwork are paid for, but that still leaves $350,000 to go. That's a lot of money. A lot if you think about it. Quite a bit, yes, a great amount of money. I gave them what I had in savings, but that wasn't much."

"Why would you only clear $150,000? With as crazy as the Seattle-area market has been, this house has to be worth almost a million."

"Yes, you're right. Almost right. It's listed for $985,000. Can you believe that? Seems like a silly amount of money for this house. We paid only $54,000 for it." She sighed. "But that was a long time ago."

"Then you have a tremendous amount of equity in it; you should—"

"But of course the mortgage company is quite concerned about getting their money. Can't blame them. I don't blame them. Why would I? It's not their fault."

"What are you talking about? You and Dad paid off this house years ago. And who do you owe the money to? And what for?"

"Ah yes. Paid off. That's what you thought? I can see why you would. Me too." Her mom stared out the window at the willow tree. "Do you remember we had that little party when your father announced that the house was paid off?"

"What happened, Mom? Why do you owe the money? Who do you owe it to?"

"Yes, right. I'm sorry. I keep getting distracted, don't I?" She looked at the ceiling and a little smile came onto her face. "It was a lovely little celebration, though, don't you think? Your dad did that slide show where he showed us all his before-and-after pictures of all the projects he did over the years."

"What did Dad do?"

Her mom fixed her gaze on Allison. Up to that point her eyes had been glassy, her mouth slightly open even when she wasn't speaking. Now her countenance shifted and she became the wife of a police force captain, the woman who was as fierce in conflict as any man. But a second later the look faded and her eyes glazed over again.

"Mom!"

"He had a double life." A pitiful laugh came out of her mom's mouth. "How did I miss that?"

A double life? Her dad? Not possible. He loved her mom. Never so much as glanced at other women with a roving eye.

"He had an affair? I can't believe—"

"No, not that." Her mom began to cry.

"What then?"

"Your dad had a vice, Ally. Not alcohol—we all knew about that one. And you know it wasn't women."

"What then?"

Her mom looked up at the mantel over the fireplace, at the family photo they'd taken when Allison was still in high school. Years before Joel died. A lifetime ago.

"I read once that you can sometimes tell what a pastor's secret vice is by what he rails against the most."

"What do you mean?"

"If a preacher screams about pornography, he's probably addicted. If he shouts about the horrors of gay people, he's probably gay himself. Adultery, alcohol . . . whatever. They're fighting the compulsion privately, so they can't help but come out against it publicly. It's their cry for help. A way to absolve themselves."

"What are you driving at?"

"If someone asked you what your dad was most passionate about shutting down, what would you say?"

Allison's voice dropped to a whisper. "Illegal gambling."

"Yes." A long sigh from her mom. "What was the other one?"

"Human trafficking."

"Yes."

"No, Mom. No." Allison's heart seized. "You cannot tell me Dad was part of a human-trafficking ring."

"He wasn't. Not for a long time. And he was never, ever involved like you're thinking. Never. But he started turning a blind eye. He took bribes to delay cases. Ignored tips when they came in."

"Why? That's not who he—"

"He needed the money."

"For the gambling."

"Yes."

Allison's head dropped and she closed her eyes. This was a nightmare. Not possible. Not her father.

"He won a lot apparently. Lost a lot too. Obviously. It took me a while to piece it all together. I'm told it was small bets at first. Then bigger. And it grew out of control. It got to the point where he'd win millions and lose millions. I suppose we should feel good the debt was only $550,000 when he died."

"Only?"

A nervous giggle came from her mom. "I guess at one point he was down $3.2 million."

"I don't believe this." Allison fell back against the rocking chair. "I simply can't accept the idea—"

The giggle started to move toward hysterical. "That's when he took out another mortgage on the house. And he sold his life insurance policy."

"What do you mean, sold it?"

"There are companies that will give you up to eighty percent of the value of your life insurance policy when you're alive in exchange for getting your policy when you die."

"Who are the people who want the money, Mom?"

"Exactly who you think they are, Allison."

Every image from every mafia movie and TV show she'd seen flashed through her mind. Men who broke fingers, shylocks who showed up in the middle of the night to put a gun to your head, men who killed with as much remorse as they felt tossing a bottle of wine into the garbage.

"We have to go to the police, Mom."

Her mom looked at her as if she were a little girl again.

"Wouldn't that be wonderful?" She patted her knees. "Yes, let's go to the police. Let's do that. Shall we do that right now?"

The irony of that idea struck Allison like a brick. Sure, they'd walk into her dad's old precinct, gather all the cops who served under him, and explain that the man they called the greatest to ever run the place, the one they'd loved and showered with accolades, had been living a lie. Everyone had secrets. But her father's would rock their world.

"We go to them anyway."

Her mom shook her head. "It's not what you're thinking. No, it isn't. The reason we can't go to the police is that there's no crime. This isn't the mafia we're talking about. The loans were legitimate. The men your father borrowed the money from are not criminals. They're businesspeople. Not savory, no. But there's nothing illegal about the way they loaned your dad the money."

"The ones who gave him money for looking the other way are criminals!"

"Yes, but there are no records of that. And those aren't the ones behind this loan." Her mom drew both her hands down her face. "It's bad, Ally. The men didn't know about your dad's cancer, and he always came up with the payments, and then he'd get ahead and pay them back, but then a run of bad luck kicked in, and—"

Allison opened her palms. "Then you file bankruptcy."

A frightened look came into her mom's eyes and she whispered, "No, don't say that."

"Why not?"

Her mom glanced around the room as if looking for hidden cameras.

"They told me if I tried to file for bankruptcy, life would get extremely unpleasant for me and for you and for Parker. They weren't bluffing, Ally."

"Now they are committing a crime."

"No, they're not. You know that. How many times would your

dad come home with stories like this where there was no hard evidence to even arrest someone? No proof. There was nothing he could do then, and there's nothing we can do now."

"You're telling me there's no way to get out of this."

"Only by paying off the debt." Her mom stopped and peered at the spot where the last professional photo of her mom and dad had sat. "It's funny. I can't even look at his picture. I can't believe he did this. Can't believe he did it to you, to me, to Parker . . . and yet I still love him. I can't help it. I still love him." She glanced at Allison. "Does that make any sense?"

It made more sense than Allison wanted it to. She wanted to lash out at him for the lies, rush up to him and scream at him for the horrible things he'd done. She wanted to hate him and rip him from her memories. Hate him for all the harsh comments he'd made through the years, hate him for being married to his job instead of her mom, hate him for always harping on following the rules, hate him for loving Joel more than Parker or her.

She took a moment to settle and push the anger from her mind.

"So we'll owe $400,000 once the house sells?" Allison asked.

"We? No, not we. This is my problem, not yours."

"And the debt is accruing interest every month."

"Yes."

They sat in silence, glancing at each other uncomfortably.

Finally Allison said, "When were you going to tell me?"

"I wasn't. I mean, I was going to get into an apartment first, then bring you over and—"

"With what money?"

"I don't know."

"That's why you were up on the ladder, isn't it? Trying to fix the gutters before potential buyers start dropping in."

Her mom's head bobbed in affirmation.

"You should have told me. There's no reason to carry this alone."

"Yes, there is. I didn't want to drag you into—"

"You didn't. I'm choosing to jump in." Allison pulled out her phone and started making notes.

"Okay."

"I'm going to get Parker to help."

Her mom released a bitter humph. "Good luck with that. You'd have to find him first."

"I will. And I want the contact info on the loan sharks."

"Okay."

"You said they wanted their money sooner rather than later. What does that mean?"

"I told them I was selling my house, so they'd get at least $150,000 soon."

"After you get them that, how much will the monthly payment be?"

"They want a minimum of $12,000 a month."

Allison blew out a low whistle. "Wow."

"How is your business going? Can it help? I'll pay you back, of course."

Allison stared at her mom for ten seconds. She wouldn't lie to her mom, but she didn't want to add another stone of worry to her mom's load by describing the lack of accounts or her strained relationship with Kayla. And yet Allison had to let her mom know her floundering business wouldn't be much help in paying off the massive debt.

Even if she stripped her expenses to the bone and combined that money with what her mom brought in from teaching, they'd still be thousands short each month.

"Al?"

"It could be better."

Her mom frowned. "I thought you two were getting accounts."

"We are, we have . . . but the accounts are small. Sporadic. We get one and lose one. We haven't found that anchor client yet. We're making survival money but not big money yet. So we don't have an assistant, which would allow us to—"

"I can quit the school and come and—"

"Nope. Let's not make this about me. We are going to get you out of this. Somehow. Some way. First, you're going to move in with me immediately. That way the house will show clean, and I can take care of you while you heal."

They stared at each other for what seemed years, till her mom dropped her gaze and slumped back on the couch.

"I have some money saved from the divorce," Allison finally said. "And I can take out a home equity loan."

"You can't do that."

"Yes, I can." Allison glanced at her watch. She had to go. "I have an appointment, Mom."

"Yes. Go."

Allison stood, walked over to her mom, and kissed her on the forehead.

"What are we going to do, Ally?"

"Simple. We're going to pray for a miracle."

The miracle came twenty-four hours later.

four

ALLISON'S CELL PHONE RANG AS she and her mom watched a new Netflix series, and she stared at the caller ID for five seconds before answering. Derrek Wright? Calling her in the evening? Curious.

Derrek Wright. Her business associate for six years. Early fifties with twenty-five years of success behind him. Friend. Sort-of mentor. Encourager. He'd offered sage advice as she and Kayla started their architecture firm. Listened to her struggles to find decent clients. Even sent them potential clients who didn't fit Derrek's ideal customer profile. Didn't matter that ninety percent of them were time wasters and the others never paid. His intentions were good. They'd had coffee once or twice a quarter over the past four years, sometimes with Kayla, sometimes just the two of them, always professionally appropriate. She hadn't talked to Derrek in at least three months. The last two times she'd called she hadn't heard back. So he was due to reach out. But after work? Odd.

"Hello?"

"Hello, Allison." His deep voice held a hint of laughter. "How are you this evening?"

"I'm fine."

"Good." The smile was still there. "Did I catch you at an inopportune time to chat for a few minutes?"

"Not at all."

"Okay then." The smile in his voice vanished. Which meant this wasn't personal. It was a business call.

"How is your firm doing?"

Allison waved at her mom to keep watching and stepped into the kitchen. "Two steps forward, one step back. Too often it's two steps forward, two steps back."

"I understand." He paused and blew out a slow breath. "More importantly, how is your relationship with your partner going? Kayla, isn't it?"

She laughed. "I thought marriage was hard. In some ways, this is harder."

"Ah yes." Derrek chuckled. "The reality of being around your business partner for longer hours than your life partner. And under conditions often more stressful. This is a common occurrence."

"Exactly."

"What I've seen is that this predicament can often change if you choose the right partner. For example, Rod and I haven't had one disagreement in the past six years."

"But then again, Rod's been gone for the past four years, hasn't he?" Allison asked.

Derrek chuckled again, and this time it sounded forced. "Good memory, but even so, we were the right fit for each other till he decided he liked the sunshine of Hawaii better than the rain clouds of Seattle. And he's actually still an owner in the company. We're working on a plan for him to sell his shares. Should be fully out in another three or four weeks. That puts me in an interesting position. I need another Rod in my company."

This was crazy. He was talking about her, wasn't he?

"I want to grow my firm. I don't need any more money—I make far more than necessary—but I do want to see how big I can make this company. And I can't do it alone. I need someone who can not only draft but go after new clients. Drawing skills and people skills. I need someone who can balance me out. I need someone who understands the mentality of not working for someone else, who understands being their own boss."

He paused and went silent.

"Derrek?"

"Yes, Allison."

She hesitated, not quite believing the words that were about to come out of her mouth. Not believing that God could be answering her prayer in a way beyond what she'd imagined.

"You're asking me if I want to be your partner."

"Yes. That is correct." He chuckled. "I am."

"I'm . . . I don't know what to say. My mom . . . I mean . . . Derrek, I'm a little speechless right now. This is—"

"I should back up half a step, Allison. What I'm asking for right now is if you'll take time to pray about it. See if God is part of that idea. That's what I've been doing for the past week, and now it's your turn. If you don't feel like God is leading you to this, that is completely acceptable. However, if you feel—after praying about it—that you want to pursue a course where we join forces, I think there would be an exciting road ahead for both of us. I'm not getting any younger. Someday—not for years, mind you—I'm going to be more interested in navigating the waters of Puget Sound on my sailboat than navigating the intricacies of new client contracts and designing new buildings."

Allison's mind reeled. How many days ago had she prayed? Two?

Three? Derrek's company was one of the top ten firms in the Puget Sound region. Could this be happening? Yes, but she had a major problem. What about Kayla? She couldn't break off her partnership with Kayla. It wouldn't be fair. There was no way she could leave her without a partner, without someone who could handle the drawings as well as Allison could. But this would save her mom. Wasn't this the answer she'd dreamed of? No. It was better.

Lord? Lord, is this happening?

"Are you still there, Allison?"

"Yes. Yes." She ran her fingers through her long blonde hair and tried to breathe steadily. "I'm sorry, I'm just . . . This is a surprise."

"I understand. And I'm sorry to disturb you after hours, but I didn't want to put you in an awkward position by calling during the day, when perhaps you wouldn't be able to talk freely, with your partner perchance nearby, or at the very least put you in a position to have to explain a phone call from me and concoct a story that wasn't true about the nature of the conversation."

"No. Right. I mean, yes, I'm glad you called now."

"Good. Then let's proceed in this manner if it's acceptable to you. I'll let you think about it, talk to any confidants, and pray about it. Then I'll wait to hear from you. Please know, there's no rush for this to happen. Whenever you're ready."

"Sure, yes . . . I mean, I'll get back to you soon." Allison shook her head. "No, wait, I'm ready right now. This is . . . an answer."

Derrek chuckled. "I've gotten along okay without you here, so like I said, take your time. I'm ready for as long as it takes you to decide what God wants you to do and what you want to do. Not that those two things are mutually exclusive."

"Derrek?"

"Yes?"

"What I mean is, your call is a direct answer to a prayer. I want to meet."

"All right, then let's make that happen sooner rather than later."

"Great."

"I can meet you tomorrow morning. Say ten?"

"Can we make it ten fifteen? I have a conference call that's going to last till—"

"I'd prefer ten, but if your conference call is critical, I can—"

"Not a problem, Derrek. I'm a competent juggler. I can make ten work."

Derrek chuckled. "Then ten it is. Do you have a preference as to where?"

Yes, she did. She wanted it to be on her turf. A place where she felt at home.

"Let's meet at The Vogue."

"Fine. I'll see you tomorrow."

After ending the call, Allison stared at her phone till all the blood had rushed from her hand. This was it. The miracle. A miracle with a major problem. Yes, she'd wanted to kill Kayla lately, but Kayla was a partner she loved. A partner who was a sister. A partner she would never leave hanging.

But wasn't that what she'd be doing to her mom if she didn't take the partnership with Derrek? A partnership with Derrek meant serious money, not only from a monthly salary, but from profit sharing. With Allison's sales skills and Derrek's reputation, she could imagine them easily snagging two or three major clients within six months. And a slew of minor ones would be tantalizing frosting on top of the cake.

Allison leaned on the kitchen counter, palms wide, then stood up straight and paced, fingers rubbing both temples. The answer was simple. Clone herself. Argh! There had to be a way to take care of Kayla and be able to work for Derrek. But there wasn't. Wait. She could ask Derrek if Kayla could come too. No. Stupid idea. They didn't have the relationship she and Derrek had—they'd never clicked actually. Even if he did take Kayla as well, it certainly wouldn't be as a partner. And now that Kayla had tasted the freedom of working for herself, it would be almost impossible for her to go back to working for someone.

Allison went back into the family room and joined her mom on the couch.

"What is it, sweetie?"

"I think our miracle might have just arrived."

She relayed the phone call to her mom, and tears formed in both of their eyes.

"Do you really think this is our answer?"

"Quite possibly." Allison squeezed her mom's hand. "But what do I do about Kayla? I can't just leave our partnership."

Her mom shifted on the couch. "Forgive me for saying this, but Kayla isn't my biggest concern right now."

five

ALLISON ARRIVED EARLY FOR HER meeting with Derrek—she'd rescheduled her conference call—and looked around The Vogue, the coffee-wine bar she'd loved for years. It was a gathering place for people who still loved the idea that community could exist in the midst of a huge metropolis. The baristas remembered her name, and she remembered theirs. Long and narrow, The Vogue was painted with dark oranges mixed with reds. Paintings and photos for sale from local artists hung on one wall.

Shelves of wine lined most of the opposite wall, along with notices for events happening around town. Toward the back a small stage held two black leather chairs arranged under four paintings of guitars. Every Friday and Saturday night, local and semilocal musicians would come and play for tips.

Allison knew most of the regulars by face if not by name. It was her place. A place she would feel comfortable talking with Derrek Wright about her new life as a partner in Wright Architecture. Allison ordered coffee, settled in, and found a table between two men talking in earnest tones on one side, and what looked to be a college student working on a laptop on the other. She glanced at her watch. Ten minutes till ten. Enough time to review her journal entry from two nights back, then start on a backlog of emails that had piled up while she'd been taking care of her mom.

By ten o'clock she'd done her review and clipped through all of Monday's emails. Allison paused, took a sip of her coffee, and glanced up at the men who sat at the table to her right. The one doing most of the listening was taller, with thick hair the color of sandstone, just starting to go gray, and eyes a shifting shade of sea green, intense and gentle at the same time. Midfifties, she guessed. The other man was younger, had wire rim glasses, and wore a Western Washington University sweatshirt a couple sizes too small. His gaze bounced back and forth between the older man and a leather-bound book—no, it looked more like a journal. Gorgeous. It appeared to be old, the leather a rich tan color with dark markings in places. Was that a tree on the cover? She couldn't tell from this distance, but it looked like it. A thin, flat piece of leather was wrapped around the journal. The edges of the pages were creamy off-white and looked slightly thicker than normal.

The younger man patted the cover with one hand while the other cradled its spine. Strange. She felt herself drawn to it. Maybe because she had been journaling since ninth grade, when her English teacher, Ms. Flowers, had encouraged all her students to start writing down their hopes and dreams, sorrows and triumphs. Not on a desktop or laptop, but by hand, preferably with a beautiful wooden pen. Allison had done so nearly every day since.

She pulled her gaze away from the journal to find the two men looking at her. The older man smiled, his eyes bright.

"I didn't mean to stare." She smiled to lighten the mood. "But your journal is quite captivating."

"Well said." The younger man nodded and patted the journal again. "It certainly is."

She turned back to her laptop, slightly embarrassed. But while her eyes were focused on her screen, she didn't see anything. All her concentration was focused on the men's conversation.

"When I look back on who I was before this, it staggers me."

In her peripheral vision, Allison saw the man tap the journal three times with his finger. "What was I before this entered my life, Richard?"

"A man on a journey."

"Yes, 'tis true." The man rubbed the journal with his palm. "Well, I'm stunned at what has happened to me. And will be forever grateful for this journal."

"It's been a gift to know you," the man who must be Richard said.

"So this is goodbye?" the other man asked.

"You're the one moving in a few weeks, not me."

"You know what I mean."

"For a time." Light laughter. "Only a short time, for time is shorter than any man wants to confess."

The man rubbed the cover of the journal once more. "One more choice."

"One more. I know you'll choose well. Don't rush the decision, yes?"

"No, I won't."

Allison's head was down as if she were looking at her laptop but tilted to the right. If they'd glanced over, they would have seen her eyes as far right in her head as she could make them go.

Richard took both of the man's hands, squeezed, then let them go and stood. He started to move away, then turned and shoved his hands in his pockets and stared down at Allison. Whoops. Caught. She looked up into his smiling face and met his eyes. A moment later he gave a quick, polite nod and strode away. There'd been laughter in those eyes, and a knowing Allison couldn't explain. Her gaze turned to Richard's friend, who slipped the journal into a satchel at his side and left the table without looking in her direction.

A sensation of wanting to talk with Richard lit up her mind like a Fourth of July sparkler. Allison pushed the thought aside and glanced at her watch. Ten after ten. Wasn't Derrek the one who had pressed for a ten o'clock meeting? Not a problem. She would plow through more of her emails, respond to a client to confirm a meeting on Friday, answer a question from her and Kayla's accountant. Send out payment reminders to three clients. Compose a short intro letter for a pitch they'd been working on. She glanced at her watch again after she'd finished her mental list and gotten through twenty emails. Ten fifteen. She sighed and dove back into her inbox.

"Hello, Allison."

Derrek's bass voice floated down from his six-feet-five-inch frame.

She looked up and said, "Hi, Derrek."

Derrek Wright. Tall. Lean but well-muscled. Dark blond hair with a cut straight out of the mideighties.

"Thanks for meeting me here." He glanced around the coffee shop. "I'll grab some coffee and we'll get started if that's all right with you."

"Of course."

After five minutes, Allison looked up to see where Derrek was. Venti-size cup in hand, he stood at the far end of the shop, laughing into his cell phone. Her minute hand crawled to ten twenty-five.

She'd texted Derrek earlier that morning that she had to be out of there by eleven to make her rescheduled conference call. He'd promised the meeting would go no more than twenty or twenty-five minutes. Another five minutes dragged by before Allison stood, walked over to Derrek, opened her eyes wide, and held out her hands.

Derrek held up a finger and nodded. She shuffled back to her table, sat, and pressed her lips together, arms folded. A few minutes later Derrek's long strides brought him across the length of the coffee shop in seconds, and he settled in across the table from her.

"Thanks for considering this partnership, Allison."

"Why me?" She spread her hands on the table. "Yes, I did well at my former company, and Kayla and I are doing okay, but we're not setting the world on fire."

"I know what you did for your former company. Exceptional. That's the kind of person I need. Someone without inborn athletic talent who nevertheless went out in high school and pushed herself to win the state title in the 800 meters and place second in the 1,600 meters. The kind of person who was ASB vice president. The kind of person who competed in track at the college level and, although she only won a few races, was named most inspirational on her team three out of the four years she ran. The kind of person who was graduation speaker in both high school and college. That's the kind of person I want to partner with. I need those qualities to grow my company to the level I see it becoming."

"Whew." Allison sat back and blew out a puff of light laughter. "I'd like to meet this woman."

Derrek smiled.

"You've been doing a bit of research on me."

"A bit. Not hard these days."

"No. I suppose not."

"Well then." Derrek patted the table with both palms. "Since our talk last night, have you had any hesitations about moving forward?"

"I have a few questions."

Derrek paused and gave a tiny nod. "Yes, I expected that."

"Your wife? She's good with you bringing on a partner? And a woman?"

"She's fine with it. More than fine. She's fully behind your joining us. Your being a woman has no bearing for her one way or another."

"Good. But I'd still like to speak with her about it, make sure she's okay, woman to woman."

"Not necessary, although I appreciate the gesture very much. She prefers to stay out of the business, and I respect that and so allow her to remain in that posture. I'm sure you understand."

"Sure."

Allison glanced at the notes on her phone she'd made for their meeting.

"Last night you talked about Rod and finalizing things there before we sign our contract."

"Yes, yes, that's right."

"Where are you in that process?"

"Close. As I told you on the phone, we're about three weeks out on that matter. I'll be buying out his shares in the company. As soon as that's final, those shares will be transferred to you. I'll be setting up a meeting with Rod soon to finalize everything."

"So if we are going to partner together, we need to wait till—"

"No." Derrek reached into his briefcase and pulled out two sets of papers. "Look this over. It's an agreement between you and me. While you're correct in implying we cannot sign it till Rod and I make the final dissolution of his and my partnership, this maps out all the details of how our arrangement will work. If you like what you see, you can start working for me immediately. We'll start you at a base salary just to get things in motion, but as soon as the partnership kicks in, your pay will jump substantially."

"Working *for* you?"

"With me. There's no point in delaying. We trust each other or we wouldn't be having this conversation. And the sooner you come on board, the sooner we can take over the entire world of architecture in the Emerald City."

Allison smiled. "Low ambition I see."

Derrek matched her smile. "Then, as soon as Rod and I finish, we'll get you your Lexus, and—"

"Lexus?" Allison couldn't keep her astonishment from splashing across her face.

Derrek chuckled. "Don't get too excited. It won't be new. A couple of years old. But yes, a Lexus."

She focused on the papers Derrek had prepared. Page one. Good. Page two. Good. Page three, unbelievable: her monthly salary once the deal was done, plus a bonus structure based on each month's profits. She would start making serious money immediately upon signing. Miracle in black and white.

"You would keep fifty-one percent of the company, I'd get thirty-nine percent." She tapped her pen on the papers. "The remaining shares?"

"Those will be held in reserve for the possibility of another partner coming on board in the future. I see this company growing significantly, Allison." Big smile. Big chuckle.

She turned to the last page. A noncompete agreement. "What's this?"

"A simple noncompete agreement that says you won't go to work for another architecture firm for six months after working for Wright Architecture. Everyone at the company signs one. It's not significant, and it's not something I would ever hold over you if you wanted to leave. Plus, it won't apply to you as a partner. It's simply standard procedure until we finalize the papers on our partnership. At that point the partnership supersedes the noncompete agreement." Derrek leaned forward slightly. "What do you think? Can we move forward?"

"What happens to the accounts at my company?"

"You split them fifty-fifty with Kayla, I would assume."

"What if I wanted to let Kayla have all the accounts?"

"I'd be fine with that." Derrek chuckled. "I'm not wanting to marry you for your dowry, Allison. It's for the skills you bring, both in design and sales, and the mentality of someone who has owned their own firm."

She nodded and read slowly through Derrek's pages once more.

"This is excellent, Derrek." She patted the papers. "I'll read through them again, see if I have any other questions, and let you know."

"I can sense your hesitation." Derrek's voice grew soft. "Do you want to tell me why?"

Allison stared at him. More perceptive than most men she knew. Did she want to tell him? Why not? If they were going to be partners, secrets did not make for strong alliances.

"My partner, my current partner, Kayla. We started our company together. She's my best friend, and while the partnership has been hard on that relationship, I still love her. I'm having a hard time imagining leaving her high and dry, even if she gets all the accounts."

"If you give her all your accounts, I'm not sure I understand how that would be leaving her high and dry."

It was about more than accounts. More than money. It was about history and friendship and taking care of each other. And she knew Kayla would never do well as a solo act. She needed someone alongside her. Allison paused and bit her lower lip. She had to get the words out before she never said them.

"You don't know how timely this partnership with you is, but I can't do it. As wonderful as everything you've laid out is, I can't leave her on her own. I can imagine how it would feel, and it would devastate me. So I can't go, not without her being taken care of some way, somehow."

"Wouldn't it make the most sense to trust that Providence will figure out that part of the equation?"

"Yes, that's exactly what makes the most sense. That's exactly what I'm going to do."

"You'll let me know then?"

"The moment I get the answer."

Derrek paused and steepled his hands. "How soon?"

"Unfortunately, God isn't working on my time frame; I'm working on his."

"Well said."

Late that night Allison took a long shower and pondered the fight she'd had with Kayla earlier that day. They couldn't decide which one of them should go through their mail first. So stupid. And exhausting. They were fighting about anything and everything these days. As the water poured down on her, she prayed.

"If this partnership with Derrek is you, God, you have to show me. I have to see something to prove it. Sorry for the lack of faith. I want to take the job with everything in me. I believe it's you, but there's no way I'm leaving Kayla in the lurch. So, God, help me out. If this is you, really you, then I want something crazy. I want a friend of Kayla's, one of her friends who has her own firm—like Becca Carter or Mila Matthews—to call us, ask to do a three-way partnership deal. Okay? Please? Take care of Kayla. That's it. I'm letting it go."

It was ludicrous. Sure, out of the blue another architect would pick up the phone and propose the idea of joining forces. It didn't matter that it wouldn't happen. She'd tossed the idea out, then let go of it. It was in God's hands, at least for a while.

That night she didn't go to sleep till past two a.m., too many possibilities churning through her mind. When she did finally nod off, she slept far better than she had for the past four restless nights. God was in this, right? After her divorce and the financial struggle for the past two and a half years, and her dad dying, and now this catastrophe with her mom, wasn't it time for something to go her way?

Allison woke early the next morning to the sound of her cell phone ringing.

six

ALLISON OPENED HER EYES A millimeter and peered at her vibrating cell phone. Caller ID said it was Kayla. Way too early to have a conversation with anyone, let alone Kayla, who believed getting up at four thirty was "sleeping in."

She probably wanted to work things out from yesterday. They'd figure it out. Always did. They always made the time and found the place where they could agree. But this early wasn't the time, and her bed certainly wasn't the place. She turned her pillow over to the cool side and pulled another pillow over her head to block the light from the window. That meant it was later than she thought, but she was making up for her lack of sleep since her mom's revelation of financial apocalypse.

Just before drifting back into dreams, her cell buzzed again. *Should have turned it off.* She lifted the pillow. Kayla again. What time was it? Allison squinted at the phone. Whoops. Quarter to eight. Allison reluctantly sat up and let her legs dangle over the side of the bed. She needed her slippers. Her coffee. And an excuse to go back to bed.

Hard to do given what was going on with her mom. There wasn't time to sleep. Had to figure out an answer. Wait, hadn't she met with Derrek Wright yesterday? Yes. Not a dream. Real. It had been real! She glanced at her phone. Time to call Derrek and accept his offer.

No, couldn't do that. Kayla. Had to take care of Kayla first. She rubbed her eyes. She wasn't thinking straight. She needed to wake up.

The buzzing stopped. She waited till the phone chirped, telling her Kayla had left a message. She'd get it after coffee. Then text and apologize for sleeping in. Somewhere in the back of her groggy mind she recalled a brainstorming session they'd scheduled for that morning. Or was that tomorrow?

Wait. Was this Friday? No, Wednesday. Oh no! They had a meeting with a new client today at nine thirty, didn't they? Adrenaline shot through her as she pulled up the calendar on her phone. A moment later she flopped back on her bed and breathed a sigh of relief. No meeting today with a client. No meeting with Kayla. She really needed to get in the habit of waking up before she decided to think.

After her first cup, she checked on her mom, who was still asleep in the downstairs guest room. Good. Best thing for her ankle. Allison listened to Kayla's voice mails as she made her way back upstairs to take a quick shower.

"Hey, girl, I gotta talk to you about something. Pretty interesting idea. Like extremely."

She deleted the message and opened the second one.

"Call me, soon as you can. This could be big. Really big."

Allison deleted the second message and texted Kayla.

Hey. Sorry. Still waking up. I got to sleep really late last night.
Got your calls. I'll call you on the way in.

She sent the text, set her phone on the bathroom counter, and stepped over to the shower. But before she could slip off her pajamas and turn on the water, her phone rang.

Kayla. Might as well pick up.

"Hey."

"Sorry, this can't wait, Ally."

"Okay, no problem."

"I got a call this morning." Kayla giggled.

"From?"

"Mila Matthews." Kayla laughed again.

The bathroom suddenly seemed empty of air. "What?"

"She wants to join us. Can you believe it? A three-way partnership. She'd bring all her accounts. And get this—she'd split them with us. And she has some big ones. It wouldn't be a ton more money, but at least a twenty percent bump, and she'd be a great addition to our company."

A thimbleful of air puffed out of Allison's mouth as she stared at herself in the mirror. This couldn't be happening. Could it? Pray one day. Get an answer the morning after. This kind of thing only happened in cheesy made-for-TV movies. Not real life. "Too good to be true" in Allison's life had often meant she needed to cover her head because the second, third, fourth, and fifth shoes were about to drop.

"Al? Did you hear me?"

"Yes, but . . . tell me what happened. What she said."

"She's been thinking about it ever since she mentioned it to me a year ago. Did I tell you she made a casual comment about it last year?"

"No." The word barely made it through Allison's lips.

"Anyway, doesn't matter. She's been thinking about it a bunch, and then she realized it's tons more fun to work in a partnership than for just yourself. I mean, it can totally be exactly that, and better than that—if it's the right people—and like I just said, she would bring all her clients over. Think about this, Al!"

Through the phone Allison heard thumping and pictured Kayla jumping up and down.

"When does she want it to happen?"

"Now. Yesterday. As soon as we agree, we write up the partnership paperwork, get it signed. We make it simple. Thirty-three percent each, and the extra percent goes into a general fund for extracurricular company activities."

"I . . . uh . . ."

"Mila has worked with some of the biggest contractors in the state, Al! She has the clout to get us in front of some really big fish. It will still take time, but the three of us . . . Oh wow, just thinking about it makes me want to party."

Party? Allison agreed. But not for the same reason. This was her out, her answer. Clear as crystal.

"What do you think?"

"I think I'm stunned."

"I know. Me too."

"I think this is a direct answer to prayer."

"Prayer? Yeah, sure, I know you've been doing your thing in regard to this. I guess it worked!"

"I didn't believe, even a little bit, that it would."

"But it did." Kayla laughed. "So you're in? I can call Mila?"

It worked. It had really worked. God had come through. Kayla would be taken care of. She'd exchange a good partner for a great one. And Allison would get exactly what she needed to save her mom. Plus, she'd get to work for her friend. No, not work for him, *with* him, be his partner! A man who shared her faith. A man she could learn a great deal from. A man who had hinted at her someday buying him out and taking over the company. Her mom would really, truly be okay. Crazy. Absolutely crazy.

"Al?"

"Sorry, I was just trying to figure something out."

"What's that?"

"Nothing. We can talk about it later."

"What's your definition of later?"

"I don't know. I have to make sure my mom's okay."

She realized showing up at work meant Kayla would know she was hiding something and pry it out of her. Plus, she needed time to think. Away from Kayla. Away from her mom. A chance to jot down the debate raging in her mind. Go work with Derrek? Stay? But there was no debate, not really. It was only her love for Kayla telling her there was still a decision to be made. No, she was supposed to go. How much clearer could the answer be? This was God as front and center as she'd ever seen him. But it would still hurt Kayla, even if she joined with Mila. And yet they were tearing each other apart.

"I'm probably going to work from home or the coffee shop. I want to be close by if she needs anything."

"We need to talk about this now," Kayla pressed.

"We will. Tonight."

"What's tonight?"

"Sip and Paint, right?"

Kayla laughed. "Right. Good timing. We can celebrate our new account and celebrate our new partner. I like it."

"I'll see you there."

"You okay, Allison?"

"Yes, sure. I'm fine."

"You don't seem fine. I can hear it in your voice."

"I am. Just a lot on my mind."

"Like?"

"I'll see you tonight."

Allison hung up, sprinted downstairs, and found her mom easing slowly into the kitchen. "You're not going to believe the phone call I just had."

"Oh?"

After a quick review of the call, she saw the flicker of a smile on her mom's face. "Maybe God is in this, Ally. Maybe he's going to help."

Allison nodded.

"So what are you going to do?" Mom asked as she settled into a chair and propped her gray aluminum crutches against the wall.

"I have a client meeting, then a lunch, then two more clients to see, and then I'm going to the coffee shop for the rest of the day. I'll get a bunch of work done on my laptop and have some alone time to think about what I'm going to say to Kayla."

"You're not going to the office?"

"No, I don't think I can be around Kayla with this on my mind. Plus, I want to be close in case you need—"

"I told you, I'm fine." She motioned at her crutches. "I can get anywhere I need to on those."

"But if you fall—"

"Do you see any ladders in this room? Or in any of the rooms in your house?"

Allison laughed. "Not unless you've hidden a few."

"Don't worry. Do what you need to do. I'm fine." She smiled at Allison like she did when Allison was a child. "I'm giving up my high-wire act. Promise."

"Good to hear, Mom."

"Speaking of hearing, have you heard anything from Parker?" A wistful look passed over her mom's face. "It would be nice to know if he's okay."

"I'm sure he's okay, Mom."

"How? How do you know he's okay?"

She didn't. She'd called his cell three times since her mom's accident, but he hadn't responded. Probably because she'd told him Mom was fine on his voice mail. Should have said they were going to amputate her foot.

"Since hearing from Parker is the rare occurrence, *not* hearing from him, or anything about him, is probably a good thing. And that means he's good."

"Nice try, Al."

"Thanks." Allison grabbed a bagel and cream cheese. "But I mean it."

"I know you do. It would just be nice to hear from him."

"We will. I promise."

She went back upstairs to shower and get dressed and pray she was right.

seven

FIVE HOURS LATER, AFTER FINISHING her lunch and meetings, Allison settled into The Vogue's darkest corner farthest from the counter. She needed coffee, needed a spot to think, needed answers before facing Kayla tonight. But didn't she have her answer already? Yes. Without question. But she had no idea how she would tell Kayla in less than three hours from now that she was breaking up their partnership. Maybe she could paint a picture at this Sip and Paint thing that would tell the story. Drowning woman offered a life preserver has to take it in order to save her mom.

She pulled out her journal and begin freewriting, not thinking, jotting down anything that came to mind, whether it made sense or not. A peace started to come over her, which rarely failed to happen when she wrote. By the end of three pages, she sat back and took in her surroundings with a different view of life than when she'd stepped through the front door forty minutes earlier. It would be okay with Kayla. Somehow they'd be okay.

As she sipped her drink, she let her gaze meander around the shop and was surprised to see the journal man from the other day on the opposite side of the shop. Western Washington Sweatshirt Guy. He was alone this time. No Richard. Perched on his chair, writing slowly in a journal, but not the gorgeous leather-bound one. He wrote, then paused and studied the writing. Wrote. Paused. Wrote again, a smile tickling the corners of his mouth.

Without warning, he jerked up his head and stared right at her. A sweet grin of surprise came to his face, then he nodded at her as if he'd just figured out a rather difficult puzzle. He stood, pushed his coffee cup and plate to the center of his table, glanced back at her for an instant, then stuck the journal under his arm and loped out of the shop.

She felt like he'd told her half a secret, and she had to know the rest. Allison stood and strode after him, pushed through the front door of The Vogue, and glanced to her left. Not there. Right. There he was. Loping away, long legs taking him down the street, where he blended into the river of people meandering up and down the sidewalk. A few seconds later he disappeared from her line of vision. She shook her head.

The look the man had given her was like nothing she'd ever seen. Wasn't inappropriate. Wasn't romantic by any stretch. Wasn't him being curious about her or even wanting to meet her. The only way to describe it was as a knowing, as if he'd been waiting for an answer and had received it in the instant their eyes locked. He had a confidence about something that involved her. Allison had no doubt a kind of connection had just happened, one that neither of them had been expecting.

She wandered back inside The Vogue, ordered a sandwich for dinner, and after finishing it went to her car, started it up, and headed to meet her soon-to-be ex–best friend.

eight

As Allison merged onto I-90, she called her mom.

"Same," her mom said.

"What?" Allison frowned.

"Same."

"What do you mean, same?"

"This is the fourth time you've called to check on me, and each time I've told you I'm doing great, so this time I thought I'd speed up the conversation, because I think you're driving and I don't like the idea of you driving while you're talking on the phone."

"I'm on a Bluetooth. It's totally legal."

"Did you ever see that *MythBusters* episode where they proved that talking on the phone while driving is as bad as being drunk?"

"Does that mean I shouldn't tell you about the three cosmopolitans I had before I got in my car just now?"

"That's not funny."

Allison laughed. "I can't help it if I love you, Mom."

"I suppose not." Her mom paused. "You're going to be fine tonight. Kayla will understand."

"I hope so."

"Wake me up even if it's late. I want to hear how it went."

"Will do."

Allison turned on music to drown out her imaginations about the coming conversation with Kayla, but thirty seconds later her phone rang again. Speak of the best friend.

"We still on for that Sip and Paint class tonight?"

"I'm on my way now," Allison muttered as she changed lanes.

"Good!" Kayla laughed. "For a minute I thought you were going to stand me up. But we have to celebrate. Plus, you just went through a breakup after dating a guy for five months—which classifies it as semiserious—and you know the bylaws of our friendship say we can't allow each other to stay at home when there's the potential of meeting an eligible man at the painting class."

"Everyone there is going to be female."

"Do you know this for certain, or are you guessing?"

"I'm not ready to meet anyone yet." She slowed as traffic bottle-necked. "Someday. Not now."

"Until you meet the right one. That's what unbreaks a broken heart."

"My heart isn't broken."

"Yes, it is." Kayla paused. "But that's all right."

"Okay."

"You liked this guy. A lot."

"Okay."

"But he wasn't right for you."

"Okay."

"You're just saying okay to get me off the phone."

"Okay."

They both laughed.

"I'm ten minutes out, Kayla."

"I'm nine. See you there."

Twelve minutes later Allison walked through the door of Sip and Paint's small retail shop in the middle of a strip mall. Three long rows of tables filled the space. Every few feet a blank canvas sat in front of tan steel chairs. Brushes and paints were next to the canvas. Fifteen or so women wandered through the space, and a few more had already settled into their chairs. No men. Allison smiled.

A voice behind her called out, "You made it!"

Allison turned to find Kayla standing in front of her, a wide grin on her face. "This is going to be so much fun."

"I've never painted anything before."

"That's why these things are so great. Most of the people haven't. So there's no pressure."

They found some seats. Their instructor was a woman with short reddish hair who looked to be in her late sixties. She spouted instructions on how to paint the river that flowed through the middle of a lush green forest.

After they had started splashing greens and blues and creating boulders on the side of the river, Kayla turned a spotlight on Allison's hidden agenda.

"I told Mila we're in." Kayla grinned and nudged Allison with her elbow.

"You what?"

"What do you mean, what? I told her that the Supremes are going to happen."

"The Supremes?"

"Come on, Al. Motown? One of the greatest girl groups ever? And we're going to be one of the greatest women-owned architecture firms ever."

"You told her yes? We didn't decide—"

"Yes." Kayla dropped her paintbrush on the thick tan paper in between their two canvases. "We did decide. This morning."

"No, we did not."

"When we decided we were going to be celebrating tonight, what exactly did you think we were going to be celebrating?"

"You decided it was a celebration, not me. I said we'd talk about it tonight. Not decide. Talk."

Allison glanced at the woman to her right and then the one over Kayla's shoulder. Both glanced down as soon as their eyes met Allison's.

"I think we should probably step outside to have this conversation, Kayla."

"What is there to talk about? Are you saying we're not going to join up with Mila?"

Allison stared at her friend for a long time, waited till the fire in Kayla's eyes dropped a few degrees, then spoke in a whisper. "You're joining her. I'm not."

Kayla cocked her head, stared at Allison for a few seconds, then turned her gaze to the ceiling. Finally she turned back and said, "What in the universe are you talking about?"

"I'm going to work with Derrek Wright. And you're going to partner with Mila."

"You're right." Kayla's eyes narrowed. "We're going outside."

———

As they stepped onto the sidewalk, Kayla yanked her arms across her chest and glanced up at the darkening sky. Rain was coming.

"Go ahead," Kayla spat out. "Tell me all about this stupid idea of yours."

After Allison finished, they stopped under the awning of a clothing store that had closed for the night.

"You're really, truly leaving our partnership?" Kayla shook her head and glared at Allison. "I don't get you. At all."

"I already told you. I have to."

"No, you don't have to. You're choosing to."

"I prayed about this like I just said. If Mila hadn't called you, there's no way I would be doing this."

"No." Kayla wagged her finger. "Don't bring all your God-talk into this. That's an excuse to do anything you want. It's not going to work on me."

"We're tearing each other apart."

"But we've always figured a way through it."

"No, we haven't." Allison sighed. "We're both battered and exhausted. And we promised each other that if it ever got to the point where our friendship was being destroyed, we'd end the partnership."

"But things will change once Mila comes on board."

"True. Then we'd have another person to muddy up the mix. It would get worse."

"It wouldn't."

"It would!"

Kayla clenched her teeth and shook her head slowly. "Well then. If you're set on dumping me, big congratulations are in order." Kayla slowly clapped her hands together three times. "Way to go. Woohoo. Let's have a party in celebration of you waltzing off to the big successful firm, making beaucoup bucks, and leaving me here with nothing."

"I'm not doing this to make big bucks. I'm doing it because Mom is in serious trouble and because God—"

Kayla waggled her finger.

"Plus, I'm not taking any of our accounts. You get them all. And when Mila comes on—"

"If! *If* she comes on. Now that you're leaving—"

"She's your friend, not mine. Without me there to split things three ways, it will be even more attractive."

"You don't know that."

They walked again, neither speaking till they'd circled the block and stood outside their class.

"I'm sorry, Kay." Allison pleaded with her eyes. "You know I'd never do this unless—"

Kayla took Allison by the arms.

"Okay, I'm over it," she growled. "Actually, I'm so ticked off at you, but at the same time I love you enough to say this."

"What?"

"I don't trust Derrek Wright, Al. I don't. I never have. This is not about me and you. It's about you. He's . . . I just . . . There's a snake factor with him, I know it. Just be careful, okay?"

"I know you don't believe like I do, Kayla, but this truly is God. He's in this so strong and so clear, I can't not do this."

They walked back inside, picked up their unfinished paintings, and tried to make small talk as they shuffled back out and made their way toward their cars. In the parking lot they both cried and hugged, but the hug was quick and Allison knew it was a perfunctory gesture at best.

———

Allison pushed through her front door at nine thirty-five and went to find her mom. Not in the guest bedroom, which would be her mom's room till she literally got back on her feet. Not watching TV. Had to be in the kitchen. She was, reading a book about how to grow lush gardens in tiny spaces.

"Hey, Mom."

"How'd it go?" Her mom took a sip of what smelled like pumpkin spice tea.

"It went."

"That bad?"

"It will be okay. I hope." Allison poured herself a cup of tea and joined her mom at the table.

"Why do I feel like the bad guy? It was God who did this. If it's anyone's fault, it's his."

"When do you start with the new company?"

"It'll take at least three days to wrap everything up with clients, and with Kayla."

"No chance for a little time off in between?"

Allison laughed. "Unless Dad's business pals want to stop the clock, I'd say no."

nine

MONDAY MORNING, TWELVE DAYS LATER, Allison came downstairs and looked in the mirror. Dark straight-legged jeans, black ankle boots, her mom's oversize gray cashmere sweater, and a long necklace with a Tree of Life emblem—which Parker had bought for her twenty-fifth birthday. She adjusted the sweater slightly and gave a quick nod. Perfect.

She went into the kitchen to say goodbye and found her mom staring at her plate, hands in her lap.

"Mom, you okay?"

"Fine."

"You don't have to pretend with me, Mom. Right? Tell me, please."

"Worried. I didn't sleep well last night. I think I told you that yesterday morning. And the morning before that."

"You did, but you can tell me again and again." Allison sighed. "Are you going to finish my world-famous mushroom-and-spinach omelet?"

"Sure."

She'd taken only two bites and hadn't touched her toast.

"You have to eat, Mom. I know your stomach is busy getting itself tied in knots, but you have to, okay? For both of us."

"Okay."

"We're going to get you through this. I promise."

"I don't know what I'd do without you, Ally."

Allison tried to laugh. It came off weak. "Then it's a good thing you decided to have me thirty-four years ago."

"Have you and Derrek finished your partnership agreement yet?"

"Soon. We're going to get it done soon."

"Good. And once you do, and once we get things paid off, I'm going to pay you back. You know that, right, Ally?"

"Yes, Mom, I know." She backed away. "I gotta go, Mom. Don't want to be late."

Five minutes later Allison inched down the on-ramp that fed I-90 and would take her to Wright Architecture. Day nine of her new adventure. For the most part it had been good. The fourteen staff members seemed friendly. The only person she didn't click with was Linda, Derrek's longtime executive assistant, but one out of fourteen wasn't bad.

She glanced at her watch—eight twenty already—then at the cars in front of her. Puget Sound gridlock. One of the downsides of partnering with Derrek: her commute time had tripled. And with an accident like the one showing up on her GPS? Forty minutes to travel sixteen miles. Two more cars ahead of her waited for the metered ramp stoplight to flash from red to green.

A few seconds later her phone buzzed. A text from Linda.

Where are you, Allison? What are you doing? Derrek would like to meet with you. I'm quite surprised you're not at the office already, or at least let us know where you are and what has caused your delay. Our workday starts at 8:00 a.m.

Eight? Good to know. As if she hadn't been able to figure out what time the office officially opened. Where was she? The same place she'd been every morning that week. Getting her mom ready for a day without assistance. Making sure she had her medication and a charged cell phone. Wrapping up niggling details with Kayla so she wouldn't have to do it at her new office.

What was she doing? Feeling guilty when there was no reason to feel guilty. Trying to figure out how to respond to a scolding from a woman who unofficially was Allison's employee but acted like she owned the company.

Eight fifty came and went before Allison pulled into her spot in the parking garage in the heart of downtown Bellevue. She got out and jogged across the gray concrete, lugging her light tan briefcase, which felt heavier now than it should, and passing pricey late-model cars. The kind Derrek had promised her but hadn't mentioned since their meeting at The Vogue. She didn't really care. Would it be nice? Sure. But the rest of the agreement was what mattered. Today she would get him to finalize it. She had to.

She slipped into the elevator just as the doors slid closed and faked a smile for the two ladies and a man who hadn't tried to catch the door for her. She forced herself to settle into long breaths in and out before the elevator reached the twenty-third floor. *Get out, get into the office, get your game face on.*

ten

AS SHE STEPPED THROUGH THE door into the offices of Wright Architecture, Linda glanced up from the copy machine and drilled her with a look that said, *I've got you now.*

"Good morning, Linda."

Linda leaned to her left, pulled the copies out of the tray, and lined them up. Glanced at her watch, then cocked her head. "He's waiting for you in his office."

Allison dropped her coat and briefcase off in her office first. Her office was next to Derrek's, and in a bit of creative construction, there was open space six inches wide that ran from the ceiling to halfway down the wall, which allowed her to hear Derrek's conversations. Her hearing was exceptional—family and friends had always joked about her ears having nanotechnology—and in this case it allowed her to stay on top of the ebb and flow of the office without having to meet with Derrek every few hours.

She made her way into his office and stepped to the center of the room. Derrek's focus was on his laptop, fingers pounding the keyboard, his ever-present Bluetooth earpiece over his right ear. Allison studied his wall-to-wall shelves full of books, photos with the important and powerful from the Seattle area and beyond, and exotic trinkets from Africa, Rome, Thailand, and Antarctica.

Three minutes slipped by. Five.

"Be right with you, Allison."

Seven. Ten.

"You want me to come back, Derrek? I can—"

"No, no. I'll just be a few more seconds. Thanks for your patience."

A few more seconds slipped into a minute, two minutes. Three.

"There!" Derrek tapped the mouse pad on his laptop with a flourish, turned to Allison, and motioned to the seats in front of the desk.

Allison sat in the chair closest to the door.

"Well then. Good morning, Ms. Moore."

"Good morning."

"Do you have time to chat about a few things?"

No. She didn't. She had an email she had to send out by nine thirty that she'd be done with by now if she hadn't just burned fifteen minutes standing in Derrek's office. Plus, two proposals that needed to get out by noon.

"Sure."

"Good." Derrek leaned back and locked his hands behind his head. "As you're aware, we're trying to inculcate a certain decorum in our office. An attitude, a statement, an ambience of professionalism."

Allison nodded.

"To achieve those things, a certain standard is required. To be specific, our dress needs to communicate that standard. To be even more precise, I'd like you to start wearing business suits."

"What?"

Derrek smiled.

Allison frowned. "We're not a law firm, we're an—"

"Yes, I understand that, and you're going to say your style is more casual, and that's the way you did it at your old company." Derrek chuckled. "But I'm not interested in one of us being the straight man and the other being the cool gal who dresses so casually our clients think she's trying to be hip, which they perceive as a veiled statement about our creativity. Our creativity is demonstrated in our designs, not our dress."

"I dress well. Casual, but sharp."

"I know you do, and if it were just me, I'd have no problem seeing you here in shorts and T-shirts every day." Another throaty chuckle. "But we have clients dropping by from time to time, and we need to be battle ready at all times."

"That means?"

"As I just said, business suits. Skirts. On rare occasions slacks and blouses." Derrek released his hands behind his neck and leaned forward in his chair. "At some point we might move a few inches more casual on Fridays. But for now this is the way everyone in the office will continue to dress."

Unbelievable. Allison hadn't worn skirts or formal business suits—except for weddings and funerals—for five years. Even at the company where she and Kayla worked before starting their firm, the dress had been smart but relaxed. Where was Derrek living? In the fifties? Formal wear at work? Yes, business suits and skirts did send a message. A message that Wright Architecture was as stiff as Sheetrock.

Derrek turned to his laptop.

"Anything else other than the dress code, Derrek?"

"Um, I think Linda already addressed our arrival time, didn't she?"

"Arrival time?"

"We start at eight."

"Yes, and we end at five. And I've been working past seven every day since I started, and working at home as well. One of the perks of being a partner is the freedom to come in when I need to and leave when I need to."

"I know, I know. I understand."

"Then what's the problem?"

"Of course you can come and go as you like, but since Linda is the office manager, out of respect for her, and to set a good example for those working for us, what do you say? Can you make a concentrated effort to be here by eight?"

"Sure, Derrek. No problem."

"Thank you, Allison, I appreciate it."

He turned back to his laptop.

"Anything else on that?"

"No." Derrek smiled with a twinkle in his eye that said they were done.

"Then can we talk about finalizing the details of our partnership?"

Derrek looked up, but his fingers stayed on the keyboard. "Thanks for bringing that up, Allison. I'd like to, and I know you've been patient in regard to that subject, but—"

A voice from the doorway interrupted him.

"I'm sorry to interrupt, Derrek, but can I ask Allison a quick question?" Linda stood just inside the door, a plastic smile at the corners of her mouth.

Derrek raised his eyebrows to Allison, who slowly nodded. Linda. Perfect timing. Not the first time this kind of thing had happened. *Think positive thoughts. Try to believe it's a coincidence.* Allison gave Derrek a weak smile and twisted in her chair. Linda strolled into the room, her maroon skirt long and pressed sharp, arms cradling a stack of yellow file folders. When she reached Derrek's desk, she leaned against it and cocked her head.

"What was so important that you came in late, Allison?" Linda tapped her fingers on the files. "It's not a serious issue. I'm simply curious."

"It was . . ." Allison stared at her, trying to keep her frustration in check. She wanted to describe Linda's eyes as kind, but they weren't. The first layer maybe, but there was ice underneath. A cruelty. The kind that forces a child's hand onto a hot stove to teach her not to touch and justifies the action when the behavior changes.

"Why don't you go ahead and tell us, Allison?" A half smile now only made her eyes colder. "I think Derrek might like to know as well. Because as Derrek just alluded to, we have a policy around here of being on time. Every day. And this is the second time you've been late since you started working for Derrek. And that's only been nine days."

Allison almost laughed. Working *for* Derrek?

Linda didn't want to know why she'd been late. Didn't care. Was just trying to make her squirm. Allison glanced at Derrek. He was buried in his laptop as if Linda and she weren't there.

"I saw a homeless man who looked painfully thin. I pulled off and bought a breakfast sandwich and gave it to him. I'm sorry that made me late."

"Really? That's what you did, Allison?"

"No." Allison stood till she was eye to eye with Linda. "You know that's not what happened, Linda."

"What is the truth then?"

"That it isn't an issue you need to be concerned with."

Linda pulled her files tight to her chest and glared. "Let's be on time from now on, shall we, Allison? To set a good example for the staff."

Allison offered nothing more than a thin smile.

Linda sat, crossed her arms and legs, and stared at Allison with eyes that said, *Leave now.*

Allison leaned in toward Derrek.

"When are we going to finish our conversation about the partnership?"

"Soon. Let's set a goal of having that discussion before the end of next week, if not before. As I mentioned, I know we need to get the details finalized."

"Can we set up a time?"

"Yes, I'd like to, but right now I need to meet with Linda on a few things about the company structure."

"I should be here then."

"No, it's nothing major that would require your input. I'll call you if needed. Thanks, Allison."

The rest of the day moved by with enough demands to keep Allison's mind occupied, but as she left the office at five that evening, only one thing filled her mind. The fact that Derrek had once again pushed their partnership into the depths of the forest where the sun didn't shine. But late that evening, as she glanced at her Tree of Life necklace, another thought jockeyed for position. The man she'd seen at The Vogue, and his gorgeous journal that had somehow fully captured her imagination.

eleven

FIVE DAYS LATER, ON SATURDAY afternoon, Allison blew out a long, low breath as she dropped two dollars in the tip jar and picked up her vanilla latte at The Vogue. Now to find a quiet spot to think, to journal, to figure out how she could speed up the partnership process with Derrek. Or maybe take the easier route and get in good enough shape to run a sub-three-hour marathon.

"Allison?"

Allison turned back to Marque, the young gal who had started nine months ago with no experience but already made the best drinks in the shop.

"Yes?"

"You doing all right?"

"Sure. Yes."

"Okay, jus' checking. Your smile's been hiding a little lately."

"It's still here." Allison pointed at her mouth and smiled. "It's just that work is super stressing me right now. And having my mom living with me is stressing me. You know, life."

"Yeah, I get it."

"You? How are wedding plans?"

"We should have eloped."

Allison laughed. "I hear it's a lot easier."

"Without a doubt. Thanks for asking."

She turned to go.

"Hey, Allison, almost forgot." She spun back as Marque went to the back counter, picked up a nondescript box, and brought it back to Allison.

"Here."

"From you?"

"No."

"Then who?"

"I don't know. Mike told me to give this to you."

"Mike?"

"You know . . . Mike." She waved her hand in the air. "The guy who owns this place."

"Right."

Marque pointed at a folded piece of paper on top. "Looks like he wrote a note. That might explain it."

"Mike wrote it?"

"No idea. Like I said, he just told me to give this to you." Marque smiled and motioned toward the espresso maker. "Sorry, gotta go."

Allison worked her way to the back of the shop, sat at her usual table, and set her satchel on the floor. She leaned against the dark maroon wall. She placed the small rectangular box on the table, took a sip of her drink, and opened Mike's note.

Hi Allison,
    Apparently this is yours.
        Mike

Allison set the note aside, lifted the cover of the box, and gasped. Inside was a leather-bound journal. The one Western Washington Sweatshirt Guy and Richard had talked about. Allison lifted the journal out of the box as if it were a parchment from a thousand years ago and set it on the table. She slid her fingers over the leather. Softer than she'd imagined. A texture that came from years, maybe decades of use. The surface felt warm.

She stared at the cover. Gorgeous. The image of a tree was carved into the leather. An image she knew well. The Tree of Life. Allison ran her fingers over the image of the tree, and as she did, a sense of peace swirled around her mind. An urge to open the journal swept over her, but she gave a tiny shake of her head. Of course not. It wasn't hers.

After staring at the journal for more time than seemed appropriate, Allison stood and walked to the front of the shop. She caught Marque's eye a few minutes later.

"Did I mess up your drink?"

"Never." Allison held up the journal. "This is what was inside the box. It's not mine."

Marque blinked. "Beautiful."

Allison nodded.

"I think I know whose this is. I mean, I don't know him, but he had it the other day when I was in here. I don't think he's a regular, but do you guys have a lost-and-found in case he comes back? I think this is something he'd come back for."

"I would too." Marque frowned as she poured a liberal dose of caramel into a cup. "But we don't have a lost-and-found. I guess we used to, but so much stuff piled up. Plus, Mike and Janice don't want to be responsible 'cause of some weird thing where they got sued a while back. So now we hang on to things till the end of the day, then have to toss 'em. So if the guy doesn't come back by the end of the day . . ."

Allison stared at the journal and spoke more to it than Marque. "The journal ends up in the dump."

"Yes, sorry."

Allison shuffled back to her table and glanced at her watch. The shop closed in thirty-five minutes. Which meant she would stay till closing and hope the man showed up to recover the journal. And if he didn't? She'd describe him to Marque and ask her to keep an eye out. No way would she let this journal end up in the trash.

At six ten, Marque said, "Sorry, Allison, I have to kick you out. We gotta clean."

"I've never understood why you guys close so early. You're a coffee and *wine* bar."

Marquee laughed. "You'll have to take that one up with Mike and Janice."

She stood on the sidewalk outside the coffee shop till six thirty. No man in wire-rimmed glasses and a Western Washington University sweatshirt came by looking for his lost journal. Time to head for home.

As she turned her car down the street where she lived, Allison glanced over at the journal that sat on her passenger seat.

"How am I going to get you back to your rightful owner?"

After she pulled into her driveway and stopped, she picked it up and undid the leather cord that bound it shut.

"Easy. I'm going to open you up and find a name and address." Who put their name and address in a journal? She didn't. But maybe Western Washington Sweatshirt Guy did. Allison opened the journal, looked at the top of the first page, and laughed. Right there, in dark blue pen at the top of the page, in a man's large handwriting, was a name and an address.

ALISTER MORRISON
43417 WHITETAIL LANE
PRESTON, WA 98888

No phone number. No email. But the address was enough. Preston was close. After she had dinner and caught up with her mom, she'd google Alister's address and see where he lived. She'd write him a note and tell him she had the journal. Maybe just drive by his place. Under his name and address was what looked like a poem, in different handwriting.

Who we are, and truly are,
A matter of perception.
Choose the truth and find yourself,
Step through the veiled deception.
Know it from the inside out,
Not from the outside in.
Though fear and trepidation wait,
It's time that you begin.

Allison frowned. Wow. Quite the introduction to Alister if he'd written it, and quite the inscription if it had been written for him. She went to put the journal into her satchel, but curiosity got the better of her, and she turned to the next page, then the next, then the next. All of them were blank.

She riffled through the next ten, twenty, thirty pages. No writing on any of them. The rest of the pages as well. It made little sense. Why would Alister tell Richard that the journal had been part of changing his life when there was nothing in it? Sure, the poem was intriguing, but while it raised questions, she couldn't see where it gave any answers. And hadn't he said he'd written in it?

After a quick dinner with her mom and a long conversation about how they shouldn't worry about Allison's partnership being delayed, she unpacked her satchel and set her things on the kitchen counter. As she did, her mom sipped on her chamomile tea and wandered over.

"Did you get yourself a new journal? Where did you find it?"

"I didn't find it, more like it found me. By mistake." Allison laughed. "It's not mine. It belongs to a guy from the coffee shop, and he—"

"Can I see it?"

"Sure." Allison handed her mom the journal. "The owner's address is in the front, so I'll try to find him online or mail him a letter. Probably just mail him a letter. Go old school."

"It's beautiful."

"I agree. I'm going to ask the guy where he got it. I'd love to have one like it."

Her mom ran her fingers over the journal. "The leather is so soft. And the tree, my, it's lovely."

"Like you." Allison leaned down and kissed her mom on the cheek. "I'm going to take a shower, Mom. Be back downstairs in a bit."

"Take your time, honey."

After a long shower, during which Allison nudged the water hotter than usual, she toweled off, slipped into an old pair of sweats, a T-shirt, and her Running Is Cheaper Than Therapy sweatshirt and headed downstairs to chat with her mom. Allison found her sitting on the couch watching *An Affair to Remember*. The journal sat next to her.

Mom looked up as Allison slid into the overstuffed chair next to the couch.

"How's the movie?"

Her mom looked at her furtively. "I peeked inside the journal. At all the pages."

"Good."

"Good?"

"Now I don't feel so guilty." Allison giggled. "I peeked too."

"I think you should keep the journal."

"I can't keep it, Mom. It's not mine. It's Alister's. And I'm going to get it back to him."

"How are you going to do that?"

"I told you. I'll send him a note." Allison held up her cell phone. "Or I'll plug the address into my phone and just drive to his house and drop it off."

"How are you going to do that?"

Allison frowned as a tiny laugh escaped her lips. "Are you okay, Mom?"

"How are you going to do that?"

"Mom, really, are you all right? Like I just said, I'll write a note using the address Alister put in the front of the journal, or I'll drive over there. Yes, I'm assuming that's his address. Why wouldn't it be?"

A crack of a confused smile appeared on her mom's face as she handed the journal to Allison and spoke in a whisper. "What address?"

Allison took the journal from her mom. It felt heavier. She held it for more than a few moments before gently lifting the cover, already sensing what she would find. She stared at the first page for a long time. A page without a name. Without an address. Only a poem that no longer felt intriguing, but ominous.

twelve

ALLISON SLID OUT OF BED at six the next morning, pulled on a sky-blue tank top, running shorts, socks, shoes, and a light jacket. Eight miles on the schedule today—after she reached the trailhead, which was 1.7 miles away from her home. No problem. At least physically. Felt like she could do eighteen. But emotionally she was closer to being able to do half a mile. Still, she had to rid her body of the stress of the day before, and the days before that, and try to forget about this weird journal thing for a few hours.

There had been an address. There was no doubt in her mind, and she was far too young to be losing it. *Alister Morrison* had been there, written in thick black pen along with an address in Preston. Those words *were* written at the top. She could still picture it in her mind! But when her mom had handed Allison the journal, the words and numbers simply were not there. Impossible. There had to be a reason. Not invisible ink. Maybe it was another kind of ink she didn't know about that only appeared with heat. But that made no sense. She hadn't applied any heat in the car yesterday when she saw the name. And why would it be hidden anyway? What was the point of writing your name and address in a journal if no one could read it?

She shook the thoughts from her mind and took off down the

street. Allison reached the trail at the base of Tiger Mountain and stopped to stare at the clouds. Heavy with rain but no drops falling. Yet. Allison cinched the hood of her jacket a hair tighter and launched herself onto the trail. The dirt was soft from yesterday's deluge, but manageable. It would probably mean nine-minute miles instead of seven, but the workout would be just as grueling. No one was on the trail at this time of the morning. On occasion Allison would meet another runner slaloming through the fir trees this early, breathing the crisp morning air, but rarely till the weather grew warmer.

Forty-five minutes later she reached the top of the trail where acres of trees had been cleared for radio towers. She slowed and strolled over to the lookout spot on the north side of the mountain, which gave a 240-degree view. To her west: the rolling forested hills of Issaquah and then Bellevue. To the east: Mount Si and North Bend. She already felt far better than she had upon waking that morning. As if on cue, the sun struck through the clouds in a few places, promising her spring—and hope—was coming.

For the next ten minutes she closed her eyes and didn't let herself think about her job, her mom, Kayla, the money—nothing except that at this moment she was free of all of it. And then, as if with the flick of a light switch, an image of the journal popped into her mind. With a tiny shake of her head, she opened her eyes. She blinked against the sun, which had taken over at least half of the sky, and sighed.

What was that? Movement in her peripheral vision to her left. She turned and spotted a man seventy-five or so yards away, gazing west toward the Bellevue skyline. His height, his hair, his frame. All familiar to her. Did she know him?

She took a dozen steps closer. Was it him? Yes, no question. Richard. The man who'd been with Alister Morrison that day in the coffee shop. *Oh my gosh. Answers.* She clipped toward him, but after she'd taken only a few steps, he turned slowly away from her, stretched quickly, then started to jog back down the trail.

"Excuse me!" She picked up her pace.

He didn't turn, and his jog turned into a run.

"Hey!" Allison called louder as she broke into a run of her own. "Hello!"

The man was already around a corner in the trail, the trees hiding him from sight. By the time Allison rounded the corner, he was gone. No, wait. There he was, at least a hundred yards in front of her. She pushed herself into a full sprint as he disappeared around the next switchback. No doubt she could catch him. She'd slowed since her days on the track in high school and college, but not that much.

But by the time she reached another straightaway, the man was easily 150 yards out. Allison's sprint faded to a jog, to a brisk walk, to standing still. No chance of catching him, which surprised her. She was no slouch when it came to running. The guy appeared to be in decent shape, sure, but pushing his midfifties. Probably an ex-athlete competing in masters competitions.

The sound of her heart pounded in her ears as she leaned forward, hands resting on knees. Hadn't he heard her? Seemed unlikely, but why would he ignore her if he had?

When she pushed through her front door an hour later, the smell of muffins filled the kitchen. Allison found her mom curled up on the brown leather chair in the den.

"Did you have a good run, Al?"

"I did."

"What's wrong?"

"Nothing's wrong."

Her mom tilted her head and gave that funny little smile that Allison loved and hated at the same time.

"How do you know there's something wrong?"

"Because—"

"You're my mother. I know. You can tell something's wrong even when my back is turned."

"Yes. It's a superpower most moms have." Her mom sighed. "But it also comes at the price of worrying about your kids too much."

"I don't always like your superpower."

"Too bad." Her mom wiggled her fingers. "Speak."

"Let me get some tea first."

"Hurry."

Allison turned and rolled her eyes as she walked out of the room. "I saw that!"

Her mom laughed and Allison smiled. Maybe her mom really could see around corners.

She heated a cup of water in the microwave as she pulled a tea bag from the pantry. This conversation called for strawberry-pomegranate herbal tea, because she had few doubts her mom would want to hear every single detail about her encounter—or nonencounter—up on the mountain. At the moment Allison would prefer to give only headlines.

The microwave dinged. She brought out the cup and placed her tea bag on top and watched it sink into the near boiling water. She drew in the smell of the tea and closed her eyes. Perfect.

As she settled into the other chair in the den, her mom clapped her knees. "Now tell me."

"In the coffee shop, the first time I saw the journal, there was a man there with Alister. A guy named Richard." Allison paused. "I saw him on the mountain today. At the top. No question it was him. But when I called to him, he ran off."

"Ran off?"

"Yes."

"How do you know he heard you?"

"I don't."

Her mom rubbed her upper lip. "Then how can you say he ran off when he heard you?"

"I didn't say that. I—"

"Yes, you did. You just said it."

Allison took a long sip of her tea. "I'm *guessing* that's what happened. It seemed that way."

"You're sure it was the same man who was in the coffee shop?"

"Yes."

"What did he want?"

"Mom, how would I—"

"I don't mean that." Her mom waved her hands as if to excuse the comment. "I mean, what do you think he has to do with the journal?"

Another long sip. "I don't know."

"Tell you what, sweetie." Her mom leaned forward in her chair. "Go get your journal. I think it's a sign, seeing this Richard character."

"My journal?"

"Yes. The new one."

"Mom, stop. It's not mine."

"Go get it."

Allison squeezed her lips together. "Mom?"

"And bring it back here."

"Mom, I—"

"I'll wait right here till you get back."

"All right, Mom."

Her mom nodded as if giving Allison permission to leave. Allison set her cup on the cherrywood stand next to her chair and rose. She grimaced at her mom and strode from the room. She'd set the journal on the coffee table and it was still there, but not exactly in the spot she'd left it. Her mom had moved it. Looked at it. Not a surprise. The journal was captivating.

When she came back into the den, her mom's head was down.

"Okay, Mom. Now what?"

"I think you need to start writing in it."

"I told you, it's not my journal."

"I know what you told me." Her mom leaned forward in her chair, and her face turned to stone. "But you should. I feel it deep inside."

They locked eyes. The gentle countenance Allison had known all her life had vanished. Her mom's eyes were full of grit.

"Open it."

"Why?"

Her mom nodded toward the journal.

Allison slowly undid the leather cord that wrapped the journal and let it fall to the side. Then she lifted the cover and fixed her eyes on the first page. Once again there was writing at the top. A name. And an address.

Her name. And her address.

thirteen

ALLISON'S HAND WENT NUMB, AND the journal slipped from her hands and thumped onto the carpet next to her feet. She barely noticed. She stared at her mom, words sputtering out of her mouth.

"What?" She poked her finger in the direction of the journal. "Did you do this, Mom? You shouldn't have done that. It's not yours or mine to write in."

"I didn't write in it."

She knew it wasn't her mom's handwriting, and the air grew thin in face of the fact there was no explanation for how the old name and address had vanished and hers had replaced them.

"Then . . . who . . . who . . ."

"Breathe, sweetie." Her mom rose and limped over to her. "It's okay. Just breathe for me, all right?"

Allison forced herself to slow her breaths, then eased back into the chair she'd been in before the world had gone crazy.

"Who wrote in there, Mom, if it wasn't you? Who did this to me? What is that thing?" She jabbed her finger at the journal again as if it were alive.

"I don't know what it is, and I don't know who wrote in it, but I have a theory."

Allison's mind continued to spin. "I don't think any theory is going to stop me from freaking out."

Her mom gingerly bent down, lifted the journal, and settled onto the corner of the chair next to Allison. She set the journal on her lap as Allison inched away from it.

"The writing is on the wall."

"What?" Allison scooted another inch farther away from her mom. "What do you mean? Are you saying I should have seen this coming?"

"That's my theory." She opened the journal and tapped the writing at the top. *"Mene mene tekel upharsin."*

"Oh, that explains everything. Thanks, Mom."

"Daniel chapter 5, in the Old Testament, the story of Belshazzar's feast. That's what I think this is. You remember the story, don't you?"

"Not really." Not really? That was a stretch. She didn't remember it at all. The last time she'd cracked her Bible to the Old Testament was three years ago. Her mom looked at her as if she knew the truth but decided to ignore the white lie. She pulled her cell phone out of her pocket and half a minute later began to read.

"King Belshazzar held a great feast for 1,000 of his nobles and drank wine in their presence. Under the influence of the wine, Belshazzar gave orders to bring in the gold and silver vessels that his predecessor Nebuchadnezzar had taken from the temple in Jerusalem, so that the king and his nobles, wives, and concubines could drink from them. So they brought in the gold vessels that had been taken from the temple, the house of God in Jerusalem, and the king and his nobles, wives, and concubines drank from them. They drank the wine and praised their gods made of gold and silver, bronze, iron, wood, and stone.

"At that moment the fingers of a man's hand appeared and began writing on the plaster of the king's palace wall next to the lampstand. As the king watched the hand that was writing, his face turned pale, and his thoughts so terrified him that his hip joints shook and his knees knocked together. The king called out to bring in the mediums, Chaldeans, and astrologers. He said to these wise men of Babylon, 'Whoever reads this inscription and gives me its interpretation will be clothed in purple, have a gold chain around his neck, and have the third highest position in the kingdom.' So all the king's wise men came in, but none could read the inscription or make its interpretation known to him. Then King Belshazzar became even more terrified, his face turned pale, and his nobles were bewildered.

"Because of the outcry of the king and his nobles, the queen came to the banquet hall. 'May the king live forever,' she said. 'Don't let your thoughts terrify you or your face be pale. There is a man in your kingdom who has the spirit of the holy gods in him. In the days of your predecessor he was found to have insight, intelligence, and wisdom like the wisdom of the gods. Your predecessor, King Nebuchadnezzar, appointed him chief of the diviners, mediums, Chaldeans, and astrologers. Your own predecessor, the king, did this because Daniel, the one the king named Belteshazzar, was found to have an extraordinary spirit, knowledge and perception, and the ability to interpret dreams, explain riddles, and solve problems. Therefore, summon Daniel, and he will give the interpretation.'

"Then Daniel was brought before the king. The king said to him, 'Are you Daniel, one of the Judean exiles that my predecessor the king brought from Judah? I've heard that you have the spirit of the gods in you, and that you have insight, intelligence, and extraordinary wisdom. Now the wise men and mediums were brought before me to read this inscription and make its interpretation known to me, but they could not give its interpretation. However, I have heard about you that you can give interpretations and solve problems. Therefore, if you can read this inscription and give me its interpretation, you will be clothed in purple, have a gold chain around your neck, and have the third highest position in the kingdom.'

"Then Daniel answered the king, 'You may keep your gifts, and give your rewards to someone else; however, I will read the inscription for the king and make the interpretation known to him. Your Majesty, the Most High God gave sovereignty, greatness, glory, and majesty to your predecessor Nebuchadnezzar. Because of the greatness He gave him, all peoples, nations, and languages were terrified and fearful of him. He killed anyone he wanted and kept alive anyone he wanted; he exalted anyone he wanted and humbled anyone he wanted. But when his heart was exalted and his spirit became arrogant, he was deposed from his royal throne and his glory was taken from him. He was driven away from people, his mind was like an animal's, he lived with the wild donkeys, he was fed grass like cattle, and his body was drenched with dew from the sky until he acknowledged that the Most High God is ruler over the kingdom of men and sets anyone He wants over it.

"'But you his successor, Belshazzar, have not humbled your heart, even though you knew all this. Instead, you have exalted yourself against the Lord of heaven. The vessels from His house were brought to you, and as you and your nobles, wives, and concubines drank wine from them, you praised the gods made of silver and gold, bronze, iron, wood, and stone, which do not see or hear or understand. But you have not glorified the God who holds your life-breath in His hand and who controls the whole course of your life. Therefore, He sent the hand, and this writing was inscribed.

"'This is the writing that was inscribed:

"'MENE, MENE, TEKEL, PARSIN.

"'This is the interpretation of the message:

"'MENE means that God has numbered the days of your kingdom and brought it to an end.

"'TEKEL means that you have been weighed in the balance and found deficient.

"'PERES means that your kingdom has been divided and given to the Medes and Persians.'

"Then Belshazzar gave an order, and they clothed Daniel in purple, placed a gold chain around his neck, and issued a proclamation concerning him that he should be the third ruler in the kingdom.

"That very night Belshazzar the king of the Chaldeans was killed."

Allison's mom set her phone down and gave a satisfied nod. Allison shook her head. "Are you saying God wrote in that journal? That he wrote the poem? That he's trying to tell me something? Like I'm going to die?"

Her heart rate spiked.

"No, not that part, just the writing part."

"So the writing in that journal came from God."

"Do you have a better explanation?"

"Sure. There're a million things that could explain it." Her mind scrambled for ideas and didn't land on any inspired enlightenment.

Highly unlikely someone sneaked into the house and erased Alister's information, then sneaked in again and wrote down her name and address. The invisible ink theory was laughable, and unless some angel— Oh boy, she'd returned to God in two quick steps.

"God writing in there? That's crazy. God doesn't do things like that anymore."

"God is the same yesterday, today, and forever. If he did it thousands of years ago, why couldn't he do it today?"

"I'm not sure I believe he did it thousands of years ago."

"Maybe not." Her mom patted Allison's leg. "But is there a better answer?"

Her mom's words made a memory pop into Allison's mind. A philosophy class from college where the professor had lectured on Occam's razor.

"For each accepted explanation of a phenomenon, there may be an extremely large, perhaps even incomprehensible, number of possible and more complex alternatives. However, the simplest answer tends to be the correct one," the professor had said.

Allison stared at her mom. "If you're right, what do I do now?"

"If that really is God's hand, then apparently it's your journal now. So I think you should do what you always do with journals. I think you should write in it."

"I don't know if I can do that."

"I don't think you have to know at this point. Just think about it. Pray about it. Then decide. For now, just be open to the idea."

Her mom had always been able to make things simple.

Allison extended her arm and mouthed the word *Okay*.

Her mom set the journal in Allison's palm as if it were a butterfly's wing and gave a little smile. Allison opened it and looked at her name and address, then read the poem again.

Who we are, and truly are,
A matter of perception.
Choose the truth, and find yourself,
Step through the veiled deception.
Know it from the inside out,
Not from the outside in.
Though fear and trepidation wait,
It's time that you begin.

Allison peered at the writing. From a black pen. A strange style, with the edges of each letter bleeding onto the page as if the paper had soaked up too much ink.

The words were written in a thin, flowing script. An artist's penmanship. The words intrigued her. Even more, she was captured by the feelings they stirred inside her. Scared. Excited. And more than those, a sense the poem was written for her.

"My journal, huh?"

"For now apparently."

"But why me?" She closed it and rubbed the supple leather. Stared at the Tree of Life tooled into the cover. Imagined herself taking a pen to the journal's thick, creamy pages.

"Why *not* you, sweetie?"

"I don't know, Mom."

"Do what you do with journals. Get it out. Whatever's inside you."

She turned the first page and ran her finger down the blank paper. Maybe tomorrow. Maybe.

fourteen

ALLISON WOKE THE NEXT MORNING long before the sun would crest the horizon, with an image of the journal filling her mind. She gritted her teeth. Couldn't she get a few moments to wake up first without thoughts of the journal crowding her brain? Her mom would say it was God trying to talk to her. She wasn't so sure. Allison shuffled past the den and glanced at the journal, which sat in the middle of her desk. She shouldn't have glanced. Her mom's words about writing in it flooded back in, and she had to make a conscious choice to push on toward the kitchen.

What was wrong with her? Why was the idea of writing in the journal so hard for her? Because it was someone else's. Not a compelling argument, because apparently it was hers now, decreed by the very hand of God. How about because she liked her old journal better, and she always finished filling out an old journal before she started writing in a new one?

Lame. If God really was part of this journal, how could she turn down his invitation? The real reason came from the little voice inside. The one that told her if she went down this path, there was no coming back. That if she took pen to paper she would have to face things about herself she didn't want to face. Truths a little voice said she'd be crushed under. Truths she couldn't handle. And that, of course, was where the little voice inside made a mistake. Because as much as the idea frightened her, the part of her that refused to back down from a challenge was a fraction more persuasive.

After fixing herself coffee, toast, and two scrambled eggs, she went to the den, got the journal, then moved into the family room, where she snuggled up in an ultrasoft throw with a snowflake pattern she'd bought for herself last Christmas. She glanced at her watch. Almost five thirty. Had to get in the shower and get ready for work. Had to beat everyone in. Had to keep building her case for getting the partnership finalized soon. There was no time to write in the journal now. Tonight, however, she might, probably would, but certainly not until she took one more shot at finding Alister. But how? A Google search hadn't shown her anything useful.

Allison arrived at the office at six sixteen—she even beat Linda in—and had made it through a complex set of drawings and was about to start another when Derrek knocked on her office door. Allison glanced at her watch. A few minutes past nine.

"Good morning, Allison."

"Hi, Derrek."

"I trust your weekend was refreshing."

"It was all right, thanks." She gave him a smile she hoped looked sincere. "Yours?"

"Fine, fine." Derrek chuckled as if he'd just recalled a joke.

"Good."

"Do you have a moment?"

"Sure."

"I wanted to commiserate with you in regard to the Thompson project. I think it wise to set a target date for completing the first set of drawings."

"I finished them a minute and a half before you walked in here."

"Really." Derrek glanced up as if counting the days in his mind. "That was extremely rapid."

Allison pushed back from her desk as the scent of cinnamon rolls floated through her door. She glanced around Derrek and spotted Ellie scooting around her reception desk with a box of Cinnabons in her hands.

"Thanks. It came together well, I think."

She had worked on the project over the weekend and put far more hours into it than she'd meant to, but it was a way to solidify her position and show Derrek her worth.

Derrek stepped inside her office, shut the door halfway, and lowered his voice.

"Have you called him yet, Mr. Thompson, told him the drawings have been completed?"

"No, not yet." Allison pointed to her laptop. "Like I said, I just finished them. He did send an email about ten minutes ago asking how they're coming along, and I just started a reply. Do you think I should call him instead to let him know we're finished?"

Derrek reached over and eased her door closed.

"That course of action might not hold the maximum long-term benefit for us."

"What are you saying? I should call, or I should email?"

"Neither. I'm saying do not call and don't email. Not yet. At least not to tell him we're finished."

"Why would I put it off?"

"Let's think through this, shall we?" Derrek stepped up to her desk and leaned against it.

"If you provide him the drawings this quickly, it will train him to expect this level of response every time. That is not to our advantage. This time we finished early. What happens next time when it takes longer, due to unforeseen impediments?"

Allison frowned. "If we give him a timeline and something out of our control happens, we call and explain it. He's a reasonable man. He wouldn't be upset."

"Possibly." Derrek glanced behind him. "But unfortunately, after the initial conversation, he would only remember that we didn't deliver as efficiently as the time before, which could cause him to doubt our acumen. We have an opportunity to build in a cushion here for a time in the future when we might perhaps need it."

"What do you want me to say?"

"Tell him you're working on it but have hit a number of complications that will take time to work through. But they are only minor delays, and we don't see anything on the horizon that would prevent us from being finished in three or four days."

Allison stared at Derrek and gave a tiny shake of her head.

"In other words, you want me to lie to him?"

"No, no, of course not." Derrek chuckled and glanced at the closed door of Allison's office again. "That's not what I'm suggesting in the least."

"Then what are you saying?"

"We tell the truth, of course. We say we've been working diligently on the project, that we are confident the drawings are going to be to his liking. That we are going through our five-phase process to make sure we have met all of his requirements. And that we will deliver them at the end of the week at the latest. None of that is a lie. It is all truth, and yet at the same time we take advantage of the opportunity to—"

"It's still a lie, Derrek."

"Let me ask you a critical question." Derrek moved toward the door and placed his hand on the knob but didn't open it. "Have you gone through the five-phase review process yet?"

"What five-phase review process? We've never talked about—"

"It's a process we do on all projects. Apparently I haven't gone over it with you yet."

"No, you haven't, but that doesn't change the fact I've finished the drawings and—"

"If you've finished the drawings, then you're through with the first part of the project. But since you haven't gone through the five-phase review, then obviously you aren't prepared to show them to Mr. Thompson yet. Are you?"

"Using that logic, no."

"Good, good. I'm pleased that we're in agreement." A wide grin. "I'll cover the review process with you in the next day or two; then, when you've completed it, you can send out the drawings."

Allison stared at him, any coherent response gone from her mind. What could she say? *You're full of air so hot it would scorch the sun.* She'd never heard of a five-phase review process till this moment, yet she'd had multiple projects go out the door. But this wasn't the time to press the issue. After the partnership was sealed? Then she'd confront the man who had spin-doctoring mastered.

Allison made it to The Vogue by six o'clock and was thankful to find Mike and Janice, the owners, both in the shop. Marque could probably explain to them why Allison wanted to put up little flyers asking Alister to contact her, but it was better coming from her.

She was three sentences into her request when Mike held up a hand and she stopped. "Can't do it," he said.

"You have a policy against customers putting up flyers in the shop?"

"It's not that," Janice said and offered her a tender smile. "It's that you don't need to."

Allison's heart skipped. "You know who he is?"

"Nope. Neither of us has any idea," Mike said as he wiped coffee grounds off the counter. "But we do have something to give you."

Janice went to the shelf on the wall behind the counter and plucked up a small square envelope. She handed it to Mike.

Mike said, "The other day he comes in and hands the journal to me. Says it's yours."

Now Mike's note made sense. *Apparently this is yours.*

"And then, after I take the journal, he gives you that note," Allison said as she pointed at the envelope in Mike's hand.

"Yes."

Mike leaned his tall frame down, elbows on the counter. "Guy says his name is Alister, describes you, says when you come in next time to give you this." He handed the envelope to her.

"What else?" Allison glanced back and forth between them. "Who is he? Did he give you any way I can reach him?"

"Nope," Mike said, stood tall, and shuffled off.

"I did ask this Alister fellow who he was and why he'd given you the journal." Janice patted Allison's hand. "But he just smiled and asked if we could make sure you got the envelope. He was in and out in less than a minute."

Allison turned the envelope over in her hands. Nothing on either side.

"Thanks." She slid it into her back pocket. "If he comes in again . . ."

"I sure will."

———

She waited till she got inside her car, then pulled the envelope from her pocket and tore it open. Before she slid the thick paper out, Allison asked God for the note to provide answers. God must not have been listening. Allison stared at the words till her eyes blurred.

Write in the journal. It truly is yours now. Write. Not for me. For you. Just write.

There was nothing else on the card. *Fine.* Tonight she would log her first entry.

fifteen

ALLISON TIPTOED PAST HER MOM'S bedroom, listening for the soft snoring that proved she was asleep. Yes. There it was. Now she felt free to write in the journal. This was not a moment to be interrupted, and if her mom spotted her writing in the journal, there would be a flurry of questions and suggestions.

She went to her den, found her favorite pen, lit a sandalwood candle, then curled up on her overstuffed chair and lifted the journal from the stand next to the chair and onto her lap. A deep sigh. Open the journal. Turn to the second page and begin.

May 20th

First, I have to say it feels incredibly strange to be writing in a journal that's mine but isn't mine. How honest should I be in these pages? I suppose that's the point. If I'm not willing to be honest here, then I shouldn't be writing anything down.

If God is truly in this, then I need to be fully in it as well. So I will be. And I also know, or feel—how can I know for sure?—that if I do this, if I go all in, life will change. And in this moment I have a choice. To stay safe. Or to jump.

Allison paused and peered at the rain pattering on her window. Did she really want to jump? She put pen back to paper a few seconds later.

> I'm stalling. What do I want to say?
>
> That I'm adrift. That a sadness has surrounded me.
>
> That leaving Kayla and going to work with Derrek—no, right now it's *for* Derrek—has been like going from the frying pan into an active volcano. He's not the man I thought he was. I need to get the partnership finalized. For Mom. And if I'm honest, just as much for me.
>
> When Derrek called and asked me to partner, it made me feel so good and wanted and valuable. And now, with Linda lording her power over me and Derrek putting me off, I don't know where I stand.
>
> And I'm alone. Never expected my marriage to end. Does anyone? So alone. I wasn't made this way, yet here I am.
>
> I have no power. I'm not in control. I have few choices. I'm scared. What do I do?
>
> I've never been strong. Not as strong as I want to be. As strong as I need to be. Help me, Lord. I want to believe in myself, believe I can do this.
>
> God, if this really is you, I want to know it for certain. I want to know you'll show me. Please?

Enough for the first entry. She gently closed the journal, wrapped the thin leather strap around it, and tucked it in under itself. The candle flame flickered as if to approve of her writing, and a warmth settled into her mind.

Allison turned the book over in her hands, then again, then

peered at the tree on the thick leather cover. In that moment the journal did feel like hers. Completely.

The next morning Allison rose early, went for a two-mile run, then went to her den and picked up the journal to read what she'd written the night before. But three quarters of the way through she stopped cold. The words had changed. And some had vanished altogether.

sixteen

SHE STARED AT HER ENTRY and took short, quick breaths through her nose. Impossible. But it had happened. The writing had changed. Hadn't it? Those were her words, most of them, yes—but not all of them. Words had disappeared, a few replaced by new ones, in her handwriting, a few simply gone. How was that possible? Heat washed through her.

She squinted at the words.

> I have power. I'm in control. I have choices.
> I've been strong.
> Help me, Lord. I believe I can do this.
> God, if this really is you and you really are going to speak to me through it, I know you'll show me.

This couldn't be happening, could it? Her heart pounded as if she were running six-minute miles. Allison tried to steady her breathing. As she slowly got herself under control, she peered at the words again. It was impossible. But the professor's words about Occam's razor flashed into her mind, and she stopped the wrestling match in her mind.

"Is this really you, God?"

Allison shut the journal and glanced at her watch. Six ten. Had to start getting ready for work soon, but also had to talk to someone about the journal. Her mom might be up by now. She went to the guest bedroom and opened the door a crack. Her mom sat in the small chair in the corner of the room, staring at her laptop, wrapped in a shawl.

Allison knocked and her mom said, "Come in."

She eased into the room, journal behind her back.

Her mom glanced up but didn't say anything.

"What are you doing?"

"Watching a documentary called *The History of the Eagles*. It's good."

Her mom's voice was flat.

"You don't have to watch it in your room."

"I know, but sometimes I want to give you your space. I'm sure you miss the peace and quiet of morning time."

Her mom turned up the volume on the laptop.

"Mom, I want to talk about the journal. Something just happened that's beyond bizarre, and I'm not sure what to do, but I do know I need to get some answers. Right now."

"Did you know Don Henley used to live right above Jackson Browne? And that Jackson Browne gave the song 'Take It Easy' to the Eagles?"

"No, I didn't." Allison stepped farther into the room. "Mom, please, you have to listen to me. Something weird just happened with the journal. Like, off the charts."

"Okay." She paused the show and set the laptop aside. "Go ahead."

"Are you all right?"

"Sure. Just tired."

Allison wiggled the journal. "I wrote in it last night."

"Really?" Her mom motioned for Allison to sit down. "How was that for you?"

"At the time it was good. It felt right. A little strange, but that might have been my imagination. But this morning it turned into more than my imagination."

"What happened?"

"I went back to read what I wrote and the writing had changed."

"What?"

"Not a lot, a few words. Replaced by different words. And some words vanished completely."

"I told you," her mom muttered. "This is God. The hand of God is writing in your journal."

"I don't believe that."

"Yes, you do. I can see it in your eyes. With your heart you've already accepted it. Soon you will with your mind as well."

The words were right, but the pace of her mom's voice was at half speed, and her tone had grown more somber.

"What's going on, Mom?"

"Nothing."

"Tell me."

"I need to send a payment off today, and I don't have the money."

"I know."

"You do?"

"I suspected." Allison gritted her teeth. "You have to stay on top of this, Mom."

"Yes, yes, I know I do." She sighed. "But right now—"

"Right now you're going to relax because I've been working on it. I applied for a home equity loan and it should be finalized soon. I couldn't get a lot. I don't have much equity in this house, but if the loan comes through we can get this payment and next month's taken care of, then have some in reserve. And by that time my partnership will be finalized and I'll be making plenty every month."

"But I need to send it today. It has to get to them in five days, and the mail can be slow sometimes."

"As soon as the loan comes through, we can transfer the money. We won't need to mail it. You know how to do that?"

"Yes." She glared at Allison. "I'm not a Luddite."

"Why don't you just let me take care of it?"

"No, this is my debt. I need to handle it."

Allison stood and slowly backed out of the room as she watched her mom pick up her laptop to start the show again. But before she did, she turned to Allison and said, "What are you going to do?"

"I'm going to work, and then I'm going to call on the loan, and then I'm going to find out what this journal is. And where it came from."

"How are you going to do that?"

Before her mom finished the question, Allison knew exactly what she needed to do.

"I'm going to go see Parker."

She needed to talk to him about the journal. He'd be fascinated by the idea God was writing in it. Didn't matter that Parker wasn't sure God existed. He wouldn't think she was crazy. Or he might. But if anyone could give her a theory on where the journal came from and what it was, it would be Parker. "A student and scholar of hallowed iniquities," he called himself.

"Parker? How would you do that when you don't know where he is?"

"I don't know. But if God is leading this strange dance, then he's going to have to show me some new moves."

The new move arrived within days.

seventeen

ALLISON PULLED UP TO HER street's bank of mailboxes after work Friday afternoon and took out the usual stack of bills and junk mail. But the letter in the middle of the pile was far from usual. Parker's handwriting. She knew it in an instant. She ripped the envelope open and began to read his nearly illegible scrawl.

Hey Sis,
    Yeah, of course I'm alive. Tell Mom, okay? She'll believe you more than she would me. I want to write to her, but I'm not sure how, you know? Her losing Dad and all. Us too, but she's the one who needs words talking about how because he's moved on, she needs to move on too, and I don't know those words. The right words, that is. You're the writer-type person, not so much me. And tell her I love her and think about her and all that stuff too, all right?
    Doing fine here. Just processing things the way I process them, ya know? You probably want to know where here is, don't you? I ended up getting off the grid—that's a big shock, huh?—out in Mazama. Still in Washington, so Mom should be happy about that.

Do you know where that is? I didn't till I found it.
Hadn't even heard of it. It's pretty close to Winthrop,
that cowboy-themed town north of Lake Chelan. Built
a place for myself here in the middle of nowhere. Didn't
take long because it's small. But it's got a couch if you
ever want to come visit. I hope you're well. Hope you and
Kayla are killing it with your architecture stuff instead of
killing each other. Hope you and Mom aren't missing me
too much. I'm guessing you aren't, but I might be wrong.

If you ever want to come visit, I wrote out directions
for you. But if you don't feel like making the drive over
here, don't worry about it. I'll be coming back to say hi
pretty soon. I hope. Don't ask me to define soon.

I have my cell, but the coverage is lousy, so it's shut
off most of the time. But you can write to my PO box.
It's on the envelope. I check it every week or so.

Love to you, Sis, and love to Mom,

Parker

Parker Moore stood on the edge of the cliff and stared down into
the craggy valley below. Five thousand feet down. Maybe 5,500. He
grabbed a loaf-size rock in one hand and held his stopwatch in the
other. He tossed the rock over the edge, starting the timer at the same
moment the rock left his fingertips.

He squinted at the stone as it rocketed down the face of the cliff,
then shattered against the massive boulders below. Parker peered at the
readout on his watch and did a quick calculation. Best guesstimate:

just under 5,000 feet. He repeated the exercise twice more. The average of the three tosses came in at 5,100 feet. Plenty of height for a serious rush.

He'd spotted this peak in the heart of the North Cascade Mountains two years ago, but he'd never had the time to scale it till now. Odds were few had climbed to the top. It had required four hours of hiking through rough trails to reach the base, then another four hours of climbing, several of them in clouds with intermittent rain and less than one hundred feet of visibility.

Long before he reached the top, the trail had vanished. He'd crossed large open areas with no guidance or direction. Which was fine. It was exactly what his life had become. The unknowing had become his companion, and he sank into the comfort of only having to understand one step in front of himself at a time.

Now, as he stood on the cliff in the fading twilight, he smiled, knowing the odds were even lower that anyone had ever done what he would do in the morning: leap off the cliff five thousand feet above the ground with a wing suit snugged up tight around his body and a parachute on his back. BASE jump where no one had jumped before. Something about the risk fueled him like nothing else in life, and this would be his most insane jump yet.

He didn't sleep well that night—not a surprise, since he never slept well before he tempted fate with one of his "insanity missions," as Allison called them—but the feeling during and for a time after his jumps made a little insomnia well worth it.

The light from the east woke him at a few minutes past six thirty. As he munched on his last Mountain Bar, Parker eased over to the edge of the cliff and gazed down. A smattering of clouds moved toward him along the base of the cliff to his left. He needed to hurry. He was crazy, but not crazy enough to jump into a cloud bank that obscured the ground. Parker had found his exit the day before, an old abandoned logging road that ran parallel to the cliff. He could just make out the line as it snaked through the logged-out ground, where new growth had yet to fully reclaim the land.

He packed up, slipped into his wing suit, and checked his pack once more before strapping in and walking to the edge of the cliff. He stared into the valley with its rock-strewn, thick-treed tapestry sprawling out before him.

Then, as always, came the best moment. And the worst. Both at the same time. The anticipation, the slam of his heartbeat spiking, the monsoon of fear, the embrace of the fact he could be dead in less than thirty seconds all crashed through his mind. He glanced at the clouds. No more time to savor the prejump rush of emotions. Time to go.

Eyes closed. Always eyes closed for fifteen seconds before a jump. Enough time to pray to God, if God existed, to tell his mom and Allison he loved them, and tell Joel they might be reunited sooner rather than later. Then open his eyes, no hesitation, and go.

A quarter second later Parker was no longer the man who'd stepped off into nothing. He was Iron Man, the Human Torch, a sentient comet streaking through the sky going wherever he chose. A bank to the left on a whim, then right, then straight, then right again, the rush of the wind pummeling his face, the rush of the ground coming up to meet him—but not yet, not yet.

All concerns, worries, inadequacies disappeared. Nothing existed except this moment. His body felt like a fighter jet, able to maneuver with great agility and speed. The shrug of a shoulder, the pointing of his toes, and the suit changed the speed and angle of his glide.

Parker laughed and dove straight at the ground till he gathered enough speed, then planed out, achieving the sensation of weightlessness.

Too soon—every time it was too soon—the ground filled his vision and Parker pulled his rip cord. A second later his chute would fill and he'd slow from over a hundred miles an hour to less than ten. He pulled. No chute. And he continued to rocket toward the earth. *No!*

Panic yanked on his mind, but Parker refused to give it quarter. *Think! Calm. Find your secondary chute.* His hand flailed for the ring. He'd practiced it a million times, but never when he was plummeting toward the earth at terminal velocity. No panic. No time for anything but getting hold of the ring and pulling.

He glanced at the ground. *C'mon!* Had to release it at least four hundred feet above the road. Any less and the chute wouldn't open in time. His fingers latched onto . . . No, that wasn't it. *Find it! There!* He grabbed, yanked hard. Seconds later his reserve chute popped open and relief flooded him.

He pulled hard to the left. Only seconds to adjust so he could catch the edge of the road. His boot clipped the branch of a young Douglas fir tree but nothing else. A few seconds later he yanked down on his cords and skidded to a halt on the old logging road.

Adrenaline pumped through him more powerfully than he'd ever known, and he fumbled to unclip himself from the chute. His breath came in ragged gasps, fear still tightly clenching him. But then a sliver of laughter started deep down and grew till it filled his entire being.

Parker gazed up at the cliff he'd just launched himself off of, and his fear transformed into the biggest rush of exhilaration he'd ever had. He'd done it. Yet again he'd cheated death, conquered the fear of jumping off into nothing, not knowing how it would end. And for a moment, more than a moment, he felt like a man.

When Parker reached Mazama five hours later, he stopped at the gun store in town, strode up to the front counter, and watched the twenty-something clerk behind it. The kid was on a short ladder, pulling two boxes of ammo off a shelf about ten feet high. Parker tapped his foot in double time to the insipid song from Nickelback or a band like them that poured out of the speakers overhead. Molasses. The kid must cover himself in it before work every morning. Would be impossible to move that slow without some kind of assistance.

Finally the kid came down off the ladder, handed the ammo to the guy in front of Parker, then asked, "Is that all you need, Billy?"

"Yeah, thanks, Bo." Billy twirled the toothpick in his mouth.

"You headed up into the hills this weekend?" the kid asked.

"Gonna try. I figure we'll have to head up there on Saturday if we're gonna go, 'cause I checked the weather, and it's saying the clouds are going to be spitting pretty good on Sunday."

The kid jabbed a finger of each hand in two different directions and grinned. "Which route you thinking of taking?"

Parker's foot was now tapping triple time. He squeezed his lips together and moved up next to Billy Joe Hunter, then started rapping his fingers loudly on the glass counter.

"You mind, pal?" Billy said and turned back to the kid. "I'm thinking we're gonna head up Cooper Canyon."

"Sounds good. I've been wanting to get up there for a couple of months now."

"Yeah, gonna get up there, get something hopefully, maybe camp up there, maybe not. Just don't know, you know? We'll find out when we get up there and see the lay of the land. I'm gonna spend the night. I got a new tent, supposed to be good in the wind, rain, snow, probably earthquakes too!"

Billy laughed at that, and Bo joined in.

"Excuse me," Parker said.

Billy turned, eyes cold. "Yeah?"

"I'd like to grab some ammo before the moon comes out." Parker tried to smile, but it probably came out more as a grimace.

"That right? Well, I'd like to finish my conversation with my friend here."

Parker nodded and stepped back a pace.

"So as I was saying, it's a new tent. I got a new pack—well, not completely new—but the guy said it was only used twice, didn't even look like it was used once, so I made a good offer on it and the guy takes it, so I'm trying out all this new gear, and should be a good trip."

"Excuse me, Bo? Is it possible for you to grab me some ammo while you're talking to Billy?"

"You got a problem, pal? Maybe somethin' you wanna say to me?" Billy shuffled into Parker's private space.

"Me? No." He narrowed his eyes. "You. Yes. You want to tell me you're going to give me a minute to buy my ammo and get out of here."

"Really, you want to tell me more about that?"

Billy's breath stank.

Parker started to speak when his dad's voice barked into his mind. *"A true man knows how to hold his frustration in. A true man is patient. A true man doesn't fight petty battles. Instead, he fights the ones that change the course of the world. A true man . . ."*

Parker stood up to his full height and moved forward an inch. Bumped the toes of his boots into Billy's feet.

"I asked you a question, pal," Billy said.

The distance between their noses was now less than three inches. The guy was taller than Parker by an inch, maybe two, but Parker was thicker, and the thickness had grown into solid muscle over the past six months. Billy? His thickness wasn't from muscle.

"I was thinking about asking if you wanted to step out . . ."

"A true man . . ."

"No, let me back up. I wanted to say something else." Parker clenched his teeth.

Shut up, Dad.

"Yeah, wanna tell me what it is? Sounded like you were 'bout to invite me to a party outside. That about right, cowboy? I love parties." Billy grinned as he twirled his toothpick and winked at the kid behind the counter.

"A true man . . ."

Parker slid his right boot back half an inch. Then his left boot joined the right.

"My name is Parker," he said as he forced his tone to mellow. "I haven't been much beyond my property and a couple of miles around it, and I'm looking to expand a bit. Wondering if you could suggest a good spot for me to do a little light hunting. Where I'm not going to disturb any of the locals."

Billy stared at him for at least five seconds, his countenance moving from ticked off to puzzled to playful.

"Sure, friend. I can let you know where to go." He thumbed toward the kid behind the counter. "You mind if I finish up with Bo here first?"

"Not at all. Take all the time you need."

Parker moved away and perused the fishing poles along the wall to his left. Five minutes later Billy the hunter strolled up to him.

"Billy Culver."

Parker took Billy's extended hand. "Parker Moore. Pleasure."

"Agree."

For the next fifteen minutes Billy described the best places to hunt, to hike, to fish, to explore.

"Thanks for all that, Billy. I appreciate it."

Billy nodded and said, "What kept you from taking a poke at me a few minutes back?"

"My dad. Heard a few of his sayings ringing in my ears."

"Yeah." Billy chuckled. "Dads can do that to ya. The good, the bad, and sometimes the brutally ugly."

Billy sauntered off but turned before he'd made it five yards. "Would've been a heck of a fight, Parker. But ya woulda lost." Then he grinned, turned, and kept going.

Parker meandered back to the counter.

"I need to grab some nine millimeter ammo from you and some targets."

"No problem." Bo still moved like an ice-encased slug. But it was okay. At least for today.

After a stop for groceries, Parker headed to his cabin. Thirty-five minutes later he reached the edge of his property and parked his ATV under a small lean-to he'd built in a cluster of aspen trees to shelter the four-wheeler from the harsh winter he'd heard would visit him in the late fall. He'd walk the rest of the way. As soon as his cabin came into view, Parker moved to the right, behind a cluster of trees and thick bushes, and slowly circled his home. He stopped as he peered into each window, looking for movement. This was his routine. Stupid? Probably. But to learn to think like a cop, he needed to learn to think like a crook, and this was how they'd approach a break-in. The good ones anyway. At least according to what his dad used to say, and his dad would have known.

Parker finished the circle and made his way to the back door. Another part of his routine. *"Never go through the front door. That's a good way to get killed."* He listened for a moment, then pushed through. He never locked it. Few even knew his place existed. And there wasn't much to steal. His laptop maybe. That was about it. If his imagined criminal wanted in, they'd get in, locked or not.

He shoved his groceries into the fridge, then pulled the ammo out of its sack and headed back out the door. He wandered back and forth at the edge of his property where the trees kissed the small meadow, till he reached the ten-feet-tall and ten-feet-wide hay bales he'd stacked. Parker secured a paper target at chest height and marched off the distance once, then turned around and marched it off again, to be sure. The precise distance used at the academy. He pressed the toe of his boot into the dirt and drew a line. He set his feet, clicked off the safety, and pointed the gun. Gaze down the target. Forget that a kick was coming. Relax. Deep breath. Ease the trigger back. *Boom!*

Parker grabbed the binoculars that hung on his belt and lifted them to his eyes. First shot. Almost perfect. Almost dead center. Parker looked skyward.

"How was that shot, Dad? Huh?"

Half-second pause, then pull the trigger again. *Boom! Boom!*

Another two shots dead center.

"Those two, Dad? What about them? Will that work for you?"

Three more, all within an inch of each other.

"Good enough? Want me to step back? Yeah? How far? Three feet? Five? How far? Just let me know."

Parker reloaded and took aim. Dusk began to settle and Parker exhaled his breath slowly. Glanced at his watch. Two hours. Enough practice for today. He slogged over the bumpy ground, slowed as he approached the target. A jagged circle of holes ringed the center of the target. Not good enough. All had to be inside. Then he'd step back five paces. Then another five. Just fifteen feet more till he reached his brother's distance.

As Parker made his way back to his cabin, he studied the sky.

Only a hint of clouds. Bright star hovering. Probably not a star, probably Venus or Mars looking down on him, telling him it would be all right tonight.

Parker tacked the target to the wall above his kitchen table and stared at it. Then fixed his gaze on the target next to it, the one he'd fixed in place the day before. And the day, and day, and day before that.

He turned one of the stove's three burners to high, filled a pot with water, and set it on the burner. Nothing fancy tonight. Nothing fancy any night. Simple and filling was fine with him. He took a package of deer meat from one of his three kills out of the fridge and set it on the counter. He'd whip up some noodles to go with it and be done.

While he waited for the water to boil, Parker strode out the front door and over to a small detached shed he'd built. But not for tools. For training. The walls were mirrored, the floor padded. There were three grappling dummies, a punching bag, even a wooden muk yan jong sparring post he'd built from one of the trees he felled for the cabin. Free weights lined one wall. Training bands and ropes and a variety of handcuffs lined another.

Parker marched up to the muk yan jong and sparred with the inanimate post he imagined was real. Five minutes later sweat poured down his back, and his forearms and legs ached from the punishment. Time to throw noodles in the pot, meat in the oven.

He patted his stomach. Getting stronger. Felt his upper arms. Little fat left on those prime cuts of meat. Guns. For the first time in his life, he could call his arms guns. He'd earned it. Twenty-four pounds lighter since getting here five months back. Ten more pounds to go to hit his goal weight. Dad would be so proud.

Yeah. Sure he would be.

After dinner and cleanup, he went to his makeshift desk and picked up the notepad and pen that sat in the center. Maybe he'd write Allison another note. It gave him a way of talking without having to talk. She must have gotten the first one by now. Maybe she'd write back. Maybe someday she'd come see him. He needed that more than he wanted to admit.

Allison found her mom in the kitchen making guacamole on Friday evening.

"Can we talk, Mom?"

"Of course we can. Anytime."

"I need to take a little trip tomorrow and want to see if that's okay with you. If you'll be all right without me for a day or two."

"My ankle is doing great. You can see how I'm getting around. I'm fine, so go. Go."

Her mom opened a bag of chips, poured half of them into a bowl, and brought the guacamole to the table.

"If Parker were here I'd have to double that amount."

"True." Allison slid Parker's note out of her pocket. "Speaking of Parker . . ."

"Yes?"

"He's doing well."

Her mom's eyes went wide. "You talked to him?"

Allison slid his note across the table. "He wrote to us."

Her mom opened the note and read for a few seconds. "It looks like he wrote to you, not us."

"Read the note, Mom."

When she finished, tears spilled onto her cheeks.

"He loves you, Mom."

"I know. I know he does." She wiped her cheeks. "I'd just like to see him every once in a while."

"You keep forgetting he's a guy." She reached over and squeezed her mom's hand. "They process things differently. He's going to be okay."

"That's where you're going, isn't it?" Her mom blinked back more tears and sat up straight. "To see Parker."

"Yes," Allison said. "He needs to know about what's going on with us, and I want to ask him about the journal."

"Do you have to tell him about your father?"

"Yes, Mom. I do."

eighteen

ALLISON LEFT HOME THE NEXT morning at ten, and by eleven fifteen was taking exit 149 off I-90 to head north over Blewitt Pass. Though still early enough in the year for the threat of snow at the top, the only thing she encountered was intermittent drizzle.

She was pushing midafternoon by the time she reached Highway 2 and passed Rocky Reach Dam on the Columbia River. Mazama was still two hours away, and based on her brother's description of how to get to his hideout, she would have at least an hour on foot. So be it. The light wouldn't fade for a few more hours, and she had her iPhone's flashlight.

Allison pulled into Mazama just over two hours later, spotted the sign Parker had mentioned, then took a road off to the right a few yards past it. His directions said to stay on that road for three miles. She glanced at her odometer and 2.9 miles later slowed her Honda to a crawl, then stopped.

What was the next part of the directions? She glanced at her phone. No service. Wouldn't have helped anyway. Parker hadn't given her a physical address, just a series of directions that sounded like they came out of a board game. She grabbed the sheet of paper he'd mailed to her and studied it.

Take highway 20 into Mazama. When you hit the sign that says Deer Skinning For Free, take a right. Check your odometer. Three miles later, take a right at the huge woodpile. That road will go from paved to dirt after six miles. Keep going till you get to a wooden sign nailed to a tree about ten feet up that says, "If you don't know exactly what you're doing here, turn around." You'll see a gate with a combo lock on it. The combination is 9–36–29. Stay on that road for 2.7 miles. It will get narrow. Keep going. When you see a wide spot, park there.

Put a sign on your car that says your name and that you're my sister. Make it big. Stay on the road for 0.7 miles. Take a left on the trail you'll see right next to the stream. It's wide enough for a small car, but nothing but a quad is going to make it, so don't think about trying to drive it. Stay on the trail for half a mile. You'll find me at the end.

Allison spotted the woodpile, took a right, and reached the "If you don't know . . ." sign twenty minutes later. After another ten minutes of navigating a track that was a road in name only, she found the wide spot and parked, then put the sign she'd made in her windshield.

Allison glanced at her watch as she locked her car. She wouldn't beat sunset by much, but she'd make it. She slung her daypack over her shoulder and headed toward the trail that would take her to her brother.

They'd always been close. At least growing up. Maybe they were still close, but the fact he'd left without a word and been out here for five months without letting her or their mom know where he was—that was not cool.

She and Parker hadn't seen each other much during college. Out-of-state school for her, Parker working insane hours getting his moving company going . . . Their schedules didn't line up. During holidays, yes, but that was about it. Then the summer after her junior year of college, she'd decided to take a year off school. She'd broken up with a boyfriend and announced her plan to hike the Pacific Crest Trail from southern Oregon to southern Washington. Parker joined her, and they grew closer than ever. But now? He'd checked out. Gone off the grid. Found someplace off in the middle of nowhere and gone silent.

Allison trudged on, hand shoved in the pocket of her jeans, hat pulled down low over her face. She checked her pocket odometer. Getting close. Another fifteen minutes and she should be there. There had been no one else on the road in and no one on the trail. Parker had wanted to get away from it all? Mission accomplished.

Sixty feet farther up the trail, Allison spotted a No Trespassing sign nailed to a tree on the right. Twenty feet more, another one on her left. Then a Private Property sign. They were weathered but not much.

A trail leading off to the right at a forty-five-degree angle made Allison hesitate. Parker hadn't mentioned it in his letter, so the logical choice was to stay the course. She trekked on in silence till a sound out of place in the forest stopped her cold. Then movement to her left. A second later a man stepped out from between two small trees and pointed a shotgun at Allison's chest.

"Stop moving, little lady. Unless you want a hole in your chest the size of a beach ball."

nineteen

SWEAT BROKE OUT ON ALLISON'S forehead as the man slowly trudged toward her.

"You blind?" The voice sounded like it hadn't been used in months.

Allison raised her trembling hands and gave a tiny shake of her head.

"I think you gotta be blind." The man cocked his head, eyes narrowed.

"I don't—"

"Blind people don't see signs that say No Trespassing. But people who can see, they spot those signs. And they turn around. Or maybe you can't read. That it?"

Allison pressed her lips together, glanced to her right and left.

"What're you looking at?" The man slid a half step closer. "You keep your eyes locked in on me. Got it? Yeah?"

"I get it." Her voice quivered. "Yes."

Fear swept through her as the look in the man's eyes switched from crazed to mischievous back to crazed.

"So what is it? Can't see or can't read? Gotta be one of the two."

"I saw the signs, but—"

"Then why'd you ignore them and keep coming?" He winked. "Huh?"

"I'm—"

"Shut up."

The man was over six feet, dark baseball cap, blue eyes that looked highly intelligent. Short dark hair. He circled Allison slowly, his steady breathing the only sound. When he finished his circle, he lowered the gun a few inches and Allison started to lower her hands.

"Nope. Let's keep those up for a bit longer, okay?" The man motioned with his gun. "And by the way, if you try to run, I will shoot you. No hesitation. I don't like threatening a woman, but that's just the way it is out here. We understand each other?"

Allison nodded and raised her hands back up.

"You have a gun?"

Her eyes narrowed. "Yes."

"Well, well." The man cocked his head and gave a couple of small nods. "Where?"

Without lowering her hand, Allison pointed to her hip.

"Then let's keep those hands up nice and high, eh?"

Allison didn't respond.

"So you're out here stomping around, miles from the nearest real road, breaking the law, trespassing on my land, pissing me off, making me have to call the sheriff."

"I'm not staying long."

"Wha'd you say? Not living long?" The man grinned, obviously pleased with his joke.

As Allison's heart rate slid down closer to a normal amount of beats per second, she studied the man. If she was betting, she'd say not crazy.

"I'm here to see my brother."

"Oh, is that so?"

Allison nodded.

"Not sure I believe you. Ain't no one out here for a ten-mile radius 'cept me."

"He moved out here recently. Five months ago. He told me he's at the end of this road."

"What's his name?"

"Parker."

"Does he know you're coming?" The man squinted.

"No."

"In other words, you do want to get shot."

"No." Allison took a half step back.

"Then you're just stupid."

Deep inside, something stirred. Her fear shifted to something more powerful. A fire began to build. A fire she liked. A fire she didn't embrace nearly often enough.

"Maybe."

The man lifted the shotgun a few inches. "Maybe?"

The fire shot to the surface.

"Yeah. Maybe. You didn't hear me, huh? What's your problem? You deaf?"

The tiniest hint of a smile played at the corner of his mouth. She narrowed her eyes and lowered her hands and stepped toward him.

"I know you're not blind, so you must be deaf. Huh, old man! Are you?"

Allison took another step toward him. "You want to shoot me? Go ahead, tough guy."

The man's smile burst into a grin and he pulled back the shotgun, then dropped it to his side. "Same eyes, you and him."

Allison glared at the man.

"Who's older?"

"I am." The familiar voice floated up from behind her. Allison whipped her head around. Parker!

Her brother stood ten feet away. Hands on hips. A bandanna around his head. Green pants. Flannel shirt. Work boots. He stepped toward the man in the cap and raised his voice a notch.

"You don't put that shotgun behind your back in less than a second, I'm going to take it outta your hands and knock you to the ground and then hit you again to make sure you're out cold."

The man grinned at Parker and slowly put the gun behind his back. "Hey, Parker."

"Nathan." Parker nodded.

Nathan jabbed toward Allison with a calloused finger. "Says she knows you. That she's your sister."

"That's what she says, huh?" Parker eased forward slowly.

Allison studied him. Couldn't tell if his eyes were playful or ticked off.

"What are you doing here, Allison?"

"Nice to see you too."

"Congrats on not getting shot before I got here."

"Thanks."

"You must not have tried anything stupid."

"Must not have." She glared at Nathan, whose smile threatened to break out into laughter.

"Not many people make Nathan smile," Parker said. "How'd you win him over?"

"The only way it's done," Nathan said. "Show a little backbone."

Parker smiled as if recalling a number of similar scenes involving himself, then turned to Allison. "He likes people who assert themselves."

Nathan hacked out a laugh. "Was just having fun."

Parker nodded and focused on Nathan. "Thanks for looking out for me, but you do that again to Allison, you'll be eating dinner through a straw for a long time."

"Understood."

Seconds later Nathan vanished, and Allison and Parker stood alone together for the first time in ages. They stared at each other. She brimmed with so much she wanted to say, but had no clue where to begin. He finally grabbed her for a long hug. She buried her head on his shoulder.

"It's good to see you, Al."

"You too."

After they pulled apart, Parker asked, "You hungry?"

"Famished. It took me longer to get here than I thought it would."

He gave a thin smile that hinted at the way he used to be before Joel died. "It feels longer the first time you hike it."

"It gets shorter the more you do it?"

"Yes. Absolutely it does," Parker said.

"You want to explain that?"

He turned and tramped down the narrow, rock-strewn trail, his legs chewing up the path fast enough that Allison had to jog for a few paces to catch up. Parker glanced at her as she pulled alongside.

"It's the way our minds work. It will feel like a shorter hike on the way out. Simply the way our synapses process data."

Allison waited for him to elaborate, but Parker didn't say any more. No doubt he could have given her a detailed explanation. He graduated from the University of Washington with a degree in engineering even though he'd never used it. If Parker said that's the way the mind worked, she believed him.

They walked the rest of the way to Parker's camp in silence, though she guessed he had as much to say as she did. Couldn't have that much conversation with Nathan or the others who might live out here.

In under five minutes they came to an oval clearing, a little more than an acre. A half ring of trees stood to the north. To the west a slice of the mountains poked above a line of clouds. In the middle of the clearing was a small log cabin made from what looked like aspen trees. Two large windows flanked the front door. On the side Allison saw another window. Smoke curled up from a chimney in the back corner of the roof.

"You built this?"

"Most of it, yeah. I had help."

"Nathan and friends?"

"No. I sold my company. Didn't clear much, but enough to hire a company out of Mazama. And it doesn't take a lot to live out here. So I'm getting by fine."

He led her inside. It wasn't more than twenty by twenty. But for one person it was plenty. Two thick, dark brown rugs covered the wood plank floor. Parker's kitchen was in one corner, his bed and a simple dresser opposite. A woodstove sat on the same side of the cabin as the kitchen. Two bookshelves stood on either side of the front door.

"You want to stay in here and talk while I cook us dinner, or would you rather walk around the property while you still have a little light left?"

He wasn't asking. He was telling.

"I think I'll do some exploring."

"Sounds good."

She slipped outside and walked through the meadow to the hay bales. She studied the hay at the height of a man's chest and knew immediately what they were there for. Target practice. After all these years, it had never left him. The need to please their dad. A burning passion. No, not passion, more like a soul-sucking obsession.

She'd tried to talk to him about it after their father died. But Parker had closed it off, bottled it up inside. The cork needed to come out. Maybe that's why God had sent her out here. To find the hay bales peppered with bullets, to have her ask what he was doing. Maybe.

After another fifteen minutes she wandered back to the cabin, stepped inside, and studied her brother. He'd lost weight. Looked strong. Lean. His hair was longer—not a shock that he hadn't cut it. He probably didn't care how he looked. Allison strolled over to the stove.

"Why Mazama, Parker?"

"I like it here." He stirred the potatoes and didn't look up.

"Why?"

"Lots of reasons."

"Like?"

"It's only twenty-eight miles from the Canadian border." One corner of his mouth turned up. "I could get across on my quad in a few hours if I needed to."

"What're you doing that might make you need to get across the border?"

"I'm just saying." A soft smile.

"That's why you came here? Get across quick when you pull off the perfect crime?"

"It's an interesting area. Mazama was the launching point for the mining towns in the Harts Pass area. For a long time it's been little more than a crossroads, but it's growing. People are putting it on their maps for vacations. Getaways. You think you're in the middle of nowhere, and in one sense, you are. But in another, you're in a hidden paradise. A lot of summer weddings here. It's home to one of the

world's longest cross-country skiing trails, plus heli-skiing and moun-
taineering. Plenty of rock climbers wind their way up Goat Peak. A
few high-end lodges too. But it's largely unknown, even to people who
live in the state."

"You're not going to tell me why you came here."

"You know why."

"To practice. To become the son you thought you never were. To
go on your crazy adventures where you try to kill yourself using the
stupidest extreme sports ever created."

"Good. We got that over with. Now can we get on to other things?"

"Dad loved you."

"I'm not saying he didn't." Parker scowled. "Just loved Joel a thousand tons more. Then he went and got himself killed in the line of
duty, which made him even more of a god in Dad's mind."

"You have to let it go."

"Oh really? Like you have?"

"Yes, like I have."

"Have you? Or have you just buried it better than I have?"

He was right. She hadn't let it go, just pushed it deep down where
she could ignore it most of the time, but not so deep down she couldn't
feel the ache. Like on late spring days like this one. They never failed
to remind her of what it had been like at track meets growing up.

A championship meet from her freshman year of high school
flashed into her mind. Parker was a sophomore, Joel a senior. All
three were on the team. Allison ran long distance. Parker did the shot
put and discus. And Joel sprinted. The 100, the 200, and the 4x100
relay.

*Their mom and dad sat in the stands, ready to see how their sons and
daughter would fare in the district championships. Allison came in*

fourth, the first time a freshman had placed in the top five in the history of the school. Parker? He took second against a slew of acclaimed juniors and seniors.

But of course Joel blew everyone away. First place in the 100. First in the 200. And the only reason his team didn't win the 400 was that he had too much time to make up running the anchor leg of the relay. He nearly did that too. Five-tenths of a second short.

After the meet, as the three of them meandered out of the stadium and searched for their parents, Joel said, "Both of you, outstanding performance. Well done."

They thanked him and a minute later found their parents. Both of them beamed. Their dad strode up and looked at Allison first.

"Hey, Al, that was a good run. Nice." He patted her on the back, then focused on Parker.

"You too, Parker. Good job." Their dad flashed her brother a thumbs-up.

Then he turned to Joel. "Come here, kid."

Joel stepped forward, and their father grabbed Joel in a huge bear hug. "You're not a kid. You're a man. And today out there on the track, you ran like a man. Ran like a Spartan. Ran like a god!"

"Thanks, Dad." Joel grinned. "Parker and Al were pretty amazing too."

"Sure," he said, never taking his eyes off Joel. "What are we going to have to do with you? Bronze you? The 100 and the 200, those are the glory races. The ones people love. And you crushed them."

He threw his arm around Joel's shoulder and strode off, the two of them silhouetted against the darkening sky.

Their mom said, "You two were terrific. What wonderful performances! I'm so proud of you."

And of course they thanked her and smiled, and Allison tried to ignore the ache inside for her dad to speak the same kind of words to her that he'd said to Joel.

A similar scene played out again and again throughout their child-hoods. She and Parker always did "fine." Their dad often said, "Good job." But they were never a god or a goddess in their dad's eyes.

"Let's not do this," Allison said as she pulled herself from the memory.

"That's what I was saying. Let's be done with it."

Allison sighed, and they ate in silence for the next few minutes. Parker filled her water glass and said, "Lots for you to do here if you're staying for a few days."

"I'm staying tomorrow. But I'll head back on Monday. I have to work on Tuesday."

"I was hoping you were here to hang out for a while."

"I'm here because I need your help with something weird that's going on."

"Not because you wanted to see me."

"I do." She grabbed his forearm and squeezed. "You've been gone too long."

"It works for me out here."

"It doesn't work for me." Allison took his hand. "I miss you."

"I know, Al. I know."

They lapsed once more into silence and finished their meal before either spoke again. Parker got up and loaded the woodstove with another three logs. "Probably don't need the heat, but I like it."

"Me too. It feels good." Allison cleared the plates to the kitchen counter. "Are you the only one that lives like this out here?"

Parker grinned. "Are you kidding? Lots of us."

"Like your pal Nathan?"

"Yep."

She started scrubbing the plates, glasses, and silverware, but out of the corner of her eye she could see Parker staring at her.

"What?"

"Nathan had the shotgun pointed at your chest."

"What about it?"

"Why aren't you like that with other people?"

"Like what?" Allison kept her head down, dropped it a few inches closer to the sink.

"You stood up to him." Parker pushed his hip into the counter and leaned over till she glanced at him. "Called his bluff. Backed him down. Whatever you want to call it. Why did you stand up to him? Why aren't you like that around everyone?"

"Because most people don't scare me like he did."

"That's my point. Most people would cower if a lunatic backwoodsman pointed a shotgun in their face. They'd start begging. Or panic. Not you."

"Whatever."

"No, not whatever." Parker took her shoulders and turned her toward him. "Tell me. Why don't you do that with other people?"

"You mean like you do? Picking fights with people all the time?"

"They're not fights. They're heated discussions. Fights mean fists. I've gotten much better at not doing that," Parker said. "Back to you. Why don't you do what you did with Nathan with other people?"

"I do that with other people."

"No, you don't. Not like you should. Around people you know really well, sure, you take a stand, but everyone else? Nah, not so much."

"So you were there watching me with Nathan longer than I thought."

"I was there for a few seconds before I spoke, yeah."

"Why?"

"Because something told me to watch you for a few. So I did. And I liked what I saw. I think you liked what you saw inside yourself. And I think you like that it didn't stay inside."

Allison pulled away and went back to the dishes.

"You need to talk about this."

"Yes, I probably do." Allison wiped her hands on the checkered terry-cloth towel that hung next to the sink. "And you need to talk about why you've done a vanishing act. I want to know why you left. I want to know—"

"You know why I left!" Parker slammed his hand down on the counter.

"Then let's talk about it." She stepped toward him and narrowed her eyes.

"Fine. You talk about why you can't stand up to most people, and I'll talk about what I'm doing in the middle of the middle of nowhere."

Allison nodded. "Someday."

"Now."

"No." She glared at him. "I said someday."

"Nice." He grinned. "You just stood up for yourself again. Well done, sis."

"Thank you. If only I didn't know you. Then you'd really be impressed."

After they finished cleaning up, they sat on either side of the woodstove listening to Van Morrison, an album Allison hadn't heard in years, and for those moments she and Parker were back in their Bothell home growing up, sneaking out together during high school nights, pranking their friends, and getting into more trouble than their mom and dad could have imagined.

When the album finished, Allison said, "That brought back some good memories."

"Yeah, indeed."

———

In the morning they had target practice together, then sat outside and talked about nothing and everything. Time had reversed itself and they were in their teen years again, being closer than most brothers and sisters ever were.

"You still shoot well," Parker said. "Do you still take your gun with you everywhere?"

"I think Dad would come back from the dead if I stopped lugging my gun around." She laughed. "Kind of drilled it into my head when he trained me. Plus, it's a way to feel like he's still here."

"Yeah, I get that."

"Or a way to make him proud of me."

"I get that too."

Again, a peaceful silence.

"Do me a favor, Parker."

"Maybe."

"Think about coming over. Seeing Mom for a few days. She misses you."

He stared at her for a long time before saying, "Okay, Al. I'll think about it."

Over a late breakfast on the cabin's small porch, she said, "I want to talk to you about that weird thing I mentioned last night. Something you might be able to help me out with."

"Right!" Parker popped his forehead with the heel of his hand. "I spaced. Talk to me."

Allison went inside the cabin to the small sofa she'd slept on—she refused to let Parker give her his bed, even though he'd pushed her—and grabbed her backpack. When she returned to the porch out front, she pulled out the journal and handed it to him.

"Wow," he said after studying it. "Nice work. Where'd you get this?"

"That's a story."

"Beautiful leather." Parker ran his finger over the engraving of the tree. "That is crazy good work. Look at the detail."

"What can you tell me about it?"

Parker studied it again, taking more time this go-through, and when he finished, asked, "Can I open it?"

"Sure."

He looked at the first page. "Your name, but it doesn't look like your handwriting."

"It's not."

"Whose is it?"

"That I would love to know."

Parker gave her a curious look, then turned back to the journal. As he studied it, Allison studied the trees and then the mountains in the distance. Sporadic clouds rested among the peaks. Beautiful. Peaceful. No wonder Parker loved it here.

"I'm guessing you're going to tell me you didn't write the poem either."

"You guessed right."

"What's the story, morning glory?"

She smiled at his pet name for her. She loved getting up early and he loved sleeping in. As kids she couldn't resist waking him up at sunrise to go off on adventures together. He said he hated her for it, but she knew deep down he'd always loved it.

"It's a weird story."

"Hit me." Parker leaned his chair back against the cabin wall.

Allison started with the first time she saw the journal and finished with her writing changing the morning after she'd written it. When she finished, Parker let out a low whistle.

"So the guy's name was Alister Morrison, and it changed to Allison Moore." He squinted at her. "You sure you weren't smoking a little weed and wrote your own name in there?"

Allison glowered. "I'm not the one on this porch who's indulged in that area."

"Jus' saying . . ."

"No. I did not write my own name in there and give the journal to myself as a gift and forget I'd done it."

"Then you have some serious crazy-train action going on here."

"You could say that."

"You're *sure* you didn't forget what you wrote?" Parker tilted forward and the front legs of his chair thudded onto the wooden porch.

"Yes."

"Positive?"

"Yes! I'm not a wacko."

"Okay, okay!" Parker held up his arms. "I'm just saying I'm not sure I believe the writing in the journal changed."

"It did."

"Whatever." Parker rubbed his hands together.

"Not whatever." Allison gave him a light shove.

"Moving on. From what you've told me, you getting this journal wasn't random."

"Meaning?"

"You see the two guys in the coffee shop, this Alister and this Richard, then the Alister guy gives you this knowing look, and wham, a few days later your friend at the coffee joint is handing you the journal."

"Yes."

Parker studied the journal again, a look of concentration on his face as he bit his lip. "I've read about these journals, I know I have."

"What? There's more than one?" Allison's heart sped up.

"There's something about them that's . . . Wow, I'm blank. But . . . these are more like from legends I've read about."

"I need to find out more, Parker." She leaned toward him.

"Okay." He nodded, a strange look in his eyes as he handed the journal back to her. "I know someone. He's into unusual artifacts, runs a store in Ballard. Antiquities, curiosities, art, the stranger the better. If anyone can tell you anything, it will be Carl."

Parker jotted down Carl's name and the name of his store, then handed the slip of paper to Allison.

After cleaning up breakfast, they drove up to Rainy Pass and took a long hike north till they reached Cutthroat Pass. The view was spectacular and their conversation playful. For eight glorious hours there were no problems, only her and Parker and the mountains and lake and streams.

But that evening, before bed, Allison brought up their mom.

"One thing before sleep," she said.

"Yeah?"

"I need to talk to you about something serious."

"What?"

"Mom's in trouble, Parker."

Parker's head pulled back. "Not cancer."

"No, not her physical health."

"Then what?"

"Money."

"What's going on?"

Allison told the story, and when she finished Parker stared at the last embers of the fire in the woodstove and gave a few slow shakes of his head. "Never saw that one coming."

"Nor Mom. Nor me."

"He screwed us over, Al." Parker kicked the floor hard. "In life and now in death. So now we get to deal with all his crap."

"Yeah, he did. And yeah, we do."

"It's going to take a while to get over this one," Parker growled.

"No question about that."

Allison stood and stared out the window at the last traces of light above the mountains to the south.

"I have to sell this place. Give Mom the money. Move in with you guys."

She turned to him. "This is all you have."

"So what?"

"How much could you get for it? Total. Land and building?"

"Thirty-five thousand."

"Maybe. If you're lucky."

"Yeah."

"Don't. It's going to be okay. Kayla and I split up, and I'm going to be a partner in the firm I'm working at. And I'm going to have a very generous wage and a percentage of profits. I can cover it."

Parker blinked in surprise. "When did this happen?"

"Four weeks back."

"Big firm then?"

"It is, and once we get the deal finalized I'll be able—"

"What do you mean? It's not done?" Parker crossed his legs and scowled.

"Not yet."

Parker turned and stared at her.

"It's going to get done. Soon. Let's talk about something els—"

"Nah, I don't think so. We're going to talk about this right now. You have to get this done."

Allison slumped back into her chair. "I know."

"What's the holdup?"

"Derrek has to finish things with his old partner. And he's been busy."

"Finish what?"

"There are a few issues. A payout, a—"

"What you just told me is that he invited you. Not the other way around, yeah?"

"Yes."

"So the deal with his old partner is not your problem. It's his. He brought you over as his partner. A month ago. You trusted him. And now he's stringing you out."

"No, he's not, he's . . ."

But Parker was right. That's exactly what Derrek was doing.

"Yeah, he is, Al. And you know it."

She did.

"You need to take care of this. If you don't, I think I might show up—"

"I'll get it done, Parker."

"I'm just saying the longer you wait, the easier it is to—"

"I'll get it done." She folded her arms across her chest and leaned back in her chair.

She hoped her voice held more confidence than she felt. All she could picture was Derrek continuing to deflect and put her off. But the hard truth was, it wasn't his fault. It was hers. She shouldn't have started working there till their deal was finalized.

But going to work for Derrek was more than an answer to her prayers. It had come directly from God, as direct as those kind of decisions can be. Hope had extended her hand and Allison had taken it. It would happen—the partnership, the increased salary. She simply had to be patient and trust God it would get wrapped up soon.

"I'm not saying you need to take care of it for Mom and her money issues, although that might be part of it. You need to do this for you."

"What does that mean?"

"I think you know exactly what it means."

She did know. And it scared her.

twenty

THE NEXT DAY, AFTER THE long drive home and a long conversation with her mom in which Allison assured her over and over that Parker was well both physically and emotionally, Allison took a hot shower, then settled into her chair in the den to jot a few notes in the journal before bed.

Monday, May 27th

Seeing Parker was wonderful and horrible. I ache for him. Still trying to get Dad's approval. It will never happen. He'll never get accurate enough with his gun, never be in good enough shape, never dive off a tall enough cliff to turn Dad's spotlight in his direction.

I want to shout, "He's gone, Parker!" But of course Dad isn't gone. He's right there in Parker's head every moment. He has to let it go. So do I. But how?

And then there's Derrek. Am I letting him string me along because I don't think I'm worth better? Parker's right, I have to get the partnership finalized. Why haven't I? Because I don't stand up for myself. I start, but then I don't stay standing and I back down.

But it's there, deep inside, like a fire hidden by too many trees, but I can feel the heat. I like the strength of that fire. And I like the moments when I let it out. Like with Nathan. I like that Allison. Where do you go? Why don't you come live with me more often?

And why does it matter what Linda thinks of me? Why do I long for her to compliment me?

'Cause I'm messed up inside, of course. And I continue to wonder if I did the right thing going to work with Derrek.

With that, she closed the journal, made her way upstairs, and was asleep in minutes.

In the morning Allison woke a few minutes before her alarm was set to go off. She lay on her side with only one thought streaking around her mind. Her entry in the journal from last night. And whether it had changed.

Part of her didn't want to look, but the stronger part did, and she made her way downstairs, adrenaline pricking at her body. By the time she reached the den, her pulse had jacked up as if she were in the middle of a low-minutes-per-mile run.

She strode up to the journal, pulled it off the stand next to the chair, and unwound the leather cord. Closed her eyes for a moment, then opened them and the journal. Allison skimmed through the entry. No, nothing had . . . Wait! At the bottom. Again. Words missing. And a few added.

I stand up for myself. I stay standing and I don't back down.
I like the strength of the fire inside me.
I live with that fire often.
It doesn't matter what Linda thinks of me.
I did the right thing going to work with Derrek.

Heat washed through her. She shoved the journal off her lap, rubbed her eyes, and waited for her mind to stop spinning. Then she picked up the journal and peered at the page again. How could this be happening? Impossible. But obviously not impossible.

What was the name of that shop? The one Parker told her to call? Ballyhoo Curiosities. That was it. Carl something. She opened her laptop with shaking hands and did a search for the store. Three seconds later she had it. They opened at ten o'clock.

During a quick breakfast, Allison's mom asked if she was okay.

"I'm fine. Work pressure, you know."

"What aren't you telling me?"

Allison sighed. "I'm not telling you that I wrote in the journal again last night."

"And?"

"The writing changed again."

"It wasn't me."

"I know. And it wasn't me, so that leaves only one option. And it's freaking me out." Allison motioned in the direction of the den. "Right in there, some *Twilight Zone*, sci-fi/fantasy thing is going on just like on TV, except this isn't TV, and—"

Her mom shook her head. "It's not science fiction and it's not fantasy. I think it really and truly is God."

"That would be amazing, but I've never heard of God ever doing something this weird."

"Sure you have. We just talked about this. How in Daniel, God wrote—"

"No, not some story from a million years ago. This is today."

"God hasn't lost his power of creativity. He can still reach people in extremely unusual ways. Do you remember me telling you about the time my Bible study group was supposed to be praying for Sue

Rowley's situation at work, and she ended up getting healed of asthma right there at the meeting?"

"I have to go." Allison grabbed the rest of her toast and filled her coffee cup. "Traffic is going to be heavy today with the rain."

"Don't work too hard, Allison."

"Okay, Mom. What are you going to do?"

"Look for money in your couch."

Allison wished her mom was kidding, but she probably wasn't. They had enough, barely, to take care of next month's payment. After that? No idea. That home equity loan had to come through!

She made it to work with two minutes to spare and tried to work on a proposal for a condo project in downtown Seattle, but she couldn't remember what she'd written for more than a few minutes and kept repeating herself. Her mind was too consumed with her watch, which seemed to be moving in slow motion.

At nine fifty, Allison started glancing at her watch every few seconds as if doing so could speed things up. The moment her watch hit ten o'clock, she dialed the number for Ballyhoo Curiosities.

twenty-one

THE PHONE WAS ANSWERED ON the seventh ring.

"Ballyhoo Curiosities."

"Carl Pugliese?"

"Yes. Who is this?"

"My name is Allison Moore."

Carl didn't respond.

"Are you there?" she asked.

"Yes." He coughed. "We're not open yet."

"I thought you opened at ten."

"We do."

"It's ten."

"So it is." The mumble that followed could have been an apology. "What can I do for you?"

"I'd like to show you something. My brother, Parker, said you might be able to help me with an unusual item."

"Ah, Parker." Carl's voice grew a few degrees warmer. "Yes, a good man, your brother. How is he?"

"He's fine."

"Good, good."

She glanced at the office lobby and saw Linda looking her direction.

Allison went to her door and shut it. She didn't need Linda, or anyone else for that matter, overhearing the conversation.

"Now," Carl said, "what, pray tell, is the item you'd like to talk to me about?"

"A journal."

"Journals are not unusual."

"This one is."

"How so?"

"I'd rather discuss that in person." She pictured the journal tucked away safely in her desk drawer at home.

"Fine. Do you have the store hours?"

"I'd like to show you the journal in private."

"And I'd like to keep my policy of never meeting with clients outside of store hours unblemished."

"I'm not a client."

"You're not looking to sell this item?"

"No, I have no desire to sell this journal. But I do want to try to understand some things about it. Learn the history. Ask you questions about it."

"That will cost you."

"I see." Allison swallowed. "How much?"

"That depends, naturally, on how long I need to examine the journal to provide you with the answers you seek. And since you have not deemed me worthy enough for you to describe the journal over the phone, I have no idea how much time it will take."

"It's old. Seems to be, to me."

"And do you mind telling me what that assessment is based on?"

Allison blushed. "I felt it."

"Ah, I see. A serious scholar."

"It's just a feeling."

"Anything else you'd like to tell me before we meet?"

Allison paused. Should she tell Carl now or wait? She swallowed and said, "Words that were in the journal when I got it disappeared. And new words showed up a day later. And then I wrote in it, and then those words that I wrote changed." Allison paused, then added, "And I'm not crazy."

Carl didn't respond.

"Are you there, Mr. Pugliese?"

"Not Mr. Pugliese. Carl, please." The voice warmed at least five more degrees.

"Sure."

Again, silence.

"I'm not making this up. It happened. I'm an extremely stable person."

"Hmm."

All Allison heard was Carl's breathing.

"Carl?"

His voice was quiet and almost monotone. "Do you mind repeating what you said a moment ago, so that I'm clear? About the words?"

"I said there are words that have disappeared and reappeared in it. And words I wrote—and I know what I wrote—have changed."

Carl's voice was now quite warm. "When do you want to meet?"

"I can leave work today at six. I can be to your store by seven, maybe a few minutes earlier."

"Fine. I'll see you then."

———

A few clusters of people wandered up and down the sidewalks on both sides of the street as Allison parked her car on Main Street in downtown Ballard. She got out and clipped toward the address she'd pulled up on her phone. The two restaurants she passed were crammed to capacity. The smell of Mexican food surrounded her as she scanned the buildings to her right for Ballyhoo Curiosities.

There. Found it. Allison read a wood sign that hung from a thick iron beam.

WHAT ARE WE? SOMETHING BETWEEN A LIBRARY OF THE STRANGEST TOMES, A NATURAL HISTORY MUSEUM, AND AN ANTIQUE STORE. STEP INSIDE TO DISCOVER AN ECLECTIC ARRAY OF ALL THINGS UNUSUAL, UNIQUE, AND POSSIBLY NOT FROM THIS PLANET. WE CELEBRATE THE ART THAT EXISTS IN NATURE AS WELL AS THE ART THAT HUMANKIND HAS ACHIEVED BOTH CROSS-CULTURALLY AND THROUGHOUT HISTORY.

Allison cupped her hands around her face and peered inside. Darkness shrouded the store. She could make out shelves on the right and left, walls full of books and what looked like masks. In the middle of the store, three long tables sat but were covered in too much shadow for her to make out the objects lying on them. One looked like a skull.

At the very back of the shop, a thin slice of light pressed out from under a door. The light dimmed, then grew bright again, then dimmed, as if a person paced behind the door.

Allison knocked and the light held steady. She waited. Five seconds. Ten. The door stayed shut. Allison rapped on the doorframe again. Harder. A few seconds later the door at the back opened a quarter inch, maybe less. A finger of light now framed the door in a warm gold tone.

Another ten seconds ticked by. Allison was about to level a third knock on the door when the door at the back swung halfway open and the person Allison assumed to be Carl stepped into the frame. The lean man couldn't have been over five six. He was backlit, the light from his office putting him in silhouette.

He stood that way for three or four seconds. Staring at Allison? Allison couldn't see Carl's eyes, but she felt them. Five more seconds before Carl patted his doorframe twice, then strode toward Allison, weaving in and out of the tables like a cobra. As he did, a shiver slid down Allison's neck. Not from standing in the cool night air. From a thick sensation she shouldn't have come.

twenty-two

THE DOOR OPENED ON WELL-OILED hinges, and Carl waved
Allison inside. He flipped a switch that bathed the shop with a low
level of light.

"Ms. Moore, I deduce."

"Yes. Allison. Thanks for seeing me."

"Pleasure. My apologies for not having the lights on when you
arrived. It couldn't be helped."

"Why couldn't it—"

"Now, if you like, let's scuttle back to my office and have a look
at what you've brought."

Carl spun and snaked back through the tables, starting on the
opposite side of the room on the way back. Allison followed him at
a slow pace, giving her a chance to glance at the shelves and tables.
They were packed and stacked with ancient-looking books as well
as newer ones, mostly old maps with worn corners and artwork, and
jewelry that looked handmade. *Odd* was the best way to describe the
collection. The name of the store and the description on the wooden
sign were apropos.

When they reached Carl's office, he offered Allison a chair under
a brass diving helmet attached to the wall.

"You don't care for tea, do you?"

"I love tea, but I'm fine, thanks."

"Good. I don't have any."

Carl laughed at his own joke with great enthusiasm, and Allison offered a polite smile.

"Now that hospitality has been attended to, let us take your journal and give it a cursory examination."

Allison reached inside her coat and brought out the journal she'd stopped by the house to grab. She hesitated for an instant, then handed it to Carl. He reached out with both hands to take the book and cradled it like a robin's egg. He brought it up close to his face and smelled the leather.

"My, my, isn't this interesting?" Carl said, far more to himself than to Allison.

Carl set it delicately on his desk and stared at it from all angles, holding each gaze for at least ten seconds. Then he turned it over and studied the back. Finally he unwound the wide leather cord around the journal and pulled back the cover. He ran his fingers on top of the first page as if stroking a rose petal. Then he took the cover and rubbed it between thumb and finger. Bent down and smelled the leather for a second time. A quick search through his right desk drawer produced a large magnifying glass, and he ran it along the top of the inside cover, then did the same along the inside of the back cover.

"Yes, yes. It's there." He stared at the journal with awe in his eyes, then turned and said, "You have no idea what you have here, do you?"

"That's what I'm trying to figure out."

Carl's only response was to nod and say, "Hmm."

After another minute, he glanced up at Allison as he pointed at the journal. "May I? The final test, to be certain."

"Certain?"

"To be certain the journal is what I think it is."

Allison assumed he intended to look through the pages of the journal. She nodded. With one quick motion, Carl pulled matches from his desk drawer, lit one, and held it under the leather.

Allison lurched forward and knocked Carl's hand away. The match fell to the floor.

"What are you doing?"

Carl's face was puzzled. "I asked. You nodded your acquiescence."

"No. No!" She glared at him. "To open the pages, yes. Not to burn it!"

"I see. My apologies for the misunderstanding." He lifted the journal and studied the spot where he'd held the flame. "No mark. Not a surprise. There's no need to place flame against it again."

"I'm so comforted."

"Good. Good."

"Why would you burn it?"

"Burn it?" He looked at her, sincere confusion on his face. "I would never do that."

"You were starting to do exactly that."

"No, what I was doing was confirming what I already knew to be true."

"Which is?"

"This leather." Carl tapped it with his forefingers. "It is not common. It's been treated with a substance that prevents it from being damaged by fire, by water, by mold."

"It's indestructible?"

"No. Not completely. The pages can be torn with some effort. And it could be charred with fire, I suppose, if hot enough. It would have to be quite hot. And it certainly could be damaged by water with significant exposure. But it is highly resistant."

Carl closed the two overlapping covers, then opened the journal again. He turned to Allison, a question in his eyes.

"What?" Allison asked.

"May I look through its pages?"

Allison hesitated. She didn't want him reading her entries, but there were only two, and if he lingered she could encourage him to move along. "Sure."

Carl opened it, seemed to read the poem, but only glanced at Allison's entries. Then he riffled the rest of the pages quickly, closed the journal, and handed it back to Allison.

"This is astonishing. Truly." Carl leaned back in his chair, hands folded across his gaunt stomach. He seemed to be studying an ancient-looking map on the wall next to the door. "Who else knows about the journal?"

"No one."

"No one?"

"My mom. My brother. The guy who gave it to me. And the guy I saw talking to him. Richard."

"Gave it to you?"

Allison told the story of how she wound up with the journal. When she finished, Carl nodded and said to himself, "Yes, that's the way it would be, wouldn't it?"

She peered at him, at the funny look on his face. Carl turned to her and rubbed his lower teeth on his upper lip.

"'The way it would be'?" Allison asked.

He picked up the journal and turned it over and over, his expression now that of a boy delighted by what he'd found.

"I believed they existed, I believed that part, but I don't think I ever really believed the second part. That adjunct was simply legend. Still might not be factual. We'll have to find out, won't we?"

"Carl?"

"However, even if it is fraudulent, it is still a remarkable moment to hold a hoax of this magnitude. Few people know about them—the narrative, that is. But of course I do, which is why Parker sent his sister to me—"

"Carl!"

He shook his head and flashed her an irritated look as if she'd awakened him from a sound sleep.

"Yes, what is it?" He blinked.

"The journal. What is it? Please."

"Oh. Right. Yes, of course." He rubbed his hands together and leaned forward. "There is a legend, quite a fascinating legend. Would you like to hear it?"

"Yes," Allison said through a forced smile.

"Well then, let me share it with you." Carl rubbed his hands together. "The legend says that five hundred years back, an aging monk was led by God into the mountains to pray, to listen, to hear what the last—and greatest—work of his life would be. After three days he heard the voice of God, who told him to create seven journals, each the same and each different. The same because the design, the way the leather was cured and tanned, the paper inside, would be as close to identical as possible. Different because on the cover of each journal a differing image would be carved."

He paused and rubbed his finger over the journal. "One of the images was the Tree of Life."

"Are you saying—"

"After the journals were finished, the monk placed them in a thick wooden box and mentioned them to no one, for God had told him to keep their existence a secret. They were discovered upon his death. A note written in the monk's hand lay atop the journals. The note said, among other things, that the journals were created by him, yes, but also by the hand of God, and that they were to be distributed to seven locations throughout the world. Seven monks from the monastery were to be chosen to deliver those journals to a holy place in each location."

Carl paused, as if picturing the monks on their journeys, and smiled. "But the note did not say where the locations were, nor did it name the holy places. Stories—just rumors really—of the journals showing up here and there cropped up through the centuries. No one could ascertain if they were true until a man named Higgins wrote a detailed account of having seen one of the journals in 1903. He held it himself, only for a few weeks, but long enough to run a number of tests on the journal and declare the legend true. Over the years I've heard reports—well, just whisperings actually—of the journals showing up in Ireland, South America, Japan, Albania, the Netherlands . . . and many other countries."

For the first time since starting his story, Carl turned to Allison. He smiled and said, "It appears that you have in your possession one of those seven journals."

"Even if your story is true, how could the journal be in such good condition? And how does that explain why the writing would appear and disappear? And how my name would show up inside and—"

"That is the part of the legend that I'm not sure I believe." Carl adjusted his glasses. "But as you say, seeing this journal in this condition, I can almost believe it's true."

Allison pressed her lips together. Why couldn't the guy spit it out? Get on with it! But she smiled and blinked and waited for him to continue.

Carl gestured to the journal as if it were the *Mona Lisa* and said, "Because the journals were made with the assistance of God, they are highly resistant to damage, as I mentioned a moment ago. The only change to the covers over the years is for them to become more beautiful, bearing the oils of the fingers and hands that have carried them."

"That still doesn't explain—"

"Seraph Journals, Allison." Carl winked. "That's what they are. The Seraph Journals. Each one of these journals is guided by an angel tasked with giving them to the people who need them. And once the journals have done what they are to do with each person, they are passed on to another person."

"You can't be serious."

"I'm only telling you what the legend says. I'm not telling you if I believe it." Carl cocked his head and peered at her. "However, you told me strange things have happened with your journal already, yes?"

"Yes. Words have vanished. And appeared. And the meaning of what I've written has changed. Changed to the opposite of what I meant."

"Ah, interesting." Carl nodded. "You didn't tell me that part."

"You believe me?"

"You're Parker's sister. You seem quite normal. You seem as surprised as I suspect someone would be if the like happened to them." He winked again. "If it's true, I imagine an angel would have little problem adding or subtracting any kind of writing to its pages."

"But what's happening is impossible."

"Oh? How do you know that?"

"I . . ."

Carl picked up the journal and handed it back to Allison.

"For the moment it seems it doesn't matter what you believe. Only what you choose to do with what you have in front of you right now."

He rose and she followed him out of his office, through the store, and to the front door.

"Good night, Allison."

"Thank you, Carl."

She started to go when his voice called out. "One more thought before you go."

"Yes?"

A brightness like a firefly's shone in his eyes.

"The legend says the lives of those who have encountered the journals are never the same."

On the walk back to her car, Allison dialed Parker's number. He didn't answer. Not a surprise. Probably wouldn't get the message till he went into town next, whenever that would be. But still, she wanted to thank him. And she needed to talk to someone about it, even if it was a one-sided conversation.

"Hey, bro, it's me. I met with your friend Carl. You're right, he was the guy to talk to. I'm not sure I believe what he's telling me about the journal, but I'm definitely going to write in it more. Carl says it will change my life. It already has. I feel like I'm on one of your wild rides, Parker. Jumping out of a plane or off a cliff. Just in a different way, you know?

"Anyway, hope you're doing well. It was so good to see you. Call me."

By the time she got home, her mom was asleep, which was okay. She needed to put the journal out of her mind and mentally prepare for a meeting in the morning with Derrek. He wanted to talk to her about something. What, he wouldn't say.

twenty-three

Let me show you again."

Derrek held up his right forefinger, then his left as he stood in Allison's office the next morning.

"One plus one equals three."

"I see only two fingers." Allison smiled as she spun in her chair across from her drafting board to fully face him. "Am I supposed to see three fingers?"

"No. But the two still equal three."

"Do you care to explain that?"

"There is this space." Derrek peered at his right finger, then his left. "There is this space . . . and there is the space in the middle. One. Two. Three."

He smiled at Allison as if he'd revealed an important secret. "And the third space, the one in the middle, is quite often the most important. Architecture is too often focused on the spaces we create instead of the spaces we leave out. An inch more width on a window or a wall, or an inch higher on a ceiling, can create ambience that otherwise would not have been possible to achieve."

Derrek pointed to the drawing on Allison's board and tapped his finger on a wall she'd started to sketch in. "This wall, for example, is a fell stroke of wonderful imagination. You've created a charming third space by doing what you've done. That small nuance will be noticed by many, mostly on a subconscious level, but I do believe it will be noticed and enjoyed to a greater degree because of it."

"Thank you."

"You have a real talent, Allison. In areas where I don't. You see things I don't. You apply them in ways I don't apply them, as I never imagined them in the first place."

She stared at him, hoping the surprise she felt hadn't spilled onto her face. She couldn't remember the last time he'd given her a compliment as thorough as this one.

"Thanks, I appreciate that."

"You're welcome."

She did appreciate it. Compliments from Derrek were rare. He'd never made any specific positive observations about her drawings. Only suggestions for what she might change. He was never harsh in his assessments, but he rarely took time to point out the strengths of a design.

Before she could stop it, gratitude welled up in her. This was all she wanted: to be recognized, to be appreciated for what she could bring. She was about to speak, but the emotion was too close to the surface, so she swallowed and simply nodded.

As if sensing the awkwardness of the moment, Derrek stepped back and said, "'Good buildings come from good people, and all problems are solved by good design.' The British architect Stephen Gardiner said that."

Allison smiled. "All problems?"

"Yes. All."

Allison hesitated a moment, then said, "That's what you wanted to meet with me about this morning? To tell me about how one plus one equals three?"

"Yes." Derrek smiled like a little boy who had blown a perfect bubble. "And to tell you that I appreciate your gifts. I don't do that often enough."

The warmth of feeling appreciated and deep gratitude toward Derrek both surged. He saw her. Saw who she was.

No. She couldn't let herself trust him till they finalized the partnership. But still, the moment was rich with promise.

Derrek turned to go, but before he could step from her office into the hallway, Linda slid inside and said, "May I speak with you for a moment, Allison?" She didn't wait for a response. "I noticed that you were over your budget for client lunches last week."

"Oh really?"

"Yes. That's not acceptable."

"I think we're okay." Allison clasped her hands together. "I didn't have any client lunches the week before that, and only one the week before that. So I'm way under budget overall."

"We don't average here. Each week stands on its own."

"Oh." Allison glanced at Derrek, who had apparently become fascinated with his wedding ring. "And how much was I over last week?"

"Three dollars and seventy-four cents."

Allison glanced at Derrek again, then back to Linda. Was Linda joking? Doubtful. This was not a woman who joked about anything.

The fire inside Allison flickered. "You're worried that I was over budget by three dollars and seventy-four cents?"

Linda narrowed her eyes. "I'm not worried about it. I am simply telling you to stay within company structure from now on. If you can't abide by that, we'll need to have another, more serious conversation."

"Please tell me she's kidding."

Derrek shook his head, a tiny smile in the corners of his mouth.

"Is that what you want, Derrek? For me to make sure I don't go over budget by three dollars and seventy-four cents for a client lunch? That's what a partner in this company is required to do? If so, it's ludicrous. Who actually runs this company?"

Derrek chuckled his hollow chuckle and held up his hands as if at gunpoint. "I'm not weighing in on this one. Linda is the office manager, so she runs the ins and outs of the weekly budgets. Consequently, I defer to her in this case."

Linda pressed her lips together and nodded as if the matter were settled. As she walked out the door, she said, "Thank you for your cooperation, Allison. It's appreciated."

The fire inside her grew, and Allison started to stride out the door after Linda, but she pushed it down and stayed silent. And hated herself for doing it.

———

That afternoon Allison left the office at four thirty, steam still building inside her mind. Ridiculous. Four dollars? Linda was hammering her over four bucks? Asinine.

But a few minutes later a sliver of good news arrived. The bank called. Her home loan had come through. Relief washed over her. It was a reprieve. Not for long, but for the moment they could breathe.

By five fifteen she pulled into her driveway, happy about the loan but still ticked off about Linda. She needed a way to exorcise her frustration. She strode inside, greeted her mom and gave her the good news about the loan, then went to her room to get ready for a run. She glanced at her watch. Plenty of time to get up the mountain and back before twilight settled over Issaquah.

Allison's heart pumped like a jackhammer as she pounded up the mountain, pushing herself harder than she had in months. It hurt and felt good at the same time, each step squashing Linda's pathetic control issues into the ground.

By the time she reached the top of the mountain, her lungs burned along with her legs, but her spirit felt release, and the peace that often comes after extreme physical exertion washed through her. After her breathing returned to normal, she strolled over to the lookout and gazed down over the cars on I-90 likely streaming their drivers home. Clouds were thick on the horizon. Rain was bound to arrive soon. The sky would darken early. She should head back home.

She turned to go and her breath caught. On the far edge of the clearing with his back to her stood Richard, the man who had been in the coffee shop the day she'd first seen the journal. Had to be him. Same running outfit from ten days back. Same hair, height, build. As she marched toward him, he began to stroll away from her. No. Not this time. This time she would catch him, and get answers.

twenty-four

Richard!" Allison jogged toward him.

To her relief, he didn't break into a run back down the mountain. He turned, his eyes quizzical as she approached, hands stuffed in his blue windbreaker.

"Your name is Richard, isn't it?"

"Yes, it is." He peered at her. "Have we met?"

"Not exactly." She stood with hands on hips, studying Richard. The same look of gentleness and intensity she'd seen in The Vogue that day filled his eyes. "I saw you in The Vogue toward the end of April, you and another man. I sat at a table next to yours. He had a journal and he said his life had been changed."

"Yes. That's right, we did see each other." Richard smiled at her the way Joel used to do, and it peeled something back inside her. "So you eavesdropped on our conversation."

She couldn't tell if that bothered him or if he thought it amusing. "Yes, I did."

He didn't comment.

"Can I . . ." She stopped. What did she want to do? "Can I talk to you about the journal?"

"Sure." He glanced at the sky. "Might we chat as we walk back down the trail? Looks like rain is coming."

"Good idea."

They made their way back to the trail. Just before starting down, Richard offered his hand. "My name is Richard. But you obviously already knew that."

"Yes, I did." She took his hand. Large. Warm. "My name's Allison."

"Pleased." He smiled. "Impressive to remember a name you've only eavesdropped on once." He winked.

Good. He wasn't offended.

"Your conversation made an impression on me. I've been journaling my whole life, so it was hard not to pick up on your discussion. I love all kinds and styles, but the one I saw that day is one of the most exquisite I've ever seen."

"*Is* exquisite? Not *was*?"

"Is." She peered up at Richard. "I have it now."

"Oh really? I'd like to hear all about that." Richard motioned down the trail. "Would you like to lead?"

"That's okay. I'll bring up the rear."

"As you wish."

They hiked down the path, and as they weaved in and out of groves of trees and collections of boulders, she told Richard about getting the journal, talking to her mom, and mustering the courage to write in it. She told him about her conversation with Parker, and about going to Carl and learning of the monk who created the journals and of the legends surrounding them.

Richard asked a quick clarifying question here and there but otherwise spoke little till she'd finished.

"And you've told me all of this, Allison, for what reason?" She wished she could have seen his face as he spoke the words. Was he kidding?

"First, I want to know why your companion, Alister, gave the journal to me."

"Because you're the one he chose."

"Chose?"

"Yes." Richard turned and gave her that warm smile again. A dad smile. A smile she'd longed for from her own father. "He chose you to have the journal next. As you said, the legend is that these journals are passed from person to person. You apparently are the next in line for this particular journal. Anything else?"

"I only have three or four hundred more questions."

Richard laughed, a hearty laugh of peace and thunder. "Ask away."

"I want to know more about the journal. Everything I can. You obviously know something about it because of your friendship with this Alister guy."

She stepped over a log fallen across the trail and scraped her leg on its bark.

"Here are a few of the things I know: I know Alister believed the journal was special. Supernatural, you might say. I know he wrote in it, and he told me he often felt the journal spoke back to him. I know he was a different man after having the journal than he was before."

"How do you know him? Where can I find him?"

"How do you know he wants to be found?"

"I don't. But I need to find him."

"Why?"

"Because I want to find out what the journal is. What it does. What I'm supposed to do with it."

"From what you've told me, you know what the journal is, you know what it does, and you know what to do with it."

"Tell me about Alister. Please."

"I met Alister a year ago. We got together a few times a month, sometimes more, sometimes less. A coffee shop. Hikes. He needed a friend. I became one to him."

"How did you meet him?"

Richard laughed. "You're not a reporter, are you? Talk-show host?"

"No and no. I'm an architect." She held up her hands in mock defense. "But I'm motivated to find out everything I can about this journal. Sorry about all the questions."

"Don't be." Richard glanced at the sky and picked up his pace down the trail. "I was Alister's parole officer."

"You're a cop?"

"Used to be. Guess I'll always be, in some ways."

Allison sniffed out a soft laugh. Of course Richard was a cop. Nice way to remind her of her dad. God certainly had a sense of humor.

"My dad was a cop. Leon Moore."

"I know of him. But I never met your father."

Her dad would have liked Richard.

They lapsed into silence for five or so minutes and Allison slowed. Richard was right. She did know what to do. Write in the journal. And she knew what it was—if Carl's words were true. She picked up her pace and caught up to Richard.

"So you believe there are seven of them? That they're angel journals?"

"What do you believe, Allison? Has anything strange happened since you started writing in yours?" He turned and walked backward down the trail a few paces, somehow avoiding the rocks and roots that could have easily tripped him up.

"Yes."

"Do you want to tell me about that?"

Did she? She barely knew this man, yet the answer was yes, she did want to. Not simply because the warmth that seemed to radiate off him invited her to believe this space was safe; her intuition whispered that the more open she was with him, the more open he'd be with her.

"I've written in the journal, and the words I've written have changed. It wasn't my imagination. They changed. Not once, but two times now."

"Alister said the same."

"So it's real? The journal? It really is the hand of God writing in the journal, or changing the writing?"

Before she finished her question, the clouds opened and rain poured down. Richard glanced back and said, "Mind if we pick up the pace and get off the mountain?"

Allison shook her head and they both broke into a run. Little pockets of the trail turned to mud, and dodging the larger puddles made her think of playing hopscotch as a kid. But after another half mile, her shoes and socks were drenched with fresh rainwater and ancient mud, and she gave up trying to stay out of the muck. No chance to get her question answered till they got to their cars.

But when they reached the parking lot, the rain had turned into a torrent, not exactly conducive to finishing their conversation.

"Can we talk again?" Allison shouted to be heard over the deluge.

"Anytime you'd like."

"Where?"

Richard yanked open his car door, pulled out a business card, and handed it to her. "Call me. Or text. I look forward to next time."

With that, he jumped into his car, waited till Allison was safely in hers, then drove off, leaving Allison enlightened, bewildered, and inspired all at the same time.

twenty-five

Wednesday evening, May 29th

    I don't know what to think about what is going on in my life at the moment. Work. This journal. And Mom. She's at the point where she doesn't need to live with me any longer. Her ankle is doing well. But where would she go? With her house now sold and all the proceeds gone to the loan, there's no other option. It's fine having her here but would be nice to be back on my own again. She asks about the journal a lot, and I don't mind that much. I tell her about it, but there's a big part of me that wants to—no, *needs* to—go on this journey, whatever it is, on my own.

    And the money. Always the money guillotine hanging over my head. Payment next month? Yes. But when my home loan is gone . . . then what?

    Then there's this Richard guy I met today. What's his story? Why is he willing to talk to me about the journal? Is he just another father figure who will let me down in the end?

    And of course my ongoing struggle with Derrek. He wants me to lie to clients, he continues to put off getting the partnership finished, is aloof for long periods, then turns around and tells me I'm talented and gifted and he appreciates me. I hate the mixed messages! Because it opens me up and gives me hope for what things can be like at Wright Architecture. I went there thinking it would be the last place I'd ever work. But now? I don't know. Have to, have to, have to get the partnership finalized. And life can settle.

Which brings us to Linda. Why does she hate me? And why don't I stand up to her? And why can Derrek praise me one moment, then throw me to Linda the Wolf the next?

And what are you going to tell me, Journal? How are you going to rearrange my words to change the meaning of what I've just written?

I need answers, God, and direction and guidance and all of the above. Change the words, Lord. Show me what to do.

But in the morning, when Allison checked the journal, nothing had changed. As strange as it had been before to find certain words of hers taken out, and words that were not hers put in, to find her entry exactly as she'd written it was somewhat shocking.

She could talk to her mom about it, but the person she really wanted to chat with was her brother. "Where are you, Parker?"

———

Parker had watched Allison trek away from his homestead, equal parts peace and sorrow. He'd missed her, and the time they'd had together over Memorial Day weekend wasn't enough. She'd been his closest friend all through junior high and high school. Even during college when they were apart too often. She was the person he could tell anything to. And right now she was right. He needed to talk.

But he didn't want to. The hermit life agreed with him. Maybe too much. And then there was the matter of their mom. What if Al's new partnership thing didn't work out? What then? Could he leave Al hanging? Leave Mom hanging? No way. What he should do is find the loan sharks, stick a gun in their faces, and tell them to forgive the loan. Yeah, sure he should do that. Perfect solution.

Al said things would be fine. Yeah, maybe they would be. But there had to be a way for him to help. In the morning he'd head into Mazama and make some calls to some old friends. Find work.

Parker got to Mazama at eight o'clock Tuesday morning. By late afternoon he'd found a job. After that he put in a call to Allison.

"Hey, Al. It's me. I know we're supposed to talk on the phone tomorrow, but I have a better idea. Let's do it in person. I'm coming over. I'll be there on Thursday, late afternoon, early evening. Hang in there. We'll figure out this thing with Mom together. I've figured out a way I can help."

On Thursday midmorning he drove his quad to the mechanics garage where he stored his Ducati 1098 motorcycle. Paid the guy twenty dollars a month to keep it there. The bike was twelve years old but in great shape, and it could still shred a highway. And right now Parker wanted to shred the North Cascades highway.

He marveled at the scenery as he headed west. The skyrocketing mountains shooting up to the sky never failed to impress. Traffic was light, affording him the chance to punch the gas on the straightaways and take the corners only slightly slower.

Just over the pass, he saw a straight shot, and something inside told him to go for it. See how far the speedometer would climb before the curves appeared that would force him to slow down. He'd had this bike over 140 only once, and once was far from enough.

Parker kicked the bike into fifth gear and eased down on the throttle for a few seconds, then opened it up wide. The torque almost lifted the front wheel off the highway, and Parker focused on the pavement sliding by underneath him. *Speed, baby. Pure speed.* The engine screamed as he hit eighty. One hundred. One ten. When he hit 120 a wry smile formed. When he reached 130 it was a fun grin. At 150 laughter poured out of him. No one holding him back. No one holding him down.

Three seconds later a yellow sign came into view. Curve ahead. Parker braked, then dropped a gear and glanced at his speedometer. Eighty-three. The curve came into view, long and gentle. *Should be able to take this pup at ninety.* He gave the bike gas and leaned into the curve, the rush of danger filling him.

Fifty yards in, a white car with lights on top came into view and his heart skipped. A half second later Parker shot past him and caught a glimpse of the cop's face. Not happy.

The cop pulled out, lights whirling. Parker looked in his rearview mirror as the cop's car pulled a U-turn. Parker's stomach lurched and he glanced at his speedometer. Thirty-five over. This was going to be expensive. Not just this ticket, but his insurance was sure to bump him to higher premiums. Getting four speeding tickets in less than two years will do that.

He slowed and pulled over on the shoulder, toed out his kickstand, but didn't get off his bike. The officer pulled in behind him five seconds later, popped out of his car, and strode toward Parker. As he did, Parker took off his helmet and goggles.

The cop was tall. Lean, strong jaw. Eyes hidden behind mirror shades. Parker kept his hands on his handlebars, stared straight ahead, and waited for the crunch of the cop's boots on the gravel shoulder.

A temptation circled his mind. *Tell the cop about Dad.* The guy probably wouldn't know him, but there was a chance. And then what? The cop would let him off? Yeah, right. Parker kept his mouth shut and pressed his lips together.

The cop scraped up next to the bike, hands loose at his sides. He didn't speak for a few seconds, and Parker didn't turn his head.

Finally, "Do you know why I pulled you over?"

Of course he knew. What a stupid question. How often was anyone pulled over when they didn't know what they'd done wrong?

"Yep."

"You know?"

"Yeah. I do." Parker glanced at the cop, then turned back to staring straight ahead. "You think you're looking at an idiot?"

The cop drew in a hard breath and stepped closer. Parker could almost feel the tension rising.

"You want to tell me?"

"Nope, sure don't." Parker gripped his handlebars harder. "I mean, I did want to tell you at first, but then I thought about it for a few seconds and changed my mind." Parker cocked his head and looked at the cop.

The cop placed his hand on his gun. "You should be on late-night. I'm busting a gut."

"Thanks." Parker shifted his weight. "I work on my material a lot. Especially for cops."

"Guess what all the comedians I meet out here get."

"What?"

"Maximum penalty allowed."

Parker nodded. "Not surprising."

"I'd like you to tell me why you think I pulled you over. Right now."

Parker leaned his head back and stared at a hawk circling above them. Freedom. *Fly, baby, fly.*

"I was speeding. Way over. Doing probably ninety in a fifty-five when you spotted me. Stupid move. Really idiotic. But there hasn't been a rash of great decisions in my life lately."

The cop sniffed out a laugh. "I'm going to have to document this. First time I've gotten an honest answer in eight months."

Parker didn't respond.

"I clocked you at eighty-eight miles per hour."

Parker nodded. "Sounds about right."

"You want to tell me why you were in such a hurry?"

"Because the speed felt good. And I haven't had much good lately. I've been doing the hermit thing, and it's not always the best choice for my mind."

"Oh?" The cop shifted his weight. "Any other reason?"

"That's it."

"Okay," the cop said. "License and registration, please."

Parker handed him both and the cop started to stroll back to his patrol car, but after five paces he stopped, spun on his boot, and meandered back.

"Your license says your address is in the Seattle area. What are you doing on the east side of the mountains?"

"Uh, no. I don't live over there anymore. Life got weird. I decided to make a change. Move to Mazama. Build a place on a remote piece of land. Get away from everything and everyone. Start over. And I feel really stupid telling you all this like you're a bartender or something, but like I said, I haven't talked to too many people lately."

"Your last name is Moore."

Parker resisted the urge to comment. This cop was brilliant. Apparently he knew how to read. "Yes, it is."

"Might be a painful question to answer, but I'm curious. Are you any relation to Joel Moore?"

"Yeah. You're right." Parker pinched the bridge of his nose. "Painful."

"So you knew him."

"My brother."

The cop tapped Parker's license on his hand for a few seconds.

"I'm sorry for your loss." The cop took off his sunglasses. "Joel was one of a kind."

"Thank you, I appreciate that." The words were rote. Automatic. He'd said them so many times over the past two and a half years they didn't mean anything. Yes, he did appreciate it. At least he tried to. But it was tough being reminded he'd never measured up to the family's golden boy.

The cop cleared his throat. "I met Joel back in 2010. He and I went through the academy together. We stayed in touch. Phone calls a couple of times a year. Christmas cards. But what I'll always remember is the time I mentioned I needed a car. Boom. Three days later he shows up on my doorstep with an old beater he'd found and just gave to me. That's the kind of guy he was. They don't come better than him."

Parker swallowed. He glanced at the cop. Were those tears in the man's eyes? *No. Come on. Please.* Parker swallowed a second time. Coughed. *Say the words. Get this over with.*

"No, they sure don't make 'em any better than Joel."

The cop returned Parker's registration, license, and proof of insurance.

"I'm letting you off with only a warning."

"What?"

The cop put his sunglasses back on. "Because of Joel."

The saint saves the sinner from a speeding ticket. Even in death, Joel was the hero.

"Thank you."

"Again, I'm sorry for your pain."

"Thanks."

"No problem." The cop tapped Parker's rear tire with the toe of his boot. "I know it's tempting with a bike like this, but keep it down from now on."

"Will do."

After the cop pulled back on the road, did a U-turn, and headed back to his lookout, Parker sat on his bike till the chill of the day seeped through every inch of his jacket and clothes. Allison had the wisdom to be born a woman. Didn't have to deal with any of the pressure. All she had to do was be Daddy's girl. Besides, she was an architect and would soon be pulling down the big bucks in her new partnership gig. Yeah, they had to get their mom's debt paid off, but after that she'd have a career, a direction, esteem from others that overshadowed the fact she'd never measure up to her dead brother.

twenty-six

FINALLY," ALLISON SAID AS SHE stood at the window and watched Parker's motorcycle pull up to the curb in front of her house early Thursday evening. He'd made it.

"Mom?"

Her mom answered from the kitchen. "Yes, sweetie?"

"Parker's here."

Her mom came around the corner, tears already forming in the corners of her eyes. She gave Allison a quick hug and said, "I can't get too emotional."

"Sure you can. Your son's been off the grid for five-plus months, not truly knowing if he's alive or . . . That can't be easy to go through, given the past."

"It's not."

"So get emotional, Mom. You've earned it."

Allison smiled, trying to infuse a hope into her mom that neither of them felt.

"Things are getting better, Mom. All the time. We're going to reconnect with Parker. We're going to get your problem taken care of—he told me on the phone he has a way to help—and life is going to be good again."

"I hope you're right, Ally. Really, I do."

"I am."

The doorbell rang, and Allison pulled away to answer it. She yanked open the door and threw her arms around Parker. "Mom is feeling a little emotional," she whispered. "So make her feel like you want to be here."

"I do want to be here."

"You know what I mean."

Parker stepped into the living room, strode up to his mom, and gave her a long hug. "I'm sorry, Mom, I just had to get away for a while."

"I know you did. I know." She wiped away tears. "I was just worried. Moms are supposed to be."

"I should have been in touch. I blew it. Really. I'm so sorry I put you through that."

Their mom waved her hand. "It's over. You're here now."

Parker's face went blank.

"What's wrong?" Allison asked.

"I'm not here for long."

"Why not?"

"I'm going to Alaska."

"What?" Their mom squinted at him. "What for?"

"Money. So I can help you out." Parker rubbed his thumb against his fingers. "Fishing boat. I have a friend who has a friend. One of the crew got hurt. They needed someone quick. Perfect timing. A lot of hours, a lot of fish, a lot of money."

"Those boats are dangerous," their mom said.

"Yeah, that's how some people would describe it." Parker grinned. "Me? Should be a rush."

"You don't have to do that, Parker," Allison said.

"I don't?" He peered at Allison. "So you got your partnership thing figured out?"

Allison gave a tiny shake of her head.

"Then I do. Even if you were already pulling in the big bucks, Al, and the school gave you a huge cash prize, Mom, for doing something cool, I would still need to help out."

Tears welled in their mom's eyes.

"Besides, I need to try civilization again."

Allison scoffed. "I'm not sure I'd call a fishing boat in the Bering Sea *civilization*."

Parker laughed. "I'm easing back in slowly."

They sat down together around the coffee table. After Parker described his life in Mazama and he got an update on his mom's ankle, she sighed and said, "We should probably watch this."

"Watch what?" Allison and Parker asked in tandem.

"One, two, three, four, five, six, seven, eight, nine, ten, jinx!"

Allison laughed, and a second later Parker joined in. And they were kids again, he a little boy, she a little girl. Like they'd been when they hid out together in Parker's tree house talking about nothing and everything. Dreaming about what they'd be when they grew up.

"You got me, Al. These will be the last words I speak till you release me."

Something about his eyes shot to her heart, and there was nothing more in the world she wanted to do than free her brother from his pain and fill his longing. They stared at each other, not needing to speak, knowing exactly what the other was thinking.

She forced her tears down and said softly, "I release you, dear brother."

He nodded, and maybe it was only her imagination, but she thought she saw moisture in his eyes.

After the moment settled, their mom cleared her throat and said, "I was going through a few of your dad's old things in the boxes we brought over to Al's garage from the house, getting rid of stuff, and . . . well, I came across an old VHS tape. Apparently your dad never threw out his old camera, and he filmed something he wants us to see. There was a note on top that said, 'Play this please when I'm gone. It's for you and the kids. Love, Leon.' So I hooked up the old VHS player to the TV and I think we should watch it."

"Wow." Parker leaned back and put his hands behind his head. "This should be interesting. You sure you want to see this, Mom? Since the revelation of . . . uh . . . certain things none of us knew about?"

"Yes." Her mom's face was somber. "I'll only wonder about it till I see it."

"Me too," Allison said.

"Okay," Parker said. "Let's go."

Allison pressed Play, and an image of her father filled the screen. He sat in his favorite gray camping chair out in the backyard on the lawn. Its edges were frayed but not badly. Based on how the chair looked last summer, the video had to have been shot at least a couple of years ago.

"Hello, my dear. Hello, Allison. Hello, Parker."

He rubbed his face and laughter sputtered out. "I can't believe I'm doing this. But I've always liked those parts in the movies or on TV when the character makes a video and says, 'If you're watching this, then I'm dead.' Now I get to be the one saying it, and you're the people watching. But I didn't think it would come this early." A sadness crept into his eyes and he tried to laugh again, but the laughter died in his mouth.

He paused and a pensive look came over his face, as if he was gathering his thoughts. After folding his hands across his lap, he continued.

"Having that heart attack a few years back made me finally admit I'm not going to make it out of this thing called life alive. And then when the cancer followed up, I knew immortality wasn't in the bag for me. So in case I go before any of you, which is pretty likely, there's a few things I want to say.

"First, there were times, a lot of times, I wish I'd done things differently. But more times where I'd do it over again in exactly the same way. Second, I wasn't the best father, but I love you, Parker. I love you, Allison. Third, I wasn't always the best husband, but I love you, sweetie. With all my heart. Last, don't cry for me. I'm in the place now where all your dreams come true. And I'm with Joel again. Finally I'm with my boy again. And what could be better than that?"

It looked like tears were coming to her dad's eyes. Cry? He never cried. But if they were tears, they didn't spill over. Another deep breath and he continued.

"I leave you with my love, most of all. I'll see you all soon."

Her dad smiled, then reached forward, and the clip ended.

Allison sat stunned, not wanting to turn and look at Parker, but she had to. Had to see how much damage her dad had done from the other side of the grave.

"There're things he wished he would have done differently? Like not leave us hundreds of thousands of dollars in debt? And he's excited to be with Joel?" Parker's voice started out low but grew in volume with each word. "Like he wasn't with Joel every single moment of every day, even after Joel was dead?"

"Don't say that, Parker."

"Why not, Mom? It's true. He was with Joel before he died and with Joel even after he died. He certainly wasn't here with us. Ever."

"Please, Parker."

Parker stood, marched to the edge of the living room, and spun. "Every conversation—I am not exaggerating—every single conversation I had with Dad, somehow we ended up talking about Joel, the superstar of the universe, the man who barfed up nuggets of gold when he was sick."

"Stop, Parker," his mom said.

"Good for Dad. What could be better than leaving us in debt so he can go be with Joel again? Certainly beats being here with his sorry excuse for a son." Parker threw his hands in the air in mock praise. "Be with wonderful, glorious Joel! Way to go, Dad!"

"Don't say that. You loved your brother."

"Yeah, I did. But he wasn't perfect. Did you know that?"

Allison went to Parker and took his arm. "Let's talk, you and me. Let's not make this about Dad. Let's make it about the three people in this family who are still living."

Parker gave a slight nod and said, "I love you, sis. Always will."

"Me too, Parker, so let's—"

Parker pulled away and said to their mother, "I love you too, Mom, but I'm out of here."

"What?"

"I'll call you both when I get back from Alaska."

He strode for the door.

"Parker, stop. Please." Allison rushed after him. "Let's talk about this, find a way to let this go."

"Good call." He stopped in the doorframe, the edge of the door in his left hand. "You do that, and let me know when it's all figured out."

He yanked open her front door, strode through it, then slammed it behind him. Allison pulled it open and went after him.

"Hey, talk to me," she called out to his retreating figure. "Stop!"

Parker marched up to his bike and stopped but didn't look up. "What?"

She worked her way down the steps and made her way to Parker's motorcycle.

"You're not the only one who was an afterthought to Dad."

"I know, Al. I get it. Sorry."

"Where are you going?"

Parker still didn't look up.

"Job starts right away."

"Be careful."

"Hey, it's me." Parker got on his bike and gave her a thin smile. "You know I won't be careful."

twenty-seven

AT A STOPLIGHT ON THE way home from work the next day, Allison pulled out Richard's card and stared at the number. She wanted to talk to someone other than her mom about the journal. Mom was great, would drop anything to talk for as long as Allison liked, but the subject matter was too close to home. Plus, Richard hadn't answered her question about the writing being—or not being—from God. This guy knew something. Had to. And he'd said he'd talk to her anytime.

She dialed his number, and he answered on the second ring.

"Richard here."

"Richard? It's Allison Moore. We met on the—"

"Have you dried out?" Warm laughter came through the phone.

"Yes, thanks. You?"

"Yes." She could tell he was smiling. "I'm sorry we didn't get a chance to finish our conversation. You wanted to know if I thought the writing in your journal was the hand of God or something else."

Allison almost laughed. So she wouldn't have to drag it out of him. How refreshing.

"I did. You're right." She paused. "So can we talk?"

"Love to. When? Where?"

———

They met the next afternoon at The Vogue, and Allison didn't waste any time with small talk.

"The first two times I wrote in the journal, it changed, but the third time it didn't. What does that mean? And the first two times when it did, are those changes from the hand of God?"

"That's what Alister came to believe. And if it is God, then I suppose he gets to choose when he changes the writing and when he doesn't." Richard leaned back and crossed his legs. "What do you think, Allison?"

"I don't know."

"Which is why you want to know what I think. As if my opinion is the one that matters, which I don't think it does."

"Yes, it does matter."

"Why is that?"

"Because you were with Alister. You were around during the time he had the journal. You had to have gained some kind of insight or knowledge about the journal."

"Regardless of what I saw, it's still only my opinion. What matters more is yours."

"Will you tell me what you think anyway?"

"Yes." Richard uncrossed his legs and leaned forward, hands clasped, elbows on the table, and lowered his voice. "I do think the journal is real. I do think something supernatural is going on with regard to the writing in your journal."

"What do I do about that?"

"Read what it says, embrace the changes."

So simple to say, so hard to do. Time to shift gears.

"Why did Alister choose me?"

"He told me he would listen to the Spirit and give it to the person he thought the Spirit told him to. Apparently that is you."

"But what's happening in that journal is impossible."

"Is that so?" Richard arched an eyebrow. "We're talking about a God who can create a universe so vast we cannot comprehend it, a God who makes blind eyes see. This is a God who raises people from the dead, a God who makes lame men walk. You think he isn't capable of putting things in motion to change a word or two in an ancient journal?"

"Those miracles were thousands of years ago."

"No, they weren't. We are bound by time. God is not. Those miracles happened just a moment ago." Richard smiled as if Allison were his daughter. "Yesterday I saw a man's leg grow to match the length of his other. Two weeks back I watched as a man who hadn't heard in twenty years regained his hearing. And a month ago I watched a woman extend forgiveness, truly extend forgiveness, to her sister, who had defrauded her out of her life's savings. God still does miracles in this day and this age. But then again, you just met me. Maybe I'm making those things up."

"I want to believe they happened. I'm trying."

"'It will happen to you just as you have believed.'"

"Don't go all spiritual and start using the Bible against me."

"Sorry, won't happen again." Richard laughed. "I hope."

"I'm still having a hard time wrapping my mind around this."

"Maybe you're right. Maybe there was no change. You imagined it, or you're simply going crazy." He winked at her and smiled.

She didn't. "I've considered that."

"You're not going crazy."

The sounds of U2's "I Still Haven't Found What I'm Looking For" floated down on them from the speaker above.

"Where do I go from here?"

"Good question," Richard said as he tilted his head toward the speaker above. "My suggestion, dear Allison, is to climb the highest mountains that come into your world. Scale the city walls. Keep running even when this journey overwhelms you. Believe your bonds have been broken. Believe Jesus carried the cross of your shame. Believe in kingdom come. Not in some age to come in the future, but right now. Choose to believe the kingdom is in your midst and is here to set you free."

twenty-eight

PARKER'S SLEEP WAS FILLED WITH constantly shifting images of the ocean, and men with thick forearms and multicolored nets, and the sensation of sitting in rocking chairs that wouldn't stop rocking. He felt like he woke up multiple times but didn't have the strength to stay awake and kept slipping back under. Finally he settled into a dream where he stood on the edge of a stream that reminded him of eastern Oregon. A hot summer sun blasted down from above. But it invigorated him. Thick underbrush and grasses filled the other bank and spread out for miles till they reached a low range of mountains. Behind him was a lush forest.

The river water was crystal clear, and all he wanted to do was sit on the soft turf along the bank and soak his feet in the stream. Forget his life. Pretend his dad had loved him as much as he loved Joel, and he and Allison were as tight as they'd been in the old days. He breathed in the peace of the dream. But the solitude didn't last. A man appeared on the other side of the river and strode toward Parker. Cap on his head. Flannel shirt, worn. The dense foliage reached almost to the top of the man's beat-up jeans, but he cut through it without effort. His thick forefinger was pointed at Parker's chest, and the scowl on the man's face said he wasn't camping in the land of milk and honey.

"Get up!" he growled.

When he reached the edge of the other bank, he stopped and screamed the command again. The third time, Parker realized the voice wasn't coming from his dream.

Parker pried open his eyes and found himself staring into the dark brown eyes of a man whose face was less than a foot from his. The man had a forest of a beard, with eyebrows almost as thick. His head was covered in a dark red stocking cap, and he wore green rubber coveralls that came up to his chest. A thin scar ran down the left side of his chunky neck, and his voice sounded like he had half a potato stuffed in his cheek.

"Where . . . who—"

"The fish are running, and they're not going to wait for your lazy glutes to get on deck. So move! Now!"

"Wow. Overslept, didn't I?"

The man pointed a sausage-like finger at Parker. "A pal of yours vouched for you. Said I should hire you. I took a chance. Gave it to you even though the other three votes aboard this little luxury liner were against you. People would kill for this gig, guys younger and probably in better shape, so don't screw with me. Got it, Rook?"

"Yeah. Got it. Back off." Parker pushed himself to a sitting position and scooted back. The cold hull of the boat pressed through his T-shirt.

"Wha'd you say?"

Parker gritted his teeth. "I said I'll be right there."

"That's what I thought." The man slammed his boot into the base of Parker's cot. "You sleep in again, you're going swimming. Got it?"

"Hey, it was a long flight. I didn't sleep. I haven't been—"

"Shut up. I don't want to hear it. This boat has a limited number of weeks left to make or break the entire year. So unless you shut your mouth and start working, I'll give you a new set of teeth about half the number you have now."

The man turned and lurched out of the cabin. He slammed the door behind him, but the wood didn't mute his final instructions. "Two minutes and you're on deck or I'm throwing you overboard, and don't think for a second that I'm kidding."

Parker's gaze whirled around the tiny cabin to take in what he hadn't been able to see in the dark when he arrived last night. Five bunks. Work clothes. Boots and gloves and hats. Not much else. He crept out of the small bunk and tried to get his footing on the stark gray floor. The boat lurched and Parker almost went down. Had to be rocking back and forth at more than thirty degrees. No picnic working on a boat moving like this.

He pulled on his jeans, a long flannel shirt, a thick coat, and his work boots. The boat pitched hard. Parker lost his balance and slammed his elbow into a small wooden shelf to his right. Pain shot through his arm. Nailed his funny bone with perfection. Funny bone. Yeah, hilarious. What a stupid name for a part of your elbow and what a great start to the day. He finally staggered through the door of the sleeping quarters, then up the stairs that more closely resembled a ladder.

The wind buffeted him as he stepped onto the open deck. Not bad but still cold. The rocking targeted his stomach. He formed a fist and punched his gut. He wouldn't allow himself to get sick. He could do this.

Two men stood with their backs to him, their legs braced wide, their arms resting on the railing. A third man stood by himself on the other side of the boat. The two at the rail turned, glanced at him, then resumed gazing out over the black waves dusted with dawn's gray light. The tall, older man on the other side studied Parker from head to toe.

The man who had woken him pointed at the men near the railing. "Guy on the left is Dawson. Don't piss him off. The one on the right is Fredricks. Don't piss him off either. The one over there is Abraham. You met him last night when you arrived, so he's probably already told you to call him Abe. My name is Logan, but you'll call me Captain."

The big man started to turn to walk away but hesitated, then called to Dawson, "Anything you want to add to the rook's education?"

"Yeah." Dawson glared at Parker. "Don't screw up."

"Fredricks?"

"Same." Fredricks grinned at Parker. "It won't go well for you if you do."

"Abe?"

Abraham shook his head. "We will see what we will see." He glanced at Parker as if to say, *Hang in there.* But it might have been Parker's imagination.

Parker's stomach heaved again and his head pitched forward as he gagged. *No. Keep it down.* These were not the kind of guys he wanted to see him throw up. Wouldn't make the right first impression. But it was already too late. Parker lurched toward the railing and just made it to the edge as whatever he'd last eaten spilled over the side.

"Yeeee-haw! Looks like we've got a puker, gents!" Dawson leaned back and shouted at the sky. "Gotta love the pukers."

Parker glanced back at the grinning faces. Even Logan joined the merriment, although his only way of showing it was to allow one corner of his mouth to turn up, and a glint hovered in his eye for a moment. A second later it vanished and he pointed at Parker.

"You get a drop on my ship, Rook, I'll take off your ring finger. Got me?" Logan's eyes said he was dead serious. Parker stumbled forward two steps and grabbed at the railing as another heave overtook him.

"Bait!" Fredricks hollered. "Feed the fish, baby!"

"You're gonna love going across the gulf, Rook." Dawson grinned again. "Can get a little choppy at times. Roller coaster of the seas."

"This isn't choppy?"

Fredricks laughed. "Don't worry, we won't be headed that direction for another two weeks. Plenty of time for you to get your sea stomach."

Logan drilled Parker once more with his eyes and strode off. Parker glared at the back of Logan's head and muttered, "That man needs to go down."

He glanced at Abraham, who must have had Superman's hearing, because he shook his head, and his eyes said that trying to take down Logan would be a poor decision. Parker wandered over to Abraham. His hair was graying slightly under his baseball hat, but he looked to be in good shape. A cigarette was tucked behind his right ear. As soon as Logan was out of sight, Abraham pushed himself off the railing and strolled forward.

"You ever smoke, kid?"

"I'm thirty-five, not a kid."

"Everyone younger than me is a kid. Nothing personal."

Parker stared at the dark green, four-feet swells off the side of the boat and a horizon of low-level mountains in the distance. "Where are we? What part of Alaska? The guy who dropped me off last night didn't think it was worth his breath to tell me."

Abraham handed Parker a pair of worn brown gloves.

"You're not going to answer my question, Abe?"

Parker studied Abraham. Laughing eyes even when he wasn't smiling. Eyes that said he was a decent man. Hard to ignore a guy like that, especially since he might be Parker's only hope for a friend on this boat. What had he gotten himself into?

"We are looking at the saline waters of the great state of Alaska about five miles off the coast of Ketchikan, catching the freshest salmon the world has to offer. Your turn."

"I smoked once or twice in high school." Parker pulled on the gloves. "Tried it a dozen times in college. That's about it."

"Why'd you do it?"

"Trying to be tough. Tick off my dad."

"Ah, good reasons."

"Good?"

Abe gave him a thin smile.

"What about you, Abe? Why do you smoke?"

"Did I say I smoke?" Abraham grinned.

Parker pointed at his ear. "Then what's that?"

"A cigarette." Abraham slipped it out from behind his ear and stroked it. "A reminder."

"Of?"

"Lung cancer. A friend of mine got it. Took him early. It reminds me to treasure the moments I have on this earth."

Logan appeared around the corner of the boat's cabin. He reached Parker in two strides and grabbed his neck with a hand large enough to easily palm a basketball.

"I wasn't kidding about tossing you overboard if you don't work. But since it's your first day, I'm going to cut you a break." He shoved Parker backward toward Abraham. "Do exactly what Abe tells you, and start doing it now, Rook."

"My name is Parker." Parker grabbed Logan's hand and yanked it down. "Not Rook. Not Puker. Parker. Got it?"

"You're on my boat, so I'll call you whatever I want to call you. You asked to be here, so you'll follow my rules. You eat, you sleep, you work hard every second you're on duty, you stay out of the wheelhouse, and you keep your mouth shut unless someone asks you a question. Are we clear?" Logan snarled at him as he stepped away.

"Yeah." Parker looked down and muttered, "They must have loved you in charm school."

Logan whirled back. "What did you say?"

He glared at Logan as his dad's voice echoed in his mind.

A strong man knows when to fight and when not to fight. A true man controls his emotions. His emotions do not control him.

Logan's face seethed with anger. "You want to give me lip? Give it to me right here with your fist." Logan stuck a thick finger into his chin. "But if you don't want to mix it up with me, then shut up and work. Eat. Sleep. Work. Stay out of the wheelhouse. Are. We. Clear?"

Parker glared at the man. "We're clear."

Logan started to go, then spun back and launched his fist into Parker's jaw with the power of a jackhammer. Parker crumpled to the deck. As darkness took him, he heard Logan mutter, "Now we're clear."

twenty-nine

WHEN ALLISON WALKED INTO HER office Monday morning, she found two construction workers putting up Sheetrock to cover over the six-inch opening between her office and Derrek's.

"Why are you doing that?"

One of the men said, "I dunno. We were hired to close up this space," and turned back to the work.

They finished half an hour later, and half an hour after that, Derrek poked his head into her office and said, "Can I chat with you for a moment in my office, Allison?"

"Sure."

She stepped inside Derrek's office and found him hunched over drawings for a set of three resort cabins along a lake in eastern Washington. He glanced up at her, then focused again on the drawings.

"How much work have you done on this account since you got here?" He tapped the drawings.

She motioned toward the wall between her office and Derrek's. "Why did those guys fill in the opening between our offices?"

"Oh, yes, that." He didn't look up. "I'm sure I've been making too much noise and wanted to make it quieter for you."

"You didn't. And I liked that we could—"

"How much have you been involved in this account?" He pointed at the drawings again.

"You don't want me to overhear you?"

"Truly, Allison, it was only done for you. I've been having quite a few meetings in my office lately, and I'm only looking out for you as I know you enjoy silence when you work." He looked up and smiled. "Perhaps I should have spoken with you first. We could have saved a few pennies, but now what's done is done, so can we focus on the subject at hand?"

She closed her eyes for a few seconds, then moved closer and looked at the drawings.

"I've done a fair amount of work with this client."

"That's what I thought." He glanced up again, then tapped the client's name at the top right corner of the drawings. "And how many times have we met with them together? Four? Five?"

"It's been five times."

"Excellent." Derrek sat back and gave her his full attention. "They like you. Your work on their account has been solid."

He grinned at her as if she should know where he was going with this.

"Thanks."

Derrek leaned forward, his arms and palms stretched out on the drawings. "How would you like to take over the account? Be the lead on it?"

"What?"

"Be their main point of contact. Craft the proposals for new projects. Oversee the work on the account."

"Uh, yes . . . I'd like that."

Allison tried not to look shocked. Kalimera Resorts wasn't a huge client, but they weren't small either. Derrek's suggestion that she carry the account was a huge vote of confidence in her abilities.

"And, as you might imagine, I can move a bit more salary in your direction for handling the account. Plus, it will free me up to work on some larger projects." He started to roll up the drawings, then stopped and waited for her answer.

"That'd . . . that would be great," Allison said.

"Good. Then it's settled. I'll have Linda set up a meeting with them, and we'll let them know." He finished rolling up the drawings and slipped a rubber band around them.

"Derrek?"

"Yes?"

"Thank you."

"You're quite welcome."

_____

That evening, after all light had faded from the sky, Allison fixed herself a second cup of Earl Grey tea and headed for her den. She picked up one of her writing pens and returned to her chair, opened the journal, and began to write. The action filled her with the feeling of being in the exact spot in the universe where she was supposed to be.

Monday, June 3rd

The day today outside my body was beautiful. Inside, not so much. I'm still trying to feel my way and discover where I fit in . . . and know who I am and what role I play at the company and in life, for that matter. Easier said than done. I'm frustrated that the partnership is still not finished. It's been more than a month already, but Derrek says there have been accounting mistakes, not from my side of things but others, and $100,000 was flushed down the toilet, so the timing isn't right. Will it ever be?

On the positive side of things, Derrek gave me a sizable account today, but I love it and hate it at the same time. Love it because it says he believes in me and trusts me to do a good job for them. Love it because it's going to mean extra income while I'm waiting for the partnership to be finished. Love it because it's going to be a fun project to work on.

And I hate it because of what it does inside me. It makes me hope—no, believe—that things are going to be okay. But there's still this part inside that thinks it's never going to work out. And I hate it because when Derrek believes in me, I believe in me, but why does it take something or someone from outside of me to make that happen? Why can't I believe in me all by myself?

Far too much of me wants desperately to know that Derrek likes me, respects me. It's easy to figure out why. I need a dad to show he loves me, since Dad didn't know how. I know my longing isn't going to be solved by finding a doting father figure, but that doesn't stop the longing from welling up inside me.

And then there's the issue of closing the opening between our offices. How am I supposed to see that but as a sign of distrust?

Show me truth, Lord—please show me all the truth I need to see.

Allison slept well that night with no dreams, and when she woke, the gray of dawn had just started to creep into the early-morning sky. She showered, dressed, and ate breakfast, all the time picturing the words she'd written in the journal the night before. Finally she went to her den to see if the words had changed this time. Within seconds of opening the journal and turning to last night's page, she saw the changes.

> Monday, June 3rd
> The day today outside and inside my body was beautiful. I'm discovering where I fit in and who I am and what role I play in life.
> Derrek gave me a sizable account today. I love it. It's going to be a fun project to work on.
> Things are going to be okay. I believe in me. It's going to work out.

Allison shut the journal, went to the kitchen, grabbed her cell phone, and called Richard.

"Yes?"

"Richard? It's Allison Moore."

"Good to hear your voice, Allison. You're up early."

"Sorry."

"Not at all. I've been up for an hour."

"I need to talk." She closed her eyes and gritted her teeth.

"I'm guessing you've had words change on you again."

"I have. Can you get together?"

"I can. How about a late lunch?"

"Perfect."

They met at Suprema's Deli, and after their meals arrived Allison told Richard about her journal entry and how it had changed.

"Tell me why you're frustrated," he said.

"How do you know I'm frustrated?"

Richard offered a kind smile. "It might be the scowl etched into your forehead."

"It's that obvious, huh?" She pulled up a photo she'd taken of the journal entry that morning and waved at it. "Yes, I am frustrated. The words change and they change the meaning on paper, but I need more than that."

"What do you need?"

"I need change in here." Allison pointed at her chest. "It has to be more than pretending I believe in myself. More than positive thinking. It has to be real."

"I agree." Richard took a big bite of his pastrami sandwich and, when he finished chewing, said, "All men, all women, live in two worlds. The one beyond them, of circumstance and insinuation and friendships, of words spoken to them in jest and joy and anger and sorrow, in encouragement and cruelty. And then there is the world within. The world of words we speak to ourselves. What we know about ourselves. Truly know. In there, if we allow ourselves, we face our glories and horrors. Our moments and days and years are about the connection between those two worlds. About the gate we construct to allow the outside world in and the inside world out. And most folks allow too much of the outside world to inform their inward world.

"They look to friendships, wealth, status, politics, religion, drugs, food, and many other things to fill them, but the thirst man has will never be quenched with those things."

"So what do I do?"

"The same thing I suggested last time we talked." Richard leaned forward. "Be willing to climb the mountain, even though you know it will be one of the highest you've ever scaled. And when God shows you the whole truth, be willing to step into it, no matter the cost."

thirty

PARKER FOLLOWED ABRAHAM AROUND THE boat, working the nets, hauling in the catch. Dawson and Fredricks only glanced at him with disinterested eyes, and Parker didn't see any point in engaging them in conversation. It was obvious Abraham was his best chance for an ally, so that's where he focused his energy.

During a quick lunch break, Abraham explained that they were aboard a type of boat called a purse seiner and gave a brief history of the type of fishing they were doing.

"Seine fishing has been going on for ages. There are seine nets in Egyptian tomb paintings dating from as far back as 3000 BC. Pre-European Maori deployed seine nets over one thousand meters long from their canoes.

"Native Indians on the Columbia River wove seine nets from spruce root fibers or wild grass. Here in Alaska we're just doing a modern version of what they did. The net hangs vertically in the water. The bottom edge is held down by weights, and you can see the top is held up with buoys. Fish swimming near the surface are surrounded by this net wall, then the net is drawn tight, or 'pursed,' so it is closed at the bottom as well. Then we pull 'em in."

Abraham pointed at a large drum-like object. "We're using a drum seine, which, as you can see, uses a horizontally mounted drum to haul and store the net. We pull the net over the roller, and the spooling gear makes sure it gets wound tightly on the drum."

Parker glanced around the boat, then focused on Abraham. "Not that much has changed."

Abraham shook his head. "Why are you here, Parker?"

"Excuse me?"

"You heard me."

"Are you always this direct?" Parker laughed.

"Most of the time, yeah." Abraham chewed slowly. "You here to escape?"

"I'm here to make money."

"Oh."

"A friend needs help."

"Ah." Abraham peered at Parker as if seeing right through him. "Why here? Why come to the middle of nowhere?"

Parker took a bite out of his sandwich and gazed over the water at the thickly forested coastline. Alaska was far more beautiful than he'd imagined.

"The job was available. Pays what I need. And I like the middle of nowhere."

"Fair enough."

Parker stood and tried to stretch his back. "How long are we working today?"

"When the fish are running, we work. Period."

"That's gotta be like five in the morning till nine at night."

"Pretty close, yeah. But not quite. Try four till midnight. Or three till midnight. Or two till midnight."

"Are you kidding?"

"Long days, you betcha." Abraham sighed. "Hard days, won't lie.

Logan is shooting for twenty sets today. That's pushing it, so we're going to be doing some back busting. We'll be hurtin' for certain."

"Sets?"

"Laying out and bringing in the net full of salmon equals one set."

By the time Parker reached his bunk at ten past midnight, his body was shot. He'd wanted to shed his final extra pounds. This job would do it, or give him a heart attack.

By the end of three days, he was spent, but Abraham kept pushing him. Not like Logan probably would have—the captain still acted like he was going to toss Parker overboard at any moment—but enough that Parker had little time to think about home.

————

On the fourth morning Abraham tossed Parker a protein bar as they started work. "You're doing fine so far."

"I don't think I've ever worked this hard three days in a row in my entire life. But it's okay. It's taking my mind off . . . my life."

"Good not to think about life for a while, and glad to hear it's okay, 'cause you get to do the same thing for the next thousand days. At least," Abraham grinned.

"I can't wait."

"More good news then. You don't have to wait. We got at least eighteen hours ahead of us today. But we might get three or four minutes for lunch and dinner."

"How do you survive out here?"

"Like I just said, it's only three months. Sometimes less." Abraham shrugged.

"But it's three months, averaging two to four or five hours of sleep a day. That's insane. I don't understand how anyone makes it without collapsing."

Abraham stopped moving and lasered his eyes on Parker. "You gotta choose, kid. What are you going to fix in your mind, huh? How this is making you stronger, or how it's tearing you apart? Take pride in busting your butt on this job, or whine about how your feet are killing you? Think about the fact you're not suffocating in an office building, or that you're living a crazy adventure? Fixate on lack of sleep and the constant stink of fish guts, or think about seeing firsthand some of the most stunning landscape ever created?"

Abraham gave him a light pop in the chest. "Who's the real Parker, huh? The weak one or the strong one? Who are you at your core?"

"I don't need this, Abe."

"It's exactly what you need. You have to accept that the muscle that gives out first isn't in your legs or arms or back or hands or feet." Abraham studied him for a few seconds, then tapped his head. "The one that always gives out first is right here. And it doesn't matter what anyone else tells you. All the people in the world can tell you you'll make it, but there's only one voice that matters."

thirty-one

THREE MINUTES AFTER ALLISON WALKED into the office after her lunch with Richard, Derrek appeared in her doorway, his face blank.

"Allison, do you have a moment to discuss an important matter?"

Have a moment? No, given the extra work he'd dumped on her the previous Friday, she'd have to clone herself to get it all done, and plus, Derrek's "moments" were never three or four minutes, but at least fifteen-plus.

"This really isn't the best—"

"Good, good, thanks for taking time. It's minor and won't take long, but I'd like to get clarity on it right away, get your input, so we can incorporate it into our company culture immediately."

"I really can't, Derrek. I need to . . ." She trailed off. If Derrek had heard her—and there was nothing wrong with his hearing—he would continue to ignore her protests. Better to simply get it over with.

Allison followed Derrek down the hall. He stopped outside his office and let her step through his door first. As she walked in, her jaw tightened. Three chairs. One for him, one for her, and in the third chair rested Linda's ever-present notepad—a relic from another generation that still thought pen and paper were the only tools for taking notes.

"How is your day going, Allison?" Derrek asked.

"Fine, thanks." She pointed at the chair Linda's notepad rested on. "We're waiting for Linda?"

"She should be here any—"

Before Derrek finished, Linda strolled into the room with a plastered-on smile and said, "Good afternoon, Allison. Good afternoon, Derrek."

"Good afternoon, Linda." Derrek motioned toward Allison. "Allison was just about to tell me about the first part of her day."

"Oh, lovely."

Allison glanced at her watch. "I'm sorry, but I have a set of drawings that are due in ten minutes and I need fifteen to review them. So can we cover this quickly?"

"I'm sure they're fine. You do excellent work, Allison." Derrek nodded. "But in light of your time constraint, we will get right to the subject at hand."

Derrek stood, shut the door, then took his seat, back straight, eyes distant.

"Linda and I have been talking about a number of recent mistakes that have cost the company money. We've decided to change our policies on how to handle these losses."

"What kind of mistakes?"

"As an example, when a budgeting error is made on a client's account."

Derrek stopped as if that was all the explanation needed.

"Such as?"

"If we get a defined budget from a client and it is allocated for a certain amount of billable hours for a project, and it turns out that a clerical error was made in the execution of that budget, the company suffers."

"I still don't understand."

"I can see how it's not easy to understand," Derrek said, but the mocking twinkle in his eyes suggested she was too stupid to comprehend what he was driving at.

"Let's say one of our clients gives us $15,000 to develop a set of plans for a vacation home. But due to an error during the planning stages on our spreadsheet, the client actually gave us only $12,500. We have lost $2,500 by overspending in error. Do you understand now?"

Allison held his gaze and didn't respond.

"Good, good, I knew you'd be able to grasp the idea."

Allison glanced at Linda. The woman smiled at her as if congratulating a fourteen-year-old on figuring out how to tie a shoelace.

"What does that have to do with me? I don't set the budget. I don't enter them into the spreadsheet."

"Yes, but you do handle the account."

"And?"

Derrek glanced at Linda, then out the window before focusing on Allison again.

"We feel it's only right to let you know that when you are issued your paycheck next week, it will be a bit lighter than usual."

"What?" Allison's face went hot. "You're taking money out of my paycheck?"

"Yes."

"You are not going to do that."

"In this particular case your check will be reduced by thirty-five percent, as the mistake was sizable. But the pay period after that will only be fifteen percent. We wanted to give you the benefit of having it spread out over two paychecks to ease any discomfort that could potentially arise."

Allison blinked as a squeak of disbelief escaped her lips. "You're going to do what?"

Linda cocked her head. "I think you heard Derrek. The money

lost due to the accounting mistake is going to come out of your next paycheck."

"You are not going to take money out of my paycheck." Allison gripped the armrests of her chair and glared at Derrek.

"Oh really?" Linda gave a mock frown. "And why is that?"

"I didn't make the mistake."

"That's a good point, and I acknowledge it." Derrek folded his arms behind his head. "You did not make the mistake. However, it is your account. Entrusted to you. So ultimately, you are responsible."

"No." Allison shook her head. "This is insane. I don't have a problem taking responsibility when I should, but I haven't been shown the full budgets of any of the clients I'm handling. I don't have anything to do with setting up budgets or billing clients or running numbers."

"I'm sure you faced this type of situation when you were running your own company." Derrek tapped his fingertips together. "When you and Kayla made an accounting mistake, it ultimately meant less money for you and her. Even if Kayla was the one who made the mistake, you still shared in the loss."

"This is different!"

"How so?" Linda leaned in, a thin smile glued to her face.

She glared at Derrek. "Because with Kayla, I was a partner. Here? Still waiting."

Derrek sighed. "Allison, this isn't the time or place to have that discussion."

"Fine. Then let's talk about now. At this moment I don't have the control I did when Kayla and I were together. I don't send out the budgets. Dianne does." She stared at Linda. "And you are the one who approves all the budgets before they're implemented."

Linda's eyes went dark, and she slowly tilted her head to the right as if deciding how to fillet Allison.

"Allison." Derrek undid his hands and leaned forward, elbows now on his desk. "This company is not in the habit of blaming others."

"I'm not blaming. I'm simply pointing out that I had no control over whether that mistake was made. So I don't see how—"

"This isn't a debate, Allison." Linda's eyes narrowed. "We are simply explaining to you how we will conduct this part of our business going forward so there are no surprises when you open your next paycheck. This is a courtesy conversation. And hopefully it will spur you to check the budgets from now on."

"This is flat-out wrong. You know it. I should not have to bear the responsi—"

"Do you think we should take it out of Dianne's check?" Linda snapped. "She makes far less than you. She can't afford the loss to the degree you can."

"How do you know what I can and can't afford, Linda?" Allison's voice rose, and she struggled to keep from shouting.

"We have been paying you generously," Linda said with sticky syrup in her voice. "But whether you can or can't afford it doesn't matter. What matters is doing what is right. And this is how we've chosen to have things rectified when errors are made."

"How are you paid, Linda? A percentage of profits?" Allison turned to Derrek, her cheeks hot. "Dianne and I are on a fixed salary. You, and I suspect Linda as well, take a significant percentage of the profits of this company every month."

Derrek chuckled. "I'm not sure if you understand—"

"Before I came here, you explained that the company has been extremely profitable, and since I came here, we've added five new clients. Five. In three months. I had a minor hand in two of them, and a major hand in three. How can you laugh at me and tell me I don't—"

"I'm not laughing at you, Allison." Derrek betrayed himself

instantly with a broad smile. "But there are factors you are not comprehending. There are a great many elements that go into a company's profitability. Ones I haven't taken the time to explain in detail, but trust me, there are months Linda and I barely take any money home at all."

"Barely take any money home at all" meant what? Derrek had told Allison before she'd come that he was making $490,000 a year. What was "barely"? Twenty-five thousand a month? Twenty? What was Linda scraping by on? Fifteen grand a month?

"It's not right." Allison glanced from Derrek to Linda, then back to Derrek. "I'm being penalized for mistakes I had no hand in making. And despite what you think, Linda, I can't afford to lose that money."

Derrek nodded, a look of deep understanding on his face, and for a moment Allison thought he would agree with her. "I know it can't be easy. And I feel bad things had to come to this, but it's the way it's going to be for the time being. Linda and I have talked about this extensively. Sought God's counsel. We know this is what he is directing us to do. Please know we did not enter into this decision lightly or without extensive time spent in prayer.

"Once we get our feet back under us, we can revisit the policy. Odds are we'll go back to the way it was, with the company absorbing mistakes such as this one. And I wasn't going to tell anyone this, but due to your consternation, I'll let you in on it early. We've already talked about a long-term solution. There is a strategy in place for everyone in the company to become part of a profit-sharing plan at the end of the year. Likely before. So there is an excellent chance you'll be able to make up the money and more."

Derrek smiled at her like he'd just told Allison that her mom's financial tsunami would be taken care of, that she and Parker would connect again like in the days before Joel died, and that a wonderful man would come into her life—all in the next thirty seconds.

"An 'excellent chance' doesn't take care of my finances right now." Allison tried to hold down her voice, but it rose in volume. "I have obligations that must be met now, not from money that might be coming at the end of the year. It doesn't work that way!"

Allison slumped back in her chair and shoved down the tears trying to force their way out.

"Linda?" Derrek asked. "Might I have a moment with Allison alone?"

Linda nodded. Allison wanted to slap the smugness off her face. Derrek waited a few moments after his office door had closed. He folded his hands and unfolded them. Fold. Unfold.

"As much as I would like to help you, and as much as I sympathize with your position, my primary responsibility is to this company. I must keep it healthy so all of us can stay healthy. There are eighteen people on the payroll. I want to keep them on the payroll. To do that, sometimes difficult measures must be taken. This is one of those times. It won't be the last. But trust me, good times are coming as well. And you're a big part of that. You've been doing excellent work. I believe in you, possibly more than you believe in yourself."

"Derrek, please, I can't—"

"Have you considered that this might be a very, very good circumstance for you, Allison?" Derrek stared at her, a somber look on his face.

"How could this possibly be a good thing?"

Derrek picked up a Bible off his desk and set it on his knee. "God's Word says that he works all things together for good. It also says we are to count it all joy when we go through trials and testing. If you are going to consider this a trial, then you might also consider looking at this temporary condition as joyful even, and trust that your heavenly Father knows what he is doing."

She stared at him. "You're serious, aren't you?"

"Yes."

"I'm not at liberty to say why, but reducing the salary we agreed on is not an option. I must have that money."

"Be patient, Allison. God is at work."

He turned to his laptop and began to type.

"Derrek, this is wrong. You know it."

He looked up. "Perhaps you don't trust me. That's fine. But make the choice to trust God. Provision is coming. Soon. I promise. We will find you other accounts. Now, if you'll excuse me, I have some work that must be finished."

Allison staggered back to her office, her mind reeling. How could she fight this? Once again Derrek had played the God card. If God had told him to do this, then how could she argue against it? It was brilliant in its simplicity. Despite how obvious the ploy was, if delivered with deep conviction, she could play no trump card against it.

And yet the blaze stirring inside shouted the truth. She could speak out against what Derrek had done, right now, God or no God, but once again she hesitated and soon convinced herself the time for that wasn't now. But at her core, she didn't believe the lies she told herself.

Allison stared at the drawings she needed to review without an ounce of strength to do so. But she had to. Deep breath. Move forward. After reviewing the drawings faster than she liked, she sent them off and slumped back in her chair. Allison glanced at her watch. One forty-three. Still a long slog till the end of the day. She had to get out of this office, get some fresh air, clear her head. Ask God if he really was in the business of stealing money out of her paycheck.

thirty-two

AFTER HER MOM WENT TO bed, Allison watched TV, trying to get her mind off the money, and even more, trying to get her mind off Derrek and Linda. But she couldn't ignore it forever. She needed to get her thoughts down, try to make sense of nonsense. She pulled the journal onto her lap, opened it, and began to write.

Tuesday, June 4th

What are you doing, Lord? What the hell is going on? Is this the mountain I have to climb? I'll keep climbing, believe me. I won't give up, but this is insane. I need answers. Now.

My checks are going to be even less now? Because of someone else's idiocy?

In these quiet moments in the stillness of late night, I wonder why I'm working so hard. The things I wanted—the freedom to enjoy my life, the ability to free Mom—will those things come? Doesn't look like it. I don't know how much longer I can be caged at work. Always looking over my shoulder. Getting antsy taking two extra minutes in the morning because I'm not getting there early. Feeling like I'm punching a clock when I've been working so many hours already. Warned not to let lunches with friends go too long. All the things I got away from when Kayla and I started our firm, and now I'm back in them. I'm stressed. Stressed because I'm tired of waiting. I don't want to be resentful of Derrek, but it's hard. Money for other people's mistakes comes out of my paycheck? Are you kidding? This job is a roller coaster where there are no seat belts and I could go flying out of the car at any moment. Derrek gives me an account and the next moment I'm losing all I've gained and more.

Life has been tougher these days than I thought possible. I struggle to see the light in all of this. All I see are shadows. I've never been under this kind of stress. Why are you taking me through this? Why? I don't understand. I want to embrace it, believe good will come out of it, but it is not easy. I'm burned out. How can I reconcile what Derrek promised Wright Architecture would be and what it has become? Putting off and putting off and putting off the partnership?

I don't want bitterness to take hold, but it is beckoning me. Is suffering all life is? Is it only pain and disappointment till you die? Enduring till the end? And even if I could escape Derrek, do I truly want to? As strange as it seems, there's still part of me that believes in him, believes in what we could accomplish together. Believes the partnership is finally going to be finalized and we will do amazing things. Am I crazy? Probably.

I have to find a way out, but there isn't one. Would Derrek sue me for breaking the noncompete? Yes. Without question. Apparently he did it to someone else a month before I got there with little cause. So I'm stuck there. What would happen to Mom and the debt then? Not good. But something has to change. My home equity loan money is running out. Unless July decides not to show up this year, we're going to be in serious trouble. I'm just praying Parker's job works out and that the payment when he's finished is big. Has to be.

I need to see some changes in the journal this time, Lord. Show me. I need some hope. Please. I'm believing, I'm pressing in, but where is the path? Show me!

———

In the morning Allison checked the journal, but there was no change, which was the perfect intro to a day where Linda was on her case from the first moment she stepped into the office. By the time Allison pulled into her garage early that evening, all she wanted was a hot bath, hot tea, and sleep. Lots of sleep.

She stepped through the door from the garage into her house and stopped. Faint voices, her mom's and two male voices she didn't recognize, came from the living room. Mom hadn't said anything about guests, and given the fear in her mom's voice, these were not friends. She closed the door softly behind her, pulled her cell phone out of her purse, punched in 9–1–1, and slid it into the front pocket of her slacks. Just in case she needed to dial it fast if things went south. Then she lifted her gun out of her purse and flipped off the safety.

She eased forward, listening. The voices grew louder, and her mom grew desperate. Time to move. Allison strode into the living room and stood strong, feet shoulder-width apart. Arms at her sides, gun in one hand.

She found herself staring at a man sitting in the center of her couch, legs crossed, arms spread out on the cushions, a soft smile on his face. He was late middle age, attractive—not like the models in older singles ads, but the kind of man who didn't care if he was handsome.

Another man sat in one of the two chairs on either side of the couch. Her mom sat in the other. Her eyes went wide when she saw her daughter, a combination of relief and fear.

"Allison!" her mom sputtered.

"Ah yes, Allison." The man on her left smiled and gestured to her mom. "Your mother has been telling us about you."

"Who are you and what are you doing in my house?"

"It's okay, Allison," the man said.

"No, it's not." Allison stepped forward. "Are these friends of yours, Mom?"

"No, they're—"

"Since you're not a friend of mine or of my mom's, you're going to get up and get out of my house. Right now."

"True. Not friends."

Allison raised her gun slightly. The man glanced at the gun and smiled.

"We'll leave shortly. Just need to take care of something first."

"You'll leave now." She raised her gun slowly and gripped her wrist with her other hand.

"Oh?"

"Yes."

She glanced at the man on the couch, then at the other man, who had a look of amusement on his face.

"Is this the moment you tell me you know how to use that gun since your dad trained you for hours and hours?"

"Do you know how many cops love our family?"

"My dear Allison, let's clear up an obvious misconception right away. We have no intention of hurting your mom or you. None at all. We didn't force our way into your home. Your mother let us in. We are not interested in violence. We are interested in getting our money."

Allison motioned to her mom. "Why don't you come join me here?"

Her mom rose slowly and shuffled over.

"Are you okay?"

Her mom nodded, eyes still full of fear. Little doubt the men had threatened her before Allison arrived. She turned her attention back to the man on the couch and glared at him.

"So you're the loan sharks."

"Yes."

"Then let me ask you again. What are you doing here? We've been paying. On time. Which means there's no reason for you to be here. So get out. Now."

"Have been? Yes. February, March, April. And we got that nice lump sum a short time ago from the sale of your mother's house. But we applied all of that to the principal as your mom requested. Which means we still needed a payment for May."

"We sent—"

"No. You didn't."

Allison turned to her mom. "Mom?"

"Honey, I'm sorry . . . I just—"

"No need for apologies," the man said as he waved a check in his hand. "We're fine now. Your mom has us all caught up. But of course you understand why we were concerned. Who knows, your mom might have held back some of the funds from the sale of the home and disappeared. It's happened, as you can imagine. Plus, we hadn't met your mom yet and thought it past time we did."

"Get out."

The man stood, buttoned his suit, and sauntered to the front of Allison's home. The other man lumbered after him. Before opening the front door, he turned and smiled at Allison.

"Thank you for your time, ladies." He paused. "One more quick little detail."

"What?" Allison growled.

"We wanted to make sure you understand your payments are going to increase starting next month. Fourteen thousand."

"What?" Allison strode toward him. "We're giving you $12,000 a month! That's not enough?"

"No. Even as poor at math as I am, I know that $12,000 times twelve equals $144,000. And your mom still owes us $400,000. That will take almost three years to pay off. Too long. And of course with— "

"Shut up. I read the entries. He only borrowed $550,000 from you. We've already paid $200,000. So you're right, you aren't good at math."

The man picked at his fingernail. "Interest."

"It's only been six months!"

"The contract said he would pay it back in six months. If he didn't, then a more aggressive interest rate would kick in. If you did indeed read the history of the transaction, you know this to be true."

"That's extortion."

"No. It's business. It's all in black and white. It's a loan. Nothing illegal about it. *You* might call it unethical, but your father agreed to it."

The man wiggled his thick fingers at his partner, who handed him a packet of papers. He opened them and turned to the back page and held it out for Allison. Her father's signature was on it.

"Let me see the papers."

The man handed her the packet. No. Not good. Right there in black and white. Stupid! Why hadn't she studied her mom's copy of the document more thoroughly? Because she'd been so caught up in getting her mom moved in and paying these thugs on time and getting a home equity loan and establishing herself at work—it was a poor excuse. She should have gotten a full understanding of what her dad had done. But would it have made a difference?

"You're trying to destroy my family."

"No, we are not. We are in the business of making money. Your father had a hobby that was about spending it. We worked with him for a number of mutually agreeable years. Now? We are simply collecting on his debt."

"I've given you all my savings. I took out a home equity loan, and every month we're turning over as much of our salaries as we can."

"Then I'm sorry. You're in a difficult situation. But that's not my problem. Please don't make it my problem by not meeting the terms of the agreement."

Allison jabbed her finger at the front door. "Get out of my house, now!"

———

She didn't sleep well that night—no surprise—and woke early. She would get into the office early and make final preparations for a lunch meeting she and Derrek had that day. The account could be huge, and now she had even more motivation to bring business into the company: commission. This could be the client that kept her and her mom afloat. They could replace the money being taken out for others' mistakes and handle the payment increase. Today would be a make-or-break lunch.

thirty-three

WHEN ALLISON CAME DOWNSTAIRS SHE found her mom's school bag packed and sitting by the front door.

"Mom?"

Allison found her in the kitchen finishing breakfast.

"Are you going somewhere today, Mom?"

"To work."

"Work? You're teaching today?"

"Yes. Lois is picking me up and I'm going to school. She'll be here any second."

"But—"

"I didn't have a heart attack, Al." Her mom stood, lifted a bag off the table, picked up her crutches, and made her way toward the front door. Allison followed her.

"It's only been—"

"It's been six weeks. I'm fine. I don't even really need the crutches anymore. I'm feeling great, so I'm going to finish out the last couple weeks of school. Every little bit is going to help us right now, so I'm going to help."

"You don't have to—"

"Yes, I do." Her mom's jaw was firm. "Absolutely I do."

Allison drew her mom in for a long hug. "We're going to get through this."

"And you're going to get that client today. I can feel it."

"I hope so."

"You'll let me know?"

"Right away."

Ten minutes later Allison was on her way to work, praying as hard as she had in years, for her pitch later that day to be a success.

———

The client lunch had been going well when a tingling sensation started in Allison's feet. No, not exactly a tingle. More like a vibration, almost electric, that gave her feet and legs the sensation of being squeezed, then released, squeezed, then released.

The feeling moved up to the top of her legs, over her hips, into her stomach, then around her chest like a cobra. Then the snake slinked away, replaced by a claustrophobic fog that settled into her marrow and screamed at her to move! She had to leave. Get up. Get out of the booth. Now!

"Allison, do you agree?"

Derrek turned to her, a studied look on his face that she knew was an act. The same concerned act he put on in front of all their clients.

"I'm sorry, what was the question?"

Derrek chuckled. "Allison has been a sensational part of my team for a while now, but every now and again her mind wanders off into design mode."

Part of the team? What happened to partner? The last time they'd been to lunch with a prospective client, he'd introduced her as his partner. Allison stared at the wall over Derrek's head. Was it getting darker?

It was. No, couldn't be. Unless someone had dimmed the lights. Then the walls of the restaurant moved toward her. She glanced at the ceiling. It sank toward her. Or was the floor moving up? No, all in her mind.

She had to get a grip! This was not the time or the place to lose it. The walls continued to draw closer. Allison grabbed her water glass and took a drink. This wasn't happening. Couldn't be. It was in her head. Allison stared at the potential clients. Calm, bored even. They weren't seeing anything. She stared down at the table. Hadn't moved. Had it?

No, of course not. This was all in her imagination, but it didn't matter. The pressure of the seat underneath her, the back of the booth shoving her forward, the wall to her right pressing in . . . Derrek's tall, thick body pressing in from the other side. And the air! Not enough of it. Thin, as if she stood on top of Everest, sucking in breaths with all her strength, but getting far from enough.

Derrek was asking her the question again, wasn't he? She saw his face, his mouth moving, but the sound was light-years away. She blinked rapidly. Sweat seeped from her body. Cold. In her head, not real. Imagined. *Not real. Not real! Plenty of air to breathe.* But the feeling *was* real. More real than the booth she sat in.

She had to get up, get outside. Find air! No, had to stay here. Make a good impression on the client. Answer whatever question Derrek had asked her. Close the account. Get them to sign the deal. Get more commission, more money trickling into her bank account. Had to close this. She had to take the lead. If Derrek asked the closing question, he would claim the account. Just the way he played the game. Had to be hers. The lunch was almost over. *Stay with it. Come on!* Another fifteen minutes. That's all it would take.

The rational side of her brain calmly told her with soothing tones that there was no reason to be feeling this way. It was okay, would be okay. She could make it.

Her hands tingled. The air grew still thinner. Derrek on her left, closing in, scooting right up next to her. Too close. Edge of the table pressed against her blouse. Her heart shifted into double time, then triple.

"Ex . . . excuse me . . . Derrek, can you move for a moment? Please?"

"Are you quite all right, Allison?" He stared at her but remained fixed in his seat.

"Yes, I'm fine . . . I just need to . . . I have to get up."

"We're in the middle of a meeting, and I think we can all respect that fact. Can this be postponed for a few minutes?"

She stared at him as short, rapid breaths puffed out of her and she tried to speak. "I . . ."

He didn't wait for an answer but reached into her leather folder and pulled out her copy of their proposal, then slid it to the center of the table. "As you can see, this is a deal-point memo that covers the major items we've just discussed. I'll give you a moment to look it over and then answer any questions you might have."

A wave of anxiety attacked Allison from inside. That's what it was. A panic attack. Had to be. She'd always pooh-poohed others who claimed to have them. *Buck up. Face the music and get on with life. Stress is part of living. Dealing with it is what strong people do. Fight it.* But she took back all the thoughts in an instant. She'd been wrong. This wasn't something she could fight. While her mind spoke with a detached calm, her body screamed for space, for air, as if she stood at thirty thousand feet.

"I have to go," she sputtered. "Please."

Derrek eyed her for a few seconds, then slid out of the booth and stood. Stared down at her with a bemused look on his face.

"Please excuse Allison, you know how ladies can get sometimes." Derrek opened his eyes wider and gave a mocking smile.

The men chuckled as Allison slid out and staggered to her feet. She tried to drill Derrek with her gaze, but the most she could do was glance at him, swallow hard, and try to draw more air into her lungs than the room would allow. She stumbled through the front door of the restaurant and into the parking lot, her breath coming in stops and starts.

Breathe!

She shuffled between two cars parked too close together. Turned sideways to get through. Didn't need to, did she? There was enough room. No, there wasn't.

In seconds she found an open spot in the parking lot and tilted her head back. Long. Slow. Breaths. She focused on the sky, a cloud, one that looked like Hawaii. Then took a slow walk from one end of the parking lot to the other. Then back. Repeat. After her third trip, the ocean of panic receded. Not much, but enough. A few more seconds and it was one of the Great Lakes. After three more minutes Lake Washington, then Green Lake, then a small pond. Calm surface. Yes. She would make it.

She turned and headed back toward the restaurant. This was not his deal—it was hers. She had prospected for it, wooed them. She would close it. If she didn't, Derrek would take it. Fifty feet from the door, she watched it open. Derrek and the two clients shook hands, laughed, and parted. They didn't acknowledge her as she half jogged toward them, realizing there was nothing she could do.

On the drive back to the office, Derrek asked her for the second time if she was okay.

"Yes, I'll be fine."

"Good to know." He glanced at her, his expression indicating he doubted her. "What occurred during lunch?"

"I'm not exactly sure. Nothing like that has ever happened to me before."

"Panic attacks are common, Allison."

"Why do you think it was a panic attack?"

Derrek continued as if he hadn't heard her. "There's no shame in having one. Really. My younger sister used to have them. And one of the guys in my band has them from time to time. They can be extremely frightening. My thought is you should take the rest of the day off. Tomorrow as well. Collect yourself and recalibrate. Relax however best you can."

"I can't. I have work to do."

Again, Derrek continued as if she hadn't spoken.

"Then, when you've had a rest and feel you're yourself again, and only then, we can talk about going forward with the account we just signed."

"They signed?"

Derrek gave a slow nod. "They were a bit concerned about your leaving, but I explained that you'd been dealing with some stress at home and you simply needed a breath of fresh air. I assured them they could have every confidence in your ability to handle their account."

The last lingering bits of the panic she'd felt faded. Derrek had stood up for her. She frowned and asked softly, "It's still my account? I'm still the lead?"

"Of course you are."

Allison slumped back in her seat and hope beckoned once again.

thirty-four

THREE DAYS LATER PARKER SIPPED on bitter, burnt coffee and stared at the ocean as their boat slipped through the late afternoon toward the next fishing zone. He needed the jolt to get through the night, as it was likely to be a long one. The sea was as calm as he'd yet seen it. The wind was only a flutter, and the sun warm. Logan stood at the bow of the boat, binoculars out, his head and shoulders swiveling back and forth. Dawson and Fredricks sat at the stern in T-shirts, on the railing, their legs hanging over the edge of the boat. Parker wandered over to the center of the boat.

"You gonna join us, Puker?"

"I'm good here." He shifted his weight.

"What? You have a problem with the ocean? Scared of it?" Dawson grinned. "I've noticed you avoid getting too close when you can."

"Not scared of it. Respectful."

"Heard it before a thousand times, Rook," Dawson said. "That's rookie-speak for 'I can't swim.'"

"Not true. I can swim." Parker didn't add *barely*. Yeah, he could get across a pool okay if he had to, and he didn't mind lakes . . . as long as the water was clear and he was standing on a dock. But him and the ocean? Not friends. Ever since that day ages back when he almost died.

He'd been on the beach with his family and his aunt and uncle and their three sons.

Parker poked at a small sand castle he'd built as he listened to Joel and his cousins talk about exploring the tide pools.

"You guys ready?" Joel asked their three cousins.

"Just a sec. Let me finish my sandwich," one of them said.

Parker scooted up next to his mom. "I want to go with them, Mom. Can I?"

"I dunno, Mom." Joel squinted down the beach in the direction of a mound of rocky crags sticking out into the ocean. "It's kind of treacherous, and I think Parker might be a little young to—"

"I won't go anywhere except the safe spots. Promise!"

Parker's dad rapped his beer can on the arm of his beach chair. "Let the kid go, both of you. It'll give us a few moments of quiet here. And Joel will take care of him."

Parker's cousins scowled. Especially Tommy. A mean kid. Always had been.

"Do we have—"

"Yes, you do," Tommy's dad said. "So shut up and go."

A few minutes later the five of them started down the beach. When the adults were out of earshot, Tommy stopped and jabbed his finger at Parker. "Speaking of shutting up, that's what you're going to do the whole time, you hear me?"

Joel stepped up beside Parker. "Lighten up, Tommy."

"Yeah? That's what you want me to do?"

"Yeah," Joel said. He got in Tommy's face even though their cousin outweighed Joel by thirty pounds. "That's what I want you to do."

"Fine, let's just go."

When they reached the tide pools they spread out, and for the first ten or fifteen minutes Parker had a blast finding starfish. But then Tommy motioned them over to something he'd found. "Come check this out, guys."

It was a pool about five feet deep with a sandy bottom. Only a few mussels and sea anemones clung to the rocks.

"A hot tub!"

Tommy and his two younger brothers jumped in. Parker was about to join them when Tommy held up his hand. "No, squirt, only for us."

"Come on!"

Parker glanced around, searching for Joel. His brother was at least 150 yards away, poking around a set of rocks to the south.

"No. Go find a clam to stick up your nose."

"I'm coming in," Parker said. "You can't stop me."

"Yeah, we can." Tommy glared at him.

Parker just grinned and leaped into the water. The water was warmer than Parker expected, and he could tell the cannonball he'd done was a good one. Had to be a big splash. His tailbone thumped into the sand at the bottom of the tide pool. He pushed off the sand for the surface, but his head slammed into something. A hand. Holding him under.

Parker reached up and grabbed the hand, but it was too strong. He kicked at Tommy—it had to be Tommy—but even on the surface it wouldn't have done any good. He opened his eyes and saw Tommy's big stomach and tried to punch it, but again the water stopped his blows from having any effect.

He flailed, his hands breaking the surface of the water, and his lungs screamed for air. He dug his fingernails into Tommy's arm, and Tommy shoved his head deeper into the water. Panic buried Parker, and with the last of his strength he yanked on Tommy's arm, but it did nothing. Laughter filtered down through the water as his hands slipped *from Tommy's arm. Parker sucked in water and darkness started to seep in.*

Then a muffled voice. "Hey! What are you doing!"

Joel.

An instant later Tommy's hand was gone and a different hand grabbed hard on his forearm and yanked him up. He broke the surface and hacked out a mouthful of water, then another as he was lifted out of the tide pool and laid on the craggy surface of the rocks surrounding the water.

"You're okay, you're okay."

Joel's voice.

Parker continued to hack up water and gasp for air. The fire in his lungs was like nothing he'd ever known, and for a time he was convinced he would die. Tommy was punished severely, and Parker recovered physically by the end of the day, but emotionally he was still crippled and always would be.

"Rook? Hey, Rook, you listening to me?"

Parker shook himself from the memory and blinked at Dawson. "What?"

"I said, if you're a swimmer, we'll have to take a dip sometime before the season ends."

"That'd be refreshing."

"Yeah, sure would be. It'll get up to at least fifty-four degrees this summer." Dawson laughed. "You'd last a good twenty minutes or so before your muscles would start to freeze up and you take a slow, one-way trip to the bottom." He laughed again.

Parker wandered back to Abraham, sat, and tried to choke down more of the ship's coffee. "This isn't coffee. It's tar."

"Seattle coffee snob, huh?"

Parker stared into his cup. "Nah, not me. But a friend of mine is. Grinds his coffee every morning, times how long the coffee stays in the water, the whole thing. I've had a few of his cups. Spoiled me, I suppose. I never knew coffee was a fruit till he told me. The way he makes his coffee you can taste it."

Abraham gave Parker a light elbow. "You're doing good. I don't think Logan will sling you overboard. At least not today."

"Wow. So nice to know that."

Abraham grinned. I'm going to check in with Dawson in the wheelhouse."

"I'm coming with you."

"You are?" Abraham stared at him like he'd just suggested breaking into Fort Knox.

"Yeah, is there a problem with that?"

"Your choice, Parker."

Yeah, it was his choice. He liked Abraham, wanted to hang out with him a little longer. Plus, it was a chance to push a few of Logan's buttons. See if his whole stay-out-of-the-wheelhouse thing was only for show.

thirty-five

FOR THE NEXT TWO WEEKS life almost worked, but on Thursday evening when she got home, it blew up. Allison found her mom at the computer in the den, a strained look on her face.

"You okay, Mom?"

"Yes. I mean . . ." She pointed at the computer screen. "I'm having a little problem here."

"With what?"

"An online business."

"What online business?"

"Um . . . mine."

Allison's hands went cold. "You don't have an online business."

"I do now." Her mom gave a weak smile. "But I can't find it today."

"No, Mom, you didn't." Allison stumbled toward her laptop.

"Didn't what?"

"Sign up for—" Allison stopped as she stared at the screen. "You didn't give these people any money, did you?"

Her mom pressed her lips together.

"Mom?"

"I wanted to help. They promised I could make up to $1,000 a week . . . and that would help us a lot, you know? So I gave them . . ."

She trailed off, and Allison asked the question she already knew the answer to. "You gave them your bank info."

Her mom stared at her hands, her voice a whisper. "I wanted to get started right away."

"Not the checking account. Please tell me it's not from there."

"No."

"Which account?"

"My savings account."

"That's our grocery money and living expenses, Mom. For the next six months."

"I know, but the business was only $750. So there's still plenty left."

"When? When did you give them the information?"

"Yesterday."

Allison grabbed the laptop, sat on the couch, and logged in to her mom's bank account. Then stared at the balance as if her gaze could change the amount that was left.

The silence in the room stretched from thirty seconds into a minute.

"Is it all gone?"

"Yes, Mom," Allison said, her voice dead, her eyes staring out the window at nothing. "All the money is gone."

The next afternoon Derrek poked his head into Allison's office and said, "Are you okay?"

She peered at him and blinked four or five times before turning her gaze out the window.

"Allison?"

"No. I'm not." Her body felt numb. "Not okay."

Derrek slid into her office. "What's going on?"

"My mom did something unwise last night and . . ." She stared at her phone. "And I just got off a call."

"With?"

How could she tell him she'd just lost the Kalimera Resorts account? He'd given it to her only three weeks ago. Derrek had placed his confidence in her, his belief that she could handle the account as well as he could. And now she had to tell him she'd blown it.

"Would you like to tell me who the call was with?" Derrek settled into a chair in the corner of Allison's office.

"No, I wouldn't." Allison bit her lip. "It was with Kalimera Resorts. They're going to go with another firm for their next three projects. I lost the account. I'm so sorry, Derrek."

Derrek cleared his throat and clasped his hands together.

"Did you and Kayla ever lose accounts?"

"Yes."

"What about before that, when you were with Mckenzie? Did you ever lose an account when you were with them?"

"Yes."

"Then what happened with Kalimera is perfectly normal. A common characteristic of doing business, which you have experienced in both your previous architectural incarnations. You didn't blow it. You did nothing wrong on the account—and I've been keeping abreast these past three weeks—and there is likely nothing you could have done differently to keep the account."

She looked at him, her mouth open a sliver. Not what she expected.

"It appears you need to provide yourself with an adequate amount of grace."

"Yes." She nodded. "I probably do."

"Let it go, Allison." Derrek stood. "Anything else?"

"No, just . . . thanks for . . . Thanks."

"You're quite welcome." Derrek patted her doorframe and smiled. "Anytime and always."

———

Friday, June 21st

    I should feel good, I really should. I lose the account, and when I tell Derrek he's not upset. But he had to be, didn't he? Whether he was or he wasn't, the point is he gave me understanding and grace, and I should be thrilled with that, but I'm not because he's yanking me all over the place. One moment he's taking my money, the next he's forgiving me for losing a major account. I screamed so loud on the way home I'm surprised I didn't break my windshield.

    I feel like I'm on a ship that's in calm seas one moment and listing forty-five degrees in a storm the next.

    And in the midst of all of it, one fact remains. I do not have a signed partnership agreement. The reality is, Derrek's grace is probably supposed to placate me. But it doesn't. Not for a second.

    And I sent in this month's payment. Which feels like I've just let go of a tree branch hanging over a cliff, because now all our money is gone.

She closed the journal. Didn't feel like writing anything more. Allison made to get up, but the ping of a text message stopped her. She glanced at her phone. Richard.

Hello, Allison. Thinking of you and the dry bones. Available for
conversation whenever you need to chat. Richard

Dry bones? Allison frowned at the text. What in the world was he
talking about? She texted back.

Did i miss something? What do you mean, 'dry bones'?

She waited two, then three minutes. No response.

Richard?

Her phone pinged a few seconds later.

Sorry, had to attend to another matter for a moment. You need
to speak to yours.

Again, Allison stared at the words, not comprehending their
meaning.

Is it possible for you to be a little more cryptic? Your meaning
is awfully obvious.

Richard texted back a laughing icon and, Let's meet tomorrow if
you can. I'll explain then.

———

The next morning Allison checked the journal and let out a soft sigh.
No change. Only the words she'd written the night before staring back

at her. Wonderful. Just when she really needed a bit of supernatural wisdom, the journal went silent. She didn't think it was a vending machine, where she could write and the journal would automatically write back, but still. Would have been nice. At least she had Richard.

They met at noon at Bellevue Downtown Park, just south of Bellevue Square. The sun shone like it was mid-July, but it still felt cold to Allison.

"Thanks for meeting me, Allison."

"Uh, I think that sentiment should go the other way."

"Okay." Richard gazed at the stepped canal that cascaded into the park's reflecting pond. "How are you?"

"Frustrated and stressed and tired of life. So . . . not so good."

"Tell me."

"I wrote in the journal last night and checked it this morning. No change."

"This isn't the first time it hasn't changed."

"No." Allison pressed two fingers into her forehead. "But I really needed it this time."

"Maybe."

"Maybe?"

"You could be right about needing it this time, but . . ."

"I could be wrong."

"Yes." Richard leaned back for a few moments and the sun lit up his face. "Maybe the journal knows what it's doing. Maybe as much as you'd like an answer, this isn't the time. Maybe the journal knows it's not good for you to rely too much on it."

"The journal knows?" She laughed. "You say that like it's alive."

Richard leaned forward, elbows on his knees. "Speaking of alive, what is it that lies *dead* within you, Allison?"

Allison frowned at him. "What?"

"Within you are things that once lived but do so no longer. Do you know what they are?"

"I'm not following you, Richard."

Richard looked to the sky as if trying to remember something, and then he closed his eyes and spoke.

"'The hand of the Lord was on me, and he brought me out by the Spirit of the Lord and set me in the middle of a valley; it was full of bones. He led me back and forth among them, and I saw a great many bones on the floor of the valley, bones that were very dry. He asked me, "Son of man, can these bones live?"

"'I said, "Sovereign Lord, you alone know."

"'Then he said to me, "Prophesy to these bones and say to them, 'Dry bones, hear the word of the Lord! This is what the Sovereign Lord says to these bones: I will make breath enter you, and you will come to life. I will attach tendons to you and make flesh come upon you and cover you with skin; I will put breath in you, and you will come to life. Then you will know that I am the Lord.'"

"'So I prophesied as I was commanded. And as I was prophesying, there was a noise, a rattling sound, and the bones came together, bone to bone. I looked, and tendons and flesh appeared on them and skin covered them, but there was no breath in them.

"'Then he said to me, "Prophesy to the breath; prophesy, son of man, and say to it, 'This is what the Sovereign Lord says: Come, breath, from the four winds and breathe into these slain, that they may live.'" So I prophesied as he commanded me, and breath entered them; they came to life and stood up on their feet—a vast army.'"

As he finished, Richard opened his eyes, full of compassion and fire, and turned to Allison.

"From the book of Ezekiel," she said.

"Yes." Richard's eyes grew more intense. "It's time for you to speak to your dry bones, Allison. Call them to life."

"How? That's just a story."

"Whether you believe it or not, you are standing before the dry bones. Your dry bones. You are in the valley. And that valley seems deep, full of darkness. But that is an illusion because the valley is full of light, if you would speak it into being. Now is your time. To speak life into them."

"What are my dry bones?"

"Ah yes." Richard held up a finger. "That is the question. What are they, Allison? Do you know?"

"It's obvious, isn't it? The partnership. Getting my mom out of debt. Having a better working relationship with Linda. And Derrek. Finding a relationship again. And the big one, letting go of the fact my dad never loved me like he loved my brother."

"Those are your dry bones."

"Yes."

"Okay." Richard nodded. "Then you know what to do."

"No, I don't." Allison clenched her fists. "I might know what they are, but I don't know how to speak them into existence. You think I can say *poof!* and all those problems will be solved?"

"According to your belief, it will be done."

"No, not that again, please."

"What do you believe, Allison?"

"No, Richard. No."

"You want God to do this for you. You want him to sweep in and make things right at work, to change Derrek and change Linda and give you what you think is yours. All humans would like it to be that way. You're not alone in that. But that is not your path. Your path is to speak into existence what does not exist. She's in there, the true Allison. I see her, but you must speak to her, draw her out. But even that is not enough. Just as the bones were upright and covered with flesh and skin but had no breath in them, you must breathe into your dry bones till they live again."

thirty-six

MOST OF THE FOLLOWING WEEK passed uneventfully. Allison worked on three different projects and tried to process her talk with Richard. Thankfully her interaction with the rest of the staff was minimal, till Derrek appeared in the doorway of her office just before three o'clock on Wednesday afternoon. He knocked twice on the frame with a soft touch and gave her a funny smile.

"Hi, Derrek."

"Hello, Allison." He stepped inside. "Do you have a moment?"

"Sure."

Derrek pushed the door closed. "Do you recall the other day when I told you God was in control and we would find you other accounts?"

"Yes."

"Thomas handed in his resignation letter yesterday. He's going to work full-time at his church as an associate pastor, which will be an excellent position for him. Consequently, we're going to disperse a portion of his accounts to you and Sam."

"What?"

Derrek smiled. "Thus, starting with your next paycheck you will have an increase in pay."

"Really?"

"Yes. The commission won't be as high as if you'd acquired the account yourself, but you will get a portion of the commission Thomas was receiving."

"I . . ."

"Would you like to know how much these additional accounts will raise your pay?"

Allison blinked and resisted the urge to pinch herself. "Sure."

"This is only an approximation—I haven't finished checking the numbers, so potentially the end result could be up or down half a percentage point—but you'll immediately start receiving an approximately fifteen percent increase in your overall pay."

Allison stared at him, not comprehending his words. This was it. It still wasn't enough, but it would be a big step toward making the increased payments to her dad's creditors. And even more, it was an infusion of hope that things would eventually work out at Wright Architecture.

"I don't know what to say, Derrek. I . . . I . . . Thank you."

"Thank you is more than enough."

He spun to go, opened the door, then turned back, a twinkle in his eye. "Also, I have an unrelated question for you. Do you have a few more minutes?"

"Sure."

"How long have you been working here?"

"Two months."

"Yes, that's what I thought." He closed the door again and leaned against it. "During that time, how often have you not shown up for work? Or taken time off?"

What now? He was going to accuse her of taking too much time off? What kind of story had Linda concocted about her being gone when he'd been on his trips?

"I've been here every day."

"Yes, that's what Linda told me." He rubbed the tip of his nose. "And I've monitored the shared computer drives. You've worked long hours every week. As well as from your home."

Allison only nodded.

"I've heard you say in the past that you enjoy the ocean, the Oregon coast in particular. If that sentiment hasn't changed, what would you think about heading down there for an extra-long weekend at the end of this week?"

What? Was he actually suggesting she take a break?

"We did some work a few years back on a hotel down in Cannon Beach, and they paid us partially in trade certificates. Certificates that expire at the end of this year. You're welcome to take enough for a four-night stay. And you can have Monday and Tuesday off without it counting against your vacation-day total."

Wait. He wasn't going to accuse her of not working hard enough? Derrek was suggesting she take a long weekend? Four emotions filled her at the same time. First emotion, warmth. He cared about her well-being? Wanted her to get rest and relaxation and play? Why?

Second, anger. If she was a partner in the company, she should be able to take as many days off as she wanted. Exactly like Derrek did. Exactly like she did for two and a half years with Kayla. She was supposed to feel good because he was encouraging her to take a few days off?

Third, relief, which swept the other two thoughts away like Seattle rain. That was exactly what she needed. A break. A chance to clear her head, take long walks on the beach. Go for even longer runs. Hike, mountain bike, explore the art galleries in Newport and Cannon Beach.

Fourth, suspicion. What was the angle behind his suggestion? Things were never free with Derrek. Yet, at the same time, he'd just given her a huge pay increase.

"It's simply an idea, Allison. You've been working hard. It would do your spirit good, I think, to get some time away. But of course you don't have to use the certificates."

"Oh, thanks . . . Um, I'll think about it."

Her spin-doctor alarm went off inside. Was he working her? There had to be something else behind the compliment, didn't there? There always was.

"If you do head down there, be sure to let me know."

"Sure."

"Oh, one more thing. Have you ever flown a stunt kite?"

"No, I've always wanted to but haven't had the chance yet."

"Well, the chance has arrived." Derrek chuckled. "I have a number of stunt kites that are a tremendous amount of fun to fly, and there's no place better to fly them than at the beach."

Allison stared at him as she sorted through another flurry of thoughts. Offering his kites? A free place to stay? Acknowledgment of her hard work? She stared at him, hoping the surprise in her mind hadn't made its way to her face.

"Thank you, Derrek. I'll give that serious thought. I would like to get back down there. It's been a long time."

"And I'm not telling you when to go. It doesn't have to be this weekend. The next couple of weeks are a good time for the company. Nothing major coming up that I need you for. And even though a couple of things haven't gone your way lately, I have no doubt they will, and I'm hoping you see the new accounts from Thomas as an indication of my confidence in you. And the start of many new accounts. However, to be in the best position to land new accounts, you need to be refreshed."

He straightened up and tapped the wall of her office. "Just let me know if you decide to head down there."

"Will do. Thanks again, Derrek."

She'd gone to the Oregon coast with her family as a kid, and she had spent an anniversary with her ex at a spot about halfway down one year, but that had been ages ago. She missed the waves, the briny air, the solitude. It was a place like few others where she connected with God. It was far past time to go back. Just before Derrek shut the door behind him, she called out, "I don't need to think about it, Derrek. I'd love to go."

"Excellent. I'll get the certificates ready as well as the kites."

Derrek smiled, a genuine smile that gave her hope, that spurred her to ask the question he'd been deflecting.

"Derrek, since we're on the subject of new accounts and company growth, can we talk about our partnership? I know you've been busy. So have I, but we need to get it done."

Derrek shifted to his left and nodded. "I'm glad you brought that up. Yes. Certainly we can talk. Here's a thought: why don't you take a few hours during your time down in Cannon Beach to determine exactly what you think the details of the partnership should look like now that we've had some time to work together, and I'll do the same. Then, as soon as you get back, we can nail things down and finalize it. It has been far too long, and we need to reach a conclusion."

Another smile and an authoritative nod.

She looked at him, stunned. He meant it. They would finally get their partnership finished. She could get her mom taken care of in months, not years. In less than five minutes her world had changed, and for the first time in ages, she let hope fully bloom inside.

thirty-seven

AS THEY CLIMBED UP TO the wheelhouse, Parker said, "Does he always treat new hires this way?"

"Nope." Abraham laughed. "Certain people tend to tick him off. That's because *he's* a little off." Abraham tapped his head. "Up here. And it makes him mean. And sometimes he loses it and takes it out on people he doesn't like. But if it helps, you're not alone."

Abraham raised his thick coat to reveal a Mr. Rogers T-shirt. He lifted that halfway up his torso to reveal a long, thin scar that ran down the left side of his body and across his stomach.

The man grinned. "At first he didn't like me. Threatened to kill me, but I got away with nothing more than this impressive scar."

"Are you crazy?" Parker stared at the scar till the tall man dropped his T-shirt and coat back over his stomach. "Why didn't you report him? Even if you didn't, why would you continue to work for Logan?"

"Good question." Abraham stepped inside the wheelhouse and Parker followed. Dawson was peering at a number of instruments, heard them, and looked up.

Parker nodded to Dawson, who only grunted, then turned back to Abraham. "Well, you have an answer?"

"There're much worse things than a small nick from a slightly deranged fishing boat captain."

"Small nick? Slightly?"

"There's a lot of good in him too. So since there is, if I were you, I'd be looking for that. Not trying to prove something."

"What?" Parker glared at Abraham. "I'm not trying to prove anything to anyone."

"Oh?" Abraham cocked his head. "Good to know."

"Where do you get that idea fro—"

Before Parker could finish, someone lashed their arms around his chest from behind and pinned Parker's arms to his sides. He was yanked off his feet like a doll. Parker flung his head back, hoping to crack his head against his assailant's chin or face, but the only thing he accomplished was to make a sharp pain shoot through his neck. His captor squeezed tighter, and Parker thought his lungs were about to collapse. It had to be Logan. Parker cracked his heels into Logan's shins, but the action was like kicking an iron post.

Logan carried Parker through the door of the wheelhouse and flung him to the deck. His knees slammed into the deck and he rolled three feet before stopping. He rose to his elbows and knees, but before he could stand, Logan shoved him over again, thrusting a well-placed boot against his shoulder. He came to rest with his upper back shoved up against the starboard side of the boat.

"Get up!" Logan's gritty voice seethed with disgust.

The instant Parker stood, Logan slammed him against the railing, where the small of his back took the brunt of the blow. "What do you think you're doing, Rook?" Logan slammed Parker against the railing again and swore as spit flew out of his mouth.

"Argh!" A bolt of pain shot through Parker's lower back and radiated down his legs.

"Yeah?" Logan pressed his face into Parker's. "That hurt? Is that what you're trying to spit out?"

Logan pressed Parker against the railing in the same spot where he'd taken the first impact. Spikes of pain shot through his lower back like a knife being jabbed into his spine.

"Or are you trying to ask permission to take a swim? Huh? Which one is it, Rook?"

Parker sucked in uneven breaths and tried to focus on Logan's wild eyes.

"What is your problem, Logan?"

"Am I stupid, or did I tell you to stay out of the wheelhouse?"

Rage surged through Parker, and he ignored the pain in his back and popped Logan's shoulders as hard as he could with the palms of his hands. The big man staggered back a few steps and his mouth turned up in a mocking grin.

"That all you got?" His grin widened. "Or is that your warm-up? Maybe it's an invitation. You want to take a swing at me? Is that it? Why not? You're not that small, and you've already lost the extra you were carrying around your gut. So let's rumble."

Logan stepped back and beckoned with both hands. "Just you and me. Right here. Right now. Come on. Let's go. You know you want to."

Logan grinned and swore as he moved toward Parker, fists up, feet shuffling. Parker had never studied any kind of martial arts, never joined his dad's training sessions with Joel or Allison, but he'd been in his share of schoolyard fights growing up, and he'd been training on the muk yan jong sparring post for months now. And the one thing he had learned from his dad was never to be scared of anyone. He'd also taught Parker the simple formula for winning fights like this one. Hit first, hit hard, don't stop. Parker stared at Logan, whose grin had grown even wider. The bigger man could probably take him out with one or two shots. Parker didn't care. This wasn't about winning. The only way to get a bully like Logan to back down was to fight till his fists were bloody.

Parker raised his fists and started toward Logan, who weaved back and forth in a tiny semicircle. But after two strides Parker stopped. Abraham slipped into his line of sight over Logan's shoulder, leaning against the stairs as if he were on a beach in the Bahamas. His gaze was locked onto Parker's eyes. He gave an almost imperceptible shake of his head. But it was the expression on his face that stopped Parker. An expression of knowledge and sadness. Parker dropped his hands, tilted his head back, glanced at Logan, then turned away.

"That it?" Logan opened his palms in disbelief. "We're not going to party?"

Parker didn't trust his tongue, so he said nothing and gave a quick shake of his head. Logan strode off without a word. In seconds, Abraham and Parker were alone on the deck.

"Why did you stop me?" Parker called out.

"Stop you?"

"Yeah."

"I didn't. You stopped yourself." Abraham strolled over as he pulled his ever-present cigarette from his ear and spun it around his fingers. "You surprised me. Didn't expect you to man up like that."

"If you hadn't been there, I would have gone after Logan with everything I have."

Abraham grinned and said, "Would've been a good battle," but his eyes said Parker would have been thrashed. "You think you have a right to be pissed off?"

"What do you mean? Are you kidding? You see how he's been treating me."

"Deal with it."

"Deal with it?"

"Yep." Abraham drilled him with his eyes. "Has Logan been starving you? Made you work longer or harder than anyone else on the boat?"

"No."

"Has he screamed and sworn at you any louder or longer than at the rest of us?"

"No."

"Wha'd he tell you to do when you first got here? Huh? Stay out of the wheelhouse."

"I get it."

Abraham turned around and jumped up so he now sat on a crate. He zeroed his eyes in on Parker, then jabbed a hard finger into his shoulder. "No. You don't."

He glared at Abe and shoved his finger away. "Logan doesn't pay you or me or any of us enough to be jerked around like he does."

"But we're not talking about Logan, are we? We're talking about you. And why you go after him when no one else on the ship does."

"Go after him?"

"Yes. You're trying to push his buttons. You went into the wheel-house to do exactly that."

Again, Parker didn't answer.

"There's a better way."

"Oh yeah?"

Abraham slipped off the crate and his shoes slapped onto the steel deck. "Let me ask you, if you were to fight him, would you win?"

"Maybe. Maybe not. Doesn't matter. I'm willing to take a pounding to find out."

"I respect your courage, because you'd get crushed, which I think you already know. So what's the thing you hope to get from a fight with Logan?"

Parker sat dumbfounded. Get? Wasn't it obvious? Respect. He'd beat the man into submission if possible. If not, he'd take out his frustration and anger on the guy by at least getting in a few good punches. Take vengeance for Logan treating him like crap.

"I want to knock some sense into the lunatic."

"And probably impress your dad."

Parker fixed his gaze on Abe and frowned. "How do you know about my father and me?"

"It's all over you. In your eyes. In the way you walk. You've got something to prove. I've seen it a hundred times."

Abraham moved to the side of the boat and leaned back against the rail. "Your problem is simple, so if you want to, you can solve it fast."

"All right, what's this better way?"

"Admit the truth."

"Which is?"

"You don't feel like you're worth much. So you try to prove your worth by being tough. Never backing down. Which is why you did so well right now with Logan. That wasn't easy for you."

Parker tried to laugh it off. "What are you, some kind of psychiatrist now?"

"And that hole inside is why you immerse yourself in extreme sports and ride your motorcycle on the edge of sanity." Abraham pulled a chunk of bread out of his pocket and tossed it in the direction of three seagulls that circled the boat. "For a moment those adventures tell you you're worth something. But then the rush fades and you're back to the reality that you think very little of yourself."

Parker sat stunned. No one had ever talked to him this straight.

This brutally. This true. He scowled. "Where do you get off psycho-analyzing me, Abe? Huh? You want to tell me? What gives you the right?"

Abe only smiled, a slightly amused look in his eyes.

"You think this is funny?"

"Yeah, I do." Abraham glanced at the deck, then back up into Parker's eyes. "And you will too, in time, once you realize how stupid it is to do what you're doing. But now you have a shot to turn it around, because someone has finally told you a truth that's been there, deep in your gut, for a long time. One you need to deal with if you want to be free of your dad."

"I don't need to listen to this."

"Depends on what you want."

"Oh really? What do I want?"

"I already told you."

Abraham turned back to the railing and gazed out over the ocean. End of the conversation? Parker could pretend it was. Walk away and bury the words Abe had spoken. Or press in. His choice. He stood watching the back of Abraham's head as it slowly moved back and forth, taking in the vastness of the sea. Maybe he was a real friend. Which would be rare in Parker's world. Lots of acquaintances, few friends.

Parker glanced around the deck. They were still alone. He shuffled over to within a few feet of the railing. "If I'm such a worthless piece of scum, why—"

"I never said that. Your dad never said that. God never said that. You're the only one promoting that lie."

"God," muttered Parker. "Like he's part of all this."

"You don't think he is?"

"Not exactly."

Abraham twisted the cigarette behind his ear. "Maybe you're wrong. Ever considered that? Ever wondered if he's right down in the minutiae of this age? Maybe it's time to stop seeing him as a distant creator who wound up the toys, then left his shop and closed the door behind him."

"I think he closed the door."

Abraham just smiled.

"So, Guru Abe, what am I supposed to do with Logan? And how do I fix the feeling that I'm crap on a stick?"

Abraham smiled and closed his eyes as his head rocked from side to side. "I have no doubt your uninvolved God will show you on both counts."

thirty-eight

TWO DAYS AFTER HER LIFE-GIVING conversation with Derrek, Allison drove down I-5 with Bruno Mars crooning in her ears and nothing on her mind except escaping for four nights and almost five days. Three of Derrek's stunt kites lay in her back seat, but that was the last thought about Wright Architecture she was going to allow into her head. No thoughts of work, of the partnership, of getting her dad's debt paid off—nothing but the sky and the wind and the waves.

The trade certificates Derrek had given her were for a hotel in Cannon Beach that she'd known about for years and had always meant to visit. She'd always headed farther south in the past.

Cannon Beach was close to the Washington border, which meant she could get there quicker and stay longer. And she'd finally get to check out famous Haystack Rock. A little online research she'd done before she left claimed Haystack Rock was the third tallest intertidal structure—one that can be reached by land—in the world. Two hundred thirty-five feet high.

As soon as she checked into her hotel, a mile or so south of Cannon Beach proper, she put on shorts, shades, and sandals and headed north up the beach. Kites and blankets and foraging seagulls dotted the sand. Brave souls jumped waves in the frigid waters of the

Pacific. She didn't hurry, stopped and admired every sand castle along the way, and said hello to all the beach walkers coming from the other direction. By the time she reached Haystack Rock, no world existed except for the one she stood in at that moment.

Allison stared at the top of the massive rock and thought it appeared even higher.

She gazed at tufted puffins with their squat black bodies, large orange bills, white faces, and tufts of yellow feathers above their eyes. An army of seagulls landed and lifted off the rock as if part of a massive choreographed dance.

She stood on the beach and watched till a rogue wave reached her toes, then till the tide crept in enough to cover her feet up to her ankles. Compared to the vastness of the ocean, she felt small. Insignificant. And that was a very good thing. A reminder that he was God, she was not, and that all along he'd had a plan to rescue her.

———

The next morning Allison rose before dawn and jogged out toward the ocean to where the sand was damp and hard, then headed north. Word from the locals was that at extremely low tide it was possible to get around the point that kept people from reaching Crescent Beach most of the time.

Perfect. It would be a chance to get in a short run—probably less than three miles—and at the same time explore an untouched beach alone. She couldn't imagine many others getting up so early. And this wasn't a morning she wanted company.

She reached the point minutes later and stared at the water lapping at the rocks. Shoot. The water was at least a couple inches deep on the outgoing waves, and probably six inches on the incoming waves. But still, she'd come this far. And what was a little water? She wasn't going to melt, as her mom had always said when she and her brothers were little.

Allison waited till the water was at its lowest point, then sprinted around the outcropping, knees high, arms raised, her shoes sending little geysers of salt water up onto her socks, legs, shorts . . . and the occasional splash onto her running jacket.

By the time she reached solid sand on the other side of the outcropping, she was half soaked. But getting drenched was worth it. She found herself utterly alone on a beach at least half a mile long. The sand was perfectly smooth, a bit darker shade than the sand she'd come from. At the far end of the beach a cape jutted into the sea about a quarter mile. Had to be Ecola State Park that she'd read about.

Allison jogged down the beach in the dead center between the water and the steep rise to her right. The cliff was lush with trees and bushes. Likely too steep for trails, but when she reached the end of the beach minutes later, she spotted weather-worn handrails at irregular intervals along the steep wall, leading up to what looked like a park on top of the cape. Must have been a trail up to the top at one point in time.

She wandered slowly down to the edge of the water and peered at a lighthouse set on a tiny island. She studied the waves that seemed to have no pattern yet formed a pattern nonetheless.

"I don't know what you're doing, God, but—"

That was as far as Allison got. She saw distant motion in her peripheral vision. She squinted and spotted two figures coming around the outcropping. They stopped for a moment, then sprinted toward her. So much for being alone.

"Thanks, Lord. Just what I needed right now. Great talking to you."

They came straight toward her, a man and a woman who didn't

slow or veer off course till they were twenty yards away. Then the man slowed, lurched almost to a stop, threw his head back, hands on hips, and shifted his weight back and forth as he caught his breath. The woman came to a halt beside him half a second later, hands on her legs, breathing heavily.

Allison stepped back a few paces, then started to turn away, when the man spoke.

"Sorry. We didn't mean to startle you, but whoever passes the tree first wins." He pointed to a huge driftwood log where the sand met the undergrowth coming down the hill.

He stepped over to the woman, kissed her lightly on the forehead, and laughed. "All tied up again."

She smiled and said, "As it should be."

They took each other's hands and strolled over to her.

"My name's Micah Taylor. This is my wife, Sarah."

"I'm Allison Moore."

"It's good to meet you, Allison."

"You too."

"You're a runner, it looks like," Sarah said.

"I try to be." She gave a quick shrug. "I ran a bit in high school."

"Really?" Micah looked at her with curiosity. "What'd you run?"

"The 800 meters, and the 1,600."

"No kidding. I ran the 800 in high school." He smiled at Sarah. "Nowadays the running is a bit limited."

Sarah laughed. "Severely limited. We have two young boys at home, so we don't get out together that often. But we work at getting time for just the two of us as often as we can."

"Are you with someone, Allison?" Micah asked.

"No. I'm not." She looked down at the sand. "I'm divorced."

Micah laughed, a full-bodied laugh stuffed full of joy. "Oh, no, forgive me. That's not what I meant. I didn't mean . . . I was wondering if you're on vacation here with anyone or on a trip by yourself."

"How do you know I don't live here?"

"We can always tell who the tourists are." Micah grinned at Sarah.

"He's not going to explain that, Allison, so let me." Sarah shoved Micah playfully and he laughed again. "When we first met, he was down here visiting from Seattle and I used that same line on him."

Allison peered at Micah. "You're from Seattle?"

"Yeah. Originally."

"That's where I'm from."

"Really."

"Well, Issaquah. I work in Bellevue."

"I was in Bellevue often. Then I came down here." Micah grinned again and motioned at the ocean and the beach. "You'd better be careful down here—you might end up wanting to stay."

"I already do," Allison said. "So you live around here then?"

"About four miles south of town. It's a good run from there to here and back."

Allison peered at them. Happy together. Obviously. Something about them was irresistible. Both were attractive, but it wasn't just physical.

"I'm surprised to see anyone else on this beach at this time of day," Allison said.

"You're right," Sarah said. "There's rarely any others here this early in the morning. Sometimes all day."

"But you're here."

"We come here every two or three months." Micah kissed Sarah on the cheek. "Either up to the top, at Ecola Park, or down here at low tide."

"Special reason?"

"It was the place we came to on our first date."

Sarah laughed. "It wasn't a date. He followed me, or tried to."

"Tried to?" Allison asked.

"Let's just say Sarah is better on a road bike than I am. But on a mountain bike . . ."

"He's still not as good as me." Sarah brought her hand to the side of her mouth in a mock whisper and said, "But sometimes I let him think he's better."

Allison laughed. There was something about the two of them that drew her like a magnet. A kind of energy, or warmth—it was hard to put into words.

"Did you work in Seattle, Micah?" Allison moved a pile of sand back and forth with her shoe.

Micah smiled at Sarah, sharing a private joke, but not at Allison's expense. "I suppose I did. In another life."

"Another life?" Allison glanced back and forth between them. "Like reincarnation another life, or a long-time-ago another life?"

"The third option."

"I didn't give you a third option."

"I know." He winked at Sarah. "It's quite a long story, with a few parts that are hard to believe. Maybe we can tell it to you someday."

"I'd like that."

"Good, because I have a feeling we're supposed to tell you everything."

"What?" She frowned at him.

"Sorry," Micah said as he looked out over the ocean. "I tend to go too deep with people too fast."

"That's okay."

Micah glanced at Sarah, then fixed his gaze on Allison. "Are you sure?"

"I'm sure."

"Do you believe in God, Allison?"

"Yes."

"So do we. And I think this is more than a chance meeting," Micah said as if that explained everything. "But for the moment we will let this rest in his hands, and we'll follow his lead when it's time to move."

"That's it?" Sarah asked. "That's not telling everything—it's telling nothing. That's all you're going to say to Allison?"

"Yes."

She turned to Allison and shook her head. "Don't feel bad. We've been married for eight years and I still can't stop him from doing that. Mr. Cryptic. But don't worry, he always eventually tells you what he's thinking."

"And if I never see you two again, which is highly likely?"

"I think that's highly *un*likely." Micah grinned again. "Like I said, not a chance meeting."

"Why do you say that?"

"We haven't seen anyone here this time of day for at least six months. And last night we had Chinese food, and my cookie said I'd meet a new friend today."

"Quite the coincidence," Allison said.

"Nah." Micah stared at her, a smile seeming to want to surface, but it didn't. "I don't believe in coincidence."

For the first time since he and Sarah had sprinted up to her, Micah's countenance went hard. Not unkind, but deadly serious. A moment later the laughter that seemed to be a centimeter below the surface lit up his eyes again.

He winked at Allison and pointed behind them. "I have good news about getting back."

"Oh?" Allison said.

"Notice anything?" Micah pointed at his and Sarah's shoes. "Dry."

"How—"

"My guess is you read the tide table wrong."

"What?"

"Yeah." Micah grinned. "We have about another ten minutes before the water gets far enough in to get us wet."

"I got my feet wet for nothing."

"That's one way to look at it."

"How would you look at it?"

"You've created a memory, one you might even laugh at years from now."

———

As they jogged back, Allison stole glances at the easy play between Sarah and Micah. They had the magic she longed for, the magic she thought she'd had with Kyle. But not enough apparently. He'd come home early that day five years ago, invited her out on their back deck, and said he had something to tell her.

"Are you okay?"

He looked sad and nervous, and he scratched at his forearms as if ants crawled on them.

"Yes, but I don't think . . . I don't think we're going to be." Kyle glanced at her, and in that instant she knew.

"You've decided to leave. Good. I should have kicked you out already." *She turned and started to walk back inside.*

"What?"

She stopped and said, "I'll give you half an hour to get out."

"What? I didn't say I was leaving or that I even wanted to."

She just stared at him. "Get. Out!"

"How do you know—"

"You want to know? Really?" She walked up to him and popped him in the shoulders. "Fine. I pretended. Did a pretty good job of it. Convinced myself—almost—you weren't doing that to us, but I guess I have to stop pretending, don't I?"

"I haven't even told you—"

Allison walked to their sliding glass door and leaned against it. "Do most men really think their wives and girlfriends are that stupid? That we can't see when your eyes are roaming over another woman? That we think your flirting is as innocent as you say? You think I missed that? The way you lingered around Tanya, laughed at her jokes? The way she batted her eyes at you like a teenager?"

"Al—"

"I know exactly what I'm supposed to do." She stared at the fledgling apple tree they'd planted two years back. "I'm supposed to fight for you. But I can't, because I have been fighting for you, fighting for us for seven years. I gave you my best. Everything that I was. Obviously it wasn't enough. So go, be with her."

"No, that's not what I'm saying." Kyle threw his hands out to his sides. "I'm still with you. I don't want us to be over, but I can't deny that I'm also in love—"

"Save it!" Allison raised her palm.

Sarah's voice cut in. "Allison?"

She blinked and looked over at Sarah jogging beside her.

"Sorry. Deep in thought."

Sarah laughed, eyes full of light. If they lived closer, they might be friends. Maybe in eternity. Sarah motioned south with her thumb.

"Do you want to take one last look at Crescent Beach before we sneak around the tip?"

"Right. Yes." Allison scanned the beach, the cliffs, the lighthouse out on the little island, and took a deep breath of the briny air. This meeting was one to remember. She didn't know why exactly, but it was. Apparently Sarah knew it as well.

"Thank you." Allison reached out and touched Sarah's arm, and Sarah took Allison's hand and gave it a quick squeeze.

"For what?"

"Having me lock this moment into my mind."

"Very welcome."

After getting around the point without their shoes touching the sea, they jogged the rest of the way back in silence. When they reached Haystack Rock, the three of them slowed.

"Allison, sorry to be forward, but can Sarah and I take you out for breakfast tomorrow morning?" He waggled his thumb toward town. "The Fireside Inn makes a mean ham and cheese omelet, and wars have been waged over the secret recipe for their french toast."

Sarah slid in front of Micah. "You don't have to pretend to laugh. Deep down he knows he's not funny."

At that, Allison did laugh.

"Is that a yes?" Micah asked.

"It is."

———

Saturday, June 29th

I met a couple on the beach today, Micah and Sarah Taylor. If I believed in reincarnation, I would say I knew them in a previous

life. I felt a connection. We're having breakfast tomorrow, and I
have a feeling that something is going on behind the scenes that I
can't see. Does that make any sense? Not really.

Probably as much sense as Richard's idea about the dry
bones, which I still have no idea how to speak to.

"Get the partnership done, Derrek!"

"A new man will come into my world and we'll fall in love!"

"Get out of my mom's life, debt!"

"Make working with Linda easy!"

The end. Amen. And time for bed.

Allison laughed at herself, but it was a bitter laugh. Richard wanted her to speak into existence those things that were not? There. She'd done it. Now what? Sit and wait till these things magically happened?

She peered out at the last flutters of moonlight on the ocean, and the view took her back to childhood vacations on the beach, in the woods, in the mountains. She turned back to the journal.

Days as a kid seem so long ago. The forts Parker and I used to
build! I'd love to have pictures of those. And the battles, oh my,
the wars we would wage. We were warriors. Covered our faces
in mud, took my bows and arrows, and practiced with them for
hours. And Parker, he had the champion of swords to beat all
champions.

Allison laughed as the memories flooded in, this time a laugh of light.

"Look out!" Parker shouted as they tore through the woods, their kingdom, a mile from their home.

Allison spun and shot three arrows into the eyes of the twenty-feet-tall giant that rumbled toward them. Parker leaped aside as the giant reached them, then gave a mighty slice at the giant's leg. Another three arrows launched. Another great carve from Parker's sword into the giant's other leg. Seconds later the giant crashed to the ground.

"We did it!" Parker shouted.

"Yes, but look behind you!" Allison cried.

More than thirty trolls with axes and hammers thundered toward them.

Allison and Parker looked at each other for a moment, then shouted, "For the kingdom!" and launched themselves at the trolls. Half an hour later, covered in mud and exhausted, with scrapes and torn T-shirts and shorts, they grinned at each other and laughed.

"Another mighty battle won!" Parker cried. "By who?" He grinned as they started their victory chant.

"By who, you ask?" Allison said as she strutted among the trees. "The greatest!"

"The greatest who?"

"The greatest warriors!"

"The greatest warriors what?"

"The greatest warriors the kingdom has ever known!"

They saluted each other, Allison with her bow, Parker with his sword, then cried in unison, "May it ever be so!"

They worked their way through the woods into their backyard, where their mom puttered in the vegetable garden and their dad read his paper.

Their mom looked up when she saw them and sighed. "Not again."

"What?" Parker said.

Their mom rose slowly to her feet and walked over to them. "I've told you, Allison, you have to stop that. You're not nine anymore. You're twelve years old. You have to start acting like a lady."

"I'm not a lady. I'm a warrior. So is Parker. We're the mightiest warriors the kingdom has ever known."

"No." Their dad's voice floated through his paper, still held in front of his face. "You're not. You're a princess. Princesses don't fight. They princess."

"No, Daddy, I—"

"Dad, not Daddy." He brought down the paper. "And you tear your clothes, you get scraped up, and you're bleeding. That's not a princess. Your mom's right. Grow up."

He pulled the paper back in front of his face. Allison and Parker turned to their mom.

"You heard your father. When you were kids, the games you two played were fine. But you're not kids anymore. You're a young man, Parker, and you're a young woman, Allison. Time to put away the make-believe games."

Over time the reaches of their kingdom had expanded to beaches and campgrounds and mountains. But the scene with their mom and dad repeated itself in various forms over the next few years after that day, and she and Parker left their kingdom behind. Parker grew up. And then, so did she.

Allison sighed and shut the journal. Enough living in the past for one day. Time to look to the future. That was what existed now. But in that moment the make-believe past felt far more real.

thirty-nine

THE FRENCH TOAST WAS AS good as Micah had said, and over the course of the next hour, Allison was captured by him and Sarah. By the time the check came, Allison and the Taylors had talked about their spiritual lives, their histories, and their favorite movies. Before she could stop herself, Allison told them about the journal, including Alister and Richard and Carl. She even told them about the words changing.

When she finished, they glanced at each other a few times before fixing their gaze back on Allison. A light seemed to flicker in their eyes, but they said nothing.

"This is the moment where you tell me it was nice to meet me, but I'm crazy and we're never going to see each other again," Allison said softly.

A serious glint returned to Micah's eyes and he said, "No. The opposite. This is the part where I repeat the fact that I don't believe in coincidence. Sarah and I were not planning on running to Crescent Beach yesterday morning, but yesterday evening Sarah said, 'I don't know why, so don't ask me, but we have to run up to Crescent Beach in the morning,' so we invited a friend to spend the night with us and be with the boys yesterday, and now here we are twenty-four hours

259

later with you. Something's going on that's way bigger than the three of us."

Allison stared at Micah, then Sarah, then back to Micah.

"You're serious."

"Deadly." Micah pulled a credit card out of a zippered pocket on the inside of his running jacket and placed it on the bill. Their waiter snagged it a second later.

Micah steepled his fingers and said, "Now comes the part where you think I'm crazy."

Allison locked eyes with his but didn't respond.

"I think I might know what you do for a living, Allison."

"Is that right?"

"Yes." Micah grinned at Sarah, then looked back at Allison. "I think you're an architect."

Allison sat back in her chair. The intensity hadn't left Micah's eyes, even when he'd smiled a moment earlier. She looked at Sarah. Her expression communicated kindness. Understanding of how strange this must be. But she shared her husband's intensity.

"How would you know that?"

"Would you believe me if I told you I got a picture in my mind just before Sarah and I started running toward you yesterday morning of a blonde woman huddled over a set of drawings?"

"I might, yes."

"Thank you for believing me."

The waiter brought back their receipt. Micah signed it and slipped his credit card back into his jacket, then looked at his watch. "I'm sorry to cut this short, but we should get going. But what's the name of your firm, if we wanted to get in touch?"

"Wright Architecture. In Bellevue."

"Are you a partner in the firm?"

Allison stared at him for five seconds before answering. "I don't know."

Micah peered at her. "I don't want to pry— Actually I do." He smiled, and in that moment Allison had a feeling she'd see them again, sooner rather than later.

Sarah bopped him playfully on the head. "No, you don't want to pry. You want to respect Allison's privacy."

"I do?"

"Yes." Sarah punched Micah in the arm. "You do."

Micah laughed and said, "Allison, this morning was an absolute delight. As are you. I hope we meet again someday."

When Allison got back to her room, she picked up the journal and glanced through her entry from the night before. Again, no change. But this time it was okay. Life was coming around.

forty

BY THE TIME ALLISON GOT home Tuesday night, her mom was asleep, but the next morning during breakfast, her mom waggled an envelope in front of her and said, "This is good news."

"What is it?"

"A check from Parker. Four thousand dollars."

"I see." Allison tried to smile as reality hit her. Yes, Cannon Beach was wonderful. And she had more hope than when she'd left. But even with her increased pay from work, they would still be short, and she couldn't pay the loan sharks with hope.

"What's the matter?" Her mom frowned.

"Four thousand from Parker? Splendid, Mom. That means there's only ten thousand to go. Due in nineteen days. No problem."

"Don't get sarcastic, Allison." Her mom patted her hand. "I'm going to get paid for the weeks I worked last month, and you're going to get your check in a couple weeks, and—"

"And we'll still be short. And we'll still have to pay for my mortgage and utilities and food and other bills."

"I thought you just said things had changed in your mind when you were down at the beach. And I thought you got a bump in pay at work. And I thought you said you and Derrek were going to talk when you got back from the beach."

Allison stared at her mom. Yes. She needed that reminder. "You're right, Mom. You are. I'm going to get the partnership finalized and we are going to get free."

When Allison walked into the office an hour later, she wore a big smile and greeted Ellie, who sat at the front desk and munched on a granola bar. Things were going to be different. New day. New start. New life.

"Good morning, Ellie."

"Hi, Allison."

There was an odd look in Ellie's eyes. Pensive. Which wasn't like her. Allison started for her office, but Ellie's voice stopped her.

"Allison? Wait." Ellie set down the granola bar and raised her hand.

Allison turned and looked at Ellie. "Yes?"

"Your office isn't down there anymore."

Allison walked over and set her briefcase on the reception desk.

"What do you mean my office isn't down there anymore?"

Ellie turned red and suddenly had a serious interest in the papers on her desk. "Derrek and Linda, they moved you on Monday afternoon after work apparently."

"Moved me?"

Ellie glanced up, then right back down to her papers. "You're in a new office now."

"They moved all my stuff to a new office while I was on vacation? Without asking? Are you kidding?"

Ellie shrugged. "I wondered about that."

"Wondered what?"

"Well, Linda said she would text you and let you know ahead of time they were going to do it, but I'm guessing that based on your reaction, the text didn't go through. Or maybe you haven't checked your texts for a while."

"I check them all the time."

Another shrug from Ellie. "Maybe Linda didn't want to spoil your vacation."

"So you didn't know about it?"

"No." Ellie shuffled papers. "I didn't hear anything about it. Yesterday morning I went to set your mail on your desk and your desk wasn't there, so I asked Linda and she showed me where your new office is."

"Did they explain why they were doing it?"

"Apparently since we're growing we need to hire more people and we need more spaces, so they're going to put two people in your old office. At least that's what I've heard."

Calm down, Allison. She needed to relax. Yes, it was incredibly disrespectful to move her office without any kind of warning, and to do it while she was gone? Unbelievable. Still, she wasn't going to let this surprise ruin her new mind-set. Besides, there was probably a reasonable explanation. She'd left Friday at noon. Maybe they'd hired someone on Friday afternoon and had to make space immediately. But why move her?

"Where did they move me to?"

The look on Ellie's face wasn't encouraging. She pointed to the office to Allison's left, three doors down. The smallest one. The only office in the company without windows.

Her stomach lurched and a soft cry sputtered out of her mouth. "What?"

Allison turned to Ellie, whose sad smile said she didn't agree with what happened, but what could be done about it?

As she shuffled over the threshold into her new office, she found Dianne at a small desk inside, clacking away at her keyboard. Allison's shoulders slumped as she stared at the back of Dianne's head. This wasn't happening.

Dianne slowly spun around and said, "Hi, Allison." Her mouth turned down. "Welcome back."

"I don't understand."

"Makes two of us."

"There's barely room to turn around in here. It's not a two-person office."

"Nope. Not even close."

"Did they give you a reason why they did this?"

"No, but do they have to?" Dianne's eyes watered. "This is the perfect spot to put people that Linda doesn't like."

"When did they do it?"

"When I walked in yesterday morning, Linda was waiting for me. Gave me her phony smile and said in a phony cheerful voice that the company was bringing on new team members, so I was going to share an office with you for a while. Since we work on the same accounts, Linda said it would be a great move for everybody."

"I don't believe this." Allison set her briefcase and purse down on a desk that was half the size of her old one. Her drafting table was considerably smaller as well. What were they thinking? She couldn't work like this.

"Is Derrek in yet?"

"Not when I came in, but I've been here for a while."

Allison picked up her phone and buzzed Ellie. "Is Derrek in yet?"

"No, not yet, Allison. Would you like me to let you know when he does come in?"

"Yes. Immediately. Thank you."

Allison accomplished nothing for the next twenty minutes except to delete a few junk mails and try to put a lid on her simmering frustration.

Her phone buzzed. "Yes?"

"He just got here," Ellie said.

"Thanks."

Allison smoothed her suit, marched out of her new office, and covered the distance to Derrek's office at a pace that would make speed walkers smile. He sat in his high-backed leather chair, laptop open, eyes narrowed. She knocked on his door three times hard, didn't wait for an invitation to come in, and marched up to his desk. Derrek looked up and sat back.

"Good morning, Allison, welcome back. How was your time at the beach?"

"You moved my office."

"Yes." Derrek stood. "We did."

"Without telling me. Without talking to me about it. That's not acceptable."

"I trust we didn't break anything in the move. I told them to take a photo of how things were laid out on your desk so all your things were in the exact same place you had them, so when you returned you'd have no downtime. We did have to give you another desk, only a sliver smaller, but that's due to having you and Dianne together."

"A sliver?"

Derrek chuckled. "Maybe two slivers."

"Tell me what's going on."

"No one explained this to you?"

"Would I be asking if they did?"

"Linda was going to text you to give you a heads-up. But she mentioned that her cell service has been intermittently cutting in and out. My guess is she did indeed send it, but unfortunately it didn't reach you due to an error on the technical side of things."

Allison stared at him. Did he really believe the propaganda that flowed out of his mouth?

"Has anyone filled you in since you got here?" Derrek waited for an answer and didn't get one, so he continued. "We hired some new folks on Friday, and we needed spots to put them. Consequently, we had to do a bit of consolidation."

"Fine. But why not move someone into my existing office? Why stick me—"

"This isn't a punishment, Allison."

"Then what is it?"

"It's a compliment." Derrek chuckled. "To you."

"What?"

"Yes."

"You're trying to tell me that putting me in the smallest office we have, with another person, and doing it without talking to me, while I'm on vacation, is a compliment?"

"Yes." The chuckle Allison had grown to hate bubbled out of Derrek's mouth again.

"I'd really like to get an explanation of how that's possible."

Derrek leaned back on the credenza his bookshelves sat on, folded his arms, and gave her the smile that used to inspire her.

"Most of the people around here don't have the strength of character you have. You're strong. You have vision. You can see the big picture. You won't take your office being moved personally, which others might do."

"I'm your partner. Why would you do this to your partner? I can't work in that small a space. My design table is too small."

Derrek rubbed his forehead just above one eyebrow and chuckled. "It's not readily apparent how this slipped my mind."

Allison stared at him, arms tight across her chest.

"I haven't chatted with you at all about the office expansion, have I?"

Again, Allison remained silent.

Derrek marched out of his office and beckoned Allison to follow. "Come with me, Allison. You need to see something."

He strode through the lobby, through the front door of the office, and down the hallway, his long legs chewing up the carpet far faster than Allison could. He didn't bother to look back to see if she was following. Derrek ducked through the first door he came to on the left.

It was closed by the time she reached it. She pushed it open to find Derrek standing forty feet away, gazing out of floor-to-ceiling windows. The space was gutted, only flecks of carpet on the floor, the walls torn out in places, paint cans along the wall to her right, electrical supplies along the wall to her left.

"See this, Allison?" Derrek grinned. "This is ours. And we're going to spend the money to make it spectacular."

"When—"

"Come here, come here. This is what I wanted to show you." He waved her over to a set of offices to the right. "See this one? It's going to be yours. Bigger than your old office, and a view to wake up nights thinking about."

Allison stared at the space. It was bigger than her old office by at least fifty percent. And the view of the Olympic Mountains was stunning.

"I had no idea . . ."

"No, I realize that now." Derrek grinned. "What do you think?"

"It's really nice."

"Good, good. I knew you'd like it. Glad you could take the time to see it. Don't worry, Allison, we'll get you in here soon. Construction should be finished in a couple of months. Three or four, tops."

"This is great, Derrek. Really is. And as long as we're talking about the future, I want to recall our conversation before I went to the beach. How we were both going to think about our partnership and get that finalized. I'm ready, so I'd like to set up a time to make that happen."

"Yes," Derrek said. "I would too. However, these next couple of weeks are going to be quite busy, so let's plan on touching base in ten days. Don't worry, we will get that handled."

With that, Derrek strode from the room, leaving Allison to consider the fact that with a small portion of the money Derrek was spending on the renovation, he could have started paying her what he'd promised her two months ago.

On the way home Allison stopped by the grocery store to pick up a few items and found herself staring at the woman two people ahead of her in the checkout line. From the back and slight profile view, it was hard to tell for sure, but it looked like Derrek's wife. Allison had only met her once briefly at the office.

As the woman picked up her bags, she turned and noticed Allison peering at her.

"Hey, Allison! Hi, I don't know if you recognize me, but I'm Sunnie Wright, Derrek's wife."

"Yes, it's great to see you."

"You too." She motioned toward Allison's items. "I'll wait for you and we can walk to our cars together."

A few moments later, when they stepped outside, Sunnie said, "So you've been working for Derrek for two or three months now, right? How are things going?"

Sunnie's name was ideal. Derrek's wife shone with kindness, and her green eyes were inviting.

"Ups and downs, you know, but overall it's been good. Just wanting to get the partnership finalized, but Derrek and I talked about that today, and we're going to take care of it soon."

Sunnie frowned. "What partnership?"

"Derrek's and mine."

"My Derrek?" Sunnie laughed and patted Allison's arm gently. "That will be the day when he lets someone partner with him again."

Allison's body grew hot as she stared at Sunnie. "What do you mean? He told me he talked to you about it. Made sure you were okay with a woman becoming his partner. I even asked if I could sit down with you and discuss it, and he said you were fine with it."

"Not that I can recall. But we don't talk that much about the business." Sunnie's face grew serious. "Are you sure?"

"There's no doubt in my mind."

An understanding look came over Sunnie's countenance. "Allison, I don't know what to say."

Allison stood stunned, her body shifting from hot to numb.

"I'm so sorry, Allison." Sunnie patted her arm once more, then turned and walked away.

Wednesday, July 3rd

Freedom Day tomorrow. Maybe for our country. Not for me.

I'm furious and frustrated and stressed all at the same time. Ran

into Derrek's wife at the grocery store this afternoon, and she
claims Derrek never told her about our partnership. Is she lying?
If not, it was an Oscar-worthy performance. Does not matter! He
said we'd get the partnership handled, and I'm going to hold him
to it. And with the whole moving-my-office thing, once again
Derrek has spun the top. Yes, if the construction he told me
about today happens, wonderful. But it feels too much like smoke
and mirrors. Tomorrow and Friday and Saturday and Sunday I will
not think about work. At all. But on Monday I'm going in with
both guns blazing. I'll get the partnership finished once and for
all. We cannot keep living like this. We are out of money and I
have to fix this. You want to change something about this entry,
mighty angel? Fine. But I'm not looking at it. The only change that
I'm going to think about is the one where my name goes from
Worker to Partner.

forty-one

"YOU WANTED TO SPEAK WITH me?" Derrek looked up from his laptop for a moment on the following Monday, then returned to studying the screen.

"Yes."

Allison stood in the doorframe of Derrek's office, her face set like flint. This would be the moment. He'd try to stall. Find a compelling reason to push off the conversation another day, week, month. No. Not today.

"About?"

"Finalizing the partnership. It's been almost three and a half months, Derrek. You've been stalling, making excuses, and I'm tired of it. I know we talked about it last week, about your busy schedule, but I'd like to talk about the partnership now. I bumped into your wife on Wednesday and brought up the partnership, and she said she had no idea what I was talking about."

"Yes, she mentioned seeing you at the grocery store." Derrek nodded, his face full of mock concern. "And you're right, it's definitely been delayed."

"Yes, it has been." She stepped inside and closed his door. "Let's take care of that."

"I have a busy schedule this morning."

"Yes, I understand that. So do I. And I'll have one tomorrow and the next day and the next. So will you. Tyranny of the urgent. But this needs to happen now, not this afternoon or in a few weeks."

Irritation flashed across Derrek's face, then his countenance shifted to amusement, then went blank.

"I see." He closed his laptop, pushed back from his desk, and motioned to the chairs in the corner of his office, then stood and meandered over and sat. Allison hesitated, then moved over and settled into the maroon chair across from him.

Derrek crossed his legs and nodded. "I know you've been frustrated at the length of time it's taken to sit down and structure our agreement, and you would classify that as wrong, but that's not truly the situation we find ourselves in. It's been a valuable time. Time that has given us both time to think. Time to listen."

"Think about what? Listen to whom?"

"Think about the partnership. Pray. Listen to wise counsel from God and from other people who know the company."

"Like Linda?"

"Yes, she's one of them."

"What does she have to do with our partnership?"

Derrek gave her a puzzled look. "Since she runs the office, has her ear to the ground with the staff, with clients, she offers a unique perspective on this company. She's been an invaluable part of my team since the day I hired her six years ago. Her insight has proved useful countless times."

"I'm sure it has."

"Good, good. I knew you'd respect her opinion on the workings of the company and how I cannot dismiss her sage counsel without careful consideration. Her bright light and gentle approach to people have been a seminal part of Wright Architecture's success. I'm glad we agree on that."

Spinning again. Yes, Linda ran a tight ship. But it was not from a well of kindness. And no, she did not respect Linda's opinions.

"I didn't say I—"

"And since you and I both agree her counsel should be held in high esteem, then this conversation could potentially be easier than I anticipated."

Allison's hands went cold.

"What is her counsel?"

Derrek folded his hands across his lap. "Her counsel is that you should not become a partner."

"What?"

"That can't surprise you. You haven't exactly won her over to your side."

Heat rose into Allison's face.

"Also, as I just indicated, I've had a chance to ponder the idea of our partnership as well. I've prayed about it extensively. Sought the views of my brothers at church. With all those considerations in mind, I've come to the conclusion that you're not ready, and consequently I'm not ready for you to become a partner in this company."

Allison's body went numb. "Are you kidding me?"

"But I do want to be clear on one thing." He smiled as if he were about to give her winning lottery numbers. "This is quite possibly a temporary decision. I believe I can say with a fair level of certainty that you will indeed become a partner in this company someday. An extremely high likelihood. You've been doing excellent work. The clients you work with have commended you often."

"Then why—"

"Consequently, my suggestion is we revisit this conversation in six months or so and see how we both feel about it then."

Six months? Allison clutched the arms of her chair as if letting go would send her toppling to the gray carpet. She stared at him, Derrek now giving her a thin smile that seemed to say everything was exactly as it should be. This couldn't be happening. But of course it could. She'd seen it coming, had known it was coming, but didn't want to admit it. How could he do this to her? Lie to her? How? Simple. Lying was what Derrek did. It was who he was.

"I can't believe you."

"Oh?" Derrek stood and strolled back to his desk, sat, and opened his laptop. "Why is that, Allison?"

"You enticed me to come over here to be a partner. A *partner*. I never would have come simply to work for you. For anybody."

Allison stood and paced, blood pulsing hard in her temples. "You said we were partners. I have your proposal. You wrote the word *partner* in memos and emails to clients for weeks after I got here. I saved those emails. It wasn't a delusion on my part. You gave me your word!"

"Now, Allison, there is no need to get upset. What you have to consider is there are different definitions of the word *partner*. I consider everyone who comes to this office to work on common goals as a partner in the work we're doing for our clients. When I hired you I did bring you on as a partner. And when I wrote those notes to clients, you were a partner, just as all of us working here are partners. I realize now—thank you for pointing it out to me—that your definition was different and continues to be different."

Allison stared at Derrek, her mind blank. She hadn't expected this conversation to be simple, but she hadn't expected a spin of this magnitude either.

"Wait a second. On one hand, you're saying Linda doesn't want me to be a partner, which indicates you know exactly what the word means. You grasp the benefits and position that come with it, because she doesn't want me to be one. On the other hand, you're saying everyone is a partner."

Derrek's face went cold. "Let me repeat, everyone is a partner. For example, Linda considers herself a partner, as she should. In her arrangement, she receives a percentage of profits, but she does not own any percentage of this company. If you chatted with any number of the people who work here, they, too, would describe their positions as partners. Just as I hope you were doing, and of course I thought you *were* doing, up until this conversation."

"No, Derrek. You're not going to spin this one. All our conversations were about partnership in the same way Kayla and I were partners. Ownership of the company. Sharing profits. My definition comes from the one you gave me when we talked on the phone and you said you wanted me to be your partner. From the paper you showed me at The Vogue that said *in writing* I would get thirty-nine percent of the company. It comes from the fact I came from a partnership with Kayla and you knew exactly what my partnership was with her, and you knew I would be expecting the same thing when I came here."

"Our expectations and reality are often quite different. Often we tell ourselves a story that is quite a bit askew from the facts of a situation."

"Why did you lie to me?"

Derrek looked up from his laptop and gave a little chuckle.

"I never lied to you. We both knew going in that we were going to take time to see how you would best work at my company. We—"

"No. We did not know that. I was patient because I trusted you."

"I'm glad to hear that." He turned back to his laptop. "I trust you as well. But let me be clear. You're not getting thirty-nine percent of this company, now or ever. As I said previously, at some point it might be God's leading for you to become a partner and share in a percentage ownership in this company. But that time is not now."

"I can't do this any longer." Tears rose to her eyes and she wiped them away quickly.

Derrek shut his laptop for the second time and folded his hands.

"This has been a profitable conversation, Allison. Let me explain why. I didn't understand the depth of your belief that you were coming over here as a partner in the same way you were with Kayla. It would have been wise of you to procure a definition and clarify that definition in writing so we could be literally on the same page from the start."

"We were on the same page! The one you showed me at—"

"However, your opportunity to do that has passed. Consequently, we need to determine a plan going forward. Perhaps your time here at Wright Architecture is coming to an end. I do not want that to be the case. I had hoped we would work together for many years. But I know money is something you have a great desire to have more of. That you want—"

"The money is not for me! I need—"

Derrek waved his hand. "Regardless of the motivation, you still find yourself in a position where you want more income. With that in mind, let me talk to Linda in the next few weeks and see if we can increase your salary somewhat a month or two from now."

"I don't have a month to wait, Derrek."

He continued as if he hadn't heard her. "In addition, if it would make you feel better, I have no problem adding the word *partner* to your business card. Perhaps we should make that offer to all who work here. What do you think?"

Allison's mind reeled. *Partner* on her business card was supposed to placate her? And yet, if he was serious about an increased salary, should she stay? And if she didn't, where would she go?

"Let me repeat, I want you to stay with me. And it's evident to me that this conversation should have happened a great deal earlier. You will make partner, Allison. You will have a percentage of this company. It's coming—I promise you that."

A battle raged in her mind. Half of her wanted to release the inferno that was swirling through her; the other half shouted to be cautious. Five seconds passed. Ten.

"I'd enjoy chatting further, but I really must go, Allison."

With that, Derrek strode out of his office without looking back.

Allison sat in her office after her talk with Derrek, no idea where she should go next. Gut it out? Gut it out for what? Even if she had it in writing that she'd become a partner on a specific future day, he'd find a way around it.

Ellie buzzed her from the front desk. "Allison?"

"Yes?"

"Phone call for you on line three."

"Who is it?"

"Didn't say."

Take the call? Yes. It would distract her at least for a moment. She swallowed and closed her eyes for a moment. *Game face on. Act professional whether you feel it or not.*

"Hi, this is Allison Moore."

"Hey, Allison, this is Micah Taylor. I have you on speakerphone 'cause Sarah's here too. We met down in Cannon Beach."

"Hi, Allison!" Sarah called out.

Allison's breath whooshed out of her in a deep sigh. "I cannot tell you how timely your call is."

"Really?" Micah laughed. "Why's that?"

"Just another brutal day at work. You guys are a breath of desperately needed air."

"Glad to help," Micah said. "Listen, Sarah and I are going to be up in the area, and if you're around, we thought we'd swing by, see where you work, take you to lunch and catch up."

"Yes to all of the above, except the lunch part. My turn."

"We might wrestle you for that," Sarah said, "but we'll wait for the battle till we get there."

"When are you guys going to be here?"

"Eleven days from now, on the nineteenth. Will that work? Pick you up at eleven thirty?"

"Yes, I'll see you then."

Allison called Richard on the way home.

"Can we get together?"

"I'm sorry, Allison, I can't. I'm in the middle of something that needs my full attention."

"Can you talk now?"

"For only a few moments, I'm afraid."

"I'm never going to be a partner. My mom is going to drown in debt. We don't have the money to make this month's payment, and my love life is nonexistent. I spoke to the dry bones, but they did not come to life."

Allison changed lanes as Richard seemed to be gathering his thoughts.

"Tell me something you believed when you were young that you now know as impossible, but back then you had no doubt whatsoever that it was true."

"What?"

"Tell me."

"Flying."

"Tell me more."

"When I was a kid I knew I could fly. I didn't believe it—I knew it. All I had to do was run fast enough. All I had to find was the right wind, and when I did I would catch it and fly. Not like a bird. Not way up in the air and for long distances, but for ten yards or twenty yards. Or I'd jump off a slide with my umbrella and float on a current across the park and land softly on the grass."

"Yes," Richard said. "That is the key. You must believe like that again."

"But do I—"

"When boys and girls are young, they don't think about their gifts and abilities and interests and desires. They simply act on them. They don't judge them. They act. They don't have to think about who they are—they simply are. They don't worry about their true selves slipping away. But then they do slip away, and they don't know how to find themselves again."

"But how do I do that?"

"I'm so sorry, my dear friend. I must go. Believe, Allison, believe."

When she got home, Allison's first move was to check the journal. It had to have changed this time. *Please!* But there was nothing more than her ink stains from five days back on the page.

"Come on, God! What are you doing to me?"

No, the journal didn't owe her anything. Yes, Richard was probably right, the journal was going to do what it wanted to, but really? No input at all after the past three entries? Why even have the thing? Why the ongoing silent treatment?

Sleep came slowly that night, and when it did it was accompanied by dreams of piles of cash just beyond her outstretched fingers.

forty-two

THE NEXT NINE DAYS AT work were uncomfortable and infuriating. Derrek avoided her, and when he couldn't he offered only a quick hello. Linda seemed to go out of her way to bump into Allison, and when she did she gave a smug little smile. Having to endure Linda's cattiness was like sandpaper on her soul.

On the nineteenth a welcome distraction arrived in the form of Micah and Sarah. Something about seeing them in the lobby gave her a sense of expectation. She gave them a tour of the office, and their countenance seemed strange almost the entire time. She introduced them to Derrek, Linda, Ellie, and eight others. They both took time to chat for more than a few minutes with all of them but were far quieter than Allison expected.

They didn't step outside until after twelve. The moment they reached the sidewalk, Micah said, "Wow!"

He shoved his hands into his pockets and glanced back at the building as they made their way to the end of the block and waited at the crosswalk for the light to change.

"That was something you don't experience every day," he said.

They stepped off the curb as Allison said, "What's that?"

"I don't think I've ever felt so much religion in my life."

"Agree," Sarah said.

"I thought I told you guys that."

"Told us what?" Micah asked.

"All of the people who work there are Christians. At least I'm pretty sure everyone is. So that's probably why—"

"That's not what I meant." He chuckled and stutter-stepped to avoid a man coming straight at him, head down, eyes on his phone, oblivious to his surroundings.

"Then what did you—"

"There's a vast difference between religion and Christianity. What I felt was an avalanche of religion burying everything in its path."

Allison stared at him. "You felt it?"

"Felt it. Saw it. Heard it." Micah gave her a sympathetic smile. "It was like trying to swim through an ocean full of jelly, and the jelly was rancid."

———

After their food arrived at the Thai restaurant they'd chosen, Micah cleared his throat and said, "I'd like to tell you about the home Sarah and I live in."

"Down at the ocean."

"Yes."

"Sure, I'd like to hear about it."

"It was designed by my great-uncle Archie. He was an architect and built the home with a company called Hale & Sons. By the way, Hale & Sons are from Seattle. You haven't heard of them, have you?"

"I haven't, no."

"Anyway, I was working in software, downtown Seattle, and I get a letter telling me this house down there is mine. I go down there, and let's just say I discovered quickly the home was quite . . . unusual in its architecture."

"How so?"

Sarah placed her hand on Micah's and looked at him when she spoke. "Someday we would love to tell you the entire story, but it would take far too long, and really, today we want to talk about you."

"Can I get an abbreviated version?"

Micah looked at Sarah and shrugged, and Sarah said to Allison, "You'll cut him off when you start getting bored, right?"

Allison laughed. "Done!"

"As I just said, I was working in software—"

"He owned the company, was making millions and millions of dollars, but he was empty inside and—"

"Oh," Micah said and pulled back from the table. "Did you want to tell Allison the story?"

"No, but sometimes you need a little color commentary."

"Thanks."

"You're welcome."

"As I was saying . . ." Micah drew out each word and mock glared at Sarah, who laughed. "I got a letter from my great-uncle Archie, telling me I'd inherited a home down on the Oregon coast, in Cannon Beach. Cannon Beach was not a place of great memories for me, so I went down there to sell it. But then things started happening in the house, strange things, and I met this mechanic named Rick who became a close friend. Rick knew more about the house than he was letting on. But all he would say about the house was that it was spiritual. Which was interesting, because my faith at that point had slipped away like the tide. Then I met Sarah, and more weird things happened in the house, and over time I slowly came to realize that the home was a . . ."

Micah stopped, glanced at Sarah, and gave a nervous laugh.

Allison put down her chopsticks and peered at Micah. "What's wrong?"

"This is the part where the story gets really weird. Which is why we don't tell it too often."

"Given the recent events in my life, I don't think much will shock me."

"Good point," Sarah said. "You want to give us an update on what's been going on?"

"I do." Allison picked up her chopsticks and motioned toward Micah. "But first, the rest of your story."

"All right." Micah grinned. "Can't say I didn't warn you, yeah?"

"Yes."

"The house down in Cannon Beach turned out to be a physical manifestation of my soul."

Allison stopped with her chopsticks halfway to her mouth. "Are you kidding?"

"No." Micah lowered his voice. "The rooms of the house were literally parts of my soul. Some rooms contained things from my past I needed to face; other rooms made me come alive in ways I hadn't for years. And at the heart of the home, there was a room that blew my mind like nothing ever has in my entire life, before or since."

Micah looked up as if recalling the room, and his eyes grew soft. "And as I was going through a mental and emotional and spiritual revolution, my life in Seattle was falling apart and vanishing, quite literally. I lost everything. And yet I ended up gaining everything by stepping into the person I truly am, the one God designed me to be."

Allison stared at Micah, glanced at Sarah, then fixed her gaze back on Micah. It was ludicrous. A home that was a physical manifestation of Micah's soul? That made her journal experiences look tame.

"No wonder you didn't balk when I told you about the journal."

"That would be one of the reasons why, yes."

"One?"

"Like we said down at the beach, we're drawn to you—not sure why—but we've learned to listen to the leadings of the Spirit and go with them. So here we are."

Sarah finished her meal and pushed her plate toward the center of the table. "Your turn, Allison. What's been going on with the journal?"

She told them about the entries and how they'd stopped changing, and the frustration of that, but also about Richard becoming a friend and the talks they'd had.

"This guy, is he like a boyfriend-type friend?" Sarah asked.

"No." Allison smiled. "He's like a dad-type friend."

"Ah yes, that makes sense," Micah said as he worked on his tom kha kai.

"Why do you say that?"

"I think God often puts people in our lives that can mentor, offer wisdom, so whoever this Richard guy is, he's probably your Obi-Wan Kenobi."

"My who?"

"Obi-Wan Kenobi from Star Wars, the guy who mentors Luke Skywalker."

"I only saw the movies once, and that was a long time ago."

"Once?" Micah leaned forward. "Once? You're kidding. What about episodes four, five, and six?"

"Once each."

"Wow, I guess that does it. Can't be friends any longer."

"Ignore him." Sarah kissed Micah on the cheek. "Can we get back to Allison please?"

"There's not much more to tell. Work has been really tough, I'm not making the money I need to make, and there've been a number of issues that have rocked me, but I'm figuring out what do to, and the journal has been a huge part of that."

They ate in silence for a bit till Micah said, "We might be able to help a bit with the financial. Not much, but a little."

"Oh?"

"Given your experiences with the journal, we think you're someone who should come see our home. We could describe more of what happened in it back when I first went there, and what continues to happen—which in some ways is crazier than anything I first went through. Then, after spending a few days with us there, getting to know our entire story, I'd want to hire you to help teach me something I've always wanted to try."

"Architecture?"

"Yes. I'm an artist. I paint, but with oils. I'd love to learn to 'paint' with metal and wood and windows. I've done a bit of dabbling over the years with Hale & Sons, the company that built my house, but I want to dive into it deeper. The way my great-uncle did."

"You're a painter?"

"Yes." Micah turned to Sarah. "And Sarah is a personal trainer. Between the two of us, we do okay, pay the bills, take care of our sons. But as I said, I'd like to learn more about architecture."

"You want me to teach you?"

"Yes." Micah smiled, and his eyes caught fire. "Would you?"

"The long answer is yes; the short answer is I don't know." Allison took a drink of water. "Right now my life is complicated."

"Oh?" Sarah said.

"Things with my mom, my brother, my job . . . this journal . . . I can't believe I'm telling you this, but at the moment my life is at about the worst point it's ever been. But I do need the money, desperately. So yes, I'll figure out a way to work it in."

Micah reached across the table and squeezed her hand for a quick second. "That is great to hear. I'm so psyched for you."

He grinned at her and gave a couple of quick nods of his head.

"What?" Allison frowned. "You're happy for me?"

"Extremely. Congrats." He took a bite and nodded again as he looked at her.

"You want to explain that?"

"When I hit my low point nine years back, I thought there was no way out. I was devastated on so many levels. But it was the storm I needed. And the light came. Breakthrough on a scale I couldn't imagine. I know that's coming for you. No doubt in my mind. But you had to get to this point first. And then, when you're through it, maybe you can help me."

"If that ever happens, I'd love to."

"Wonderful." Micah grinned and turned to Sarah. "I told you."

Sarah laughed. "You didn't tell me—I told you."

"That's what I meant." Micah's eyes grew serious. "Let's stay in touch on this, yes?"

"Yes," Allison said. "When the time comes, I'll be ready."

"I believe you will be."

When Allison got back to the office, she went to the lunchroom to heat up water for tea. As she set the kettle on the small stove and pulled out her Kindle to read while she waited, Ellie and Linda came in and sat at the far end, apparently to have a late lunch. They settled down and started talking in whispers, but their voices weren't soft enough.

". . . I don't know what I'm going to do about it," Linda was saying.

"You want to talk about it?"

Allison stopped reading. Should she leave? She didn't want to hear this. *Shouldn't* hear it. Obviously they didn't think she could hear them, but if she left now, they'd figure out that she could, and *had*. Before she could decide, Linda started in with a statement that froze Allison to her spot.

"I'm thinking of leaving Bryce."

"What?" Ellie said. "Why?"

Allison lowered her head and closed her eyes. She shouldn't be here. But she was stuck.

"Did you know I met Bryce at Boeing?"

"No, I didn't," Ellie said with compassion.

"I worked for him. We fell in love, we started having kids, and I stayed home. In the early years it was okay. Bryce took part when the kids were little. But as time went by he started coming home later. Even when he was there, he'd plop down in front of the TV. Every night. Year after year after year."

"I'm so sorry, Linda," Ellie said.

"The only time he wasn't watching TV was on the weekends when he was on the golf course." Linda paused and rubbed her eyes. "When the kids left I thought things would change. I tried to talk to him, but he was never in the mood for conversation. We never had more than the most basic of talks."

"I've known you for ten years."

"And I never let on, did I? I was committed to the marriage. I put on a brave face. Told you and everyone else what a wonderful and brilliant man he was. Great husband, excellent father to our children."

"You've always told me about the fun you guys have."

"Yes, I did." Linda blew out a long breath. "And I made up excuses why he rarely made it to church."

"And you stayed with him."

Linda didn't respond. Out of the corner of her eye, Allison saw Linda dab at her eyes. Then she rose, along with Ellie, took their bowls to the sink, washed them out, and walked from the room.

Allison stared at her Kindle, not seeing the words, just as she'd not read anything for the past three minutes. Her heart ached for Linda. Everyone had their pain; everyone had their secrets, their longings that more often than not went unfulfilled. In an instant the past three months made sense. No wonder Linda ran the office like a prison camp. No wonder she protected Derrek so fiercely. He saw her. Truly saw her, saw her as someone of great value.

Allison wondered why she couldn't be seen that way. What was wrong with her that she wasn't worthy of being a partner? And now that it was clear she'd never get what she longed for at the company, where could she go?

On the way home she prayed, begged for an answer, because she had definitely reached the low point Micah had spoken of. If breakthrough was coming, she needed it now.

forty-three

Allison groaned. Eight fifty-six. Four minutes before the weekly Wednesday morning staff meeting, and her computer was running like a slug. Perfectly horrible timing. She'd just gotten an email from her mom's loan sharks saying her mom's payment was late. She sighed. *You have to remember to send that in on time, Mom!*

Delinquent again meant another $220 late fee. On top of that, they were $1,289 short this month. Which meant they'd be paying a daily interest rate of two percent on the $1,289 till they were caught up, per her dad's contract. Plus, they could tack on another seventy-five bucks for every twenty-four hours the payment was late, which would kick in within the hour.

Allison squeezed her hands into fists, drew in a breath between her teeth, and released it quickly. She logged into her bank account. She could get this done before the meeting. No problem. Until her computer froze. Wonderful. The reboot would take at least two minutes. As she scrambled for a solution, Linda stuck her head into Allison's office and smiled like she was about to go on a shopping spree with an unlimited credit card.

"Our general staff meeting is starting in three minutes, Allison."

"Yes, I know." Allison tapped into her phone. She could log in and transfer the money from there.

"But you're still sitting at your desk."

"Yes, I'm aware of that." She snapped off the words.

"I'm not sure that tone is appropriate, Allison."

"I'll be there, Linda."

Linda stepped inside, strode up to Allison's desk, and pressed her fingers onto the wood.

"Derrek has made it clear that being on time to our meetings is one of our highest priorities."

"Have I ever been late to a staff meeting?"

Linda pressed her lips together and narrowed her eyes. "Let's not start with this one, shall we?"

———

Allison slid into an open seat at the conference table with the other staff members and glanced at her cell phone at the moment the time switched from 8:59 to 9:00. A second later Linda marched through the door.

"Derrek texted me a few seconds ago. He'll be here momentarily." She settled into her chair at one end of the table. "He's asked, while we're waiting, to go around the room and tell what projects we're currently working on and if we have any prayer requests for the week coming up."

Allison stood. "While you're doing that, I need to—"

"I feel we need to honor Derrek's request, don't you, Allison?" Linda glanced around the room, a razor-thin smile on her face that dared anyone to disagree.

"I have a critical issue I need to—"

"What is it? Perhaps we can help you solve it."

"It's a private matter. Personal."

"My thought on that is you should be taking care of personal things on personal time, not on the company's time. Would you agree?"

Linda's tone was soft, but the softness didn't mask the threat of retaliation if her wishes weren't carried out. Before Allison could answer, Linda bowed her head and prayed.

"Dear heavenly Father, we thank you that you hear our prayers and answer them in your perfect timing. We thank you for this company. We thank you for the wonderful leadership Derrek provides and that he is a man of vision and wisdom and integrity. We thank you for him and for the jobs he has provided each of us. We thank you for the clients you have brought him, and we pray for their success, heavenly Father. As we go about our day today, we ask you, blessed heavenly Father, to guide us and grant us . . ."

Linda droned on, and Allison tuned her out. Maybe she could slip out, get the money transferred, and slip back into the room unnoticed. Sure, and the office fairies would appear in seconds to pick up Linda by her hair and pull her out of the room and drop her into Puget Sound.

Allison glanced at her watch. Five minutes after nine. Linda finally ended with a request for her church's potluck on Friday night to go well. A few other people prayed short prayers. The room went quiet for ten or fifteen seconds. Then Linda closed the prayer time with another lengthy monologue.

"Amen." Linda glanced around the room, a smile on her face that looked like she'd just saved a drowning child. "What a wonderful time of fellowship together."

Allison glanced at her watch. Ten after. Still no Derrek.

"I'm sure Derrek will be here any moment, but since we might have a few more seconds before he arrives, let's go around the table and hear how you've been blessed this past week."

Unbelievable. Allison glanced around the room at the faint look of illness in the eyes of most of those around the table. Wasn't this supposed to be a business?

Linda started, saying she'd been blessed because her daughter had started working for a new massage-therapy company where she'd be making more money. Mary mentioned her sister had become pregnant after trying for two years. Three more people before it would be Allison's turn to speak. What would she say? That she was blessed to know that her time was currently being flushed down the toilet and her stress level was approaching an all-time high? She was saved when Derrek walked through the front door as the person beside her wrapped up.

"There he is!" Linda beamed and stood as Derrek strolled into the room like the guest of honor at an exclusive cocktail party.

"Hello, everyone." He smiled as if he'd just handed them all a $2,000 bonus. "I hope your morning is going well."

He gave no apology for being late. No explanation as to where he had been. But had he ever given a reason for his perpetual lateness? The odds of him starting now were low. But still, twenty minutes late to his own meeting? Classic.

Derrek set down his briefcase on the table and slowly pulled out his laptop. Allison had to figure out how to get out of the meeting and transfer the money. The meeting couldn't last more than an hour, could it? Yes, of course it could.

"Before we get started on the issues of the day and week, I want to share something I have been studying the past seven days during my time alone with God. This applies to business as well as our lives, and I believe it is critical to our success as a company and as individuals."

Derrek clicked a few keys, and the projector that hung from the ceiling sent a picture up on the wall behind his head. The first image was the word *INTEGRITY* in a bold font over an image of a brilliant sunrise.

He chuckled and pointed at the screen. "As you might imagine, I want to say a few words about integrity. It's a word we all know about, a word we all know we need to live by. We know it's a hallmark, an indication, a character trait of those who love God. Because of that, it's a principle we need to revisit and remind ourselves of."

He clicked to the next slide.

in·teg·ri·ty | \in-te-grə-tē\ *noun.* The quality of being honest and having strong moral principles; moral uprightness.

Derrek read the words out loud, then went to the next slide. An image of Dwight Eisenhower appeared, and a quote.

"The supreme quality for leadership is unquestionably integrity. Without it, no real success is possible, no matter whether it is on a section gang, a football field, in an army, or in an office." —Dwight D. Eisenhower

Derrek glanced around the room. "Our onetime president is absolutely correct. People might say they've succeeded, but deep down, even they know it's tainted."

Derrek clicked to the next slide.

"A single lie destroys a whole reputation of integrity." —Baltasar Gracián

Again, Derrek glanced at each of them before speaking. "It only takes one time, friends. Just one. And in that moment, when the lie is exposed, a reputation can be destroyed forever. It happens. But it shouldn't. As ambassadors of God, we should be above reproach."

He went to the next slide, which held a photo of Oprah Winfrey and the words:

"Real integrity is doing the right thing, knowing that nobody's going to know whether you did it or not." —Oprah Winfrey

Derrek chuckled and waggled his finger at the screen. "Although I can't agree with Oprah on many things, including her stand on spiritual matters, in this case I believe she is spot-on. We have integrity, not for what others will see and think of us, but for God and what *he* will think of us. One of the strongest witnesses we can give to the world is our integrity.

"As the Bible tells us in Proverbs 12:22, 'The Lord detests lying lips, but he delights in people who are trustworthy.'"

Derrek shut off the projector and took his seat at the head of the conference table. Allison glanced at her watch. Nine thirty-five. How long was this going to go?

"Quite a few years ago I was in the process of interviewing a highly qualified candidate and we were on the third interview. I liked him, his qualifications were stellar, and we were getting close to bringing him on.

"After chatting in my office for ten or fifteen minutes, I excused myself to go make a quick phone call, assuring him I'd return in no more than ten minutes. Now, you must know that before he arrived, I had set out a piece of paper on the corner of my desk in my handwriting. Not easily noticeable, but an observant person would spot it quickly. On it was what I would offer him in pay. Next to the word *low* I had a number; next to the word *middle* I had a number; and next to the word *highest* I had written a number. The low was what I hoped I could hire him for, the middle was where I imagined we'd settle, and the high was the maximum amount I would pay. Valuable information for the man to have during salary negotiation."

Derrek shifted in his chair, placed his hands on the table, and leaned forward.

"The words were visible, but the numbers were covered with a wooden pen holder. What my potential employee had no way of knowing was that there was no bottom on the pen set holder. Inside the holder were three hundred BBs. If he were to lift it, all the BBs would come running out."

Derrek paused for dramatic effect, and as if on cue, Linda said, "Did he lift the holder?"

"He did." Derrek smiled sadly. "The BBs came pouring out all over the place. As you might have guessed, I did not have to make a phone call when I excused myself. I left to see what he would do. As soon as I heard the BBs pour out, I walked back in and looked at him, then at the BBs, then back to him. I didn't say a word. Neither did he. He simply picked up his briefcase and skulked out of my office. As you can imagine, he was not hired."

"That was a brilliant way to figure out if the man was honest or not." Linda beamed.

Derrek chuckled. "In a way I felt compassion for the man, but it certainly was a good way to test his integrity."

A tiny alarm rang at the back of Allison's mind, but she didn't know why. Something was off about Derrek's story. A second later she had it. She'd heard it before. From Derrek? She wasn't sure. No, long ago. Way before she'd met him.

She peeked at Linda, then at Derrek, then pulled out her cell phone and googled the story. Seconds later she had her answer. Derrek had modified the tale slightly. But all the main facts were the same. She stared at him, stunned. Had he really just done that?

"I don't want to belabor the point, so let me wrap up with this thought: At Wright Architecture we will do what we say we will. Always. If we say we're going to deliver an item to our clients by a certain day and time, we get it done by that day and time. If we give our word about being somewhere on time, we will be there on time. Jesus says to let our yes be yes and our no be no. If we say yes to anything, we will do it. If we say no to something, we will not do it. It is that simple. We speak the truth in all circumstances."

Allison clenched her jaw as she stared at Derrek, utter conviction on his face. He was dead serious. Meant every word. It took everything inside her not to ask him to do a presentation next week on irony.

Derrek launched into the agenda Linda had put together and without any real effort stretched ten minutes of content into forty minutes of blather. Ten after ten. She had to get out of there and transfer the money. Finally, at ten twenty Derrek wrapped up the meeting with a short prayer. The instant he finished, Allison leaped from her chair, perspiration breaking out under her blouse. She went to her office and shut the door. Booted up her computer. Logged in. Transferred the money. Ten twenty-nine. Made it with a minute to spare.

————

After cruising through a slew of urgent emails, Allison went to the lunchroom, poured herself a cup of water, and put it in the microwave. A minute and a half ought to do it. She tore open a bag of English breakfast tea and wrapped the string around her finger. Derrek hadn't really lied when telling a story about having integrity, had he? Yes, he had. She shut her eyes and waited for the microwave to ding. When it did, she opened her eyes, and a voice interrupted her thoughts.

"Quite the presentation on integrity this morning." Renee sidled up next to her, scooped instant cocoa into a coffee cup, and winked at Allison. "If you looked up *irony* online, I'm thinking you'd see a link to Derrek's presentation."

"No kidding." Allison sipped her tea.

"Tough to listen to that sometimes."

"Sometimes?"

Renee laughed and said, "Just glad I'm not the only one who sees it."

"Not by a long shot." Allison started to leave, then stopped, slipped her hand into her pocket, and pulled out her cell phone. "Take a look at this."

She pulled up the story Derrek had stolen for his presentation and handed her phone to Renee. Allison took a few more sips of tea while Renee read the article. When she finished, her eyes widened.

"He stole the story. Didn't he think anyone would check?"

"Apparently not."

"Wow, this is a new one, even for him."

A voice broke into Allison's thoughts.

"Could you two come into my office for a moment?"

They both spun toward the lunchroom door. Derrek.

Allison's face went hot. Derrek turned and beckoned them over his shoulder with a finger. They followed him into the hallway, then into his office. When they entered, he shut the door behind them.

"I believe the kind of discussion you two were having in the lunchroom is important; however, I don't believe having it within possible earshot of other employees is conducive to positive employee morale."

Derrek went to his bookshelves and picked up a small bowl that looked African. He ran his thumb along the edge before speaking. "You're questioning the story I told during the staff meeting. You're questioning my integrity."

Allison said nothing. Nor did Renee.

"Then let me start, and you can offer your thoughts when I've concluded." He pushed off the shelves and held out his hand to Allison. "Would you like to show me what you were showing Renee in the lunchroom?"

Heat coursed through Allison as she pulled up the story again and handed her phone to Derrek.

He nodded and said, "Yes, that's the same site I found."

Derrek strolled over to his desk and shot her a condescending smile that made her feel like she was five.

"This is an aspect of leadership I thought you would understand, Allison, since you yourself are a leader in this company. And were a leader in your own company previously in a highly successful way."

Allison refused to take the bait. Didn't nod. Didn't acknowledge the comment. The candy comments used to work. Even now she felt the influence of Derrek's claim drawing her in, comforting her, making her believe in him.

No. Wouldn't work, not this time.

"And, Renee, you, too, are a senior member of the staff. While you're not officially in management, you have strong influence over many of the others, so you have an opportunity to influence for loss or for gain."

Renee didn't speak, but her jaw was clenched.

"Allison?" Derrek asked, eyes wide. "Any thoughts?"

"You were going to offer yours first."

"That I was." Derrek nodded again. "When communicating a

lesson as critical as integrity, the *lesson* is the crucial element, not the minutiae of the delivery method. To convey that lesson with enough emphasis to linger within the listeners for years, we use the power of story. I chose the story I did with care, as it is quick, memorable, and easy to visualize. I could have just as easily told a story of integrity from my own years in business, but the one I told was the best one for the moment, which is why I used it."

"But it didn't happen to you."

"In one sense, no, but in another sense, yes. I have used similar ideas throughout my years of interviewing and hiring people. Because I didn't utilize that *precise* method does not—in any way—take away from the fact that I've done the same thing."

Allison glanced at Renee, who stared at Derrek, her face blank.

"When, Derrek?" Renee sputtered. "When did you do the same type of thing during an interview?"

Derrek glanced back and forth from side to side without his head moving. "Is it possible I missed something? Am I on trial and no one made me aware of it?"

Derrek cleared his throat, and his countenance cooled. "If I chose to, I could give you hundreds of examples, but that's not what concerns me. What bothers me is you're willing to camp on such a small point of contention. You're straining a gnat and swallowing a camel, Renee."

"Whatever."

"No, not *whatever*." Derrek folded his arms. "This is precisely what I'm talking about with regard to leadership in this company. You want to be more of a leader here. You want to have a stake in it like Allison does. In order for that to happen, I need to see examples of loyalty, support, belief in the vision—in this case a vision of integrity for this company—not a rebellious spirit, which never comes from God."

Allison couldn't stay silent. "I don't have a stake in this company, Derrek. We just had that talk."

"But you will. It's coming. Soon."

Derrek settled into his leather chair and wiggled his mouse to bring his computer to life. Allison stared at him. That was it? He continued to ignore them.

"Derrek?"

"Unfortunately, ladies, I have work I need to attend to right away."

"Not before I have a chance to speak," Allison said.

"Yes, yes, of course." Derrek chuckled and glanced at his watch. "But right now I need to focus on these projects, or we might not have an office to be standing in to have those opportunities to speak." Another hearty laugh.

"No, Derrek, I'm—"

The laughter died abruptly. "Truly, Allison, we're going to have to chat later."

With that, Derrek turned again to his computer.

———

On the way home the sky opened and dumped the first rain in weeks. It seemed to increase its intensity every few minutes, and by the time Allison reached the road that led to her neighborhood, she had her wipers on high. As she came to the first of three stop signs before she reached her house, her phone chirped.

Allison glanced down. Caller ID said it was Kayla. Allison hesitated only a second before answering.

"Hey."

"Hey," Kayla said. "Been a while."

"True."

Neither spoke for a few seconds.

"Ally?"

"Yeah."

"I'm thinking we should be friends again."

"I'd like that." Allison drove through the intersection and pulled over to the side of the road. "I'd like that a lot."

"Good," Kayla said. "Me too."

"How's it going with Mila?"

"Really well. Not as much fun as with you, and not as many fights." Kayla laughed. "But I'm finally making some decent money. How 'bout you?"

"It's been tough."

"I'm sorry."

"It's okay." Allison stared at the passing red lights of the cars sloshing along the road.

"Derrek's not what you thought?"

"No." Allison sighed. "But you already knew who he really was."

"You would have seen it too if you hadn't already been friends."

"What do you mean?"

"The computers."

That was all Kayla needed to say. Instantly it was three and a half years earlier and Allison was on the phone with Derrek.

"How are things progressing for you and your new venture, Allison? About ready to hang out the shingle?"

"Just about. We're doing well. Getting everything set up. Next step is to get a couple of more powerful computers."

"I know you've been PC-based when working for other firms, but now that you're starting your own, I highly recommend you transition to Apple."

"Really?"

"Without question. They will serve you well in everything from design software to accounting to marketing."

"You're saying we should buy something like MacBooks?"

"Yes. They make an excellent product, carry an outstanding warranty, and the particular model of MacBook I'm recommending will have all the processing power you need to design with ease."

"I appreciate the counsel. I'll go to their website today and—"

"Tell you what. Let me take care of it for you. I have an order going in tomorrow, and I've purchased enough laptops and desktops from them that they are quite responsive with my orders. I'll simply add two more computers to the order and you can pay me when the computers arrive."

Neither she nor Kayla were scholars when it came to tech, so having someone put them on the right path out of the gate would be a big help.

"Wow, thank you, Derrek. That would be incredibly helpful."

A week after that, Derrek emailed and said the computers had come in. Allison sent a check for the full amount. Two weeks later she fired up her new computers, but something didn't seem right. She'd never worked with Macs, but she was surprised to see a number of files already in the documents folder. Files that shouldn't be there. Like one containing a series of songs that she knew Derrek's band played.

She called Derrek and said, "I think there might have been a mix-up. I found a few files on here and was wondering if maybe you sent us the wrong laptops."

Derrek chuckled. "No, I should have warned you about that. I was setting up the laptops for you, making sure everything worked right, then I loaded your laptop with some software that I knew would help you, and I'm guessing in the transfer process a few files might have slipped on there along with the software without my knowledge. You can simply delete those files, no harm done."

It wasn't till a year later, when a repair shop had fixed an issue on her computer, that Allison learned the truth. Her computer was a year and a half older than it should have been. She hadn't wanted to believe it. Derrek had taken the new computers and given her and Kayla his older models. She'd let it go. But she shouldn't have.

"I saw it, Kayla. But I ignored it."

"Don't beat yourself up. I'm sure I would have done the same thing."

"No, you wouldn't have."

They both went silent.

"Hang in there, Ally. Things are really crazy for me right now, but let's get together this fall, all right?"

"Yes. I'd love to, K. You made my day."

She hung up and smiled. It would take time, but she had little doubt they would be friends again, of the best variety.

———

Wednesday, July 24th

I just about lost it at work today. Master Spin Doctor of the Universe gave a talk on integrity at the staff meeting. The ultimate irony. Not quirky or funny irony, but the kind that makes me want to scream at the top of my lungs till my voice runs out. Doing the right thing. Doing what you say you're going to do. Speaking from a place of truth in all that you say.

And then he ends with a story that he stole and justifies it to Renee and me when he overhears us talking about it in the lunchroom. Unbelievable.

Renee tried to push back. But of course she was shut down by the velvet hammer.

The man is the living embodiment of a lie. Does he even know it? Has no one shown him a mirror? Even then, would he see it? Are the others in the company blind, or do they simply swallow his fairy tales for the sake of their jobs?

I was tempted at so many points to dive in and offer commentary, but I can't. Not yet. Have to take what money I can from my job. Even with Parker's next batch of money—which should arrive soon, please—it's not enough, but at least it's something. But how long will they let us make partial payments?

Micah Taylor says a breakthrough is coming. When? I sure hope it's looking at the calendar, 'cause we're running out of days.

What are you doing, God? Don't you think it's time to let me in on the plan? I could start looking for another job, but how do I do that when I've signed a noncompete? Impossible.

Richard talks about dry bones and calling them to life, and about true selves that have slipped away believing again—but believing in what?

I'm tired. And I don't see any light coming anytime soon.

Well, that's not entirely true. Kayla called me on the way home. That was a bright spot. And very needed.

In the morning Allison checked the journal. No change. Same that night. She tried to reach Richard, but his phone went to voice mail. Believe? The last of her faith had almost vanished.

forty-four

SATURDAY MORNING ALLISON WENT FOR a run and took the journal with her. She'd ignored the pounding thoughts in her mind for two days. Enough. She had to start getting thoughts down, start making a plan for where her life would go from here. When she reached a secluded lookout on Tiger Mountain, she pulled out the journal and pen. But she didn't write. Her last entry had changed.

Wednesday, July 24th
What are the dry bones?
What are your dry bones?
What are they, Allison?

She stared at the words. Never before had the journal addressed her directly. Words changing? Yes. She'd gotten used to that. Kind of. But this? A whole other level. But even that didn't shoot adrenaline through her like the rest of the entry did.

At work today I finally faced the truth about my life. Master
Spin Doctor of the Universe gave a talk on integrity at the staff

meeting. Doing the right thing. Doing what you say you're going to do. Speaking from a place of truth in all that you say.

As I listened to him speak, it was as if looking into a mirror, and I realized I am the living embodiment of a lie. I don't live from a place of authenticity. I live in a place of fear. I don't speak from a place of truth. I hide it because of what might happen to me. What I might lose. Because I want to be liked and thought well of. Why have I not seen this in the mirror of my life? Even now am I seeing the full truth of what I've become? Others in the company and in my life aren't blind—why do I expect them to accept the false mask I wear?

When Derrek was speaking, I thought I was tempted at so many points to dive in and offer commentary, but even that's a lie. If I had truly wanted to, I would have. The person I know I am deep inside would not have stayed silent. Not in the conference room. Not in Derrek's office afterward. The true Allison would have spoken out.

I can use the excuse that Mom needs every penny I'm making, but there's a deeper reason I didn't speak out. I'm in fear. I don't believe. I don't trust God. And I don't know who I am.

The dry bones need to be called to life or my true self will slip away forever. I believe now, and the light is coming. The light is coming. Now.

Allison stared at the page, at the words that had betrayed her. This was supposed to be God? Accusing her of not living an authentic life? Hadn't she sacrificed everything over the past four months for her mom? She kicked at the rocks at her feet. Wasn't what she'd given enough?

She read the entry again and screamed. Then she read it a third

time and let the truth of the words seep inside. It was true, all of it.
And as she accepted that truth, something deep inside stirred. The
dry bones. And as they knit themselves together and began to take on
life, words appeared on the page as she stared at it.

> You have girded me with strength for battle;
> You have subdued under me those who rose up against me.
> Be strong and courageous.
> The Lord will go forth like a warrior,
> He will arouse His zeal like a man of war.
> He will utter a shout, yes, He will raise a war cry.
> He will prevail against His enemies.

The writing stopped for a moment, then started up again, faster
this time.

> The Lord your God is in your midst,
> A victorious warrior.
> He will exult over you with joy.
> The Lord is a warrior;
> The Lord is His name.
> Great change is coming.

The writing stopped and a peace settled on Allison like she'd
never known. And a fire burned inside that she knew well but had not
experienced for a long time. Finally, a moment before she was certain
the writing was through, one more line appeared in the journal.

> Allison is a warrior, a daughter of the King, Allison is her
> name.

A puff of surprised laughter escaped her lips. She'd always known who she was but had been blind. The truth had been there all along. Her dry bones weren't getting the partnership or getting her mom out of debt or even finding love again. All those things could come and go like the tide. But there was one thing that could never be shaken. One thing that was as everlasting as eternity. And it was at the core of her being. She was a warrior. Had always been one. Would always be one. And it was time for her to breathe life back into that warrior. Time for the bones to grow flesh around them. Time for flesh to rise and come alive. Time to banish fear from her heart, her mind, her soul, and allow the Spirit of truth to be her strength. Time for her to fight again. Time for her to be Allison Moore.

She knew what she had to do. Confront Derrek. And tell him the truth.

About everything.

forty-five

PARKER WOKE UP ON SOMETHING hard, with pain shooting
through his left shoulder and a cold chill swirling around his body.
He reached for his blankets. Not there. Was he on the floor? He
opened his eyes and blinked. That's exactly where he was. He rubbed
his shoulder. Must have landed on it when he fell out of his bunk.
How'd that happen?

He glanced around the room, half expecting Logan to have tossed
him out of the bunk before his alarm clock went off. But the true reason he lay there became evident a second later as the floor went from
horizontal to almost vertical, then reeled back to almost vertical the
other way. They were in the heart of a storm.

As his mind screamed for him to stay in his cabin, Parker pulled
on his clothes and staggered out the door of his room and onto the
deck. Torrential rain drenched him. Ocean spray shot over the side of
the boat and pounded his face.

The deck shifted violently as the front of the boat dipped down
at forty-five degrees, reached the bottom of a trough, then seesawed
back up so the tip of the boat pointed at the lightning that flashed
through the sky. Parker clutched at the nets just outside the wheelhouse door and searched for the others.

Dawson was in the wheelhouse wrestling with the wheel of the boat like it was a bull. Abraham was checking the fish holds to make sure they were locked down. Fredricks and Logan were nowhere in sight.

Parker stumbled toward Abraham, trying to figure out how he might help. As he did, Parker heard the groan of metal against metal and glanced up. No! The ship's boom had come loose and streaked toward Abraham and him.

"Look out!" Parker dropped to the deck and whipped his gaze up toward Abraham. In that moment Parker realized crying out was the worst thing he could have done. If Abraham had stayed bent over, the boom would have gone right over him. But Parker's call brought Abraham upright, and the boom cracked into his forehead the instant he stood and turned. He dropped to the deck like a cold-cocked heavyweight boxer. The boat heaved, and the boom lurched back and forth like a whip.

"What the—" A shout came from the front of the boat. Logan. He stumbled along the starboard side, gaze riveted on Abraham. He pointed at Parker, then Abraham. "Check him!"

As Parker scrambled on his knees over to Abraham, Logan's low voice boomed, "Fredricks, get out here!"

Parker reached Abraham and squinted at his forehead. Cut and bleeding, but the injury wasn't deep. Parker set his ear next to Abraham's mouth. Thank God. He was breathing. A wave crashed over the boat and buried both of them.

"Get him over here!" Logan shouted as he staggered over the deck.

Parker nodded and tried to lift Abraham, but his boots slipped on the deck and he crashed onto his backside as Abraham slipped from his hands.

Logan's voice again sliced through the rain. "What is your problem? Get him over here! Now!"

Dawson's faint voice floated down from the wheelhouse toward Logan, but Parker caught the words. "Want me to help?"

"Do not leave that spot!" Logan jabbed his finger at Dawson. "Stay on the wheel."

"Aye!" Dawson blinked rapidly, his face white.

Not good. Dawson was seasoned. If this storm scared him, they were all in serious trouble. Again, Parker grabbed Abe, but the man's deadweight made him feel like he was made of concrete. Then Logan was beside him, lifting Abraham like he was a bag of foam. "Get below, Rook! You're just a liability."

Logan dragged Abraham back toward the wheelhouse. As Parker watched, the scene seemed to shift into slow motion. The sound of the waves and the stinging rain and the screams of the boat straining against the ocean all melded together into a rush of noise that made Parker's head spin. He tried to steady himself to keep from being tossed back and forth across the deck. And he stayed low.

The boom. Oh no. Had Logan seen it was loose?

He whipped his head up just in time to see the boom streaking toward Logan's head. At the last instant Logan threw up his arm to ward off the blow, but it was far too late to duck. Abraham fell to the deck as Logan was knocked across the boat. Momentum carried his body over the edge, his hand groping for the railing. He snagged it. Yes! He hung there as Parker sprinted toward him, his hand and forearm the only things now visible. Then Logan's fingers slipped and the captain was gone, over the edge, into the ocean.

forty-six

PARKER LURCHED FORWARD, HIS HANDS now clutching the railing where Logan had fallen into the thundering waves. The boat pitched and flung Parker to the deck. He landed on his right knee. Pain shot through his kneecap, but he ignored it and crawled back toward the railing.

"Dawson!"

No answer. Parker shouted as loud as he could. "Dawson!"

"What?" He barely heard the skiff man's voice over the roar of the storm.

"Logan is overboard!"

"What?"

The boat pitched down at thirty degrees, and Parker grabbed at the nets to keep from sliding down the deck.

"The boom knocked him over!"

Parker pulled himself up and clutched at the railing again as his eyes raked the water for Logan. Nothing. But even if he was four feet from the boat, Logan would be difficult to see in the darkness.

"What is going on?" Fredricks finally staggered to Parker's side.

Dawson twisted his head toward them and shouted instructions. "Get to the spot, you gotta light it up! Logan's over!"

Fredricks scrambled up the ladder to the spotlight and Parker turned back to the dark water. The light swept the waves as Parker squinted against the rain and spray. *C'mon, Logan.* Yes! There he was, not more than fifteen feet from the boat. But a second later Logan went under as a wave buried him, his life jacket not enough to keep him afloat.

"No!"

Parker clutched the edge of the boat, willing Logan to surface. Two seconds passed. Three. Adrenaline surged through him. He had to do something. Fast. Didn't matter that it was summertime. The Alaskan waters would suck the warmth out of Logan in minutes and drain his strength to stay afloat. The captain would kick off his boots, shed his coat to aid his mobility, but that would speed up the penetration of the cold into his extremities, then the core of his body. Not to mention the waves pounding down and tossing his body around like a waterlogged cork.

Think! Dive in? The fear he'd carried his entire life caved in on him. Instantly he was back at the beach as a kid being held under. No, he couldn't save Logan that way, but he'd find another answer.

Logan was a good swimmer, hadn't he said that? And his life jacket would keep him above the water, right? He just needed to get his bearings, and he could get to the back of the boat and climb on board. Then the sea in front of Parker lit up like God had flipped a switch on the sun. It was Fredricks's spotlight, trained on the ocean exactly where it should be.

"Can you see him?" Fredricks's voice cut through the storm.

"No! But keep—" Parker was cut off as a wave crashed into his back, thrust his stomach into the railing, and bent him over double. The blow almost knocked the wind out of him. He shook himself and scanned the surface of the water where he'd last seen Logan.

Finally Logan's head broke the surface, but five feet farther away. His life jacket had been torn off of him and floated fifteen feet away. No! Logan's mouth opened wide and gasped for air. His arms flailed and he went back under. An instant later he surfaced and jerked his head violently back and forth, searching for his life jacket. The spotlight had to be shining down in order to see the captain, but it seemed to be disorienting Logan.

"Logan. This way!"

Parker doubted his words would slice through the torrential rain and the roar of the black waves, but he couldn't stop trying. He screamed louder. If there was even a slight possibility Logan could hear his cries and get his bearings, he'd torch his voice to do it.

A wave crested and again Logan vanished from Parker's sight. No. This couldn't happen. A second later relief flooded Parker. The wave sank, and Logan was still there—above the surface, trying to swim toward the boat in long, slow strokes. Yes! But his relief was short-lived as he realized the current was slowly pushing Logan farther away. And time would soon run out, because Logan's core body temperature had to be dropping fast. How much longer before his arms and legs went numb? Two minutes? Less?

Logan went under for a third time. A line from grade school flashed through Parker's mind. "The third time someone goes under means they're about to drown." Was it an old wives' tale? It didn't matter if it was three, or four, or five. Parker had to do something. Logan wasn't going to make it on his own. Parker whipped his gaze up to the wheelhouse. Yes, that was it. Logan's only chance was for Parker to switch places with Dawson so he could get into the water and rescue Logan.

"Dawson!" Parker screamed the name with all his strength, then took a faltering step toward the wheelhouse, but before he could take another, a wave crashed over the side and tossed him to the back of the boat. Dawson turned and riveted his gaze on Parker. The man didn't have to say a word; Parker read it in the wiry man's eyes. Even if Parker could make it up to the wheel, he'd never driven a boat like this one. His inexperience meant the boat would likely go over in minutes. More likely in seconds. Time seemed to stop as he accepted the truth. Switching places with Dawson would only get them all killed. He'd never worked a spotlight, so switching with Fredricks was probably a bad idea as well. Plus, it would take time that the captain didn't have. Either he would go in after Logan, or no one would.

"Logan, hang on! Just a little longer." A little longer? Yeah, right. Hang on for what? He was going to come up with a plan in the next ten seconds that would save the day?

He had to get to the life jackets. Stupid not to grab one when he first came out. Upper deck. Had to get there somehow. Fight the rocking of the ship, fight through the waves crashing over the side. Grab two jackets and fight his way back. *Stop it!*

The thoughts were only stall tactics, his fear tossing out reasons that would only delay his taking action. Parker scrambled to his feet and scanned the deck. There! He staggered over to a long, thick rope nestled next to the wheelhouse. Next to it was a life preserver. He snatched up the ring, slung the end of the rope through it, and tied a knot he prayed would hold. Parker lashed the other end of the rope to a cleat on deck and crawled up the railing. This had to work.

He whipped his head back toward the spot he'd last seen Logan. A second later Logan surfaced and relief flooded Parker. But it vanished just as quickly as it had come because the panic that had been in Logan's eyes earlier had faded. A strange calm had settled on his face, almost as if he accepted he was going to drown. He spun in the water as if trying to spot the boat, maybe to say a last goodbye to his vessel.

"No! Fight it, Logan!"

As the words dropped into the sea, a thought flashed into Parker's mind.

Save him. Jump in and save him.

"Arrghhhh!"

Terror crawled in at the stem of his brain and painted images of him drowning alongside Logan.

Save him. Now.

Then another voice in his head joined the first.

It's suicide. You'll panic the instant you hit the water. You'll suck in water like you did as a kid and the darkness will take you. Joel can't come to the rescue this time.

Parker clutched the railing and screamed, "Joel would jump!"

You're not Joel. Besides, that's the kind of thinking that got him killed. Why kill yourself too, trying to save a man who's treated you like he has?

Then the other voice again, softer this time. *Go. Save him.*

What, you think saving this guy will impress your dad? Finally make him love you as much as he loved Joel? Not going to happen. So do you really want to die trying to save a man like him? This isn't your story— it's his.

He gripped the railing harder, leaned forward into the punishing wind. The truth? No, he didn't want his life to end. Didn't want to die for Logan. And no, saving Logan wouldn't impress his dad enough. Nothing would ever be enough.

Yes, that's it. Let it go. You can simply tell the others he went under and never surfaced again. Don't be a fool.

But then that other voice sounded in his head like a cymbal. *You only have seconds left to decide.*

"Decide what?"

Who you are.

"What?"

Are you a man who decides his worth based on what others tell him he is, or are you a man who decides who he is based on what he knows to be true at the core of his being? As you look at those waters, it doesn't matter what Joel would do or what would impress your father. It only matters what you would do. And whatever that action is, you must choose it now.

Parker's breaths grew ragged. Only seconds left to choose. He crawled up onto the railing and froze. What would *he* do? Not anyone else. Just him. Would he jump or stay?

No more time to think. Only time to choose. "God, what do I do?"

An instant later the truth struck him like lightning. The answer wasn't in him saving Logan or not saving Logan. It was in letting go of having to prove himself to anyone and stepping into who he truly was. And who was that? He knew. Parker Moore was a man who couldn't let another drown without a fight.

Parker grabbed the rope, stood for a second on the railing. The fear of drowning pressed down on him like a block of granite. The images of being held under as a kid assaulted him again.

"I'm not ready to die," Parker shouted at the waves.

But for the first time in his life, he knew who he was, so he clutched the rope tight and leaped out over the dark waters.

forty-seven

PARKER HIT THE WATER AND went under, and the icy cold bit into him like a thousand needles. A sense of panic sliced into his mind, but he fought it down as he sputtered to the surface and whipped his head in the direction he'd last seen the captain.

"Logan!"

Yes, there he was. Thank God for Fredricks, who had both of them lit up in his spotlight. "Hang on!"

Then Logan disappeared as a wave buried Parker, and the surging water tried to yank the preserver out of his hand. But he clutched the ring tighter. The water continued to stab at his skin, but he ignored the sensation and swam hard toward Logan. He must have looked like a man flailing in the water at his first swimming lesson, but Parker felt like he was Michael Phelps digging through the waves.

Ten seconds later he reached the area where Logan should be. He spun in a circle and the rope tightened around him. He spun back the other way to untangle himself, all the time searching frantically for any sign of Logan. *There!* His hat, floating right beside Parker. But no Logan. "Come on, Logan. Fight!"

Finally the man surfaced ten feet away, gasping. He went under again. Then came back up. Then under. Surfaced again. Parker dug into the water and pulled with all his strength. Seven feet. Five. He was going to make it. He kicked hard, and as he did the rope went taut. No! So close. It couldn't end like this.

"Logan! Here!"

A mouthful of salt water gushed into his mouth as he cried out. Just like when he was a kid. The water would fill his lungs and he would . . . No! Parker hacked out the briny water and stretched out his arm for the sinking man. Inches. All he needed was twenty-four inches. But it might as well have been a football field. He could no longer see Logan.

For the second time Parker had to choose. Let go and dive down for Logan? Hope to reach him, pull him to the surface, and tow him back to the ring? If he let go of the life preserver, they both would drown. Still, there was only one choice. He sucked in a deep breath and got ready to let go.

But before he could, a thick hand latched onto his right wrist from under the water and yanked down hard. Logan. Still alive. With that movement, Parker's grip on the life preserver came loose. Not good. Logan would pull them both under and drown both of them without realizing what he'd done.

But as Logan's grip tightened, Parker snagged the rope around the life preserver with his forefinger and middle finger. *Hang on!* He had to hang on. But what good would it do either of them? He couldn't hope to hold on to the rope for more than a few seconds, and then what?

The rope tore into his fingers. Pain ripped up from his fingers and into his hand, into his arm and shoulder, but he refused to let go. Logan surfaced, his eyes wild. He let go of Parker's arm and grabbed for his neck and pulled hard. It forced Parker's hand to slip down the rope, and both men started to go under. He had to make Logan let go! Parker formed a fist, reared back, and slugged Logan in the face as hard as he could. Logan's head flopped back and his grip loosened. Parker took hold of the captain's jacket and held on with everything he had.

Logan hacked out a series of coughs that sounded like they would split the man in two. But seconds later he grabbed Parker's arm with both hands, and once again the weight of the bigger man pulled Parker under and he lost hold of the rope. He sucked in a mouthful of water, clawed his way to the surface, and pulled in half a breath before a wave drove him under the water again. An instant later the world went dark.

forty-eight

TWO WEEKS LATER, THE DAY Derrek returned from a trip, Allison found him alone in his office. She knocked lightly on his door. He didn't look up. She stepped inside.

"Derrek."

"Hello, Allison." He glanced up, then back to a set of drawings. "How is everything with you?"

"Fine."

"Good, good. What can I do for you?"

Dampness crept onto the palms of her hands. "I need to talk with you."

"How long do you need?"

"Probably half an hour."

Derrek looked at his watch. "I'm afraid I can't do that right now."

"I understand. I looked at your schedule in Google Drive and saw you have a full day, but you're open at four thirty, so I'll block off that time for us to chat."

"What is this regarding?"

"That's best left for the conversation."

"Oh?" Derrek raised his chin and gave a few nods. "I see. Is there anything you can tell me to help me prepare?"

"I think it's best if we wait."

"Then I think it's best if we schedule something a bit later in the week."

"I think it's best for both of us if we have this conversation sooner rather than later." Allison stepped forward and placed her hands on his desk and leaned in. "There are a number of things I need to tell you. Truths I've learned about myself during my time here at Wright Architecture and truths about you that you need to hear."

"Ah." Derrek's eyes flashed anger and worry, but only for an instant. Then he smiled and said, "In that case let's plan on late this afternoon as you suggested, four thirty."

"Half an hour."

"I heard you, Allison."

"Good to know. Thank you."

He turned back to the drawings on his desk. "Anything else?"

"Yes. This meeting is for you and me only. No one else. And I'd like to finish all my thoughts before hearing yours."

"If that's what you like." Derrek leaned back and pulled his arms across his chest. "Anything else?"

"Not as long as we're clear on the parameters for the meeting."

Derrek chuckled and held up his palms in mock surrender. "My, my. Aren't we the little attorney today."

Allison stood straight and clasped her hands behind her back. "I'll see you at four thirty."

She strode through Derrek's office and spotted Linda standing at the lobby's front desk, her jaw set tight. Little doubt she'd heard every word, but it didn't matter. She'd locked down her time to speak with Derrek alone.

Lunchtime came and went without her stomach sounding any desire for food. At two she went to the lunchroom and heated up a bowl of soup, but after two bites she had to stop. Work on a few projects? Impossible. The thoughts in her mind continued to flit around like a frantic butterfly, and she finally gave up. Time crawled past three, then four, but finally four twenty-nine arrived and she smiled at how quickly it now felt like it had appeared. With a deep breath, she stepped out of her office and marched down the hall.

forty-nine

PARKER WOKE WITH A HAIRY face hovering two feet above his.

"How you feeling, Rook?"

He opened his eyes just enough to spot Logan leaning over him, a huge grin splitting his face.

"I'm alive?" he rasped.

"Yep. So am I. Fun swim, huh? Good times had by all. Dawson says you wanted to go for at least one lap before the season ended, so I'm glad we could take care of that request for you. Can you sit up, Rook?"

Parker tried and found it easier than he'd expected. Dawson and Fredricks stood a few feet back from his bed. Abraham sat beside Parker's bunk with a wad of thick white gauze wrapped around his head. The boat still rocked, but at a fraction of what it had done during the worst of the storm.

"Yeah, fun swim." Parker's lungs felt like they were on fire—memories of his childhood tide pool swim resurfacing—and breathing exacerbated the pain, but he was indeed alive.

Logan sat back in another chair inches from Parker's bed. He pointed his finger at Parker and nodded as the tiniest hint of a smile played at the corners of his mouth. Logan didn't speak. His eyes said more than enough—that he wouldn't be alive if not for Parker, that he was grateful, and that whatever impenetrable steel wall had stood between them had been shattered.

"You're okay, Abe?" Parker studied his friend.

Abraham nodded.

"How did we get back to the boat?"

Logan rested his arms on his lap, the big man's eyes full of wonder. "Why did you do it, Rook? Risk yourself to save me?"

"I don't know." But he did know. There was never truly an option not to go. And in that moment he'd proven his worth. As he let the knowledge wash over him, peace flooded in.

Logan folded his arms. "Abraham always says there's no greater deed than to lay down your life for a friend. So to lay down your life for an enemy, that is a truly astounding act."

Parker stared into Logan's eyes. As he did, he saw something deep in the man's eyes that shocked him. Understanding. And dare he even think it? Friendship.

"You gonna tell me"—Logan cocked his head—"why you jumped in?"

"It wasn't really about you. Something I had to do. For myself."

Logan nodded. He couldn't really know what Parker meant, but the look in the captain's eyes said he did, and for a moment Parker believed it was true.

"Also . . ." Logan tapped his cheek, which was seriously bruised. "Nice shot."

Parker grinned. "Thanks."

"As soon as you feel up to it, join me out on deck. Share a cigar with the rest of us and a kick-butt bottle of scotch."

Ten minutes later Parker did indeed join them, and Logan's

warmth intensified. Jokes and laughter and toasts filled the morning sky for more than two hours.

"A little bad news," Logan said as the conversation finally lagged. He pointed at Parker and grinned. "Don't think we're going to be able to call you Rook any longer. Not after that stunt you pulled."

Parker smiled. "I'll learn to live without it."

"Good man." Logan stood and shuffled over to Parker. He motioned for Parker to stand, then slapped both hands on his shoulders and squeezed. "Anytime you want to come back, your spot is here."

"I appreciate that."

Logan nodded and strolled off. Dawson and Fredricks stood as well and both told Parker, "Well done," before leaving him and Abraham alone on the deck.

Abe grinned at him, and when Dawson and Fredricks had pushed past the range of their voices, he said, "Almost impossible, winning Logan over to your side."

Parker laughed and said, "My life is now complete."

Abe threw his arm around Parker's shoulders and shook him playfully. "What is true? What do you know now?"

"What are you talking about?"

"Who are you, Parker?"

He frowned. "I don't know what you're—"

"You've been given the gift of sight, I think." Abe's eyes grew intense. "I hope. Sight to see how strong you truly are. To see *who* you truly are. You've lived your entire life trying to live up to your dad's expectations, but they weren't your dad's—they were yours. You've lived your entire life trying to prove to your dad you're worth something. But you don't need to. You never needed to. All you needed to do is see what has always been inside you. And now you have."

Parker nodded as a surge of emotion circled his heart.

"When you heard that your mom needed help, you didn't hes-itate. You came. You offered your strength. My guess is that's what you've done your whole life when people have needed help."

Parker could only nod as the emotion threatened to spill onto his cheeks.

"And four hours ago you again didn't hesitate to save a man who has treated you with disdain."

"I did hesitate. I almost didn't go. So close to not going."

Abraham leaned back against the railing, closed his eyes, and tilted his head to the sky. "Once a man who owned a motorcycle shop had two sons. One day he goes to the oldest and says, 'Hey, I need your help in the shop today. I want you to come by.' The oldest son says, 'No problem, I'll be there.' Then the man goes to his younger son and says the same thing. His second son says, 'Sorry, Dad. Not going to happen.'

"After looking at his schedule, the oldest son decides he's too busy and blows off his dad and doesn't go into the shop. The younger son grabs a quick breakfast, and as he's eating it he's thinking about his dad. He ends up going to the shop and helping out."

Abe opened his eyes, leaned close to Parker, and lowered his voice. "Which of the sons did the will of his dad?"

With that, Abraham stood and strolled away, whistling a song that Parker knew he'd never heard yet sounded like one he'd known all his life. After Abe slid inside the wheelhouse, Parker turned and gazed out over the water lit up like diamonds by the sun.

His world had been altered forever. *Altered* was the wrong word. Transformed. Infused with a truth that had always been there, one he'd always wanted to believe. And now he did.

fifty

Nearly everything in her wanted to put this off. Do it tomorrow. Next week. Next month. But what would change if she waited? Nothing. She had to do it now. Not next week. Not tomorrow. Now. It was far past time for the fire inside to blaze like the sun. Allison slowed as she reached Derrek's door. It was open a crack. She could see him through the sliver of the opening. She stepped up close, closed her eyes, and shot up a prayer. *Live an authentic life. No matter the outcome.* And this was her being true. To God. To herself.

The Lord is a warrior, the Lord is his name.

Allison is a warrior, a daughter of the King, Allison is her name.

Be that warrior now.

She knocked on Derrek's door and her pulse spiked. This felt like the time she'd gone bungee jumping; her ex had relentlessly pushed her to go and she'd finally given in. But at least that time there'd been a bungee cord attached to her ankles. A few more seconds went by before Derrek's voice, almost too soft to hear, said, "Come in."

Allison pushed the door open. She stood in the doorframe as she looked at Derrek, sitting ramrod straight at his desk. But he wasn't alone. Linda sat in one of three chairs on the other side of Derrek's desk, with one leg locked down tight on the other. There was a glint in the woman's eyes that Allison had grown to loathe during the past several months.

"Hello, Allison." Derrek motioned to the chairs. "Please come in and have a seat."

Allison didn't move. "I asked that you and I meet alone. You agreed. I clarified so there would be no misunderstanding."

"Yes, but I prayed about this, and I feel it's best we have a neutral party present to give a perspective that neither of us might have the ability to acquire on our own."

"You gave me your word."

Derrek chuckled, and Allison gritted her teeth at the sound of it.

"My every intention was to meet with just you, Allison. However"— Derrek pointed skyward—"when I'm led by my Lord and King to do something different, I submit to that leading."

"Enough of the God-talk, Derrek. If you refuse to talk to me unless Linda is here, fine, but don't give me the 'God told me' crap anymore."

Derrek stared at her for at least ten seconds, his face a stoic mask covering any emotions he might be feeling.

"Why don't you have a seat, Allison?" he finally said.

Allison smoothed her skirt, walked over to the chair on her right, and stood in front of it. Her face must have been like fire and steel.

"Whew," Linda puffed out. She gave Allison a cold smile. Dead eyes. "I think I'm glad I'm here. Are you sure you're in the right mood to have a conversation about . . . What did you call this? Truths you need to tell us? About you and about Derrek? Something like that, wasn't it?"

"No. There's no 'us.' I came to talk to Derrek. Period."

She turned back to Derrek, who glanced at his watch.

"I'm sorry I didn't mention this to you, Allison, but I have an early dinner appointment scheduled. I need to arrive within the next forty-five minutes, which means I need to leave here—"

"I'm not interested in playing games, Derrek. I'm sure you're not either. I told you I needed half an hour when we set up this meeting, and you agreed. You gave me your word. So I encourage you to keep your word and stay."

Derrek's mask cracked for a moment. Anger? Or just frustration? She couldn't tell.

Allison smiled. "But don't worry, Derrek. This won't take any longer than a half hour. Most of what I want to say is a simple thank-you for what you've done for me. Truly."

"That's the truth you want to speak?" Derrek narrowed his eyes. "A thank-you?"

"Yes." Allison raised her chin a millimeter. "Back in April I was in a difficult financial situation as well as a personal crisis with my former business partner. I sent out a desperate prayer when I saw no way out of it. You were the almost-instant, direct answer to that prayer. You called and asked me to be your partner in this firm. It was a dream come true. I admired you. I knew I would learn a great deal from you. We were friends, so I trusted you when you said we could finalize the partnership once I got here. But my reason for coming here was about so much more than learning the business and making the money I needed to make as a partner. Your invitation was something I've longed for from a father figure. You saw something valuable in me. Your invitation told me I was enough. Told me I was worthy. A validation I've wanted my whole life. And you gave it to me.

"But then it didn't happen. And it became apparent it would not happen unless I pushed for it. And if I'd been honest with myself back then, deep down I knew it would never happen, but I held on to the dream that I was worth something. Finally we had a conversation that confirmed the truth that you'd lied to me, and it crushed me. It told me my worth was very little, and I believed that lie."

Derrek glanced at his watch and then at Linda. "Allison, I need to stop you there. I didn't lie to you, as we discussed, and—"

"When we set up this meeting, I asked to say the things I needed to without interruption. You agreed."

"All right." Derrek slowly folded his arms across his chest.

She continued. "I floundered after that, had little idea what I was supposed to do, but soon you gave me a gift I needed desperately. Your talk on integrity." Allison walked slowly back and forth. "I went home angry because you have lied to me and to the staff and to our clients more than most politicians lie."

"Allison, you—"

"No." She held up a finger and took a step toward Derrek. "My thoughts, then yours. Keep your word, please. I encourage you not to add one more lie to the list."

Linda's breathing grew labored. Allison glanced at her. From the redness creeping into her face, Allison guessed she was angrier than Derrek.

"I thought you could tell me who I am. You can't. But in that longing I gave away my authority. So when you told me I wasn't worthy of being your partner, it was devastating. I don't know why you manipulate people like you do. I don't know why you have to lie about the things you've accomplished. I could guess, but it doesn't matter. I'm not your judge or jury. In fact, I want to thank you for the way you act, because it has set me free.

"I wrote an entry in my journal the other night about how you don't live an authentic life. That you posture and pretend and pose and stretch the truth into whatever you want it to be. But after I wrote in my journal, I went back a few days later and read the words again and ended up having to face the hardest truth I've ever had to face about myself.

"The truth is I am all those things as well, the things I accused you of being. I have not been living an authentic life because of the fear of what would happen if I did. And that fear has invaded my entire existence because I haven't believed in my own worth. Because I had a father who didn't know how to show me that." She paused and stopped pacing.

"But I've come to know my worth. I've come to see who I truly am. I'd forgotten for so long, but now I know again."

Allison sat and leaned forward, hands folded on her lap.

"As a friend from my college days always used to say, I had a severe case of plank eye. I needed to take the plank out of my own eye first before I could even start to take the speck out of yours, Derrek.

"What I realized is I had to examine my own integrity first. I had to assess whether I was being true to myself or not, and the answer was like a darkness that fell on me. I was not living an authentic life. I was living a lie.

"Even more than the money, I wanted your validation. I wanted you to tell me I was worthy of being your partner. To show me by signing the papers." She let out a small laugh. "A much simpler way of saying that is I wanted to be valued. Liked. And because of that, I didn't stand up for myself when I should have. I was quiet when I should have shouted from the rooftops. I let you spin the truth because I had spun my own deception. Because I'd forgotten who I am. But now? As I just said, I know once again. So I can stand up for myself."

She pulled a sheet of folded paper from her pocket, opened it, and read from a list she'd made.

"You lied to me about our partnership. You lied to your wife and probably many others, and I didn't speak the truth because of my fear and need to be accepted, so I lied too. You lied to our clients about other jobs we had done because you wanted to impress them, and because I wanted to be included, I never called you on it, so I lied too.

"You lied about your band doing a 'West Coast tour,' when all you did was go down and play at your daughter's wedding, but I congratulated you when you told the staff and most of our clients, even though I knew it wasn't the truth, because I wanted you to validate me, so I lied too.

"You lied to me years ago when Kayla and I bought computers through you and you sent me your used computers and told me they were new."

Linda couldn't stay silent. "Of. All. The. Ungrateful . . ." Linda's words grew too quiet for Allison to hear, but if she were guessing, they were words not sanctioned in Linda's rules for appropriate Christian talk.

"But I'm not here to—"

"Be quiet, Allison. Just shut up! Maybe Derrek promised he would wait till you were finished, but I certainly didn't." Linda's eyes were on fire. "You are a horrible person, Allison, you know that? Derrek was your friend, gave you advice about starting your own firm, and you never even paid for those computers! What kind of person does that?"

Allison narrowed her eyes and said, "Check your receivables from three years back, Linda. We paid in full. If you can't find the paperwork, I'd be happy to provide copies of my bank statements that show the money was transferred to your account. Also, I think it would be enlightening for you to check the computer that Derrek sent me. I have it at home. I'll bring it in. See, I was told by the company that fixed my laptop that it was more than a year old when I got it. That the person who bought the computer for me must have switched it out and sent me a used one. I told them that was impossible, that the person who sent it was my friend, who told me the computer was new."

Linda's face went pale, and she sat back in her chair and looked at Derrek.

"A simple mix-up, Allison. I had no idea I sent you an older version of that computer. If it is that critical to you, I'm certainly willing to—"

"It doesn't matter, Derrek. I don't want a newer version of that computer. I want what you're not able to give. Truth. Integrity. True friendship. Worth. But again, it's okay. This isn't about my fixing you; it's about me fixing me. Or at least trying to. That's why I'm grateful for what I've gone through here, because even as I sit here, I feel the joy of telling the truth filling me. So thank you, Derrek, for everything."

Derrek locked and unlocked his fingers. "That was quite the soliloquy, Allison. You seem pleased with yourself for getting those thoughts out, so well and good. Now I suppose it's my turn, time to respond to your thoughts."

Derrek steepled his fingers and tapped them against his mouth.

"I saw this coming, and by that I mean this kind of speech from you. Frankly, I'm surprised it's taken this long to surface. I've seen it ever since we first met each other years ago. A fierceness. The heart of a warrior. To accomplish the things you've accomplished in the world of sports, you have to have the spark of a warrior inside. To start your own business you must have that heart as well. There is a strength in you I believe you're just now starting to see and, more importantly, starting to believe in.

"With regard to your accusations, yes, I do have a problem with exaggeration every now and then. I'm not proud of it, and I thank you for calling my attention to it. It's something I'm working on."

Allison stared at him, stunned. She'd been ready for him to counter all of her arguments. Explain why she was in error and how he'd done nothing wrong. Justify his every lie. She glanced at Linda, who sat stone-faced, staring at the wall. Derrek kept tapping his fingers together, brows furrowed in concentration.

"As I've told you often, you have a talent for architecture and have done excellent work for our clients."

Again, she stared at him. What was this? What was Derrek trying to say? The journal said great change was coming. A thought shot through her mind. *He's going to make me a true partner.* The problem was, now that idea made her want to vomit. She'd never link her name to his. All she wanted was to keep working at his company long enough to find another job and for him to set her free from the noncompete.

"Allison?"

"Yes, sorry."

"Did you hear what I just said?"

"No, I was thinking about going forward, thinking about what happens next."

"Yes, good." Derrek straightened in his chair. "That's what I started to touch on."

"Okay."

"Your fierceness is a strength but can also be a liability. There's a recklessness about you, a lone-wolf attitude."

"What?"

"You wonder why I never signed the partnership agreement?" Derrek raised his upturned palm toward her. "This is why. Your attitude. Your rebelliousness. Your unwillingness to submit to my authority or Linda's. Your challenging me on decisions I've made. For example, my moving your office, the policy of compensation back to the company when your accounts have a shortfall, my talk on integrity, and many, many other things."

The air in the room grew thin. Allison tried to slow her breathing.

This wasn't happening. "I'm sorry you adhere to such a skewed vision of reality. I suppose we'll have to wait till eternity to see which one of us is right. However, in the meantime . . . we need to figure out what to do."

Derrek stood and walked to his window and gazed toward the Seattle skyline ten miles to the west.

"I started this company for two reasons. To make a living and to show nonbelievers how true Christians run a business. Christians who love one another. Who want to grow in their faith. Who listen and learn from each other.

"What has become abundantly clear through this conversation and during the time you've worked here is that you have no intention of listening to anything Linda and I have to say, and even if you did, you are not open in any way to the truth of what we would attempt to convey."

Derrek strolled back to his chair, placed both hands on the back of it, and leaned forward. "Your heart has hardened."

Derrek went back to the window and didn't speak for at least a minute. When he spoke again, his voice was soft.

"When one is betrayed, it presents many challenges. And yet at the same time, it presents an opportunity. The opportunity is to choose to let go, to forgive, to offer grace to the one who has betrayed you."

Derrek glanced at Allison, then turned back to the window. "You've cut me just now with your words, Allison. The knife went deep. I have offered you grace when you lost accounts. I guided you even before you came to work here, given freely of my knowledge and resources and contacts. I have washed your feet like Jesus washed the disciples' feet, offered you life, and in return you come here and speak of things that are not true. Yes, I'm hurt, but even more, I'm so disappointed in you."

Derrek turned and leaned his back against the window.

"It is understandable. When one is focused on self, when one cannot see a way to serve another, one will do things in the name of God, but the true motivation is only themselves.

"I have prayed for you, as has Linda, and we will continue to do so. However, with all that has gone on here in the past twenty minutes, and taking your time with this company as abundant evidence, I think it's clear we can no longer work together."

Allison slowly rose from her chair. "You're firing me?"

"If that's the language you want to use."

The statement should have rocked her. But all she felt was peace.

Derrek turned to Linda and said, "Before we finish, is there even a microcosm of what Allison has said that is true? Other than my slight exaggeration from time to time, is there anything to her comments? Am I blind and do not know it?"

Linda shook her head as if in great sadness. "No, you are not blind, and no, none of it is true. She is an abhorrent person."

Allison turned to Linda, and as she did, something extraordinary happened. All her anger and bitterness slipped away, and she saw the scared little girl hiding under Linda's facade.

"I've hated you, Linda. The way you've treated me has been horrendous. The disrespect, the condescending attitude, convincing Derrek I shouldn't be a partner—it hurt deeply. But I get it. I do. You're not in an easy spot in life. Haven't been for a long time."

"Oh, is that right, Allison?"

The conversation she'd overheard the other day filled her mind. "I know you're in pain. And I'm sorry for that. But you're here where you have tremendous value. And you're protecting a place where you feel special. Derrek has given you validation, and you love him for it. And you'll do anything to protect it. And I threatened that relationship.

You saw me as someone who could steal away what you've found. So you lashed out at me. But that's okay. I don't blame you. I would have done exactly the same thing."

Linda's face went hot red and she sputtered, "You are a Jezebel. I knew from the moment I met you. One of the most despicable creatures I've ever encountered."

Allison responded in a voice just above a whisper. "There is light inside you, Linda. It's shrouded by deep darkness that you have invited to be part of you, but the light is still there. You only need to see it. Just like me. You don't know who you are. You've forgotten. May you someday remember."

Linda started to rise from her chair and growled, "I swear to you, Allison, I will—"

"Enough. Please sit down, Linda." Derrek cleared his throat. "You have an hour, Allison, to collect your things and leave."

Derrek clasped his hands. Allison looked at Derrek till he dropped his gaze.

"Goodbye, Derrek."

The warrior was alive and well.

fifty-one

Sunday morning Allison opened the journal to the first page and took a picture of her entry with her phone. She did the same with each of the pages she'd written in. Someday soon she'd take the pictures and copy the words into her permanent journals. This one? She had a sense her time with it had come to a close. So she was hardly surprised that moments after she'd captured the last image, the words in the journal began to fade. Within a minute all the words had vanished.

———

Late Sunday night Allison and her mom picked up Parker from SeaTac airport. They spotted him as he trudged through the sliding glass doors onto the sidewalk on the arrivals level, glancing both ways, looking for them.

"Parker!" their mom called out from the passenger window. He spun at their mom's voice and trundled toward them. He looked tired, but only his body. There was something different about his countenance that Allison could see even from fifteen yards away. And when he got close, she saw eyes far brighter than she'd seen in forever. Allison leaped out of her car and ran around the back as she watched Parker take their mom in a long embrace.

Then it was her turn, and she hugged him fiercely.

"How are you?" she said into his ear, her arms still wrapped around him.

"Better than I've ever been. Big changes. You?"

"Same."

They released each other and grinned with the smiles of kids. They chatted nonstop on the way home, but by the time they reached Issaquah, all Parker wanted to do was grab a quick shower and go to bed. But he stopped by Allison's room before heading for the family room to crash on the couch.

"Let's grab some time tomorrow, huh?"

"I'd love that. Find a place where we can talk for a long time."

"Agreed." He whapped her doorframe and said, "Love ya, sis."

"Love you too."

The next morning Allison rose early and fixed breakfast for Parker and their mom. The three of them sat around the table telling stories from ages past, and it drew them together like nothing had in years.

After cleaning up, Allison and Parker got in her car and headed for Tiger Mountain. Not to run. To walk and tell the stories of the past four months.

"What trail should we take?" Allison asked as they headed for the mountain.

"Has to be Poo Poo Point, don't you think?"

Allison rolled her eyes. "I think you just like saying the name of the trail."

"Who, me?" Parker laughed. "Yeah, maybe, but Weyerhaeuser cleared out the trees and the stumps years back, so a lot of paragliders launch from there. It would be a kick to watch a few of them, and the view from there is spectacular."

"Promise me you're not going to talk one of them into letting you take a spin?"

"Promise."

"You know it's almost seven and a half miles, round trip."

"If you're good, I'm good." Parker patted his stomach. "Alaska fit, baby."

"And the trail rises almost two thousand feet."

"Like I said, I'm fit."

"Repeat that to me once more when we're done, okay?"

They reached the trailhead and soon were climbing up an old railroad grade through a mixed deciduous and coniferous forest. When they reached the top two hours later, they found a somewhat secluded spot away from the paragliders. Allison stared out over the view of Lake Sammamish and Bellevue and put her arm around her brother's shoulder. He grinned and said, "Okay, time to talk. You go first."

"No, you, Parker."

"All right." He stretched his legs out straight. "What a trip. Mind blowing. I thought going up there was about fishing, making money to help Mom out. And it was. But that was the smallest part."

Allison laughed.

"What's so funny?"

"I thought going to work at Wright Architecture was about making money to help Mom out, but that was the smallest part."

"I think I've heard that line somewhere before." Parker laughed. "What was the biggest part for you?"

"Finally got authentic. And did what you've been wanting me to do for a long time. I stood up for myself. Stood up to my boss." Allison smiled.

"And what happened when you did?"

"Got fired." She mock glared at him. "Thanks for the advice, bro."

"Are you serious? He axed you?"

"He did. But it was one of the best things that's ever happened to me."

"So you're not making anything right now."

"Nope." Allison laughed. "I don't know why I'm laughing—it's not funny. But it's going to be okay."

"Yeah, it will. I have some good news in that area." Parker grinned. "Not only was I paid well for the work up there, but I got a sizable bonus."

"Really? Why didn't you tell Mom last night?"

"I wanted to talk to you about it first." Parker kicked at a rock with his heel. "Plus, it's not like it's going to wipe out all of Mom's debt, but it's better than nothing."

"With me out of work, it's everything. How much?"

"Twenty-five thousand."

"And you're willing to put all of it toward—"

"Don't even try to ask me that."

Allison grinned as hope washed through her. "What'd you do to get the bonus?"

"I guess that happens when you save the captain's life."

"You did what?" She pushed his shoulder. "Oh my gosh!"

Parker told her his story from the beginning, about Logan, about Abraham, about diving into the black waters of the Bering Sea and somehow surviving.

"Wow, you saved Logan's life. After all he put you through."

"Yeah, but thing is, I didn't save his life."

"So did you or didn't you?"

Parker stopped and stared through the forest as if he were reliving the scene.

"I was part of it, the rescue, but I blacked out before I could get Logan back to the boat. No one really knows how Logan and I got out of the water. It's weird. Something about Abraham coming to and getting in the water . . . I don't know exactly. It's all a little fuzzy. But I guess the point is that I jumped in and, yeah, it helped save Logan's life, but it helped save mine too."

"How?"

Parker turned and watched a paraglider launch herself off over the mountain.

"Because as I stood there on that railing deciding whether to jump, I realized I didn't have to do it to prove anything to anyone. I jumped in because in that moment I figured out who I am. A person who would step up to the challenge and face it head-on, even if it meant dying. Who would do the right thing."

"I always knew that's who you are."

"Yeah, but I didn't. And it doesn't matter if others tell you. You have to know it for yourself."

She nodded and grabbed Parker's hand. "Well said, brother."

"I'm starting to know who I am. To live from the deep part of me that's been there all along. And it turns out that person has worth. More than I knew." Parker paused and looked down at a stick he'd picked up off the ground. "Does that make any sense?"

"More than you can imagine." Allison took his hand. "Go with me somewhere, will you?"

"Where?"

"Into a memory from another age." She took his other hand. "You are a warrior in a great kingdom. As am I."

Parker grinned and whispered, "Another mighty battle won."

"By whom?"

"By whom, you ask?" Parker said as his voice grew louder. "The greatest."

"The greatest who?"

"The greatest warriors!"

"The greatest warriors what?" Parker's voice was just below shouting now.

"The greatest warriors the kingdom has ever known!"

They saluted each other, then cried in unison, "May it ever be so!"

Both she and Parker burst into laughter, then she embraced him with all her strength and, before pulling away, repeated, "May it ever be so."

They sat in the moment till the emotion had passed, but the sweetness of it still hung in the air.

"Anything else about Alaska?" Allison said.

"I owe so much to Abe." Parker tossed his stick and watched it whirl through the air. "A lot of wisdom inside that guy."

"Have you talked to him since you got back?"

"Nah. I have his info. He has mine. Abe said he'd be in touch sooner rather than later."

"I'd like to meet this Abe."

"You'd like him. No doubt. We'll have to make that happen someday," Parker said. "Okay, your turn. Tell me about your life. Tell what you found out about that journal thing. I never gave you the chance before I left."

Allison sniffed out a quick laugh. "You won't believe it."

"Try me."

"It was one of seven angel journals created by a monk back in the 1500s. When you write in them, the writing changes in ways that make you face the truth about your life."

"You're crazy." Parker grinned. "Can you show me? Can I see the journal again?"

Allison shook her head. "No."

"Why not?"

"My time with the journal is over. It's someone else's turn now."

Allison told him about her time at Wright Architecture, about the confrontation with Derrek, about Linda and Cannon Beach and meeting Micah and Sarah and finding a strength inside her that she'd never known and yet had always known.

"You didn't know that strength was inside you? Yeah, you did. Like when you stood up to Nathan, when you stood up to the loan sharks."

"You're right, I did. But I never believed in it. Not till now." She looked at her brother and then to the sky. "Just like you, I've been figuring out that I have to live out of who I truly am. Not for others. For me. I have to realize my worth, not from getting a partnership or winning races or even having a dad who made me his favorite. But from remembering who I am. That I've always been a warrior."

They didn't get back to the parking lot till well after eight o'clock. They'd talked for over three hours straight and still there seemed more to say. They both went for a quick stretch at the exact same time.

"In sync with each other, just like the old days."

"Let's make the old days the new days, okay?" Allison took Parker's fingertips and gave a gentle pull.

"Done."

"Hey, what are you doing Monday?"

"Not much," Parker said.

"Well, I'd love for you to meet a friend of mine. Do you have time?"

"My only plan is to get back to Mazama at some point. Or maybe not. So yeah to meeting your friend. Whenever is great."

"Okay, I'll try to set something up."

"So who's this friend I'm going to meet? Male or female?"

"Male."

"Is this going to be one of those brother-checks-out-his-sister's-hot-prospect-and-makes-sure-he's-worthy-of-her type things?"

"No." Allison smiled and reached for her toes. "He's the furthest thing from that in the universe that you can imagine."

fifty-two

Wednesday morning Allison went for a walk down at Lake Sammamish State Park, and when she got back to her car she found a text message on her phone that made her smile. Micah Taylor.

> Hi, Allison, Micah Taylor here. Can you call me as soon as you get this? Thanks!

She slipped her Bluetooth over her ear and dialed Micah as she left the parking lot. He wasn't there. She left a message. As she reached the 405 freeway three minutes later, her phone buzzed. Micah calling back.

"Micah."

"Hey, Allison. How are things?"

"Life has been extremely interesting."

"Oh?"

"I'll tell you and Sarah next time we get together." She pulled onto the freeway. "What can I do for you?"

"I have a question."

"Sure."

"A mutual friend of ours says you might be looking for work."

"Our mutual friend is right."

"Do you remember us talking about my working with Hale & Sons?"

"Yes."

"Truth is, we're going into a full-on partnership with them. We weren't sure it was going to happen when Sarah and I saw you last month, so I couldn't say much, but we just finalized things."

"Wow."

"Yeah. It's a major wow. You know what that means, right?"

"You're going to start building homes together. But not normal ones. You're going to build the type that your home was. And is."

"Exactly," Micah said. "Remember my friend Rick, the mechanic? He'll be our main client. At least three-quarters of our jobs will come from him. And Rick's plans are aggressive."

"A mechanic has that kind of money to invest in homes?"

"It's a long story. Remind me to tell you sometime. The point is, we'll need a full-time architect to keep up. Are you interested?"

"Highly."

"There is one condition. Actually two."

"Okay." Allison took her exit and slowed as she came to the end of the off-ramp. "Hit me."

"Did I say two? I meant three."

In the background she heard Sarah say, "Give me the phone. Let me tell her without you stringing her along."

Micah laughed and said, "Sarah says hi and that she can't wait to see you again."

"Micah!" Allison heard Sarah shout.

"Condition one: You have to come to Cannon Beach four times

a year for company planning and meetings and playing at the beach and in the ocean."

"Done."

"Condition two: Bring your brother and mom with you at least once a year."

"Done."

"Condition three: You come on as a partner in the company. I'll send you the paperwork tonight."

"Partner?"

"It's the only way we'll do it. And there's a nice signing bonus that will give you some relief from your current financial situation."

Allison swallowed hard. "I know you're serious."

"Yes. We are. And nothing happens till all paperwork is signed."

"How do you see divvying up the company?"

"Hale & Sons gets thirty percent. Sarah and I get thirty percent. You get thirty percent, and the remaining ten percent we give back."

"You're being extremely generous to me."

"It's fair, and believe me, you'll earn it."

Allison went silent and Micah did as well. Finally she spoke. "You barely know me."

"Our mutual friend speaks extremely highly of you."

"Richard."

"Yes."

"He's not really a cop, is he?"

"He probably was at one time." Allison heard a smile in Micah's voice. "But now? No, he's not."

"And at times he probably goes by other forms of the name Richard. Like Rick maybe?"

"Yes." Now Micah was laughing. "That he does."

Allison called her mom and told her things were going to be okay.

"Really?"

"Yes, Mom. I promise. I'll tell you all about it when I get home, okay?"

She hung up, and a few minutes later her phone buzzed. Even before she looked at caller ID, she had a feeling who it was. She was right. Richard.

"I was hoping to talk to you today."

"Is that right?" he said.

"Yes. Some things have happened that I'd like to talk about. And I want you to meet my brother. He's back from Alaska."

"I'd like that."

"What about tomorrow?"

"Good day for me. Anytime."

"Parker's going to meet me at The Vogue at ten thirty, but I'd like a few minutes with you alone first."

"Sure. Ten fifteen?"

"Perfect."

Allison and Richard arrived at the same time, and he held the front door of The Vogue open for her.

"Thank you."

They both ordered white-chocolate mochas and wandered to the back of the coffee shop to find a seat. They settled at the same table where Richard and Alister had sat the day Allison first saw the journal.

"An appropriate spot, don't you think?" Allison asked.

"Why do you say that?" Richard took a drink and studied her over the top of his coffee cup.

"Because this was the spot where it began, and this is the spot I suspect it's going to end."

"End?"

"Yes. This chapter anyway." Allison let her sadness creep into her smile. "But before we get to all that, I want to tell you what's happened since we last talked."

"I'd love to hear all about it."

She told Richard about standing up to Derrek and her reunion with Parker and how rich and confirming that was, and about the job offer from Micah and Sarah.

"And I spoke to the dry bones. They came alive. I'm beginning to remember who I am."

"I'm happy for you, Allison. Truly."

"Thank you, Richard, for everything you've done and been for me."

Richard gazed at her with eyes radiating compassion. He offered a smile that spoke of great delight, then reached into the bag at his feet. Instantly she knew what was inside. Allison closed her eyes till she heard him slide a package across the table in front of her.

She opened her eyes and softly laid her fingers on top of it. "You know, don't you?"

"What?"

"That the words in the journal are gone. That my time is up."

"Yes." He glanced at the package in front of her. "I thought I'd get you a new one."

She opened the package and picked up her new journal. The Tree of Life was etched into this journal, just like the one she'd borrowed for a while. But the light brown leather of this journal was new. In time it would grow old and beautiful with nicks and scrapes and the oils from her hands. And she would fill it with words of truth and authenticity.

Allison put it back in the package. "Thank you."

"You're welcome."

She reached into a small bag at her feet and brought out the Seraph Journal and set it in front of Rick. "It's hard to let it go, but it's right."

"Why's that?"

"It was my final crutch." She took his hands and squeezed. "I had to know who I was from the inside out. The journal told me who I was—and it had to, that's what I needed—but in the end I have to know my worth regardless of anything else."

Richard's eyes grew kinder, if that were possible, and he gave a nod.

"Thank you." She wrapped her hands around her cup and brought it to her lips. The coffee tasted richer, *fuller*, if that was the right word. Rich, full of life, as full as the rest of her life had become.

"You're welcome, Warrior Allison."

She laughed and they sat in silence for a time.

"I know who you truly are."

"Oh?" A smile poked out from the corners of Richard's mouth. "Did you talk with Micah and Sarah about me?"

"Yes. Sort of. Enough."

"So you know what I am."

"I figured it out. I'm not sure I believe it, but I do believe it at the same time. Does that make any sense?"

"Completely." Richard sat back and folded his hands across his stomach.

"And from what Micah said, his friend Rick is going to be the one hiring our new company to build homes."

"That's true."

"Richard. Rick." Allison smiled and slid her finger around the rim of her cup. "It was right in front of me the whole time. I should have figured it out sooner."

Richard just smiled.

"So which name do I call you?"

"Whichever one you like."

"Okay." She took a sip of her drink and peered at him. "If you're going to be our major client, then you'll be in my life for a while longer."

"Indeed I will."

"I got the paperwork from Micah for the partnership. The salary is far beyond what I expected." Allison looked down at her cup and tapped her fingers on the sides. "I'll be able to pay off the rest of Mom's debt within eighteen months, even with the crazy interest we're paying on the loan. If Parker gets a job, which I'm guessing he will, it could be even sooner."

She went silent and looked down.

"Is there a problem?"

"Where will all the money come from to pay for the homes and my salary?"

"I'm not married. I don't sleep. I have a good head for business. And I've been around for more than a few years. So I've built up a sizable bank account." Richard paused and grinned like a little boy. "You can't imagine what the four of us are going to do together with that money."

"I can try." Allison leaned over and gave him a quick kiss on the cheek. "I don't know if that's allowed, but I don't care."

Allison glanced around the shop, seeing all the people oblivious to the being that sat among them.

"What would happen if I stood right now and shouted out who you are?"

"Feel free to try it." Richard laughed. "Most people would glance at you, then look away. Others would tell their companions you're crazy."

"But you could do a miracle to prove yourself to them."

"I could." Richard laughed. "I've often thought that. But it wouldn't convince them. People believe what they choose to believe. Most of those in here would explain it away. It's a choice to believe, no matter what that belief is, and while many people believe in angels, finding one sitting in their favorite coffee shop would test the limits of their faith."

"But you're not just an angel, are you? You're one of seven Seraphs."

"Yes." Richard's face grew solemn. "I am."

"One angel for each journal."

"Yes."

Allison sat back, stunned, grateful, astounded that she'd been chosen.

"Why me, Richard?"

"Why not you?"

"But there are only seven journals. With billions of people on this planet, how—"

"You think journals are the only way God can reach into a person's life?" Richard grinned.

"I suppose not."

"Sometimes he uses things even smaller than a journal. Sometimes bigger things, like a house." Richard winked.

"Like with Micah."

Richard only smiled.

Allison took another sip of her drink and spun through her memories of Richard.

"And do you think I'm walking alongside only one person at a time?"

"Again, I suppose you aren't."

Richard smiled the smile of a father.

Allison looked down at the journal. As she ran her fingers lightly over its surface, her heart filled with the images of how it had changed her life. Allison's gaze flitted back and forth between the journal and Richard. She laid her hand flat on the cover and said, "What happens now?"

"You already know."

"It's my turn, isn't it?"

"Yes. It is."

"Do I have to give it to someone in here?" She glanced around the shop. "Someone eavesdropping on our conversation, like I did to you and Alister ages back?"

"No, no. Anywhere you like. Anyone you like." Richard leaned in. "Simply listen. He'll speak to you, lead you to the right person."

They both took sips of their drinks and savored the moment of shared silence the way only true friends can.

Parker arrived a few minutes later. She watched her brother as he ordered his drink, then stood at the counter waiting for it to be made. She kept her eyes on him as she spoke to Richard.

"My brother is a good man. I wish he could have you in his life at some point like I've had."

A moment later Parker slipped some bills into the tip jar and scanned the room for her. They caught each other's eyes after a few seconds, and Parker started to stride toward her and Richard. But after a few yards he came to a dead stop, his eyes wide. He stood that way for more than ten seconds before slowly shuffling toward them, giving tiny shakes of his head as he approached. When he reached their table, Parker plopped into the chair next to Allison and stared at Richard with a look of utter bewilderment.

Richard leaned forward and said, "It's great to see you, Parker."

Allison's brain skipped a beat. Richard's grin went wide, and Allison could tell he was fighting to keep from laughing. She glanced back and forth between Parker and Richard. "How do you two know each—"

"Wow, it's so cool to see you." Parker lurched forward, his eyes full of confusion. "But what are you doing here, Abe? How do you know my sister?"

"Abe? Like from your boat?" Allison said to Parker, then turned to Richard and sputtered, "He just called you Abe."

"Yes." Richard smiled. "He did."

In unison she and Parker stared at each other and stammered, "How do you two know each other?"

They pointed at each other and said, "Jinx!"

Allison joined Parker in a brief bit of laughter, then sobered as she took in what this all meant. She'd wished Richard could be in Parker's life? Wish granted. For the past two and a half months, that's exactly where he'd been. He'd just told her he could walk with more than one person at a time. Proof now sat next to her in the form of her brother. The absurdity and wonder of it all coursed through her like a flash flood, and she burst into laughter.

Richard nodded and smiled wide.

"What's so funny?" Parker asked. "Will one of you tell me what's going on?"

"Yes," Richard said. "Allison will tell you. Unfortunately, I must go."

"Go?" Parker shook his head. "I just got here. We gotta catch up. You gotta tell me what you're doing here."

"You're right, we do need to catch up." Richard stood, and Parker joined him a second later. "Don't worry. We'll connect. Soon. After you talk to Allison about me, I'm sure you're going to have a few questions. I'll call you in a few days and we'll talk through it."

He wrapped Parker in a massive hug and didn't let go for a long time. "I love ya, Parker. Stay true. Know your worth. Know who you truly are, yes?"

Parker nodded as the two men released each other, and Richard peered deep into his eyes. "You're such a good man, Parker."

Then he said to Allison, "I'll let you explain it to him if that's all right."

She nodded. Richard gave each of them a wink, turned, and strode across the floor of The Vogue and out the front door.

Parker whirled to face Allison. "Tell me."

Allison took her brother's hands and grinned. "Richard, or Abraham, or Abe, or Rick, or whatever we want to call him . . . is an angel."

fifty-three

THREE DAYS LATER ALLISON STUDIED the midsixties man who sat in the corner of Kopi Kafé, the coffee shop she'd frequented before she got divorced. The man sat under a classic black-and-white photo of men eating lunch on the I-beam of a New York skyscraper still under construction.

He was reading a newspaper—at least appeared to be—but he hadn't changed the page in over five minutes. She couldn't be sure from the distance, but she thought his eyes held a deep sadness.

It wasn't the first time she'd seen him. Ages back, a few months before she and her ex parted ways, he'd spoken to her on his way out. She'd been alone, a novel held out in front of her, her coffee untouched. He'd shuffled up to her, stopped four feet away, and motioned as if asking if he could approach her table. She nodded. The man stepped closer, then smiled down on her with a look that spoke of understanding life's highs and lows. He said, "This too shall pass."

"Excuse me?"

He offered a wink and a smile and a brisk wave of his hand. "Whatever it is you're going through."

"How do you know I'm going through anything?"

"It's in your eyes." He leaned closer and whispered, "But even more than that, you've been staring at the same page of your book for five minutes now, and I don't take you for a slow reader."

"You've been watching me?"

"I watch everyone in here. The regulars, the first-timers, the only-timers. People are interesting. The pages of their faces often much more so than any book."

He spoke the words as if Allison agreed, and he was right, she did. He nodded and repeated his opening line. "This too shall pass."

With that he strolled off, then turned after he'd covered ten paces. He smiled again and mouthed the words, *It will. It will.*

He'd been right, and now his eyes held the same sadness hers must have held. Would he remember her? Probably not. She peered at him for a few more seconds. Time to find out.

"Excuse me."

The man looked up, a puzzled look on his face. "Do I know you?"

"No."

He gazed at her a few seconds before speaking. "I don't think that's true. I think we did meet, long ago. Yes?" He folded his paper methodically and set it on the table.

"We did." Allison slid into the seat across from the man. "Very briefly. Here, in this coffee shop."

"I don't remember."

"You spoke powerful words to me that day."

"Did I?"

"You did." She reached into her purse and pulled out the journal. "I have something for you."

She slid the journal across the table and patted it. "For you."

The man peered at the journal, then looked back at Allison for a moment, then focused back on the journal. With tentative fingers he reached out and stroked the leather.

"Beautiful." He looked up. "It's yours?"

"No, it belongs to a friend of mine." Allison stretched out her arm and pushed the journal a few inches closer to the man. "But for a time, it's yours. To write in. To immerse yourself in. To pour out the way you see the world."

"Why me? Why give it to me?"

Allison stood and took the man's hands in both of hers. "Because."

She let go of the man's hands and strolled away, a smile playing on her face. Without question, she'd made the right choice.

fifty-four

How long did it take you to figure him out?" Allison asked as she stood with Micah and Sarah on the deck of their home four miles south of Cannon Beach. "Who Rick or Richard or Abraham was?"

"A lot longer than it took you." Micah's smile was melancholy. "That was a tough day when he left. We were on the beach at Oswald West State Park seven miles south of here. I didn't think I'd ever see him again. But then he showed up a few years later. Then again a year after that. The next time it was a month. The next, three years. He's not predictable and there's never any warning."

"He changed my life."

"I disagree," Sarah said.

"Oh?"

"Yes, Rick helped you, pushed you, challenged you, gave you the chance to be standing right here in this moment, but you made the choice to believe all you've come to believe." Sarah gave Allison's hand a quick squeeze. "You wrote in the journal, you faced the truth, and you were willing to stand up to Derrek in the end. You."

"I agree," Micah said softly. "You were the one who stepped into who you truly are. You're the one who chose to accept it. You're the one who decided to start living it out."

The three of them watched the seagulls canter on the wind and took in the briny ocean air. After a time, Sarah wrapped her arm around Allison's shoulders and said, "Are you sure you want to go on this crazy adventure with Micah and me?"

"Yes. No question."

"Then we're going to build some spectacular homes together." Micah grinned. "Give them away to many, and watch the pages of their lives turn into stories far greater than they could ever imagine."

A Note from the Author

Dear Friend,

This was a fascinating novel to write as it is the first time I've told a story where the main protagonist was female. (If it worked for you, thank my wife. If it didn't, blame me.) But even though Allison is a woman, I still related to her since there have been many moments in my life when I haven't stood up for myself and have regretted it deeply, and other moments I'm proud of, when I *have* had enough integrity to speak the truth even though it was difficult.

My prayer for you is that you step more and more into the freedom of standing up for yourself. And that you speak to the dry bones and discover the truth of who you truly are.

Also, it was a blast to write about Micah and Sarah Taylor once again. For those of you who have read my novel *Rooms*, you know Micah and Sarah quite well. For those of you who weren't familiar with these names, they are the main characters in *Rooms*.

To bring them back for a few cameos in *The Pages of Her Life*, see what has happened to them, and discover what they'll be doing in the future, was great fun. If you want to keep up with what's going on with me and my writing, find encouragement for your journey, and receive the occasional free giveaway, you can sign up for my newsletter at JamesLRubart.com When you do, I'll send you a free instrumental song that Micah wrote (really, me) years ago when he first went to his home on the coast. And you can always jot me a note at JamesLRubart@gmail.com. I'd love to hear from you.

Finally, thank you for taking the time to read *The Pages of Her Life*. You are the biggest reason I love to tell stories.

Much freedom,
Jim

James L. Rubart
January 2019

Discussion Questions

1. What were the main themes you saw in *The Pages of Her Life*?
2. Which of the main characters could you relate to more? Allison or Parker? What parts of Allison or Parker did you relate to?
3. Have you ever had to work for a boss like Derrek? Talk about that experience. What did you learn from it? How did it affect you?
4. Often when we feel disrespected and treated poorly, we are either aggressive (which we saw in Parker), or we act passively (as we saw in Allison). Which do you do tend to do more?
5. Have you ever had a situation like Allison did when God led you into a spot where you thought things were going to be wonderful, but they turned out horrible? In the end, did you realize God did it because he wanted to help you go through significant change that would set you free? How did the experience change you?
6. At the end of the story, Allison decides to stand up for herself

like never before. Have there been times you've stood up for yourself when it was difficult to do so?

7. Are there areas of your life where you know you need to stand up for yourself but you haven't yet? What are they?

8. Do you write in a journal? If yes, how does that help you sort out your life?

9. When did you figure out that Richard was an angel and the one who was changing the writing in the journal?

10. For those of you who have read the novel *Rooms*, when did you figure out Richard and Rick were the same person?

11. Did it surprise you that Richard and *Abe* were the same person?

12. When you grew up, did you face a situation like Allison and Parker did where you felt one of your parents liked your siblings better than you? If yes, how did you respond to that? How does it affect your life now?

13. Are there areas of your life where you realize you need to be truer to yourself?

14. Have you ever considered the idea that having integrity can sometimes mean speaking up for yourself when it would be easier to stay silent?

15. For Allison, standing up for others was much easier than standing up for herself. Do you agree?

16. On the boat, rescuing Logan gave Parker the chance to discover who he truly was. Have you ever had a moment like that? What did you discover about yourself?

17. What are the "dry bones" in your life you need to speak to?

Acknowledgments

It takes a gathering of highly skilled people to birth a novel. Consequently, deep gratitude goes out to my team at HarperCollins Christian Publishing, Dennis Brooke, Rick Acker, Thomas Umstadtt Jr., Susan May Warren, Natasha Kern, Amanda Bostic, Erin Healy, Taylor Rubart, and Darci Rubart.

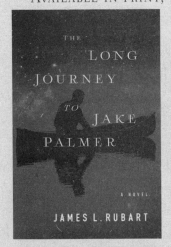

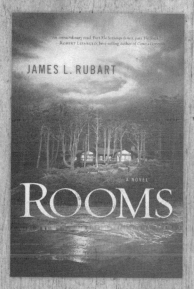
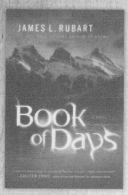

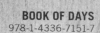

About the Author

Photo by Taylor Rubart, Bellingham, WA

JAMES L. RUBART is the bestselling and Christy, Carol, *RT Book Reviews*, and INSPY award–winning author of nine novels. A professional marketer and speaker, James and his wife have two grown sons and live in the Pacific Northwest.

Want to stay in touch with James? Sign up for his newsletter (and an occasional freebie!) at JamesLRubart.com.

———

Facebook: JamesLRubart
Twitter: @JamesLRubart